PENGUIN

The Pleasures of Spring

'Evie Hunter' is actually two authors who met at a creative writing workshop in 2010 and discovered a shared love of erotica. Since then, while they have both written fiction in other genres, they have also written a number of BDSM-themed novellas together. *The Pleasures of Spring* is their fourth collaboration on a novel, following the publication of *The Pleasures of Winter* (2012), *The Pleasures of Summer* (2013) and *The Pleasures of Autumn* (2013).

Praise for previous *pleasures* books

'More colour and better written than E. L. James and a more exciting read than any of Sylvia Day's books.' *Irish Independent* .

'A must-read if you enjoyed *Fifty Shades of Grey*.' *Daily Star*

'Evie Hunter has managed to do it again! I adore this series . . . I devoured the previous books and was so consumed by them that I felt like I was actually a part of that world . . . if you like Erotica fiction that has depth and an action-packed story line, then this book is for you.' *Totally Bookalicious* (5/5)
(full review at: http://totally-bookalicious.blogspot.co.
uk/2013/10/book-review-pleasures-of-autumn.html)

'I was riveted . . . I can't wait for the next in the *Pleasures* series and am sad that there are only four seasons.' *Books-n-Kisses* (4.5/5)
(full review at: http://www.books-n-kisses.com/2013/10/
kimberly-reviews-the-pleasures-of-autumn-by-evie-hunter/)

'These authors have once again managed to inject a special brand of magic into their writing which captivates me as a reader entirely . . . This was a sizzling, exciting read.' *Me, My Books and I* (5/5)
(full review at: http://memybooksandi.wordpress.
com/2013/11/18/the-pleasures-of-autumn-by-evie-hunter/)

'A succulent, taunting and combustible thrillride . . . an intelligent
and "smexy" read!' *Avon Romance*
(full review at: http://www.avonromance.com/post/the-
pleasures-of-autumn-by-evie-hunter)

'I had always thought that the majority of erotic novels have no
plot . . . This wasn't the case with *The Pleasures of Autumn* . . . Evie
Hunter writes well and there are none of
the clichés that I expected in my clearly misguided
preconceptions!' *Plastic Rosaries Book Blog*
(full review at: http://plasticrosaries.com/review-pleasures-
autumn-evie-hunter/)

'*The Pleasures of Autumn* is definitely my favourite of the *Pleasures*
series to date. Dynamic duo making up team Evie Hunter are
hitting their stride. [It] showcases both their writing maturity as well
as their ability to crank up the heat.' *Book Addict/La Crimson Femme*
(full review at: https://www.goodreads.com/review/
show/673611433)

'Watch out people, I'm telling you this writing duo is one to
watch. They've knocked it out of the park with two in a row
(*Pleasures of Winter* and now *Pleasures of Summer*). If you want a
well-written book to read after *Fifty* or even better than Gideon
Cross, look no further. Not only do you get all the tension with a
hell of a pay-off, you get a believable HEA at the end. Masterfully
written, artfully told, and yummy to read.' *My Book Boyfriend* (5/5)
(full review at: http://mybookboyfriend.blogspot.ie/2013/06/
the-pleasures-of-summer-pleasures-2-by.html?
zx=7e2a07f2382adc48)

'One hot read . . . but it never gets so heavy that it might leave
the reader uncomfortable. Having said that, I have to admit that
I was both surprised and intrigued by the alternative uses that
were found for both Alka-Seltzer and tiger balm in this story.
Who knew?' *Nudge Me Now* (4/5)
(full review at: http://www.nudgemenow.com/article/the-
pleasures-of-summer-by-evie-hunter/)

'Evie Hunter does it again! . . . This novel had me and wouldn't
let me go. I never had a reason to stop reading this book, and I'm
so glad that I did get the chance to read it. As erotic literature
goes, I'd say this novel would be in the top ten of amazing books
to read in the genre.' *Manhattan Reader*

(full review at: http://headstrong-tomgirl.blogspot.ie/2013/06/
the-pleasures-of-summer-by-evie-hunter.html)

'*The Pleasures of Summer* by Evie Hunter is NOT just an erotic
romp through the world of the Dom/Sub relationship, there is a
plot – honest – and it's a good one, filled with tension, danger and a
kidnapping or two! Summer and Flynn are both well-developed
(very – had to say that), dimensional (very – had to say that, again)
and their bickering and bantering back and forth is actually
chuckle-worthy at times!' *Tome Tender* (5/5)
(full review at: http://tometender.blogspot.ie/2013/06/
the-pleasures-of-summer-by-evie-hunter
.html?zx=c6d5aac4bee7872f)

'Danger, heat, obsession and unexplored desires come together
to form a combustive and sizzling tale, not soon forgotten . . . Did
I mention the chemistry that they share?! You will definitely not
need a blanket to keep yourself warm as you read this
one! . . . [It's] a knockout story that will grip readers and have
them flying through the pages at a heart-stopping rate. There
were times while I was reading that I found myself so emotion-
ally engrossed within the story and the characters that I found
my heart skipping and tears welling up.' *Romancing the Book*
(Full review at: http://romancing-the-book.com/2013/01/
review-the-pleasures-of-winter-by-evie-hunter.html)

'These authors can certainly write a hot scene . . . If you're
looking for something hot and steamy with intense chemistry, then you can't go wrong with this one. I really hope that
we get to see more of these characters in the future but I'll
be looking forward to anything that these authors come
up with.' *Feeling Fictional*
(Full review at: http://www.feelingfictional.com/2012/11/
review-pleasures-of-winter-evie-hunter.html)

'All I can say is, holy yowza, Batman! Yes, this book falls firmly
into the "What to read after *Fifty Shades of Grey*" category, but in
my opinion – and pay attention to me here, people – this book
blows *Fifty Shades* out of the water. That's right, I said it . . .
I unabashedly adored this book.' *This Bookish Endeavor*
(Full review at: http://ravingbookaddict.blogspot.ie/2013/01/
the-pleasures-of-winter-evie-hunter.html)

Quotes from *Goodreads.com* user reviews

'*The Pleasures of Autumn* has it all. Romance, mystery, suspense, a great story line and a bunch of BAAA CHICKAAA WAAA WAAAaaa . . . a great read!' 5/5

'Who needs *Fifty Shades of Grey* when you've got Evie Hunter writing up a steamy storm! This novel has got all that I love: rubies, a touch of Irish and Paris and a dollop or three of man for my sugar fix. The only thing is that it's left me wanting to go out and get the other two books!' 5/5

'The combination of eroticism and romance with suspense, action and some fabulous humour makes this book a superb read.' 5/5

'And the bonus prize goes to . . . the author for actually including a STORY! And not a bad one at that – a good plot, mystery, suspense, action, romance . . . and erotic scenes that are not there for their own sake but that actually do contribute to your understanding of the characters' relationship. And so I am thankful that my quest has been fulfilled – erotica can be well written – no more glorified porn for me!' 4/5

'The relationship between the two of them at times tended to be frustrating!!! I swear that communication is the key to a relationship and sometimes these two had none! That is exactly what makes this book so real to me. The fact that each of them was terrified to share their true feelings with each other which tends to happen often in real life, not just in stories. The makeup sex was HOT!!! It made me wish there was more book when I was finished reading.' 5/5

'Ms Hunter has done it again. Talk about a page turner. I started to read this book in bed one night and fell asleep reading it. The following morning I picked it up again and couldn't stop reading until I finished it. This is more than just a love story. The sexy scenes are HOT and the hero is halfIrish and half Scots. What more could a girl ask for? I can't wait for the next book.' 4/5

The Pleasures of Spring

EVIE HUNTER

PENGUIN BOOKS

PENGUIN BOOKS

Published by the Penguin Group
Penguin Books Ltd, 80 Strand, London WC2R ORL, England
Penguin Group (USA) Inc., 375 Hudson Street, New York, New York 10014, USA
Penguin Group (Canada), 90 Eglinton Avenue East, Suite 700, Toronto, Ontario, Canada M4P 2Y3
(a division of Pearson Penguin Canada Inc.)
Penguin Ireland, 25 St Stephen's Green, Dublin 2, Ireland (a division of Penguin Books Ltd)
Penguin Group (Australia), 707 Collins Street, Melbourne, Victoria 3008, Australia
(a division of Pearson Australia Group Pty Ltd)
Penguin Books India Pvt Ltd, 11 Community Centre, Panchsheel Park, New Delhi – 110 017, India
Penguin Group (NZ), 67 Apollo Drive, Rosedale, Auckland 0632, New Zealand
(a division of Pearson New Zealand Ltd)
Penguin Books (South Africa) (Pty) Ltd, Block D, Rosebank Office Park,
181 Jan Smuts Avenue, Parktown North, Gauteng 2193, South Africa

Penguin Books Ltd, Registered Offices: 80 Strand, London WC2R ORL, England

www.penguin.com

First published 2014
001

Copyright © Eileen Gormley and Caroline McCall, 2014

The moral right of the authors has been asserted

Set in 12.5/14.75pt Garamond MT Std
Typeset by Jouve (UK), Milton Keynes
Printed in Great Britain by Clays Ltd, St Ives plc

A CIP catalogue record for this book is available from the British Library

ISBN: 978-0-241-97003-4

www.greenpenguin.co.uk

MIX
Paper from
responsible sources
FSC™ C018179

Penguin Books is committed to a sustainable
future for our business, our readers and our planet.
This book is made from Forest Stewardship
Council™ certified paper.

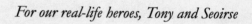

For our real-life heroes, Tony and Seoirse

Roz Spring stumbled when she saw the display of hunting knives on the wall. They were so out of place in the run-down London shopping centre that she couldn't conceal her shock. She blinked and managed to control her face, but could do nothing about the cold sweat that chilled her back.

'You all right, love?' The man in Sunny Money came from behind the counter and caught her arm. 'You turned a bit pale there.'

Roz allowed herself to lean against his arm. The heavy weight of her swollen belly unbalanced her, and she would take all the help she could get. She sagged a little, the movement taking the strain off her back. 'I'm sorry, it was those knives. They gave me such a fright.'

Mr Sunny Money turned to look at them, as if he had forgotten they were there. Six knives, long and lethal, with handles of leather, ivory and wood, gleamed evilly from their display stand on the back wall. 'They belonged to my great-grandfather. He was a big game hunter in Africa, back in the time when you were allowed to kill the animals.'

He shrugged. 'Of course, things are different now. You take photos instead of shooting them. That's my hobby.'

He smiled at her, a charming self-deprecating smile, but Roz couldn't force herself to return it. Knives freaking scared her.

She rubbed her belly restlessly. 'I'm sorry, it was the shock of seeing them.'

Sunny Money was on the first floor of Lewisham shopping centre, in a small unit sandwiched between a high-end jewellers and a boutique selling the kind of skimpy, fashionable clothes that would no longer fit her. The glass walls that divided the office from the walkway revealed neutral walls and carpet and a waist-high desk without the bulletproof protection so popular in banks. It was friendly, approachable and exactly what she needed in her situation.

Her scalp prickled and she longed to scratch it, but couldn't take her attention off the display. Roz shook slightly. Since that damp night in Paris over a year ago, she had nightmares about knives. 'Do you think I could sit down? I'm feeling a bit strange.'

Mr Sunny Money was all concern. 'Of course. Here you are.'

He pulled a chair forward and helped her into it.

Roz lowered herself awkwardly, sighing with relief when she was able to relax. She leaned forwards and rubbed her lower back. 'I had no idea pregnancy would be like this. It looks so glamorous on TV, all those glowing, happy women. It's nothing like that.'

She was close enough to read his identity badge. Dave Winston.

Dave patted her arm. 'I can see that, but you're glowing in your own way.' He paused delicately. 'You must be due soon?'

Roz averted her eyes. 'Yes, that's sort of why I'm here.

I'm due in a couple of weeks, and it's twins.' She looked up again. 'Twins! One baby would have been bad enough, but two? I had no idea they were so expensive. I'll need a double buggy, and cots, and formula and a sterilizer and clothes and all sorts of things. I have no idea where I'm going to get the money, but my friend Stella said you'd be able to help me.'

Dave smiled reassuringly.

It was a very practised expression, Roz decided.

'I understand completely. I don't suppose the father...' He allowed his voice to trail off.

'No. There's no father in the picture. My mate Stella is helping me get my child benefit organized. It will be extra with twins, but I need the money now.'

Dave patted her arm. 'That's what we're here for, love. What did you have in mind?'

She took a breath. 'Would a thousand pounds be too much?'

His smile turned shark-like. 'Of course not. Expensive, those young 'uns. Maybe you'll need a bit more. Say fifteen hundred? Repayment's only twenty quid a week, you'll manage that easily.'

Roz forced herself to look grateful. 'Oh thank you, thank you. You've saved my life. And the interest?'

'Will be no problem.' Dave helped her out of her chair and over to the counter where he handed her an application form.

Elaine O'Kennedy she wrote in the space for the name. She filled in one of the thirteen different addresses she had lived in as a child. Her dad didn't believe in settling down. She allowed her eyes to wander over the space behind the counter, searching for a locked container.

There. That was it. She scribbled a signature on the bottom of the page while he counted out the cash.

'Perfect.' Dave glanced at the form. 'Now, do you have a driving licence? I need to see some ID.' He held onto the bundle of notes.

She shook her head. 'No, I'm sorry.' She allowed a trace of desperation to sound in her voice. 'Does this mean I can't have the money?'

He frowned. 'Something else then? Your Benefit card, maybe?'

Her hand shook as she dug through her bag, looking for the card.

Dave snatched it out of her grasp and looked at the details on the forged card. 'Perfect. I'll hold onto this for a few days while I check your details.'

He unlocked the small heavy box behind the counter and dropped her card into it.

It was time.

Roz dropped the extra-fine condom she had filled with yellow-tinted water. It hit the ground with a satisfying splat, splashing the contents all over her legs and the carpet. She clutched her belly and gave a loud cry. 'My waters have broken.'

Roz doubled over. 'Ow, ow, ow. That must be a contraction. OW!'

'You said you weren't due for a couple of weeks.' Dave looked completely rattled.

She straightened up enough to glare at him. 'I'll be sure to tell the babies they're early.'

She clutched her belly again, moaning loudly. 'You have to call for help.'

Dave fumbled around the counter, looking for his phone. It had vanished.

Roz groaned again, her voice rising. 'Ow, that hurts so much.' She held onto the counter. 'I thought there were supposed to be gaps between contractions. These babies are in a hurry.'

'You can't have them here.' Dave stopped looking for the missing phone. 'Wait here, I'll go for help.'

She panted theatrically. 'Hurry, please.'

He bolted for the door.

As soon as he was gone, Roz ducked in behind the counter and grabbed the box. It was full of Benefit cards. Mr Sunny Money had being preying on her neighbours for months. Bastard. She lifted the skirt of her voluminous pregnancy dress, unzipped the top of her pregnancy 'bump' and emptied the contents of the box into it. Perfect. A lot of people would sleep better when they had those back. She quickly zipped up the 'bump' and lowered her dress, then looked around, checking to see if there was anything she had missed.

Bang! Bang!

Shots rang out, followed by the sounds of breaking glass and the screams of shoppers. Roz raised her head and caught a glimpse of a masked gunman holding a brutal-looking rifle. She dropped like a stone, praying he hadn't seen her.

More shots, screams, the noise of dozens of people running. An alarm went off.

Damn it! No prizes for guessing what had happened.

A robbery at the jewellers had gone wrong, and the thieves were trying to shoot their way out. And they were between her and the exit.

Roz stayed where she was, using the counter to shield her from the bedlam outside, but couldn't resist peering around the edge to see what was happening.

A tall figure was herding a bunch of kids down the service stairs. He was wearing an expensive looking wool coat, so it was hard to make out details, but there was something familiar about that figure.

He turned his head, and she caught a glimpse of a familiar profile.

Andy McTavish.

No, no, no! Anyone but him. The last person in the world she needed now was Andy McTavish. She had spent over a year on the run, staying one step ahead of him. She was not going to let him drag her to the nearest police station and hold her there 'til Interpol arrived. She had worked too hard, risked too much, to be caught now.

Her heart pounded. Why did they have to send someone so damn gorgeous to catch her?

Roz forced herself to crouch down behind the counter, well out of his sight. The emergency exit door closed and he was gone.

A police siren sounded in the distance, and a rapid splutter of shots told her the gunmen had a sub-machine gun as well as a revolver. Her chances of getting out alive were dropping rapidly.

She barely had time to register the shadow moving before a large body slid over the counter and onto the floor beside her.

'Oh!'

His dark eyes, veiled by ridiculously long lashes and shadowed by strong brows, were narrowed. His cheekbones were razor sharp, creating shadowed planes on his angular face. The thin mobile mouth was tight until he saw her hidden behind the counter.

She caught a wave of his scent, something woodsy and masculine that made her skin flush. How the hell could he have this effect on her?

Despite his crouched position, he took a moment to make a small bow. 'Sorry to disturb you, ma'am, but I need to borrow a couple of your knives.'

The soft Northern Irish burr was breathtakingly sexy. Even in the middle of a shoot-out with guns blazing, something inside her melted. That accent should be licensed. Typical Andy McTavish, flirting with any female he met, even in the middle of a gun battle. And he hadn't recognized her.

She quashed a stab of hurt and forced a strong Yorkshire English accent to her tongue. 'You're welcome.' Her disguise had held.

He ran interested eyes over her, stopping when he took in the bump that strained the front of her dress and his expression changed. 'Don't distress yourself, ma'am, I'll have you out of this in no time, I promise.'

'You and whose army?' she snapped. If there was one thing she hated, it was men who promised the moon and the stars, but failed to deliver.

His face changed, hardened. 'Ma'am. I'm a Ranger. I *am* an army.'

Despite herself, she couldn't help believing him.

One long arm reached up to the display and lifted down three of the knives from it. Andy tested the edges against his thumb, and nodded with satisfaction. 'I'll be back in a few minutes.' He tipped her chin up, planted a quick kiss on her forehead and said, 'Stay hidden, I promise I'll come back.'

Then he vaulted over the counter and was gone.

A stuttering round of gunfire hit the metal walkway. Sparks flashed as the bullets ricocheted, striking a shop-front and shattering the glass. More screams, but further away this time. A dull *phut-phut* as bullets hit the ceiling, spraying slivers of plaster onto his Savile Row suit.

Andy grinned and shook his head. Only a sad bastard missed being shot at, but things had been quiet lately. Even for him. What should have been a meeting with an informer about stolen art and the Eastern European mafia had suddenly got more interesting. His grin widened.

That pregnant brunette in there had doubted him? He would prove he was as good as his word. There was something familiar about her, something he couldn't put his finger on.

Another shot sounded and he dismissed the woman from his thoughts and concentrated on the job in hand.

Crouching, he tucked the smallest knife into his boot, and another one into his belt. The largest he jammed into his coat pocket, slicing the silk lining like a hot knife through butter. A gun would have been better, but beggars couldn't be choosers.

Andy moved closer to the robbery, sliding along the wall, out of sight, in the direction of the jeweller's shop, listening intently. It sounded like the idiots were trying to shoot open a safe. Two guns meant two tangos inside and there was probably a third nearby, sweating his ass off in a stolen car.

The sub-machine gun stuttered to silence.

'How was I to know the safe was on a time lock? Fucking piece of shit.' The roar came from inside the shop. More expletives followed before the gun sailed through the open doorway and over the railings to land in the fast food court below.

One weapon out of the way, but leaving empty handed would piss the thieves off and that could be dangerous.

'Get up, bitch. We're out of here.' Andy heard a different voice this time, older and harder.

'Please, no. I have a little girl. She's only four.' The woman's plea bordered on hysterical.

The sound of flesh striking flesh was startling in the silence of the empty shopping centre and she cried out in pain.

Andy's jaw locked and he forced himself to relax into his role of a businessman caught up in something nasty – the perfect bait for a pair of losers who needed a way out.

The woman emerged first, clutching helplessly at the arm around her neck. Her face was tear-stained and Andy could see the beginnings of a bruise on her cheekbone. Keeping his back to the wall, her captor moved them slowly along the walkway towards the emergency exit.

The second man exited the shop, clearly nervous.

Without a human shield he was exposed. He scanned the area as if fearful that a police sniper was already in place.

Andy came to his knees and raised his hands. 'Please don't shoot me.'

Relief swamped the younger gunman's face.

'Grab him,' the older man ordered.

Andy put up no resistance as he was dragged to his feet.

Like a chain gang from a black and white movie, they shuffled slowly towards the exit. Andy weighed his options. He needed to sort this out before the police got involved. His boss didn't pay him to spend time explaining fuck-ups in police stations.

The blaring sirens outside warned him that he was almost out of time.

Feigning clumsiness, he stumbled against the pair in front and they staggered. Andy pulled the smallest knife from his boot. As he righted himself, he stomped down hard on the younger gunman's foot. He slammed his elbow into his captor's solar plexus, driving the air from his lungs before spinning and jabbing his fist hard into the man's face. He enjoyed the satisfying crunch of bone and gristle.

Andy pulled out the second knife.

The older man turned swiftly, dragging the woman with him. His eyes narrowed and Andy could almost hear him weigh up his options. His grip tightened on the gun he was pointing at his hostage.

Acting purely on instinct, Andy let the knife fly. Like a slow-motion sequence from an action movie, it sailed through the air and the woman shrieked as it embedded itself in her captor's throat.

There was a noise behind him. Andy spun around. The younger robber was on his feet again and he was clutching the smaller knife.

Did these guys not know when to quit?

Andy reached into his pocket and grasped the handle of the largest knife but it tangled in the lining of his coat and refused to come free.

With a roar, the man lunged forwards. 'I'm gonna fucking gut you.'

The knife came straight at his eyes but Andy sidestepped. He tugged again at the knife in his pocket, but was forced to give up when the next slash grazed his jaw. Fuck. He was running out of options and time. Grasping the bone handle, Andy jerked the blade upwards.

As intimate as a lovers' dance, his assailant clutched at him. His expression slid from vicious anger to disbelief as a scarlet flood spread across his chest. 'Motherfucker,' he gasped, his knife dropping to the ground.

Andy stepped away and pulled the blade free. He forced his knife through the lining and it clattered onto the tiled floor.

'Ma'am,' he nodded to the woman as he stepped over the unconscious thief and returned to the moneylender's shop.

The brunette peeked out from behind the counter. 'What took you so long?'

'I was a bit busy,' he said. 'No kiss for the conquering hero?'

She snorted. 'You've had one already.'

He laughed. 'That wasn't a kiss.'

Was it his imagination or had her Yorkshire accent

faded? There was definitely something familiar about her. Those startling blue eyes reminded him of someone.

She struggled to her feet, her belly getting in the way, and he reined in his unruly imagination. 'Come on, I'll help you get to an ambulance.'

She froze. 'No. No ambulance.'

The woman put her foot down on something wet and slipped. As she went down, Andy was there at her side. He caught her in his arms and registered that she felt slighter than he had expected. Then something else caught his eye. Her hair had moved.

Andy put up his hand and touched it. The brown wig slipped, revealing bright red hair.

Stunned, he stepped back, staring at her. It had been so long since he had last seen her, but there was no doubt who it was. The furious blue eyes belonged to the woman who had led him a merry dance for over a year. She adjusted the wig, tugging it back into place.

'Roz O'Sullivan?' he asked, just to make sure.

He thought he heard, 'Busted!' under her breath before she straightened her shoulders defiantly. 'Roz Spring, actually.'

It was her! This was the brat who had stolen a fabulous jewel from a museum in Switzerland by impersonating her sister and had been on the run ever since. Andy had caught her once and dragged her back to give evidence at her sister's trial, but she had given him the slip right after by climbing through the second-floor window in the judge's chamber.

And here she was, glaring at him through narrowed eyes. Eyes which had kept him awake more often than he wanted to admit, but he knew this was one woman he couldn't pursue. Even if she weren't as slippery as wet soap, as trustworthy as an election promise and as cunning as a cat smelling tuna, she was off-limits: Roz was a wanted woman. He'd been on a watching brief for Moore Enterprises for the past year, with orders to pick her up if she crossed his path. The fact that Roz was his boss's sister-in-law irked Niall Moore more than he would admit.

But now Andy had her, although her distended abdomen troubled him more than the fight. How could Roz Spring be pregnant?

The usual way, fuckwit!

For some reason, he didn't want to think about Roz O'Sullivan or Spring, or whatever she called herself, with some strange man. Not that it was any of his business. She was nothing to do with him and never could be.

He caught her arm. 'You gave me a good run, but it's time to come in.'

Andy half expected her to fight him, to try to pull away and escape from him. God knows she could run. Instead, she doubled over and moaned. 'Oh, Oh!'

The stains on her dress and the pool of liquid on the floor made his stomach clench. 'Jesus, you're in labour? You're going to have the baby?'

Maybe it was the panic in his voice, but she had a hint of laughter in her eyes. 'Not quite, but if you don't get me out of here soon, I will.'

It couldn't be fucking easy, could it?

Andy ushered her along the walkway and down the stairwell. The lifts had already been shut down as part of the police emergency response. He pushed down on the

13

bar of the security door and they were immediately greeted by an ERU team.

Ignoring her protests, he lifted Roz up in his arms. 'My wife is in labour. The shock . . .'

'An ambulance is on its way, sir.'

Still carrying Roz, Andy pushed his way through the crowd. A smattering of applause came from the group of schoolchildren behind the police barrier. Shit. He couldn't afford to get caught up in this. Across the street, a taxi pulled up and Andy dodged the oncoming traffic as he ran for it. God, but she was heavy. Babies were small creatures, weren't they? How much weight did a pregnant woman gain?

He eased Roz to her feet and yanked open the door, ushering her into the back seat of the cab, before sliding in beside her. 'Which hospital?'

'None. Get me out of here.' She glared at him like a feral cat.

Maybe she was in shock. He tried again, more patiently this time. 'We need to get you to hospital, but you have to tell me which one.'

More glaring. She clutched her damp dress, raising her skirt away from her and in the process displaying a pair of shapely legs.

You're a pervert, McTavish. Andy tried to avert his eyes, but a sick fascination prevented him. He caught a glimpse of dark red panties.

Yep, you're definitely going to hell.

'Hey. My face is up here,' Roz snapped. 'And I don't need a hospital. I need to lie down for a while.'

His instinct was to get her to a doctor as soon as possible, but he supposed she would know if she needed one or not. And besides, he was certain that in a hospital, she would give him the slip again.

'Fine. We'll go to my hotel.' He nodded to the driver. 'Take us to the Savoy.'

2

She was silent on the journey. Andy could almost hear the wheels whirring inside her head. Roz Spring was a con artist and a chameleon. She was also in danger, something which didn't seem to trouble her a bit.

'You're looking well,' he ventured. The shapeless maternity clothes did nothing for her, but nothing could hide the vibrancy of her red hair, visible now that she had taken off the wig.

Roz gave him a speculative look. 'You're unbelievable, do you know that? Coming on to a pregnant woman. That's disgusting.'

'I am not coming on to you.'

'I saw you looking,' she said, raising her voice so that the driver could hear.

The temptation to snap back at her was almost overwhelming. Instead, Andy took a deep breath. She had been running for over a year and it was pure luck that he had caught up with her now. He wouldn't give her an excuse to run again.

The official reason Europe's top private security firm was still pursuing Roz was that she had witnessed a brutal murder and Interpol wanted her to give evidence in court. The police had failed to catch her, but Moore Enterprises hadn't given up.

Andy knew that the real reason his boss wanted Roz caught was that his wife would give him no peace until her missing twin was found. The sisters had grown up apart. Sinead was raised by her millionaire uncle, while Roz had been brought up by her low-life criminal father. No wonder she had turned out bad. Andy was under orders to find her and capture her, no matter what he was doing.

He smiled grimly. He bet his boss hadn't expected this. Niall Moore might be pissed off that the stolen art job was a wash-out. He wouldn't get to pose as a buyer after all, but at least the suite at the Savoy wouldn't go to waste.

He glanced at Roz again. Why hadn't she turned herself in to the police? She had a baby to protect, for god's sake. She would be defenceless against a ruthless murderer. What the hell had she been doing, getting pregnant when her life was such a mess? It made no sense. And where was the father?

She had done a good job of disguising herself, he admitted grudgingly. The nondescript clothes and brown wig had transformed her.

'Something on your mind?' Her question interrupted his musing.

'Not a thing,' he replied evenly. 'Couldn't be better. There's nothing like a knife fight to set a man up for the day.'

She paled and he regretted his words immediately. Andy patted her hand. 'Relax. You'll be fine when we get to the hotel and you can lie down.'

Roz turned away, staring at the London traffic, but as he watched her reflection in the glass, he caught a glimpse of her impish grin. She was up to something. If there was one thing he had learnt from trying to catch her, it was that Roz didn't give up easily.

Roz couldn't resist watching Andy's reflection in the window. London slid by unseen while she soaked in the sight of the Irishman who had haunted her dreams for months.

God, he was a treat for the eyes. Andy was tall and elegant but his outward appearance was deceptive. She knew that under the expensive clothes he was lean and ripped, with lightning reflexes and a body to die for. His cheekbones alone would have made him a fortune as a cover model, while those dark brown eyes could see into her soul. Black Irish. She had heard the phrase before but had no idea what it meant before she met him.

And that mouth. Mobile and sensual with a hint of wicked promise. The mouth of a man who knew how to seduce a woman.

Her dreams hadn't done him justice, she decided. She had met him twice before, once on a wild run through the streets of Paris, and once when he had dragged her along to give evidence at her sister's trial.

She had never really spoken to him before, or got close enough to smell the distinctive scent of his skin, musky and woody and male. Close enough to see the slight darkening of his jaw which signalled that he needed to shave again. The hint of a dimple in one lean cheek.

Don't think about that. She shivered.

She was too old for stupid fantasies about the impossible. Most of her experiences with men had been disappointing. Eventually, when her life was sorted out, she'd find a nice man, someone solid and reliable and nice looking.

Not a living, breathing fantasy.

The taxi pulled up outside the Savoy. Andy held her arm as he helped her out, and the taxi driver smiled the smile of a man who had been lavishly over-tipped.

Roz was conscious of her mud-coloured clothes, bought on the sale rack in Primark. The disguise had been necessary for the scam to work, but now she was hideously out of place. Around her, women dressed in real silk and fur swanned through the foyer, and the scent of expensive perfume competing with elaborate floral displays made her want to sneeze.

The immaculately polite doorman ignored her condition and saluted Andy. 'Mr McTavish, welcome back, sir.'

'Thanks Bill, can you help me look after my guest?'

The two of them herded her towards the lifts. Yes, she was definitely going to his room.

Roz allowed herself to waddle, and was rewarded when Andy winced.

He might have the beauty, but she had the brains.

Naturally, he was staying in a suite – a big, expensive one, with a king-sized bed, a panoramic view of London and a bathroom bigger than her flat in Peckham. She wondered what it cost for a night, and shuddered.

'Slumming it, are we?' she asked.

'Working.' He gave her a sardonic smile before he tipped her helper discreetly and allowed him to go. Andy guided her to the bed.

19

Roz was almost reluctant to climb onto the silk cover-let, but decided that he deserved whatever happened. Roz groaned as she lay down, a sound of relief that she didn't have to fake. That belly was heavy and uncomfortable.

'Are you all right?' he asked, with what sounded like genuine concern. His mesmerizing eyes were fixed on her.

Roz knew people. She had spent a lifetime reading them, learning how they reacted, what they would respond to. And in spite of Andy's efforts to stay detached, she thought she caught a glimpse of something more than simple concern.

'Tell me,' she said. 'Do you remember that day in Paris when we met?'

He nodded.

That day had changed her life, in more ways than one. And Andy was a part of it. Running alongside him as they raced to save her sister's life was an experience which had never left her.

'Me too,' she admitted.

His eyes darkened. 'You were the most beautiful, aggra-vating, annoying trouble-maker I ever met.' The words seemed to be dragged from him.

She almost smiled. God, it was good to know that she'd made some impression on him. The flush on his chiselled cheeks was evidence that, like it or not, Andy McTavish had thought about her, too.

'Did you ever wonder . . .' She allowed her voice to trail off.

He leaned in closer to her. 'Wonder what?'

He was so close she could smell his aftershave.

What the hell. She was never going to see him again

anyway. 'About this.' She put her arms around his neck, pulled him down to her and kissed him.

He resisted for a fraction of a second before kissing her back.

That wicked mouth could deliver on its sensual promise. Andy might be hard and angular, but his mouth was hot and sweet.

No one had ever kissed her like this. His lips brushed hers, supple and sure. He took his time, teasing and tasting her, unexpectedly gentle, but certain of what he was doing. He kissed as if she were the only woman in the entire world. As if he had all the time in the world.

He pressed a little harder, slanting his head and encouraging her to open up to him.

Roz could have resisted a head-on assault. She'd met dozens of those over the years and knew how to counter them. But kisses like this, which were sweet and tender and so unexpected, took her breath away.

As long as Andy was kissing her, she had no need to breathe.

She parted her lips a little so that he could deepen the kiss, and was rewarded with the sweep of his tongue. Still he controlled the kiss so that she could enjoy it. And she did.

He tasted smoky and male, a potent combination that teased her into sucking on the tip of that tantalizing tongue. He groaned and lowered his body closer to hers. The movement brought him against her fake bump and the strap that held it in place tightened painfully, making her gasp.

He released her instantly. One moment he was kissing

her, the next he was standing beside the bed, staring at her with shock in his eyes.

'Oh god, did I hurt you? I almost forgot you were pregnant.'

There was a dark flush on his blade-sharp cheekbones which told her he had been lost in the kiss.

She had forgotten her bump. 'I almost did, too.'

Awkwardly she sat up in the bed, the weight of the latex belly hampering her movements. She had to get it together. She couldn't let her attraction to Andy distract her. It was time to get back to business. She took advantage of the opening he had given her and groaned.

'What was that?' she gasped as she pressed her hands against the bump. 'Please say that wasn't a contraction!'

She had to fight to keep her face straight when Andy backed away from her as if he expected a baby to burst out of her belly. He was more panicked now than he had been in the shopping centre when he was taking on a bunch of armed robbers.

'What can I do? Do you want some hot water?'

What did men think labouring women did with all that hot water? Go for a swim? But it was too good a chance. 'Yes please. And some spare sheets and towels.'

He swallowed it. 'I'll call reception.'

'No, they'll take too long. You'll be quicker.' Please don't let him ask what she wanted the sheets and towels for.

As soon as the door closed behind him, Roz hopped off the bed and pulled out the wallet she had lifted from his pocket while he was carrying her to the bed. She dropped the wallet into her bump. She didn't have time to go through it now. She would sort it out and return the cards later.

It was time to get out of there.

She peered up and down the corridor, wondering which way he had gone. She couldn't afford to run into him. The lift dinged, announcing its arrival and she made a dash for it. *Please don't let me run into him.*

A young couple exited, too involved with each other to notice her, and she stepped inside and pressed the button for the lobby. The journey down seemed to take years. In the foyer, the nice doorman who had helped her earlier was busy directing a well-dressed tourist to Soho.

Roz slipped by them and into the crowded street. Only then did she release a breath she hadn't realized she'd been holding.

That had been far too close for her liking.

Half an hour later, she was back in Peckham. As usual, the lift was out of order. 'Home sweet home,' she muttered.

Roz climbed the five flights of stairs to Stella's flat. The place was clean and cosy and, most importantly, she was completely under the radar.

Stella had gone to meet her online lover in Italy, leaving the keys to Roz and giving her somewhere to live with no paper trail. There were way too many people anxious to get hold of her. She wasn't going to make it easy for anyone.

With a sigh, she stripped off the ill-fitting clothes, until she was naked apart from the latex pregnancy belly. It was incredibly useful for carrying out scams – no one ever looked at her face, just at her belly – but it wasn't comfortable to wear. The straps left red welts on her skin, and sweat had pooled beneath it. She fished out the contents of the bump, smiling when she saw how much it held.

'Shower, then shopping,' she said, her voice loud in the silence.

Roz switched on the television and listened to the news report of the aborted robbery in Lewisham. No mention of a pregnant woman, but a blonde with a black eye raved about the man who had saved her from the robbers. The management of the shopping centre were offering a reward for the mysterious hero if he would come back to claim it. The photo-fit looked more like David Tennant than Andy, she decided.

She had first-hand evidence that the body concealed by that expensive coat was far better built than any actor. And he smelled better. Roz stamped on that line of thought and, even though the water wasn't fully heated up, she forced herself under it. A cold shower was what she needed to keep her mind on business.

An hour later, she was clean and dressed in dark leggings and a colourful top which concealed her slender figure.

She riffled through Andy's wallet and found he had been carrying a lot of cash. A thousand pounds. Plus three platinum credit cards and a slim smartphone. She switched it on, impressed by the quality of the graphics and the speed of response. Andy clearly had money to burn. Niall Moore must pay a lot more than minimum wage.

She knew that Moore Enterprises was the best private

security company in Europe, known for providing body-guards for the rich and famous. It was less well-known that the company specialized in hostage rescue and provided security for medical staff in war zones around the world. She had heard that everyone who worked for Moore's was the best of the best. If Andy was an example, she could well believe it.

Roz ran her eye down the call log and took down a few interesting numbers. Oh look, Andy even had her sister's number in his phone. And contact details for her Irish relatives. How interesting. She removed the battery and SIM card, and set off for work.

The food bank was as busy as usual. Olyenka, terrifyingly efficient and refusing to be slowed by the baby at her breast, was manning the office when Roz arrived.

'Hi Oly, got a few things you might be able to help me with.'

Roz handed over the Benefit cards she had 'liberated' from Sunny Money. 'I thought you might be able to return them to their rightful owners.'

Olyenka leafed through the cards, her eyebrows rising when she saw names she recognized. She kept her hair cropped ruthlessly short, so her expression was visible. 'I won't ask how you got hold of these, but I know their owners will be glad to have them back.'

Roz tickled baby Benjamin's smooth, dark cheek. He smiled back at her without letting the nipple go.

'And I have another donation for you.'

She pulled out the thousand pounds she had taken

from Andy's wallet. After a moment's thought, she pocketed a twenty. A girl had to eat, and he owed her dinner. She handed over the rest.

'Roz, you can't keep giving us this sort of money,' Olyenka protested, even while she took the notes and put them into the cash box.

'Hey, it's nothing to do with me. It's from an anonymous well-wisher, who knows what amazing work you do here.' Well, Andy would have donated it if he knew, she told herself.

'Need a hand packing parcels?'

Her father would shit a brick if he could see her, Roz knew, but there was something therapeutic about packing boxes of pasta while chatting with the other women about their disastrous dates. Briefly, she had a sense of belonging.

3

Roz was gone. The room was empty and there was no sign of her. Andy dropped his armful of sheets and towels, picked up the room phone and found the number for reception.

'Yes, sir,' the concierge reassured him. His guest had left and no, she hadn't ordered a taxi.

What the hell was wrong with him? Okay, it had been a while since he'd kissed a woman, other than in the line of duty, but Roz Spring. Pregnant Roz Spring! He must have been out of his mind.

He didn't want to think about how her mouth felt under his. How sweet and soft her lips were against his. *Lying lips.*

His anger abated as quickly as it came. His investigation into her past had revealed that she had turned her hand to everything from stunt double to circus act. She never put down roots, never got involved and he was no nearer finding the real Roz than he had been more than a year before.

Sitting down heavily on the rumpled bed, Andy picked up the remote and flicked around the TV channels. Almost all the channels were running coverage of the botched robbery at the shopping centre and the hospitalization of the thieves.

An interview with a tearful mother described how the

unknown hero had led a party of schoolchildren to safety. Breaking news revealed that a teenager had managed to shoot some mobile phone footage of him carrying Roz across the street.

On the next channel, a pompous security adviser confirmed that the mystery man was 'definitely military' and that they were making appropriate enquiries. There was no doubt about it – he was up to his oxters in trouble.

Time to face the music. He reached into his pocket for his phone. Empty. His phone was gone and so was his wallet.

A sinking feeling hit the pit of his stomach. She couldn't have. Roz wouldn't dare steal from him. He riffled through his pockets again and even took a peek under the bed, but they were gone. That kiss had been an act, and he had fallen for it.

Andy picked up the hotel phone again and punched in the number of the last man in the world he wanted to talk to.

'Moore,' a clipped voice answered. Niall obviously hadn't looked at the caller display, but less than half a dozen people in the world had the private number for the CEO of Moore Enterprises.

'Turn on the TV,' Andy said without preamble. It was better to let him know the worst immediately.

'Any particular station?' The question was innocent enough, but the silky undertone held a touch of menace. His boss wasn't someone he wanted to piss off. He'd watched grown men quake in their boots when they had to admit that they had messed up on a mission, and Andy had done a spectacular job today. He was supposed to be working undercover, not getting his face plastered all over the TV.

'Take your pick.'

Andy heard a TV being switched on and Niall channel hopping his way through local and national stations.

'Who is the woman?'

Andy swallowed. 'Your missing sister-in-law.'

'You've brought her in? Sinead will be over the moon, she . . .'

Andy let the rest of Niall's words drift over him. How could he tell Sinead that he had found her missing sister, and let her get away again? The wounded look in her eyes would kill him. She brought out all his protective urges, making him want to slay dragons for her. And, of course, he couldn't. That was Niall's job.

A vision of another redhead, one exactly like Sinead, popped into his head, and he snorted. Roz didn't need anyone to protect her. It was the poor dragon who would need to be rescued. Let Roz near the beast and she'd end up selling him to a circus before he knew what hit him.

They might be twins, but Roz and Sinead were nothing alike.

Niall stopped talking when he realized he was getting no response. 'You've lost her again, haven't you?'

Again? Now that was a tad unfair. He hadn't expected to walk into a gun battle or Roz O'Sullivan. Come to think of it, he would have rather faced half a dozen armed tangos then go another round with the lying scheming little –

'Andy.' The sharp tone claimed his attention.

'Sorry, boss. It's been an epic bastard of a day.'

Niall grunted in agreement. They had shared quite a few days like that in the field. 'What happened?'

Andy rattled through his report of his day, skimming lightly over his feelings of shock when he found Roz crouching behind the counter in the shop. Her face pale with fear, her eyes more blue than he had remembered and her belly distended with. Fuck. He still had to drop that particular bombshell.

'And she's pregnant,' he finished his report and waited.

The silence on the other end of the line was more telling than a dozen expletives. 'She's what?' Niall sounded stunned. 'But who's the . . . ? And how did she manage that?'

Andy grinned. 'The usual way, I imagine.'

It was none of his business, Andy decided. He might have kissed her in a moment of madness, but that didn't mean that he liked her.

Niall cleared his throat. 'Find her, Andy. Call in whatever resources you need. A whole team if necessary, but I want her found within twenty-four hours.'

'Any particular reason?' There was something up with the big guy and it was more than discovering that his sister-in-law was knocked up.

'Because that's how long I have until my wife gets back from Castletownberehaven. She went to tell Granny O'Sullivan the good news. Sinead is pregnant too.'

Reeling from the news, Andy put the phone back on the hook. He now had another call to make, which would be about as much fun as the last one.

Reluctantly, he rang his office and reported the theft of

his wallet and phone, the one with all his numbers and contacts.

'You were rolled?' Reilly didn't bother to hide her mirth. 'Mr I'm-too-sexy-for-my-own-good finally got a taste of his own medicine? Wait 'til I tell the guys.'

'Tara baby, don't.'

'Not a chance. And don't try that baby stuff on me. I'm immune, remember? I'll put a trace on the phone, but I wouldn't hold out much hope. I'll work on getting you a replacement.'

Andy sighed. The petite operative was the fantasy girl for half the team, but she didn't mix business with pleasure. 'How long will it be?'

'With all the stuff you keep on it? At least an hour. Sit tight in your hotel until then.' Still laughing at his predicament, she hung up.

He would have to do this the hard way. Over the next hour, Andy rang every maternity hospital within a ten mile radius. No one answering Roz's description had been brought in and he was fed up pretending to be an anxious boyfriend or husband.

Idly, he flicked the channels on the TV, but there were few further updates about the robbery. The tangos were in hospital and Lewisham shopping centre was open for business again.

'Doh.' He tapped his forehead. Why hadn't he thought of it before? During the shooting, Roz had been in a moneylender's shop. If she was borrowing from them, they must have a record of her. He pulled on his jacket and hurried to the lobby, taking the stairs two at a time.

As he passed by the front desk, the concierge motioned to him. 'Delivery for you, sir.'

Andy tore the packet open and pulled out his replacement phone. 'God bless you, Reilly.'

He was back in business.

The shattered glass had been swept away and a gang of gawking teenagers were hanging around outside the jewellery store, jeering the police working inside. Andy stepped into Sunny Money, where it was business as usual. He waited while a middle-aged woman spoke quietly to the man behind the counter. Her son owed money to drug dealers and she needed to pay them off.

The hopeless set of her shoulders and the trembling of her veined hand as she signed for the notes told him it wasn't the first time. Clutching her battered handbag under her arm, she left, head bowed.

The assistant looked up. 'It's you,' he stammered, 'with the knives and . . .'

'Aye,' Andy agreed.

The assistant swallowed, his Adam's apple bobbing up and down nervously.

Andy glanced at the name badge pinned to his chest. 'Dave, isn't it?'

'Yes, sir,' Dave agreed, anxious to please.

'I'm looking for the woman who was here when the shooting started. She's a customer of yours, I understand.'

'I'm not sure if I can –'

'I'd like to send her some flowers,' Andy cut across him. 'Make sure that she's okay. No harm in that. Right, Dave?'

'Well, if you say so.' His voice trailed away and he handed over the clipboard stacked with loan applications.

Andy flicked through them quickly. None for Roz Spring or any variation on that name, but one form caught his eye. An Elaine O'Kennedy, who wanted to borrow money for baby supplies. Bingo! According to the information she had given, she lived less than a mile away.

Andy memorized the address and handed the clipboard back. Roz might be a thieving little bitch, but she was also pregnant and in trouble. He'd better hurry.

Number nine, Davis Street, proved to be a boarded up corner shop beside a high rise estate. The broken windows on the upper floors and the rusted hinges told him that no one was at home.

'Clever girl.' He had to admire her audacity in trying to scam the moneylender, but he was facing another dead end.

His new phone vibrated in his pocket and he fished it out. 'McTavish.'

'How much do you love me?' Reilly's cheerful voice teased him.

'Why? What did you do?'

'I've managed to trace your phone.'

'Well, in that case, let's get married immediately. I want you to have my babies.'

'And sit at home minding them while you're off flying your kite? Dream on.' Reilly snorted. 'Your target is a clever girl. The phone is dead. She must have removed the battery and SIM card, but she didn't know about the GPS locator in the battery.'

Andy laughed. 'Where is she?'

Reilly rattled off an address in Peckham.

Andy stepped into the street to wave down a passing taxi. 'Oh, I've got you now, darling.'

Andy held the door open for a dark-eyed woman pushing a twin buggy and slipped into the building. It wasn't as bad as he'd expected. The place needed a paint job, but the small lobby contained a community notice board advertising drugs awareness and a mother-and-baby group in the local church hall. Andy checked his GPS locator app for his missing phone.

Number fifty-seven was on the fifth floor. The cardboard handwritten sign on the lift announced that it was broken, so he found the stairs and began climbing. He winced at the thought of a pregnant woman climbing all those stairs. When he finally reached the fifth floor, Andy tapped on the door and waited. No response. He tapped again and then gave up. He picked the lock quickly and let himself inside.

The flat wasn't what he expected. It was neat and tidy but not the type of place he imagined Roz living in. She was wild and vibrant, with too large a personality for this tiny space.

'Anyone home?' he called, and when no one replied he took it as an invitation to search.

On the mantelpiece above the gas fire was his phone, neatly taken apart. He re-assembled it and switched it on. She hadn't made any calls, but she'd been nosing around his Yahoo account. What was she up to now?

The living room revealed little of interest, except for

a bag that contained knitting patterns and skeins of brightly coloured wool. She must have a flatmate. He couldn't imagine Roz as a knitter in a million years. Mind you, he had found it impossible to believe she was pregnant and he couldn't understand why it pissed him off so much.

The wardrobe of one bedroom was stuffed with clothes, and none of them would fit a woman more than five feet tall. Roz could change a lot of things about her appearance but she couldn't make herself short. Andy guessed she was at least five seven.

The other room was barely big enough to hold a single bed. A faint hint of perfume hung in the air and he inhaled deeply. Yes, it was definitely Roz's room.

He riffled through her lingerie drawer without a hint of shame. Roz had some nice stuff. Not a lot, but nothing tatty. He pulled open another drawer. Laid out as neatly as a department store display was a collection of gloves, ranging from fingerless workout gloves to woolly mittens and expensive evening gloves. Well, well. Looked like he'd found her weakness. He picked up one pair. The butter-soft kidskin was light as a feather. The label inside announced that they had been made in Paris.

Curiosity got the better of him. Andy raised the leather to his face and sniffed. Another faint trace of her perfume. What would it feel like to be touched by someone wearing these, to enjoy the sensation of soft leather on his skin?

'You're definitely a pervert, McTavish,' he muttered, before replacing the gloves and closing the drawer firmly.

A cupboard revealed a footwear collection that would

give a shoe fetishist an orgasm. Neatly arranged were dozens of pairs of heels in all colours. He ran his fingertips over a pair of dark blue velvet knee-high boots and sighed. He could imagine the old Roz, the one he had met in Paris, wearing these and nothing else.

The flat trainers puzzled him. The soles were thin and he couldn't imagine they would give any support. Replacing them on the shelf, he opened the cupboard. A bulky pregnancy belly hung from a hook and next to it was the shapeless maternity dress Roz had been wearing earlier.

'Holy fuck.' He reached out to touch the latex costume. The moulded form was soft to the touch and bounced back when he removed his finger. It was heavier than Kevlar and must have been a bitch to wear. No wonder she looked worn out.

The conniving wee Jezebel.

Up to now, this mission had been business, but it had just turned personal: she had lied to him and deceived him. Roz Spring, or O'Sullivan, or whatever the hell she was calling herself, had invited a whole heap of trouble into her life and he wasn't going to rest until he found her.

4

'So what are we going to do about your appalling love life?' Jake asked. He pushed a pallet loaded with bags of sugar in Roz's direction and she pulled out two from the top. The packing centre in the food bank smelled of the recent consignment of lemons.

'There's nothing wrong with my love life,' she told him. 'As long as you don't try to mess with it.'

'Me?' He tried to look harmless and injured, which was hard to do when you're six and a half foot of Polish muscle. Most people who met him assumed he was the bouncer at the food bank, not a ridiculously over-qualified manager.

'Not my fault you didn't like the guy I set you up with.'

'Alexander? He never stopped talking. I couldn't get a word in edgeways.'

Jake cut open a box of tins. 'With you in the room? He deserves a medal.'

She stuck her tongue out at him. She didn't talk that much.

'What about Patrick? He's a good listener.'

'With bad breath and he has a tendency to grope.' Of course, he wouldn't make that mistake again. She disliked gropers.

'You're impossible to please.'

The two women helping to pack food bags were listening in and sniggered.

'I am not. You keep sending me weirdoes,' she told Jake. The man was a sweetheart, but since he had married Kate, he had forgotten what dating was like.

'Okay, Roz, tell me what sort of man you would like. Is he actually human? Does he exist?'

She finished the bags she was working on and pulled over another bundle. 'Of course he does. He's tall, muscular, with long hair. Maybe blond. Blue eyes. Quiet, someone who listens. But who can make up his mind and take action when he needs to. Someone loyal.'

She had this description off by rote. It had been her ideal of manhood for a long time.

'So if Thor appears, I'll give him your address,' Natalya assured her. 'In the meantime, back on planet Earth, are there any men here that you do like?'

An image of a long, lean Irishman, with messy black hair and laughing dark eyes, pushed its way to the front of her mind. She had deliberately kissed him in the Savoy to throw him off-balance, but she was the one who had been dizzy ever since. Was it that he was a spectacularly good kisser? Or his sexy Irish accent? Or some secret Andy McTavish thing? The memory of him hadn't left her for a single second since the moment of their kiss, and her libido had gone into overdrive.

She wanted to kill him.

Roz shook her head. 'No, I know what I want. I'm not taking second best.' She looked at Jake speculatively. 'What colour is your hair when you don't shave it?'

He laughed. 'Nice try. But I will find you someone. You spend too much time alone.'

'I'm happy that way. I haven't met a man I wouldn't dump for eating Hobnobs in bed.'

Of course, it wasn't the whole truth. Roz knew her life was a mess. She was wanted by the police as a witness to a murder. At least that's what they said. She didn't trust them not to try to pin the murder on her. With her less-than-stellar record and her father's criminal and prison record, it would be much easier to lock her up for the murder than go looking for the real killer – the man she had seen slitting the throat of an elderly French antique dealer.

She shuddered at the memory, and at how close she had come to death.

She had gone to pay a midnight visit to an elderly French art dealer who did a bit of jewel fencing on the side and discovered that he already had a visitor. Roz had watched from the shadows as the big blond American had fought with the old guy. She was too far away to hear all the argument, but had heard the little Frenchman threaten to tell the police something.

Roz still flinched at the memory of the speed with which the big man had produced a lethal-looking knife and stabbed the poor man in the neck. It was done so neatly and professionally that there was almost no blood splatter, but the violence of the movement had shaken her to her bones.

She had stuffed a fist into her mouth to avoid crying out. Later, she had found teeth marks embedded in the back of her hand, but at the time she felt nothing.

The murderer ignored the dead man on the floor, picked the locked jewellery cases, conducted a lightning search and let himself out silently.

Roz felt as if she hadn't taken a single breath until he was gone.

She crept down from her hiding place and knelt beside him. She was no medical expert, but even she could see that the glazed eyes and pale skin belonged to a corpse. There was no emergency service on earth which could help him now.

She wasn't religious, but she breathed a silent prayer over him before leaving quietly, hoping that he was somewhere with lots of jewels and paintings and gullible punters.

Roz cursed her unruly tongue, which had let slip that she had witnessed the murder. She had been hoping to cut a deal with the police; trading information so that they wouldn't send her to prison for stealing the jewel. One interview with Interpol later, she knew more than she wanted to about former Navy SEAL J. Darren Hall. He had been kicked out in disgrace and was now for hire to anyone who had more money than scruples.

The door of the workroom opened and, as if her thoughts had conjured him, a large blond man walked into the dimly lit space, led by Olyenka.

For a moment, terror froze her lungs. She couldn't breathe or move. It was him. Hall had found her. Somehow he had tracked her down to the food bank, and now everyone who worked here was in danger.

'You've never heard of me,' she murmured to Jake, and slid down behind the row of packing boxes. The windows were barred and Hall was in front of the door. But there was a tiny space at the back where the smokers indulged their addiction. She crouched low and scuttled for the back door as fast as possible.

Jake, the darling, was being all managerial and official, demanding papers from the intruder.

Roz sneaked outside into the walled-in space, took a breath and leapt for the top of the wall. It was about ten foot high, but adrenaline and desperation gave her the strength to make it. She caught the top of the wall with her fingertips and ignored the slam of her body against the bricks.

A familiar calm descended. This she knew. She swung herself up, and climbed on top of the ancient red brick wall. Once upright, she balanced herself and ran along the top, jumping over the barbed wire separating this yard from the next, then on to the next one. And there, at the end of that wall, was the pot of gold – a fire escape leading up onto the roof.

Roz sometimes felt that she was part cat. There was something about being high up that reassured her. When in trouble, her instinct was always to go for the high ground. And up on the rooftops of London, she was at home.

A quick glance behind her was enough to show her that Hall had managed to figure out where she had gone, and he was already in pursuit. She felt an unexpected flicker of guilt and prayed that he hadn't hurt anyone. She had allowed herself to stay too long here, had made friends, and it may have cost them dearly.

Hall, damn him, was moving over the crumbling walls with amazing speed for such a large man.

41

She loved parkour. It had started with running away from the cops or irate marks when she was younger, but had evolved into a full-scale love affair. There was something about the freedom of the run, the unpredictability of the terrain, the adrenaline rush, the punishing workout which left her shaking afterwards. She had never been interested in doing it officially or entering competitions, but she had studied the best free runners online and learnt from their technique.

Parkour had always been an escape from her problems. Now it might save her life.

The light was fading. She hoped that would make it harder for Hall to see her in the gloom. Her jeans were dark but the multi-coloured sweater Stella had knitted for her stood out. She hated to do it, but she had no choice.

She stripped off the gorgeous jumper, leaving her in a black T-shirt. The movement cost her precious seconds, and Hall was closer. A quick glance behind revealed the soulless determination in his eyes.

Roz picked up speed. She couldn't let him catch her. The approaching night made it harder to judge distances between buildings, and impossible to see small obstacles in her path. She had to keep a sense of where she was going.

London from the rooftops was completely different from the streets, and it was essential that she didn't get trapped by a main road. She could leap across alleys but not a two-lane high street.

From the sound of his footsteps, she knew that Hall was close behind her. How did he do it? Roz knew she was one of the fastest runners in the area, and he was keeping up with her. Guess the SEALs really were supermen. She'd have to do better.

She raced across a glass roof she would usually have avoided, trusting that her lighter frame wouldn't smash it. Hall must be close to seventeen stone, all pure muscle. She gained a couple of seconds when he went around it.

The next roof was too far away to risk a jump. She swung over the edge, using the tiny niches between the red bricks as finger and toe holds until she could grab at a balcony. A startled yelp from a lady watching television morphed into a scream, but she didn't have time to do anything about it. She shuffled along the ledge to the next corner, where there was an easy jump to safety.

Roz scrambled across the roof, trying to keep her footing on the slippery slates. She couldn't keep this up for much longer. Yelling for help wasn't likely to do her much good in London; everyone thought it was someone else's business.

The main road loomed up ahead, busy with traffic and pedestrians. A double-decker bus accelerated away from the traffic lights.

Hall was thirty yards behind her. Okay, no choice.

Roz leapt for the moving bus, and landed on its roof with a thump. She crouched, desperately, trying to absorb the shock and keep her balance, wedging her fingers into a tiny row of rivets. It wasn't much, but it was enough to help her hold on while the bus rounded the corner and moved out of Hall's sight.

Pedestrians nudged each other and pointed at her. She waved back as if she were supposed to be up there, but made up her mind. She had to get off. She was attracting too much attention.

When the bus stopped at the lights, she jumped onto the top of a parked four-wheel drive, and nipped into the nearest McDonald's. She was too stressed to eat, but ordered a large soda and tried to calm her breathing.

What was she going to do now? She didn't dare go back to her flat. She had no idea how Hall had caught up with her, or if there was a chance he knew where she lived. She wasn't walking into a trap.

Roz sipped her drink and considered what she could do. London was too hot. She'd been on the news after the robbery in Lewisham and now Hall had turned up at the food bank. She had a couple of cash-in-hand part time jobs, but spent most of her time helping at the food bank. She was going to have to leave.

Her passport was back in the flat, so getting on a plane was out of the question. She supposed she could get to Dover and smuggle her way onto the ferry to Calais. She knew France pretty well and had friends there, even if it was a part of her life that she had left behind. But Hall knew that too.

Where could she go?

There had been a time she would have asked her dad for advice in this sort of situation, but no longer. Even if he weren't locked up in Pentonville, she had stopped trusting his judgment. They wanted different things, and always would.

But there was one person who had always been there for her.

She pulled out her phone and called her godfather. The

phone rang and rang, and she was afraid it would ring out. Finally he picked up.

'Fletcher here.'

Hearing his cheerful voice made her feel better.

'Frankie, I'm in trouble.'

'What's the situation?' Straight to the point. Frankie, bless him, didn't mess around with small talk.

'I need to get out of London ASAP and hide up somewhere.' Even as she spoke, she watched the crowd around her. She kept her voice quiet so that no one could overhear.

There was silence for a moment, then Frankie came through for her again. 'I'm in Ireland right now. Get your ass over here. I have a nice little job for you, somewhere I can keep my eye on you.'

Ireland! She had never considered that. It was too close to her relatives, the ones she had spent a lifetime hating. They hated her too. But right now the choice was between the O'Sullivans and Hall.

'What part of Ireland?' She was good in cities. Ireland had cities big enough to disappear in.

'Tullamore.'

She had never heard of the place. 'Where is that?'

'In the midlands. Head to Tullamore and ask for Charleville Castle.'

Roz blinked. 'Why are you in a castle?'

'Jack Winter is making a film about the Battle of Clontarf and I'm training the extras for the fight scenes. One of the stunt women has broken her arm. Think you could take over?'

Oh yeah, she could do that. The prospect of seeing

Frankie again cheered her. There were a few practicalities to sort out first. 'Do I need a passport for Ireland? I can't get at mine right now – any of them.'

Frankie laughed. 'Only if you fly. Take the ferry from Pembroke or Holyhead and you can walk on. Just bring a driver's licence or something like that as ID.'

That would be so much easier than trying to stow away on the ferry to Calais. 'I'm on my way.'

Roz finished her soda, ordered a burger to go, and headed to the garage where she kept her bike and gear.

Ireland, here I come.

An hour later, she was on the M4 heading for Pembroke, while keeping an eye out for pursuit. She rode at precisely five miles per hour above the speed limit, carefully calculated to be inconspicuous while getting her there in time for the ferry to Rosslare. There were only two sailings a day and she couldn't afford to waste time.

Roz did a mental tally of her assets – one Kawasaki Ninja motorbike, in good condition, but needing fuel before she hit Wales. She had a leather jacket, pants and helmet, which helped to disguise her. Her number plate was the right side of muddy to be hard to read.

She had a pre-paid credit card that couldn't be traced to her which would pay for the ferry trip and cover her for a couple of days. Frankie better make sure she got paid for this job. She had the twenty she had taken from Andy's wallet. A burner phone. No clothes. No toothbrush or comb. No make-up. She was lucky she had the key for her bike in her pocket when Hall arrived.

Roz was used to travelling light, but this was ridiculous. She had no wigs either. She debated buying some hair dye to cover her red hair. In London, blondes and brunettes were all over the place; a ginger stood out like a beacon and if she didn't have a suitable wig, she used a temporary colour. But there were supposed to be a lot of redheads in Ireland, so she wouldn't stand out too much. It would be fun to be red for a change.

If she were on her own, looking out for herself, it wouldn't be a big deal. She was used to being on the run. She'd been doing it for years. But there was her dad to think about. He wasn't the best dad in the world, but he was the only one she had. He had given her an interesting education. She could hack computers with ease and do sums in binary.

Pity he had moved her around so much that her academic education was screwed. She had left school without a single GCSE to her name. She knew she wasn't stupid, but sometimes it felt like the world was stacked against someone without the right exam results.

Her twin sister Sinead had been brought up by her mother's wealthy family. She knew her dad believed that she resented the luxury Sinead had lived in. She didn't. What made her seethe with resentment was the education her twin had got. Boarding school, then the best university in Ireland, then a dream job in Geneva. Some people had it all, and didn't do a damn thing to deserve it.

Karma was a bitch. Someday, Roz would even things up.

She had to slow down in Port Talbot to avoid the speed camera. By the time she got to the ferry terminal, time was counting down. Roz danced from foot to foot while she queued for the ticket machine. What the hell was the couple ahead of her doing? Changing nationality? She was so anxious that she fumbled the PIN number, but then, finally, she had the ticket in her hand and was able to ride her Ninja onto the *Isle of Inishmore*.

She was sweating by the time she parked it safely and made her way up to the lounge, where she had a chance to breathe. She got herself a coffee, loaded it up with sugar, and pulled out her phone. She hooked it up to the Wi-Fi and searched to see if there was any news coverage of her run across the rooftops of London. All she needed was one image of her on the internet with her face showing to ruin everything.

Nothing. Maybe luck was running her way for once.

She flicked through her messages. There was one from Frankie giving directions and a message on Yahoo from an ex-client in Paris, offering to lick her shoes.

She shuddered. Why did men think she would enjoy that? He'd have a job licking her parkour trainers. Someone had told her they were the least sexy footwear a woman could wear. What was it with some men that a pair of heels could bring them to their knees? It would take more than a pair of Louboutins to tame Andy McTavish.

Roz laughed. But wouldn't she have fun trying? Damn, she didn't want to think about him or the dancing glint in his eyes which promised wicked pleasures to any woman who didn't expect more than a single spectacular night with him.

She was not attracted to Andy.

She wanted a different sort of man, one who was steady and loyal. Not someone who changed his girlfriends more often than his underwear. But she did have one guilty niggle. She hadn't had a chance to return his credit cards, and she hadn't planned to steal his phone. She might be a thief, but she had standards.

He had probably replaced the phone by now but she ought to send him a message to tell him his cards were safe. If she texted him, he'd see her phone number. Way to give her location away. She screwed up her face, trying to remember what his username had been on his Yahoo app.

Oh yeah. She snorted with laughter. Typical.

She opened a message to him.

<Hi, Dark Rider. Sorry about your phone, but your cards are safe. By the way, your money has gone to a VERY good cause. CatO9tails>

She grinned, wondering how long it would take before he got it.

5

Andy swallowed the last mouthful of his over-priced Belgian beer and set the bottle down on the marble counter.

'One for the road?' the barman asked.

'No thanks,' Andy replied. He'd already been hit on by several women during the evening. If he added beer goggles to the mix he'd end up doing something stupid. And he had given up on stupid.

When are you ever going to settle down? His mother's parting words from their last conversation rattled around in his head. He adored her. She was a wonderful woman, but he didn't want to marry anyone like her in a million years. Or the daughters of her friends that she kept lining up for him. He couldn't pay a visit home without tripping over half a dozen of them, all equally pretty and interesting and, well, nice.

Nice – the most over-rated word in the English language. Women weren't meant to be nice. Give him a naughty woman, with a dirty laugh, one who kissed you like she hadn't seen you for months. Or one who would lie awake with you in a tumbled bed and tell you her heart without holding back. God save him from nice.

He couldn't remember the last time he'd had a relationship like that – the kind where he wasn't pretending, or seducing them for information, or plain downright lying.

Oh, he loved his job. Loved the challenge, but lately he'd been . . .

'Can I buy you a drink?'

The blonde eased her way onto the empty barstool beside him. Her dress was too short, her heels were too high and he almost choked on the wave of expensive perfume that clouded the air around her.

'No, but thank you.' Andy smiled, trying to let her down easily. 'Maybe some other time.'

He waved to the barman and stepped out into the street. The biting wind made it hard to believe it was March. It was bloody freezing and even though the department stores were full of mannequins in pastel colours and cheerful clothes, people were still shivering in winter coats and woolly scarves.

Andy zipped up his jacket against the breeze, almost tempted to go back to the bar and the blonde. Instead, he walked briskly to his apartment block and cobbled together a stir-fry with the stuff lurking in the fridge, then settled down on the couch. If the lads in the Wing could see him now, they would laugh their heads off. Andy McTavish turning down a hot blonde in favour of watching *Strictly Come Dancing* re-runs. Sad, very sad.

His phone vibrated, signalling a message, and he swiped his finger across the display. Who was Yahooing him now? Who the hell was CatO9tails? He opened the message and skimmed through it.

He didn't know whether to laugh or be angry at the sheer audacity of Roz Spring sending him a message like that.

<I didn't know you cared> he typed quickly and pressed send.

<Oh, believe me, I don't.>

Damn, he was losing his touch. He had to get her attention.

<I've been to your flat. I got to spend some time with the baby. Is it a boy or a girl, do you think?>

The message hung in cyberspace for a long moment before Roz replied.

<It must be a boy. He weighs as much as a full grown turkey.>

Andy laughed. <Do you have a name for him yet?>

<Oswald.>

<What sort of a freaking name is Oswald? Anyone inflicting a name like that should be charged with cruelty to children.>

<laughs>

<I don't suppose you'll tell me where you are?> Andy typed carefully.

<Not a chance. Dark Rider. What sort of a name is that?>

He winced. He used that ID when he was working undercover. Now he was stuck with it. <Better than CatO9tails.>

<Oh yeah? Come over here and say that.>

<Why? Do you plan on using one on me?>

<Only if you ask nicely.>

It was worth a shot. He typed. <Pretty please.>

The next pause was longer.

<Gotta go, Irish.>

His screen lit up with a message telling him that she had logged off. Andy stretched and switched off the TV.

CatO9tails. Roz might be missing, but she was out there somewhere and she wouldn't have sent him a message if she didn't want contact in return. He didn't know why the prospect of that intrigued him.

Did you ever wonder? She had asked him in the hotel room before that kiss. It sounded like a line that he would use, but Roz had turned the tables on him. She had rolled him and that irked his pride.

But that kiss. She hadn't faked that. Neither of them had. It had been sweet and surprisingly tender and he couldn't remember the last time a kiss had felt like that. He'd seduced enough women to appreciate the difference between skill and real emotion, and there had been something there.

If he found her, no, make that *when* he found her, they would have a reckoning.

The lounge on the Isle of Inishmore was dim and quiet, and Roz took the chance to nap. She had debated getting a cabin, but the cruise to Ireland was short and she had nothing worth stealing. She stretched out across three seats and fell asleep, feeling curiously cheered by the brief exchange with Andy.

Dark Rider indeed. The man had way too high an opinion of himself. Just because he could kiss like a dream didn't mean he was anything special. She bet that he spent more time practising than any normal man. She knew enough about clothes to know that his weren't off the peg. The coat alone would have cost a couple of grand. Did he think that because he was rich and handsome and had a body to die for that every woman he met would fall into his arms?

Not her. Roz had weapons of her own that he knew nothing about. Andy might think he knew women. But she knew men. He had met his match.

She fell asleep with a smile on her face.

It was barely dawn when the ferry docked in Rosslare. Roz grabbed a cup of coffee before she retrieved her bike and decided to get on the road before she stopped for breakfast.

The sun was rising as she set out, and the country looked unnaturally green. A city girl through and through, Roz couldn't believe how small the villages were and how quickly the countryside took over. It looked like something from a movie. By the time she got to Portlaoise, she was starving. She pulled into a roadside café and sat down, enchanted by the soft accents. She ordered a full Irish breakfast and was presented with enough food to keep her going for the entire day. And a week's supply of cholesterol. She had pulled out Andy's twenty pound note to pay when she realized they used euros here. At least they took credit cards.

Pleasantly stuffed, she poured a second cup of coffee. It was hard to think of Hall in somewhere as tranquil as this. He'd stand out a lot more than she would. Already she had seen four redheads, though one was probably dyed. She wouldn't be remarkable if she stayed with her natural hair colour.

She sent Frankie a quick text, making sure he was expecting her. He replied immediately with directions and an assurance that there was a job waiting for her.

She sipped her coffee, and couldn't resist sending a quick message to Andy.

<Did you dream about me last night? Bet you did.>

The reply came so swiftly he must have had Yahoo open on his phone.

<Can't keep away, can you?>

She laughed. <Just checking that you're not missing me too much.>

<Don't worry, my aim is improving.>

<I know, it's a problem a lot of men have. I'll draw you a chart. Women everywhere will thank me.> Roz wished she could see his face when he read that.

Nothing kept him down for long. <Why not give me a hands-on demonstration?>

<Are you sure you want my hands anywhere near you? Could be dangerous.>

<I'm willing to risk it if you are.>

Cheeky devil. As if. She typed quickly. <Dream on, Irish.>

It would have been easy to keep flirting with Andy, but Roz knew she had to get on the road.

Charleville Castle was a couple of miles outside Tullamore. The big gates were guarded by a pair of brawny security men, who looked unimpressed with her biking leathers, but Frankie's name worked its magic and she was allowed through.

She bounced along a rutted road through a dark forest, until she wondered if she was in the wrong place. Then the bike went over one last pothole, the trees opened out and she caught her first glimpse of the castle.

Holy cow! It looked like something out of a Disney film,

all towers and turrets and leaded glass windows. The forecourt in front of the castle was jammed with cars, catering vans, trucks and portable buildings, but the front door was closed, and noise was coming from around the back.

Roz parked her bike and pulled off her helmet, staring open-mouthed at the edifice rising above her. It looked like something from a fairy tale, but it was all too solid and real.

The main door, massive and studded, was locked, so she headed around the corner of the castle to the back. One more corner and she was in an open area filled with machinery, tents, caravans, dozens of people dressed as Vikings, a row of Portaloos and, in the middle, two men fighting. Half a dozen cameras followed their every move. It was all curiously silent except for the sound of swords clanging off each other.

Roz had enough knowledge of filming to know she'd be lynched if she intruded, so she stayed silent until one of the men fell to the ground and the director yelled, 'Cut.'

The victor straightened up, panting. He took off his helmet and Roz caught her breath. It was Jack Winter, even more handsome in the flesh than he was on the cinema screen.

She locked her knees against the urge to run up and ask for his autograph. She was at least ten years too old to be acting like a fan girl, even if he was the most handsome man she had ever seen. The memory of Andy looking down at her with heat in his eyes intruded. Okay, perhaps Jack was the second most handsome.

A hand landed on her shoulder and she jumped, swinging around to defend herself.

'Whoa there, it's me.' The voice was familiar, even if it was emerging from a battered helmet over a rustic tunic.

'Frankie, oh god, Frankie, I've missed you.'

Roz threw herself into his arms. It was years since she had last seen him and she hadn't realized how much she missed him.

Frankie tightened his arms around her. 'Hey, hey now. What's up?' His familiar voice was like coming home. When Frankie was around, the horrors stayed a little bit further away.

She sniffed against the tears of relief, and straightened up, taking a good look at her godfather. He was the same height as her, and wore virtually the same size clothes. He pulled off the helmet, revealing silver hair, alert blue eyes and tanned skin. He hummed with energy and never slowed down. He hadn't changed at all. She betted he still had a six-pack under the rough tunic.

'It's good to see you again,' she said. Later, she'd tell him about Hall and ask for his help. But that wasn't a conversation for now.

'And you too, pet.' He patted her shoulder. 'Come on, they're going to take a break for lunch. I'll stand you a bacon sandwich.'

Roz laughed. She'd already had three pieces of bacon today, but Frankie's bacon butties were legendary. The world wasn't such a bad place after all. 'You're on.'

The sound of the phone dragged Andy from sleep. Years of training with the Rangers came into play and he was fully alert instantly. Who the hell was ringing him at this hour? He screwed up his eyes and looked at the display.

His mother. 'Mum, what's up?'

'Oh Andrew, it's your father. He's had a heart attack.'

He didn't know how he wasn't killed on the way to Heathrow. He was red-eyed by the time the plane landed in Belfast and he climbed into a taxi and headed for Lough Darra.

The tree-lined drive led past the walled gardens and around to the back. The ruined Gothic revival house on the shores of the lake had been restored by his grandfather, having been in the family for almost two hundred years. 'House' was a misnomer. Now it was a money-pit that needed an injection of cash and new blood to bring it back to its former glory.

But while his parents put up with dodgy plumbing and wore sweaters summer and winter to keep warm, no expense was spared on the stables.

His father wasn't so much in love with horses as obsessed with them. Andy often thought that if he had been born with four legs instead of two, he might have gotten more attention from him.

Until Robert died.

With every homecoming, memories of his older brother flooded his head until he could think of nothing else. Robert had been a charmer, a daredevil and an avid climber. If Andy had been here to keep an eye on him, maybe he would still be alive.

He shook the thought away. This wasn't the time. His parents needed him now. Before he could climb out of the taxi, the door opened and Poppy Campbell McTavish hurried down the steps. Her iron-grey pixie crop framed a face that would be beautiful when she was ninety. She had cheekbones that would have made Michelangelo weep. Dark eyes overshadowed pale, papery skin. His father described her as a good-looking woman and his father was never wrong about anything.

He wasn't sure what age his mother was, she refused to tell him, but neither of his parents had been in the first flush of youth when he was born. They had congratulated themselves on managing to produce one son. A second one, born five years later, had been an unexpected bonus.

He grabbed his hold-all and paid the driver before clambering from the cab and sweeping his mother up in a bear-hug, lifting her off her feet.

'Oh Andy, it's been far too long.'

She was right. It was more than eighteen months since he'd set foot in the place and now that he was home, he didn't know how he would leave it again.

He set her down gently. 'I know. Sorry, Mum. How is he?'

Her eyes clouded. 'You know your father. It will take more than a heart attack to kill him. He insisted on checking himself out of the hospital and now he's in bed giving orders like an emperor. There's no talking to him.'

Andy could well imagine it. Dougal Campbell McTavish was as stubborn as a rock and they had clashed repeatedly when he was growing up. 'I'll talk to him,' Andy promised.

'After you've eaten. He's sleeping now and you must be

starving,' Poppy said, leading him to the kitchen. He knew there was no point arguing.

His mother sipped herbal tea from a china cup while he ate everything that the family cook, Maggie, set before him. It felt like forever since he'd had an Ulster fry. His arteries would be screaming by the time he went home.

Home.

He wasn't sure where that was anymore. His tiny apartment in London was more of a base to store his stuff than where he lived. Half the time he ended up in company apartments or hotels. International businessman, actor, arms dealer, he had played them all in operations of one kind or another. His last job had been counterespionage – seducing a Russian Mata Hari who was blackmailing someone at the MOD. Irina had been stunningly beautiful, but deadly as poison.

He never spoke of his work to his family. His father disapproved of him enough already and there was no point in making things worse. He pushed his plate away and dabbed his mouth with a napkin. 'I'll see if Dad is awake.'

He picked up his leather hold-all and headed for the door.

'Dougal can't manage the stairs, so we've moved to the green sitting room so that he can see the gardens. I've put you in the red room,' his mother called after him.

Andy paused. The largest and most opulent bedroom in the mansion, traditionally occupied by the master of the house.

He knew his mother loved the gardens. They were her pride and joy. But giving over the room they had shared

60

for more than thirty years to their son was more than a welcoming gesture. He was the prodigal son returned. They wanted him home for good and he didn't know how to break it to them that he couldn't stay. Andy dropped his bag at the bottom of the stairs and went to find his father.

The west wing was the oldest part of the house. Generations of McTavishes and Campbells glared at him from the wood-panelled walls. Most had been wealthy land-owners. A handful had been military men, but they had all returned home to Lough Darra and done their duty by the estate.

Andy could see his future mapped out before him. Marry the dull, horsey daughter of one of his well-to-do neighbours, settle down with a brood of kids and breed horses.

It wasn't for him.

The heavy oak door creaked as he pushed it open and slipped inside. The room was in darkness and he was about to leave again when his father called from the bed. 'Open the damned curtains, I'm not dead yet.'

Andy pulled back the heavy damask drapes and let the morning light into the room.

The shrunken figure in the huge bed bore no resemblance to the man who had packed him off to boarding school when he was eleven. Andy had hated every single minute of it. He had run away twice before his mother had persuaded his father to let him come home and go to a local school.

They were delighted when he went to Queens, but it wasn't what he wanted, so he had joined the army.

His parents had been convinced he wouldn't make it, or would drop out after a week, but to their surprise he had loved the rough, tough life. They were even more shocked when he was recommended for the Rangers, and survived the murderously tough training to find his spiritual home.

He'd been in Afghanistan when his brother was killed in a climbing accident. The memory of that phone call and his strong, implacable father in tears, made him break out in a sweat.

'Hi, Dad.'

Dougal Campbell McTavish grunted. 'So you're home?'

6

The following morning, his head was foggy from too little sleep in a strange bed. The portrait over the mantel stared accusingly down at him as if he were a squatter, rather than the heir to the place.

Andy couldn't remember which ancestor it was, but he looked as if he'd swallowed a lemon. In one corner of the room a dark stain and cracked plaster revealed yet another leak in the roof. Damned thing was worse than a sieve and this was a sample of what would be waiting for him if he stayed at home.

According to his mother, if it wasn't the roof, it was the plumbing, or a broken fence or Travellers camping in the meadow. Who on earth would want to live in the country?

Andy rolled out of bed. If he was stuck here for a while, he would have to deal with all the problems, but first he had to ring his boss and tell him the situation.

Niall Moore answered on the third ring. 'You've found her?'

'Not exactly. Listen, my father had a heart attack a couple of nights ago.'

'Jesus, is he okay?'

'He's as belligerent as ever but I need some personal time because –'

'No need to explain. You're due some holidays anyway.

You've barely taken a day off in the last year. I'll put someone else on finding Roz.'

'No. It's not necessary.' Now that he had picked up her trail again, he was damned if he would let any of the other guys near her.

'You know where she is?' The anxious note in the big guy's voice made Andy feel guilty. Niall was crazy about his wife, and if something was making Sinead unhappy, he would move heaven and earth to sort it out.

'Not yet, but I've made contact with her. Online.'

Niall exhaled. 'Andy. This is my sister-in-law.' He didn't need to spell it out. If Andy messed this one up, he would be out of Moore Enterprises on his ass.

'She stole my phone and she's been sending me messages. I'm trying to keep the lines of communication open.'

That almost sounded plausible, but if Niall got an inkling that Roz and he were flirting online he would tear him apart.

'Fine, but if it gets complicated, I'll put someone else on the job.'

'Understood.' The cardinal rule in this game was don't fuck the client. Well, that wouldn't be difficult. He didn't have a clue where she was and until he was sure that his dad was on the road to recovery, he didn't have time to hunt for her.

The director of the film, Mike Scott, was a down-to-earth man with a Texan twang and chewed fingernails. He looked Roz over, asked her if she could handle the job, and sent her to costume.

Frankie promised he'd take care of her paperwork, and hustled her away before Scott could ask her any more questions.

'We lucked out that the leading stunt woman broke her arm,' he told her, around a mouthful of sandwich. 'They needed someone in a hurry, so they're not too fussy about checking your Equity membership.'

Roz wasn't particularly hungry, but she'd had too many days when a change of plan had deprived her of dinner, so she wasn't going to miss a meal. She ate slowly, enjoying the man-sized portion.

'What happened to the stunt woman?' she asked.

'Broke her arm on the old stairs. She swore a child pushed her, but there are no kids on set. Probably hung-over and didn't want to admit it.'

He led her around, performing lightning introductions as he hustled her towards wardrobe and make-up. Her hopes of bumping into a naked Jack Winter were dashed when Frankie told her that the stars had their own trailers and were fitted there, but there were plenty of semi-naked hunks in the general wardrobe area.

The American actors were shameless about stripping off to be fitted for their costumes, while the Irish extras were easily identified by their pale skin and their initial reluctance to bare more than their forearms. Still, it was an impressive display of manhood.

Her phone vibrated. It was a message from Andy. <I hope you're behaving yourself?>

<Now why would I do that?>

<Don't tell me you've found another guy already?>

Did Andy McTavish think he was the only man on the planet? <More than one, but I can't make up my mind.> She'd love to see his face when he got that one. Roz typed quickly. <I love a man with a six-pack. Don't you?>

Three minutes later, she got a message back from him. <No, I prefer a woman with a soft, round ass. But if you insist.> Her phone chirped again, and a picture arrived. She choked.

A male stomach. A naked male stomach. Andy's. His muscles were strong and defined, and the fine line of hair down the centre made her lick her lips.

Oh, he was wicked. And it didn't help that he really did have a body that was better than any of the professional actors who were swaggering in front of her.

She grinned. Two could play at that game. The wardrobe mistress told Roz to take off her jeans and T-shirt. While the woman was sizing her up for a costume, Roz took a quick selfie of her own rear. The resulting photo didn't actually reveal any more than a swimsuit would, but with the flesh coloured thong she looked naked. Perfect.

She Yahooed the shot to Andy. <One like this, you mean?> and pressed send before she could think better of it.

The response came back quickly. <Exactly like that. And me an ass man. You're torturing me.>

For some reason, that made her grin all the while she was being laced into the green velvet costume of Lady Gormflaith, and made up so that she looked exactly like the leading lady, Cheyenne Knight.

The next few hours involved falling, over and over again, from a tree that no sane person would ever have climbed in the long velvet dress, and being knocked onto the ground in a battle scene.

By the time the light faded, she was aching in every limb, and covered in mud. 'Where's the nearest shower?' she asked.

Cheyenne, who turned out to be more approachable than Roz had expected a Hollywood star to be, grinned. 'You can use the one in my trailer.'

Roz gratefully accepted, and spent fifteen minutes scrubbing off the filth of a night on the ferry as well as a day fighting in the mud. By the time she emerged from the tiny bathroom, she finally felt human again.

'Wow, you look a lot more like me than I realized,' Cheyenne exclaimed, eyeing her slicked-back wet hair. 'I bet if you were dressed like me, we could pass for sisters.'

Roz felt a pang. She already had a sister, one she had spent most of her life hating, but there was something appealing about the thought of having a sister she liked. 'Unless you plan on wearing black jeans and T-shirt, we're out of luck,' she told Cheyenne. 'I managed to lose my luggage and I'm down to the clothes I'm standing in.'

'Why didn't you tell me? You can borrow some of mine.' The actress scooped a bundle of clothes out of her wardrobe and shoved them into Roz's arms.

'No, I . . .' Roz stopped herself. She was so used to relying on herself and not accepting help from anyone that she was in danger of being stupid. She did need a change of clothes, and these looked as if they would fit, even if they were ridiculously out of place for the muddy Irish countryside. One blouse had a price tag attached. It read $800. Roz swallowed. Who paid that much money for a blouse?

'Only for a day or two,' she said. 'And I'll dry clean everything before I return it.'

'Don't be silly. Designers send me stuff to wear all the time. Those are the things I don't like. Keep them. And here, you'll need these too.' Cheyenne tossed a handful of lingerie on top of the pile of clothes.

'Thank you,' Roz said. Exhaustion was catching up on her, but she knew what she had to do. 'Maybe tomorrow night we could ride into the local town and pretend to be sisters?'

Cheyenne clapped her hands, and Roz made her escape to meet Frankie.

It was dark and most of the extras had left for home. Roz supposed she could have gone into the town and found a cheap hotel or guest house, but the long rutted driveway to the castle gate wasn't appealing at the best of times, and definitely not in the dark.

Besides, while her credit card was a pre-pay in a false name, there was no point leaving any sort of money trail. 'Can I stay here?' she asked Frankie.

'Sure thing, pet. There are three stunt women sharing a trailer, or you can bunk in with me. I've got a small caravan to myself.'

'With you.' Her answer was automatic. She was pretty sure Hall hadn't managed to track her to Ireland, much less a castle in the middle of nowhere, but he was too damn good for her to take chances. The thought of a bunch of actresses taking on a ruthless killer made her shudder. Hall had tracked her down to the food bank. She couldn't put anyone else in danger.

Frankie was close-mouthed about his own past, but she had a good idea that at least some of it had been in the military. He had a much better chance of looking after himself.

Besides, she had spent so much of her life travelling around, leaving her home at short notice to start up somewhere else, that she had little experience of spending time with other people. She'd never had normal friends or done girly chat. She'd never had a sleepover, swopping clothes and make-up and tales of bad boyfriends.

Roz didn't think she'd be able to handle that much time with other women. What did girls talk about? she wondered. For all she knew, they lay in bed discussing books they had read – and that she had not.

Frankie pointed to his caravan, and she climbed in, wincing as it tipped under her weight. It was ruthlessly neat, with a single glass on the tiny table, a couch that doubled as a bed and a pile of paperwork weighed down by a hand-made leather arm protector that he used for archery.

She stowed her dirty jeans away in an overhead locker and pulled out a blanket to make up a bed on the child-sized couch at the front of the caravan. Finally, she pulled the curtains and sorted through the clothes that Cheyenne had given her.

When she finally emerged, Frankie whistled. 'You clean up better than I was expecting.'

She scowled, but was secretly pleased. 'Does this mean that I have a film star body?'

'Better than that, you have a Roz Spring body. Most film stars are ridiculously skinny. Cheyenne Knight is the only one who looks real.'

Roz was wearing a pair of skinny jeans, a bra which she suspected cost more than she would spend on an entire outfit, silk panties and the $800 blouse. It had turned out to be the most practical of all the clothes in the bundle.

'I feel like a sow's ear,' she complained. She was terrified to eat anything dressed like this in case she got a mark on it.

'Nah, it makes a change to see you dressed like a woman.'

'I can dress like a woman.' She had a vivid memory of Paris, and a red leather cat-suit which showed off every curve. It made her look far too much like the sister she hated. She had never worn it again.

Frankie handed her a glass of wine and set a plate before her. Her mouth watered. A steak so tender she barely needed a knife to cut it.

'Acting looks like a good gig. At least they feed you well.'

He nodded and allowed her to eat half of her meal before he asked. 'So, tell me what brought you here.'

She put her knife down, her appetite gone. 'I had a bit of trouble in London.'

Roz didn't have to go into details. In their world, 'a bit of trouble' explained everything. She was tempted to stay silent, but Frankie was the one person who might be able to help.

'You know that Dad's in prison?'

He nodded.

'He got caught when he was pulling a scam on the Ramos brothers. They weren't pleased, but at least when he's in Pentonville, they can't do much to him. But he's due out in a few months, and then they'll be looking for the money he cost them.'

'How much?'

She took a deep breath. The number didn't seem real. 'Half a million.'

Frankie choked. She had never seen him so shocked. Roz patted him on the back.

'Yeah, I've got to get him off the radar, or find the money by the middle of August.' It was a depressing thought.

He gave her a measuring look. 'Peter managed to get himself into trouble. Why are you rescuing him?'

Roz looked through the window at the sky. Out here in the middle of nowhere there was little light pollution and the stars were huge and luminous. She had never seen stars like that in London or Paris. 'He's not much of a dad, I know. But I can't leave him alone. He'll get himself crippled or killed.'

'He can make his own mistakes . . .'

Roz glared at him. 'Look, he's my dad. I couldn't live with myself if I didn't make sure he was safe. He's all the family I have.'

Frankie said slowly, 'He's not, you know.'

What the hell was he saying? 'If you think I'm going cap in hand to those fucking O'Sullivans, you can think again.' She got up, planning to go to bed.

He grinned, all teeth and charm. 'No, that's not what I was thinking. How would you feel about pulling off the hustle of a lifetime?'

Roz sat down again. 'Tell me more.'

'That's my girl.' Frankie topped up her glass of wine. 'It's going to be the perfect scam. No one gets hurt, and only the greedy get burnt.'

She grunted. 'No hustle would work if people weren't greedy. It's next to impossible to scam an honest person.'

Frankie nodded. They both knew that ninety per cent of all cons depended on someone trying to take advantage of someone else or get something for nothing.

'This is a good one. You know that Tim O'Sullivan is a big racing buff?'

Roz shook her head. She hated the O'Sullivans; she couldn't bear to read about them or listen when they were on the news. She wouldn't even fly O'Sullivan Air. Every piece of extravagance was a bigger contrast to her poverty. 'I didn't know that.'

'Well, he is. He has a stable of racing horses and every year he enters the Gold Cup at Cheltenham. I've talked to a few people in his yard, and they all say he would pay any money to win. It would mean more to him than winning the Grand National or Ascot.'

Roz knew nothing about horses. They were a rich man's toy. She'd never even had a dog when she was growing up and had to make do with making pets of the feral cats wherever she happened to be living at the time. The final straw had been hearing that her twin Sinead had won some sort of pony competition. Sinead got a fucking pony of her own, and Roz had a three legged cat who scratched her when she tried to pet it.

'Go on,' she told Frankie. The idea of rooking Tim O'Sullivan was gaining appeal.

'I want to show you something.' Frankie gave her a hand to get to her feet. Roz blinked; her legs were unusually wobbly. It had been a long day.

She followed him to the tent where the horses were kept. 'The castle stables haven't been restored yet,' he told her. 'They're full of rubble and mice.'

Roz shuddered. Maybe it was all the disgusting places she had ended up living with her father, but mice and spiders freaked her. She much preferred the large tent which contained about twenty horses.

The three horses at the end had big stalls and were clearly the stars. 'Those ones are specially trained, they do the stunts,' Frankie said. 'The one I'm interested in is over here.'

There, in stall seventeen, was a large horse. In spite of a couple of night lights, it was too dim for Roz to make out what colour the horse was, but he was dark, maybe black or brown. He poked his nose out when they approached.

Frankie slipped inside the stall, pulling her with him. The horse snuffled at him before turning his attention to Roz.

She shrank back against the wooden wall. This horse was huge, and smelled, and had feet the size of dinner plates. He sniffed at her, then whickered, the sound shockingly loud, and revealing teeth like tent pegs. 'Frankie,' she said, panicked.

He was busy taking something out of his pocket, but looked up. 'Don't pay any attention, he won't hurt you.'

Easy for him to say. She glared at his back. He wasn't the one being poked in the chest by a head the size of a turkey.

'Here, hold him still for me.' Without waiting for her to agree, Frankie clipped a rope onto the leather halter the horse wore on his head, and put it into her hands. He got busy rubbing the front of the horse's head with what smelled a lot like henna. He worked from between his eyes to the long nose.

'What do you think of Nagsy?' he asked her, still working away.

Roz had a death grip on the rope, and no idea what she would do if the stupid horse moved in any way. 'Nagsy? What sort of a name is that?'

Frankie shrugged. 'It's as good as any other. Until we re-name him.'

She was going to kill him. If that monster of a horse didn't kill her first. 'Frankie, if you don't tell me why we're here, I'm going to let him trample on top of you.'

He put away the brush he had been using on Nagsy's head. 'This, dear Roz, is the key to scamming Tim O'Sullivan out of half a million.'

'Are you mad?' Roz looked up at the horse. Interested brown eyes looked back at her. She supposed as horses went, this one was pretty enough. But it was only a horse. She wouldn't have paid a fiver for it.

'He belongs to a local farmer who's been riding him around the fields and to the pub. He's a nice horse. But the most interesting thing about him,' and Frankie lowered his voice, 'is that this horse is the spitting image of Shergar.'

'Who?'

He glared at her. 'Only the most famous Irish horse

that ever lived. He won the Epsom Derby by the longest margin in history, and was kidnapped from a stud in Kildare two years later. No one ever found out what happened to him. But if we could produce the Son of Shergar, we could sell it to Tim O'Sullivan for whatever price we named.'

For a moment, she was tempted. But a horse? She couldn't cope with horses. And she didn't want to get close to the O'Sullivans. She shook her head. 'Sorry Frankie. Good luck if you do, but this one is not for me. I'll sort something else out for Dad.'

'I can't do this on my own,' he said.

'Dad's in jail. I'm lucky I'm not. We can't do this, it's too risky.' She put the rope into Frankie's hand and let herself out of Nagsy's stall.

Was it her imagination that the horse sneered at her? She didn't care.

Andy wanted to throw his phone at the wall in frustration. It wasn't her pert ass that upset him. That had been a sight for sore eyes. But she had been devious enough to un-tag the photograph before she sent it. Now, he had no idea where she was. He had thought he was being clever when he had sent her a photo of his abs. A flirtatious gesture like that sometimes caught women off guard and they forgot to take proper security measures. But not her. Not Roz. She was still three steps ahead of him, but he wasn't giving up yet.

After a dribble of a shower – he didn't bother waiting

for the water to heat up – Andy went downstairs to the kitchen for breakfast. It was too early for his parents to be awake, but it would give him a chance to catch up with the rest of the household.

Maggie was surrounded by the men from the estate. The guys joked and laughed as they tucked into several thousand calories of bacon and eggs and Jesus – was that fried soda bread?

His mouth watered. No. He was not doing this.

'Sit yourself down there,' Maggie said. 'Will you have tea or coffee?'

'Coffee, please and could I have a couple of poached eggs and toast?'

'It's far from poached eggs you were reared. Have you gone soft, Andy?' one of the men asked.

Andy sat down next to Tom and elbowed him in the ribs. 'I'd demonstrate, but then I'd have to drive you to hospital.'

'Any time you want to try, laddie. Any time. So, how's yon blond giant treating you?'

'Niall? As good as could be expected.'

'But you don't get much time off?'

And there was the rub. Why wasn't he home where he was needed, instead of wandering around the world? But there was something else going on. He caught a few furtive glances and there was an undercurrent of something not being said. Andy was determined to get to the bottom of it.

'So, what are your plans for the day? A trip to the shops?'

'Ach, he's turned soft, spending all that time in London.

He's probably booked a manicure,' one of the grooms said and the others snorted with laughter.

If he hadn't been in his mother's kitchen, Andy would have shown him exactly how soft he was. But a Ranger didn't get into stupid fights.

'Pay them no heed,' Maggie said as she set a plate in front of him. 'Have ye no work to go to? Away with ye.'

Draining the last of his tea, Tom pushed back his chair. 'I'll be off then.'

The others followed him and within a minute the kitchen was silent. Andy wolfed down his breakfast and downed a mug of coffee.

'And where do you think you're going?' Maggie demanded.

'To work.' He couldn't sit around here all day watching his dad sleep. He needed something to do or he would go crazy.

Whistling, he made his way to the stables. No wonder the house was falling to rack and ruin; his father spent more money on the horses than he did on his own accommodation.

'How many does he have now?' he asked Tom.

'It varies. Twenty-two at the minute, with the yearlings he bought at the December sale in Tattersalls.'

'How much?' Andy was almost afraid to ask.

'Seven two for one. The other was a bargain at three thousand.'

'Euros?' Andy asked hopefully.

'Pounds. And that was on top of the ones he bought last October.'

He didn't have to hear the resignation in Tom's voice to

know that his dad's passion for horses was bleeding the estate dry.

'How is the rest of the place?'

'If you're talking about the deer farming . . .'

Andy sighed. The 'D' word . . . It was another of his brother's 'agricultural experiments'. Robert had been great for ideas, but without his drive and enthusiasm they had been allowed to go wild.

'The Devlins are angry about the damage to their forestry plantations. A few bucks can strip bark from a tree quicker than a machine. And as for trying to fence them in . . .'

Tom tut-tutted his disapproval. 'I could have a team mending fences day and night and I wouldn't be able to keep up with the beggars. Don't get me wrong. Your father has a good eye for the horses, but it could be a couple of years before he sees a return and at his age, it's tough. It's not like the old days. Robert might not have been the best farmer, but he was here.'

He left the rest of the words unsaid, but Andy felt the rebuke as sharply as a slap. It was a young man's game and his parents were getting on. The estate needed someone to breathe new life into it, or a new owner.

Disheartened, he returned to the house to inspect it.

Christ, he hadn't realized it was this bad. His was the best room in the house but it wasn't the only one with a damaged ceiling. The place was a money pit. Who the hell would want it? And even if they did, could he part with a house that had been in the family for two hundred years?

He was used to travelling light and he hadn't contemplated settling down. What the house needed was a new

McTavish generation, an owner who would bring a wife and a family to revitalize the place. He wasn't ready for either.

Idly, he flicked on his phone and without thinking he clicked on the Yahoo icon, but Roz was offline. He stared at the phone in his hand with a vague sense of disappointment. He was losing it.

7

<Hi baby. Missing me?>

<Not especially.> The message flashed back and Andy laughed.

He glanced at his mother who was dozing in the chair near the fire. He could do with some shut eye himself. Maybe he should take this upstairs.

'Night, Mum,' he called.

'Good night.' Poppy sounded half asleep.

Andy took the steps two at a time and opened the door to his room. The carved four-poster bed should have been a chick-magnet, but he couldn't ever imagine bringing someone here. But if it was a certain feisty redhead, he might be tempted to break his rule about bringing women home.

<Late night?> he asked.

<Not especially. I'm tired. Getting ready for bed.>

<Way to tease a guy> he typed. <Are you a PJs or nightdress girl?>

<Like you'll ever find out.>

Andy laughed. He lay down on the bed and tapped another message into his phone. <Come on. Give a guy a break. At least tell me what colour panties you're wearing.>

The message hung in cyberspace for several seconds and he wondered if he had gone too far.

<Do you ever stop?>

<No.> He waited. <So, what colour are they?>

<Pink silk.>

Andy sat up as a vision popped into his head of Roz lying beside him on the dark red coverlet wearing nothing but a scrap of silk, her long red hair on his pillow. He would lick every inch of her smooth, pale skin.

<Picture?> he asked hopefully.

<Not a chance> she snapped back. <You've already had one today.>

<It's almost midnight. I can wait.>

No response came and as he was about to give up another message arrived. <CatO9tails has sent you a photograph.>

Andy hit the accept icon and downloaded the picture.

The silk panties were folded neatly in the centre of a narrow single bed covered with a white duvet cover. There was nothing in the picture to give him a clue to where she was.

Of Roz, there was no sign and he could almost hear her laughter.

<Your turn.>

Andy debated how to respond. He couldn't ignore a challenge like that but he was damned if he'd let her get the better of him.

He slipped out of his room and down the backstairs to the utility area adjoining the kitchen. Among the pile of neatly ironed garments was a pair of flannelette pyjamas belonging to his father. The brown check pattern screamed old folks home.

Whistling, he returned to his room and laid them out on the bed.

Her reply, when she received the photograph, was unrepeatable.

<Didn't that float your boat?> he asked.

<Not an inch. Don't tell me you actually wear those?>

<Only when I'm cold.>

<Where are you? Antarctica?>

He was almost tempted to tell her, but if Roz was hiding out somewhere in England he didn't want her to think that she was off the hook because he was in another country.

<Not quite. You could always come and warm me up?>

<Dream on, babe.>

<I will> he typed. <But only of you.>

Andy waited, and when there was no response, he logged off and went to use the bathroom down the hall. If this were his home he would knock down a wall and put in a huge en-suite with a bath big enough for two. He hurried along the chilly corridor to the bedroom.

He had spent colder nights out in the field, but this was supposed to be a mansion. How did his parents live here? He eyed the pyjamas on the bed. There was nothing for it. He would have to wear them.

He slipped between the cold sheets and warmed himself with visions of Roz wearing those silky panties.

The following day was damp with occasional rain which halted filming, but Roz didn't mind. She was grateful for the chance to zone out occasionally after the previous few days.

Filming, Roz discovered, was a lot of, 'Hurry up and wait', and location filming seemed to be a combination of velvet and mud. She learnt quickly that it was not as glamorous as she had been expecting, but the chance to see Jack Winter wandering around like a regular person was worth standing in the damp.

Frankie, as expected, hovered, warning off the film crew who tried to hit on her, and Cheyenne continued to chat to her while they waited for their takes.

'This is a great role for me. Usually I get to play the ugly friend and lately I've been offered roles of mother of the heroine. And I'm only thirty-nine. Did you know that my character, Gormflaith, was supposed to be a great beauty, even if she was evil?'

Roz had been watching the sword fighting scene, all too aware that she would soon have to be in one where she was knocked off her feet and 'killed'. She turned to look at Cheyenne. 'But you're beautiful.'

The film star's perfect mouth parted. 'You must be blind. My lips aren't symmetrical, my nose is too big, my eyebrows don't match, and my agent tells me I need to lose thirty pounds.'

Roz looked her up and down, being as critical as possible, but couldn't see any of the flaws that Cheyenne had pointed out. 'You must be joking. You're gorgeous. Anyone who says otherwise must be blind. And if you're thirty pounds overweight, then so am I.'

Cheyenne opened her mouth, and shut it, clearly

deciding that this was not a fight she wanted to win. She turned back to the scene being filmed. 'Would you have liked to have lived back then, when men were men?'

Roz laughed. 'And didn't wash? I'm very fond of modern bathrooms, thank you.'

'Me too. Are we going into town tonight?'

With some surprise, Roz realized that Cheyenne was serious. She nodded. 'Of course,' she said before she got ready for her demise on the battlefield.

At lunchtime, she checked her phone and found another message from Andy.

<Hey babe, I've got some nipple clamps.>

The mouthful of diet cola went down the wrong way and she coughed until she could breathe normally again.

Time to nip this in the bud. She swiped across her phone screen.

<I don't wear nipple clamps. But if you ask VERY nicely, I'll put them on you.>

It wasn't a huge surprise when he messaged back. <Ha ha, laughing here. There is no universe in which you get to put clamps on me.>

Didn't Andy McTavish have ideas about himself? <You will wear them. And if you're not careful, I'll post the pix all over the internet.>

<Dream on, babe. They've got your name on them.>

Ass. But she was grinning when she went to help Frankie sort out the horseback scenes.

In the daytime, she found it hard to tell which horse was Nagsy. She had thought he was black or dark brown, but now could see he had a light brown coat and black mane and tail. Pretty enough, she supposed, if you were into horses.

Nagsy snuffled at her, and she tentatively patted his nose. The hair down the front of his face was a little rougher than the rest. 'What were you doing last night?' she asked Frankie in a low voice.

'The blaze down the centre of his face is exactly the same size and shape as Shergar's. I don't want to tip anyone off, so I've dyed it to conceal it.'

When the stuntmen were mounted on the horses, Roz kept an eye on Nagsy and thought he seemed to be quick off the mark. But it was an unworkable idea. There were too many things that could go wrong, even if the thought of scamming the O'Sullivans of a large chunk of change made her feel all warm and fuzzy.

She didn't know anything about horses, but it did look as if Nagsy was faster than the other horses. Maybe it wasn't impossible. Nagsy certainly looked like a horse that would like to be in a race. She noticed something else unusual about him.

'What the hell is that between his legs?' she asked Frankie.

Frankie's shoulders shook with laughter. 'I forgot you were a city girl. Those are his balls. Nagsy is a stallion.'

She examined the other horses, but Nagsy was the only one with all his bits attached. 'Is that good or bad?' All she knew about stallions was that they were supposed to be temperamental and prone to waving their feet in the air. Or was that lions? She couldn't remember.

'It's good.' Frankie grinned. 'It means that after he's

won the Gold Cup, the lucky owner can put him out to stud and make a fortune. That makes him even more valuable. You could double the sale price.'

The scene ended and Nagsy nosed at Frankie for a treat. He handed Roz a piece of carrot and told her to put it on the flat of her hand for him.

Reluctantly, she did, waiting for those enormous teeth to take off a couple of fingers. But Nagsy snuffled at her hand, his whiskers tickling her, and picked off the carrot with surprising delicacy. She rubbed his nose, thinking that horses weren't so scary after all.

Like men. They were big and dumb but would do what they were told.

'You look at home like that,' Frankie said. 'A real Irish colleen.'

She stiffened. 'I'm not Irish. Don't ever say that.'

He gave her a knowing look. 'So you've taken to lying to yourself now?'

She was so furious she wanted to spit. 'How dare you? I'm as English as you. Just because I was born in some crappy hippie commune in the west of Ireland does not make me Irish.'

'Being born in a stable does not make one a horse?' quoted Frankie. 'Your mother was Irish, your father was half-Irish, you were born here and grew up there.' He paused to let that sink in. 'If it waddles like a duck and quacks . . .'

What had got into him? 'You know damn well it was nothing like that. My mother didn't bother registering my birth. There are no records anywhere linking me to Ireland. When Dad was going to England for a job, she told him to take me with him and she kept my sister. Do you have any idea how much trouble he had faking a birth certificate just so I could go to school?'

The memory still burnt. She had been a year older than all the other children because it had taken so long to get a convincing set of documents before she could enrol. Then the other children had mocked her accent and the colour of her hair and the clothes her dad had bought her. He did his best, but he had no clue about bringing up an unruly child.

Roisin O'Sullivan had turned into Roz Spring, she had lost any trace of an Irish accent, and she had learnt to blend in.

She turned her back on Frankie. 'Discussion over, I'm going to work.' She stamped away, leaving him with Nagsy.

By evening, she was ready to call it a day. She had been 'killed' fourteen times, and knocked on her ass so often she had lost count.

She had changed into a pair of leggings and a baggy sweatshirt, and was preparing to nurse her bruises when a knock on the caravan door announced a visitor. Cheyenne Knight was outside, clutching a large bag. 'Well, are you ready?'

'Ready?' Roz had kicked off her shoes, preparing to spend the evening reading one of Frankie's books about Shergar. No harm to know a bit more, even if she had no intention of running the con.

'Yes, you said we were going into town tonight, pretend to be sisters. I can't wait.' Cheyenne looked so hopeful Roz didn't have the heart to refuse her.

She pulled on her shoes. 'Sure, I was waiting for you. Let's go.'

Cheyenne had never ridden a motorbike before, and her Versace jacket wasn't up to the job, so Roz grabbed one of Frankie's jackets for her. Cheyenne snuggled into it, looking far happier than Roz would have expected.

The ride to the gate was dark and bumpy, and Cheyenne gripped Roz's waist tightly, but the main road to Tullamore was easier going, and they could see more of the Irish countryside. The town was sprawling and old-fashioned and the hump-backed bridge over the canal caught Roz by surprise.

'Eeek!' Cheyenne exclaimed, gripping even more tightly. Roz was sweating by the time she glided to a halt in the centre of the town.

Inside the bar, it was dim and cosy. The barman assured them they could have food and handed her a laminated card. Roz saw Cheyenne grapple with the menu. It contained a lot of meat fried in different ways.

'You've no egg-white omelettes? Or sushi? Something low fat?'

The barman peered at her. 'You're that American actress, Charlene Knight, right?'

'It's Cheyenne.' The actress sighed before her face assumed a professional smile. 'If you have a low-carb option, that would be great.'

'No, we don't do that fancy stuff. Only what's on the menu, but I could do you a sandwich without butter if you like.'

Cheyenne shuddered. 'Can we have a drink while we're deciding? Something Irish?'

'Sure thing.' The barman poured out two glasses of a dark beer, letting them sit for a while before he topped them up to reveal a creamy white head. After looking at Cheyenne, he poured a measure of blackcurrant into both of them. 'There you go, Guinness and black.'

It was a lot different from her usual red wine, but Roz decided she could get used to it. By the time Cheyenne had decided on salmon and salad, and Roz had ordered steak and garlic potatoes, they had finished their drinks. Roz switched to alcohol-free beer and Cheyenne was sipping her second Guinness.

Maybe it was the food, the dim pub, the alcohol, but something snapped in Cheyenne. With almost no warning, she told Roz about her disastrous marriage.

'How was I to know he didn't like sex? They should tell you this stuff before they marry you. Or maybe it was sex with me that he didn't like.'

She took another huge gulp of her Guinness, no longer wincing at the bitter aftertaste. 'Maybe I am too fat for him. But dammit, I try. I diet and I work out and I do yoga and Pilates and swim and lift weights.'

Where had this come from? They had been talking about how hot Jack Winter was and how much he adored his wife. Roz patted her on the shoulder. 'You're not fat or ugly. You're a Hollywood film star.'

Cheyenne snorted, causing a bit of froth to hit her nose. She continued without noticing it. 'It doesn't matter how much I work out, I can't make myself younger. No man is ever going to hit on me again. Do you know how long it is since I had an orgasm?'

'Not really my business.' Roz shoved her side dish at

the older woman. 'Try some of the garlic potatoes, they'll give you an orgasm.'

'I might as well eat garlic. No man is ever going to be interested in me again. It doesn't matter if my breath stinks.'

'That's not true. You're gorgeous.'

Cheyenne sniffed, on the verge of tears. 'No, I'm fat and ugly. And look, no one has tried to hit on me once tonight.'

Roz was torn between impatience and sympathy. 'That's because they're Irish, and the Irish are even more socially inept than the English. I bet that you could have any man in this pub. Hell, you could have every man in this pub.'

'I don't believe you.'

It was time to bring out the big guns. If there was one thing Roz had learnt from a year working as a pro-Domme, it was how to deal with men. She sat up and prepared to release her inner Domme.

She pulled off her baggy jumper, revealing a slim-fitting tank top. It wasn't glamorous or sexy, but it showed the shape of her body. She looked around the pub slowly, catching the eye of every man there, and could feel the rise of sexual tension that rippled in the wake of her glance.

There, in the corner, that was the one. He was probably twenty-three or -four, but nice looking. Roz held his eyes for a long moment, and then beckoned him over. He almost tipped over his table in his eagerness to get to her side.

She held out her hand to him. 'Hi, I'm Roz, and this is my friend Cheyenne.'

He gripped it, trembling with eagerness. 'I'm Conor. Nice to meet you, Roz and Cheyenne.'

Roz lowered her voice to a throaty purr. 'It's nice to meet you, Conor.' She indicated Cheyenne's empty glass. 'I think my friend needs another drink.'

Conor whipped his wallet out of his pocket so quickly he dropped it and flushed bright red. He knelt down on the floor to pick it up.

'Oh, you look right at home there,' Roz told him.

He looked up, blushing. 'What?'

'You look right at home there, kneeling at the feet of a beautiful woman. Isn't she the most stunning woman you've ever seen?'

Dazed, not sure what had happened, Conor stared up at Cheyenne. 'Yes, she is. She's amazing.'

Tentatively, Cheyenne reached out and patted his head. 'You're so sweet.' He kissed her hand, and stayed where he was.

'Now it's your turn,' Roz told her. 'Pick out another one and bring him over here.'

'Are you sure?' Cheyenne asked, stunned by the turn of events.

Roz nodded, and watched while Cheyenne examined the men in the pub. The two women were now the centre of attention, and it was easy for her to find one who looked eager. She beckoned to him, but seemed shocked when he came immediately. 'Can I buy you a drink?' he asked.

Cheyenne nodded, and he sat down beside her.

After that, they were mobbed. Every man there

descended, looking for a sliver of attention from the two femmes fatales at the bar.

'What did you do?' Cheyenne demanded when they left an hour later.

'What we did.' Roz grinned at her while she unlocked the motorbike. 'Nothing. We allowed the men to show us how much they liked us.'

She shook her head. 'No, it was more than that.'

Roz pulled out her helmet and handed one to Cheyenne. 'Men are simple creatures. They like women. They like women's bodies, real bodies, not Barbie-shaped ones. They like being told what to do. All we did was show them what we wanted and they did it.'

Cheyenne sang under her breath on the ride home, and Roz congratulated herself on a job well done.

Back in the caravan, she realized she hadn't been applying her knowledge to her own life. It was time to remind Andy who was in charge.

<Show me your cock> she messaged him.

<What?>

<Send me a picture of your cock.> Simple, clear, direct. That should do it.

<If you insist.>

She didn't know why she was disappointed.

The minutes ticked by, while she waited in the silence of the caravan.

Six minutes later, her phone beeped. She opened it to see the picture. A black rooster with a huge red wattle glared into the camera with his beak open. <Sorry, my cock doesn't like being woken up at this hour.>

She laughed.

Her phone beeped again. <Now your pussy.>

She messaged back. <It's out. Catching mice. Good night.>

Andy glanced at his watch. He wasn't going to fall asleep again after that little exchange. And what the hell was Roz doing up at this hour? Was she drunk? Horny? He entertained himself with a brief fantasy of a tipsy, sexually aroused Roz clambering onto bed eager to take advantage of him.

Usually he liked to be in charge, but could he submit to her?

No. He decided. He was certain that if Roz got something too easily, she would have no respect for it. The woman had the attention span of a mayfly. She needed a strong man, someone who would challenge her in every way – in and out of the bedroom.

Someone like him.

No. No. No. He was not going there. He had enough troubles on his plate at the moment without inviting more into his life. Once he was sure his father was on the road to recovery he would go back to work. Hunt Roz down. Return her to her sister and get as far the hell away as he could.

8

In the early hours of the morning, Roz lay in the narrow bed, wondering how Andy was. Damn it, she didn't want to think about him. That was never going to end well, but she couldn't resist taking out her phone and checking. He was online. Roz hesitated. This online thing with Andy was turning into a habit. One that she didn't want to break.

'Oh, don't be silly. It's not as if he knows where you are.' She messaged him.

<Are you there? Or are you out having a wild time?>

The answer came immediately. <No. I'm at home. My dad had a heart attack.>

She hadn't expected that. <Oh crap. How is he?>

<Okay. He discharged himself from hospital, but he's . . .> There was a pause before he continued. <I can't believe how old he looks.>

She knew that feeling. The first time she saw her dad in prison, she had been horrified. The man who had met her wearing prison overalls looked three sizes smaller than the larger-than-life father she had grown up with. For the first time, she noticed how grey his hair was, and the lines in his face. <It's a shock, isn't it, when you realize your father is old?>

<Tell me about it. He looks like he's shrunk. I'm a terrible son. I haven't been home for eighteen months.>

94

<Let me guess, super spy stuff?> She grinned as she swiped the message.

<Something like that. I've spent more than a year chasing a redhead around Europe.>

The nerve of him. <Don't blame me! Not my fault you didn't visit your parents. It's not like you can't afford a plane ticket. I hear that O'Sullivan Air is cheap!>

<And nasty, LOL.>

She laughed. She never travelled O'Sullivan Air, even when she wasn't in trouble. There was something about their signature yellow and green colours that made her want to barf.

Andy went on. <But the problem with visiting my parents is that they don't want me to leave.>

A wave of longing went through Roz. What must it be like to have someone who never wanted you to leave? She wasn't going to say that to him, so she joked, <I'd kick you out.>

<Baby, you know that's not true.>

She laughed out loud, and Frankie turned over in his bed, so she forced herself to be quiet again. <What do your parents want you to do?>

<Take over the running of this place.>

<Poor little rich kid?> Even across the internet, the acid leached. <You don't have any real problems.>

<Unlike you?>

<Yeah, try my life for a week and you'd run back to yours. I bet you had a nanny when you were growing up and went to a posh boarding school.>

<No nanny. Mum was very hands on. And I ran away from boarding school. Twice.>

What would a hands-on mum have been like? Roz had begged her dad for stories about her mother. She had never been real to her. The one small photograph he had was black and white, and didn't convey any hint of the vibrant woman he told her about. And now the poor little rich boy was complaining.

<My heart bleeds for you. Try thirteen different schools. And most of them were kips. I had no mum, just a series of different 'aunts'.>

Andy didn't rise to her bait. <My dad is in his eighties and I have no idea what age my mum is. They have no one but me.>

<And you keep disappearing on them. Do they know what you do?>

<Not exactly. Better that way. They'd be frantic if they thought they could lose another son.>

What? She had run a computer search on Andy, but his background was a mystery. <Another son?>

<My older brother Robert died in a climbing accident while I was in Afghanistan.>

<Oh, nasty. And you're all that's left?>

<Yep.>

<So are you going to do what they want – stay home?>

<I don't know. The idea of settling down . . . you know how it is.>

She wished she did. <I've never had a home. Sometimes I wonder if it's as good as it's supposed to be.>

<Oh, don't get me wrong. The place is great. If you like dodgy plumbing and wearing layers all year round to keep warm.>

<Been there, done that. Though I doubt your home is a damp B&B in Blackpool.>

The memory of that particular place made her shiver. Frankie's little caravan, small as it was, was warm and cosy in comparison.

<Not exactly, but it's pretty old. Think haunted house.>

<Oh cool, I always wanted to see a real ghost.>

Roz paused, and then decided to go for it. There was something about the pre-dawn silence which made it easy to ask awkward questions. <So are you, like, rich?>

<LOL. Only on paper. It costs a fortune to heat the place.>

<You should see where I'm staying now. One room has three fireplaces.>

The inside of the castle had changed her mind about a lot of things. The huge drawing room took half a forest to heat. Lucky there was one outside. From here, she could hear the trees swaying in the breeze.

Andy jumped on that, of course. <And where would that be?>

<Ah ah, no more clues. Tell me about your father.>

<Tough as old boots, deaf as a post, and believes kids should be seen and not heard.>

<But you love him?>

<He's my father. I can't send him back.>

Roz laughed. <LOL. Sometimes I'd like to send mine back. Most of the time, in fact, but he's the only one I've got.>

<He's still in prison?>

That wiped the smile off her face. She messaged quickly. <How did you know?>

<Super spy stuff. I know a lot about you.>

Of course he did. Why had she allowed herself to forget who he was? <Ugh, I feel violated. And not in a good way.>

<LOL. Is there a good way? I'm only doing my job, babe.>

<That's creepy. What else do you know about me?> She might as well pump him while he was feeling chatty.

<I know that you worked as a Domme, and didn't you work in a circus?>

He knew too damn much. She shivered. <Cirque Noir isn't your average circus. I don't do that kind of thing anymore. I'm done with that.>

<So you've turned over a new leaf. Scamming moneylenders instead?>

She was happy to change the subject. <Ah, you spotted that? A friend of mine was being fleeced by them. I thought payback was fair.>

Roz was sorry she hadn't managed to take them for as much cash as possible while she was at it. Seeing Natalya crying every week when half her benefit went into the moneylender's clutches had made her break her rule about staying out of sight. It had been a stupid risk but worth it.

Like an echo, Andy messaged, <Wasn't that a bit dangerous? What if they found out?>

She wasn't going to agree with him. <Dangerous? You have no idea what my life is like. Trust me, irate moneylenders are the least of my worries.>

<Why don't you tell me?>

<Oh, you're good.>

And he was. She was surprised by how tempting his offer was. She wanted to talk to someone.

<You almost had me. But it's the middle of the night, and I have to work later today. Some other time, perhaps.> She shifted in the bed, ready to sleep.

But Andy's message stopped her. <What are you up to this time? Robbing a bank?>

She grinned, his answer changing her mood. <Treason! And murder. And maybe a drop of poison.>

<Aha! You're stealing the crown jewels.>

<Yep, that's it. I always wanted a crown.>

<I'll have the car revved up and waiting.>

She laughed.

<Seriously though, if you want a crown, there are lots of nice shiny things for a girl to play with here . . .>

<You know, someday I might take you up on that. When I'm out of trouble.>

Of course he couldn't let it go. <You'll never be out of trouble if you keep doing the same things. You can't keep running all your life.>

Weariness suddenly flattened her. <I'll stop running when people stop chasing me.>

<And that's working out so well for you.>

<Fuck you.> Why couldn't he leave her alone? She didn't want him prying into her mind or her pathetic life.

<Hey, I'm sorry. I didn't mean to push. But it must be tough being on the run all the time. Why don't you come in? Let someone take care of you?>

He had no idea how tempting that was. But he didn't mean it. Andy was just doing his job and she had to remember that. <Someone like you?> Her fingers flew over the keypad. <How naïve do you think I am? I'm a job. You don't want to take care of me out of the goodness of your heart.>

<And you lied to me and stole from me, but hey, no hard feelings.>

She wasn't going to admit to any guilt about that. <I was trying to slow you down. Your money went to a good cause.>

<Glad to hear it. But it wasn't my money. It was Niall's. And btw, you owe me a kiss.>

For some reason, she cheered up. <You'll have to catch me first.>

<I'm planning on it.>

She wasn't going there. Kissing Andy McTavish again would be dangerous. That mouth should be licensed as a weapon. And the taste of him, so seductive. When he had kissed her, her mind had stopped functioning. <Good night!>

<Dream of me.>

<Nightmare, much?>

<Baby, you know you will, why deny it? But don't get too hot and bothered. I'll find you soon.>

She shoved her phone under her pillow and settled herself to sleep, with no idea why she was smiling.

Eventually Andy gave up on sleep. There was nothing more from Roz, the house was silent and he was still awake. He would go for a run. Lord knows he could do with the exercise. After changing into his running gear he made his way through the darkened halls. It would be dawn in an hour or so. He could work up a sweat by then.

He ran around the back of the house, his feet crunching loudly on the gravel. His warm breath fogged on the cool pre-dawn air.

'Who's that?'

Andy skidded to a halt as he recognized the voice. 'What the fuck? Paddy, is that you?'

The old stable hand had been with the family for over forty years. Andy clapped him on the shoulder and was rewarded with a gap-toothed grin. 'Andy, I heard you were back. What the hell are you doing running around the place in the middle of the night?'

'I might ask you the same question.'

A guarded look crossed the old man's face. 'Me and the boys have been taking turns watching the place since, well you know . . .'

Andy's inbuilt radar for trouble kicked in. 'Since what?'

'Since the night your father had the heart attack.'

Dawn was long past by the time Andy dragged every scrap of information he could from Paddy and the other stable lads. Four teenagers in a stolen car had thought Lough Darra was an easy target for a robbery. They hadn't reckoned on his father coming at them with a hunting rifle loaded with blanks.

Dougal had been congratulating himself on a job well done when his heart rebelled. His mother had insisted on calling an ambulance despite his father's protests. The 'heart attack' had been a mild episode and his father was recovering.

Back at the house, Maggie was preparing breakfast.

Andy poured himself a coffee and tucked into a bowl of cereal. He refused her offer of another fry-up and settled for a plate of scrambled eggs instead. If he stayed long enough he would be waddling.

As he sipped his coffee, Maggie kept a monologue going of the latest news in the village. 'And of course it will be nice to see the Turners again.'

Andy made an interested noise, trying to appear polite. Weren't they the family with that freckle-faced girl his mother was always trying to set him up with? What was her name? Iris, Rose, some kind of flower.

'And Lily is back, you know. Her romance with the Scottish doctor didn't work out. He's one of them, you know?'

Maggie paused, clearly expecting a response.

'One of what?'

'Kinky folk,' she whispered before turning her attention to the stove. 'They say she came home from work early to find him wearing one of her dresses.'

Andy almost snorted his coffee through his nose. Lily had no figure to speak of. She was built like a beanpole and was as strait-laced as a nun. He couldn't imagine anyone wanting to get into her clothes, whether she was wearing them or not.

'But you won't mention it, will you? The poor girl is so upset.'

Andy shrugged. 'I'm not likely to run into her.'

A puzzled look crossed Maggie's face. 'Of course you are. Your mother has invited them for dinner on Friday night. Didn't she tell you?'

'No.' Trust his mother to plan one of her get-togethers and not tell him.

'It's a small party, no more than a dozen. Your father is a lot better and she thought you'd like to catch up with your old friends.'

'Great.' Not great. Between them, his mother and Maggie could have run MI5. The pair of them had more plots than a library full of books. What were they up to now?

It had been an easy day for Roz. The whole crew had turned up to watch the big love scene between Cheyenne and Jack Winter. It was amazing, Roz reflected, how kissing Jack Winter could look boring when you saw it happen seventeen times before the director was satisfied.

She spent a bit of time chatting to Nagsy, trying to convince herself that this horse could possibly be sold for half a million. He butted her hand with his nose, clearly hoping for another treat. Roz held out the core of the apple she had been eating, carefully keeping her hand flat as Frankie had told her, and Nagsy lipped it up without hurting her.

'I'm getting fond of you,' she told him and petted his nose. The warm, horsey scent had become familiar and welcome. There was something peaceful about the dim stable tent that made her feel safe. No one would think of looking for her here. She was a city girl through and through. Never in her wildest dreams did she imagine she'd be somewhere in the middle of the Irish countryside petting a horse and talking to him like a friend. Paris and Hall seemed a long way away.

She watched as the grooms saddled and unsaddled the

horses, admiring their fearlessness while dealing with the huge beasts.

The film set was an enclosed world of its own; so far away from Interpol, murdered art dealers and ruthless ex-SEALs that she could pretend it was all a dream. She knew it was fantasy, that Hall was still out there, but the sense of safety was seductive.

Roz got her dinner from the catering van and ate outside the caravan. It was warm enough to sit out as long as she wore a jacket. Frankie would be along later, but for now, she was enjoying the break from the crowds.

Cheyenne appeared with a plate in her hand and stood there awkwardly. 'Do you mind if I join you?'

Astonished, Roz waved her to a seat. Frankie could get another chair when he turned up. 'Of course not. But I thought you'd be hanging out with the rest of the actors.'

Cheyenne sat down carefully and set her plate on the small table. It was piled high with salad leaves and a small chicken breast. 'I needed some me time, you know?'

Roz nodded, not pointing out the obvious. If Cheyenne wanted to be alone, inside her trailer was the place to go.

'And I wanted to talk to you,' Cheyenne continued. Roz had a good idea what was coming. 'Last night, in the bar. What did you do?'

Roz shrugged. 'I showed you that you're an attractive woman.'

Cheyenne shook her head. 'No, it was more than that. I heard about women like you. Are you some sort of Domme?' She pronounced the word 'Dom-my', and made it sound like a foreign species.

'Domme,' Roz said. 'I was, but it's not a big deal.' She shrugged. That part of her life seemed a long way away.

But Cheyenne was looking at her as if she had grown two heads. 'I didn't know that was real. What did you do? How do you make men do things for you? Did you sleep with them?'

She laughed. 'God no. I didn't sleep with any of them. Do you think I'm some sort of prostitute?' She tried to convince herself it was funny, but there was an edge in her voice.

Cheyenne backtracked rapidly. 'No, I'm sorry. I don't know.'

She was so upset that Roz relented. 'It's not like that. A good Domme doesn't have sex with her submissive. She works out what he needs, and challenges him to push himself.'

'So it's not about giving orders?'

'Well, it involves giving orders. Men like clear directions and women who know what they want.'

Cheyenne ignored her chicken and pushed the salad leaves around her plate. 'Tell me more about it. I've never met anyone like you before. I thought it was all whips and chains and funny clothes.'

Roz laughed. 'It can be. Being handy with a whip is a good skill for a Domme. It's amazing how many men want to be flogged hard enough to push them into sub-space.'

'Subspace?'

Roz searched for the words to explain it. 'It's when the adrenaline and endorphins and oxytocin combine in a way that produces an altered state of consciousness.'

She saw the other woman's face scrunch in confusion. 'Don't worry about the technicalities. What matters is that they are in a headspace where they're not worrying about the hostile takeover of their company.'

Funny, Roz knew exactly how to push other people into subspace, but had never had it happen to her. She'd never had a relationship where anyone cared enough to spend the time it took.

'You've flogged men?' Cheyenne looked shocked – and fascinated.

She shrugged. 'If that's what they needed. One client wanted to be treated like a puppy. I threw balls for him to fetch.' The memory made her smile.

'And there was one man I didn't like, so I locked him in a cage to keep him out of my hair. He swears it was the best night of his life.'

'This stuff happens? For real? There are men who like it when you give them orders and flog them?'

Roz smiled. 'Oh yes, and women too. Ever been tempted?'

Cheyenne ducked her head to hide her face. 'A little. But men don't want me the way they want you,' she mumbled.

What the hell was going on? 'Why would you say that? You saw the reaction of the men in the bar last night.'

'No, that was you. Not me. Today I was doing love scenes with Jack and he barely kissed me. I tried the stuff you showed me last night and it didn't work.'

Exasperated, Roz put her glass down on the small table. 'What do you expect? He's married, and everyone knows he's madly in love.' She lowered her voice. 'And from what I've seen, his inclinations run in the opposite direction. He's a Dom.'

'Oh!' Cheyenne sat up a little straighter. 'How can you tell?'

'It's something to do with the body language. How they stand, how they sit, it's a quiet confidence that's hard to fake.'

Jack Winter had it. Roz had no doubt about it. Of course, that confidence could be because he was one of the top actors in the world, but she was pretty sure it was more than that.

The image of another man with that type of confidence flashed into her mind. There was nothing quiet about Andy McTavish, but he gave off that same vibe. Why hadn't she spotted it before? Damn, he was out of her league. She might not be a Domme anymore, but she was definitely not a submissive. For a moment, she considered faking it, to see how he'd react. She shivered. Maybe that wasn't such a good idea after all.

'Please tell me you're not in love with Jack Winter.'

Cheyenne's mouth formed a small O. 'Of course not. I know I haven't a chance and he's not my type. No, there's someone else I like, but he never notices me.'

'Who is it?'

'I'd rather not say.'

Interesting. Roz ran through the men Cheyenne had been chatting to, but there were so many on the set she couldn't pick one out.

Before she could ask for more details, Frankie stomped

through the gathering darkness. 'Hello ladies, is there room for one more?' He was holding a plate of food and a glass of wine.

Roz laughed. 'I think we can squeeze you in. It's not like you take up too much room.'

'Cheeky brat.'

Cheyenne jumped up. 'I'm sorry, I'm in your place. Please sit down.' Her cheeks were bright red.

Ah! Realization dawned. For an actress, Cheyenne was terrible at concealing her emotions. Roz stood up. 'Don't be silly. Frankie, you take my seat, I'm finished eating and need to find a bathroom. Cheyenne, can you stay and keep Frankie company until I get back?'

The other two looked at each other. There was a small smile on Frankie's face, and Cheyenne was blushing.

'Take your time,' Frankie said. 'I'll look after your friend.'

Grinning, Roz left them alone.

9

Andy twisted his neck from side to side, straining against the collar of his borrowed shirt. He hadn't packed anything suitable and if his mother hadn't insisted, he would still be wearing jeans.

The table in the formal dining room was set with the best silver and crystal. Vases containing early blooms from the garden perfumed the air. Twelve place settings were artfully arranged. He was halfway down the middle on one side. There would be no escape from his mother's guests.

The sound of car doors closing indicated that the visitors had arrived. He peeked through a gap in the velvet curtains. Friendly get together, his ass. Eight, or was it nine guests, mostly women teetering in high heels on the gravel drive. A fox would have more luck against a pack of hounds. For the first time in his life, he felt sorry for Mr Darcy. This evening was turning into a Regency farce.

He downed his pre-dinner drink in two gulps as he struggled to remember the names of his neighbours' daughters. Kirsty, the youngest, couldn't have been more than sixteen and was trouble in the making if ever he saw one.

Lily, her older sister, was almost as tall as he was. He tried not to smile as he caught a glimpse of a pair of blue Crocs peeking out from beneath a shapeless floral print dress which did nothing for her. Brenda, the middle child, was down from Queens for the weekend and was already bored.

He had the vaguest recollection of the Turner family. They had bought the farm next door around the time that he left. Deirdre looked almost as uncomfortable as Brenda and the pair sat and whispered together.

'And this is Isobel,' his mother introduced him to the eldest Turner daughter.

Frank grey eyes stared back at him and she gave him an apologetic smile. She didn't want to be here either. At least he had found one ally. 'Nice to meet you.'

His mother clapped her hands. 'I believe that dinner is ready. Why don't we all go inside?'

As he had feared, Andy was surrounded by women. Usually it wouldn't have bothered him but this evening he felt like a prize stallion being put through its paces in the stable yard.

'I believe you're in security,' Mr Turner said politely as he sipped his soup.

'That's right,' Andy agreed.

'Like in a shopping mall?' Kirsty pulled a face.

Despite himself, Andy laughed. 'No. I'm involved in the other kind of security. Personal security. Bodyguard. That type of thing.'

'Oh. And have you met anyone famous?'

If he hadn't signed non-disclosure agreements, he could have given them a list as long as his arm. 'Lots of actors, actresses, some foreign dignitaries.'

'Like who?' Kirsty was interested now.

He put his spoon down. 'Well, I looked after Jack Winter and his wife while they were on honeymoon in Scotland.'

Look after them. That was a laugh. They had spent most of their time in bed. But Jack was a friendly guy and obviously crazy about his American wife.

'What was he like?'

At this point he had the attention of all of the women at the table. What was it about Winter that made women go weak at the knees?

The soup plates were cleared away and Maggie served the main course.

'But you won't be running around the world like that forever, will you, Andy?'

His mother was smiling, but there was a brittle edge to her voice that made Andy sit up and take notice. She was getting on in years. The heart attack had given her a scare and she wanted her only son home. Not tearing around the planet from one trouble spot to another.

His voice was gentle when he replied, 'Of course not. If I transfer from field operative to running teams, I can work from anywhere.'

Poppy and Dougal exchanged a satisfied glance. He would have to talk to them later. He wasn't going to escape without an interrogation about his future plans. He wished he could say that he had some.

'Cool,' Kirsty chipped in. She shot a sly glance at her sisters. 'And do you have a girlfriend?'

His mother glanced up. Lily paused with a fork halfway to her mouth and Isobel was trying her best to stifle a smile. He could look forward to weeks of dinners like this one if he didn't nip his mother's plans in the bud right now.

'Actually, I do.'

A knife clattered at the far end of the table. He suspected it was his mother's, but Andy kept his focus on Kirsty. The child had a great future ahead of her as an interrogator.

He could hardly make up a story about someone they were likely to meet socially. The glimmer of an idea dawned. 'She works in London.'

Well, that bit was technically true. He pressed on before his mother could interrupt. 'She's one of the O'Sullivans. You know – the airline family.'

'Tim O'Sullivan keeps a fine stable,' his father agreed. 'Horsey girl, is she?'

'I have no idea, Dad.' He knew Roz was good with a whip, but he didn't know if she had ever been near a horse. 'We only got together quite recently.'

Like a few days before, in the middle of a gun battle, when he believed she was pregnant.

'And do you like her?'

His mother's question put an end to Kirsty's interrogation.

Did he like her? It was a simple question. One he should have been able to answer without thinking about it. Roz was a thief and a liar and lord knows what else. He had been on her trail for more than a year and he probably knew more about her than he did about his last five girlfriends. But did he like Roz? He only knew that she intrigued him more than any woman he had met for years.

'Yes,' he admitted. 'I do like her.'

After dinner, they returned to the sitting room and sipped drinks beside the fire. Brenda and Deirdre took turns playing the piano, earning them a smattering of unenthusiastic applause. Kirsty rolled her eyes at them, pulled out her iPhone and logged on to *E! online*.

Five minutes later, she straightened up with a squeal. 'Oh, Jack Winter is in Ireland!'

She flushed when Brenda stopped playing and demanded, 'Show me.' All eyes turned to Kirsty.

'It will be on the TV,' she said. 'Put on *E! News*.'

To avoid any more torture from the piano, Andy switched on the television and within minutes he found the news clip about Jack Winter. A student film-maker had managed to get onto the set of Jack's latest movie and persuaded the star to give him an interview. A large castle loomed in the background.

A bearded Jack was surrounded by a bunch of rough looking Norsemen who waved their shields at the camera.

Andy's attention was drawn to a group of actors in the background. One woman nodded as she listened to instructions from the director. The hood of her cloak fell back and a mass of strawberry blonde hair tumbled around her shoulders.

Under the director's orders, an actor approached the woman and aimed a blow. The redhead staggered and fell to the ground, only to get up a moment later, smiling. The delicate line of her profile was one that he had last seen in a London hotel room. Roz Spring. The latex belly was gone, revealing that she was in good shape. Excellent shape.

Excitement thrummed in his belly at the prospect of the chase. He had her. He had finally tracked Roz down. Andy gulped down his coffee and wondered how soon could he make his excuses and leave the party.

He calculated swiftly. It would take about three hours to drive there. He could imagine her face if he turned up in the middle of the night. No. That would encourage her to run. He would have to be patient. Turning up while she was working and couldn't leave the set would be so much better.

He would be able to observe her from a distance while he let Niall and Sinead know where she was. Then it would be job done. He wasn't sure why the prospect of that made him edgy. He wanted this over. Right?

As if sensing his indecision, his phone vibrated in his pocket. He pulled it out and touched the screen. It was her.

<Hi>

<Hi yourself. Doing anything interesting tonight?>

<Nothing much. Watching a movie. What about you?>

Yeah. Roz was watching a movie alright – one that wouldn't hit the big screen for at least six months.

<I'm at a party> he typed.

<Oh. Any nice ladies there?>

Andy glanced around the room. Deirdre and Brenda had disappeared. Kirsty was bored. Lily was chatting to Isobel. She looked as if she'd had a little too much to drink and Isobel was patting her hand in sympathy. They were probably talking about the kinky doctor.

<Lots. Blondes, brunettes, you name it.>

<Well, you won't need me then.> A message flashed across the screen that she had gone offline.

Andy laughed. Was she jealous? Was Roz actually interested?

'Anything important, dear?' His mother was frowning. He probably shouldn't have checked his phone. He was about to say 'nothing' but then paused. He needed to borrow a car for a few days.

'It's Roz. She's just arrived in Ireland. I'm driving south tomorrow to see her.'

The early morning traffic on the motorway south was mercifully light and Andy made good time to Tullamore. He took the road out of the midlands town and drove towards the castle. He had checked for the latest news about the movie and a company that specialized in recruiting film extras had put out a call on Facebook looking for Norsemen for a battle scene they were shooting that day.

Andy hoped that he could blag his way past security at the gate. He rolled down the window of the Jeep. 'Kate sent me. I'm here for the battle scene.'

'Corpse or fighter?'

'Fighter,' Andy replied. He could wield a sword if he had to.

'Okay, mate. Drive half a mile up the road and take the turn-off marked western meadow. They're doing wardrobe and make-up there.'

He waved him on and Andy made his way up the rutted drive of the castle. Someone had filled the worst of the potholes with gravel, but he was glad he'd borrowed a Jeep. Up ahead, a group of armed Norsemen were making their way through the woods in the misty rain.

He hesitated at the turn-off. Maybe he should 'borrow' a costume. It would make it easier to move around the castle grounds without being noticed. Andy reversed a couple of feet and took the turn for the meadow.

After parking the Jeep, he headed for the costume depot and smiled at the girl behind the desk.

'Norse or native?' she asked, giving him an appreciative glance.

Beside him, a middle-aged man was being painted up to look as if he had received a spear wound. He wasn't going there. A costume that involved chain mail might be heavier, but the long tunic beneath would at least be warm. 'Norse,' he replied.

She checked the rail for sizes. 'Haven't I seen you in something before?'

'I've done a bit of theatre and film work, but to be honest, I'm waiting for a break.'

The girl studied him carefully and brushed his hair back from his face with her fingers. 'You have great bones. The camera will eat you up. Benny might be able to use you for some scenes up around the castle. Two of the guys are injured.'

'Benny?'

'Benny D'Angelo, the art director.'

She punched a number into her phone. 'Benny, I have someone who can fill in for Rory. Do you want him?'

'Mmmm, yeah,' she continued. 'No beard, but he's dark and unshaven.'

She put her hand over the phone for a moment to ask Andy, 'Do you have weapons experience?'

He refrained from telling her that most of the weapons he used were the twenty-first century kind. 'Yes.'

'Horses?'

He'd very nearly been born on one. 'Yes.'

'Great.' She pointed to a curtained-off area. 'You can change in there and then head over to make-up.'

No wonder it cost millions to make a movie. Make-up took forever and he looked little different than before. Perhaps a bit more rough and dangerous but nothing to warrant two hours sitting in a chair being painted up like a ponce.

He made his way to the castle, itching for his first glimpse of Roz.

The area in front of the castle was full of trailers, trucks and portable generators. The men in jeans and T-shirts were obviously crew. The women carried clipboards, wore wellingtons with velvet skirts and constantly spoke into their Bluetooth headsets.

Ignoring the rule about no phones on set, Andy found a quiet corner and checked his messages. Nothing from Roz. He risked a message to her.

<Hi babe.>

There was no reply and he was about to give up when his screen flashed.

<You slept in? Sweet. Was she nice?>

Andy wanted to punch the air. He had reeled her in. If that wasn't jealousy, he would eat his chain mail, link by link.

<Not as good as you, I'd say. I bet you're a little firecracker.>

<In your dreams, Irish.>

When she went offline, Andy looked around him, checking each of the trailers grouped near the set. The door of the one furthest away opened and two women emerged, both dressed in similar costumes. Even from this distance, he recognized her. Roz.

His heart thumped. Something primal awoke in him at the sight of her. A ravening hunger licked and gnawed at his insides. Andy hesitated, struggling to process a physical reaction to her. It wasn't the usual satisfaction when he tracked down the bad guy. This was more than a job. He fancied her. He actually fancied Roz Spring. Without conscious thought, he set out across the set only to be brought up sharply by a roar.

'Oi, mate, it's this way.'

Fuck. He turned to see who was shouting at him.

The man was shorter than he was and intelligence shone in his blue eyes. His skin was tanned and his bearing looked military. Andy almost saluted.

'We're shooting a scene at the old stables. How's your sword arm?'

'A little rusty.'

'But you can ride?'

'Of course.'

The man grunted his approval. 'Which branch were you in?'

He was sharp, Andy thought. 'The Wing.'

'And what are you doing now?'

'This and that. A bit of private security here and there – you know how it is.'

'Indeed I do, my son.' He thrust out his hand. 'Frankie Fletcher, pleased to meet you.'

Old was an understatement. The stable block looked as if it had been there since the Vikings invaded Ireland and was about to collapse at any moment, but it was suitably authentic for a Norse raid. Andy was introduced to his fellow actors and he listened as the fight scenes were planned out in meticulous detail.

He had to hand it to Frankie, he knew his stuff. The guy might be in his fifties, but he was fitter than all the twentysomethings on set.

The director clapped his hands and called for silence. 'And action.'

By mid-afternoon Andy was exhausted. This was as bad as the army. Although the old stable block was freezing, it was like the Bahamas under the heat of the lamps. His shoulders ached from swinging the heavy sword and beneath his chain mail and long tunic, he was sweating.

He was never so relieved as when the director yelled cut. 'Nice work, guys.'

Andy sat down on a bale of hay and mopped his brow.

Frankie took a seat beside him and drew an electronic cigarette from his pocket. 'Filthy habit, I know. But I can't seem to give it up.'

They sat in companionable silence until one of the assistants approached them. 'Rory is going to be out of action for a week. Can you come back tomorrow? Benny has more work for you.'

Andy nodded. Things had just taken a turn for the better. There would be no sneaking around the set now that he had a job. All he had to do was find Roz.

Abbie Marshall was an average looking woman. Average size, average looks, barely any make-up, brown hair cut into a no-nonsense style that required zero maintenance. Nothing compared to the beauties dressed up for the camera. But when she arrived at Charleville, she took the castle by storm.

Her taxi swept up to the front of the castle, and she leapt out, all energy and inquisitiveness. She grabbed her small bag, threw a handful of money at the driver, and glared up at the tower.

Roz was picking up a script when she arrived, and had no difficulty identifying her. Jack Winter's marriage to Abbie had been a media storm, and the fact that Abbie hadn't taken Jack's surname had all the gossips predicting an early end to the marriage. But right now, she looked like a woman on a mission.

'Where's Jack Winter?' she asked Roz.

'Come with me.' Roz led her around the corner and pointed to where the filming was going on. In spite of the trainers under her velvet dress, she could barely keep up with Abbie. The reporter hummed with anticipation.

The director called, 'Cut!' and the actors all relaxed.

As if he could smell his mate, Jack's head came up and turned in her direction. A wide smile lit up his face, and his eyes gleamed impossibly blue. It was as if someone had plugged him into a power source. He ignored everyone around him and headed straight for Abbie.

When he pulled her into his arms, the electricity between them crackled. He kissed her, oblivious to the audience watching him. And Abbie reached up and pulled him down to her, as hot and passionate as he was.

Every single member of the set stopped to watch. It was like watching a perfect storm. The power and fury of the two lovers was mesmerizing.

The sight of them made Roz smile, but it also awakened a sense of dark resentment and jealousy. God, she wanted that. She wanted a man who would ignore the world for her, someone who treated her as if she was the only woman in the world.

That was what her sister had. And what she didn't.

Roz was never going to be the one with the prince telling her how much he loved her. Better get used to it. No one loved her. Hell, there were a few people who liked her, who were fond of her. But no one who loved her like that.

Get over it. This is your life. You live in the shadows and watch other people love.

She wouldn't cry.

To distract herself, she copied everyone else and pulled out her phone to record the scorching kiss binding Jack Winter and Abbie Marshall.

Finally, Abbie allowed an inch of space between her and her husband and saw what was happening. She wiggled enough to free one arm and pulled out her camera. She twisted around, recording all the people recording her and Jack.

Jack laughed and kissed her cheek, but was careful not to get in her way.

Roz moved back before Abbie could record her. She couldn't afford to get distracted by this, she had a dangerous stunt to do.

Andy crossed the meadow back to the castle. The damp spring air was chilling and the crew wore padded jackets and stamped their feet in an effort to keep warm. A spotlight was aimed at the turret where an action scene was unfolding.

High overhead, a desperate fight was taking place on the battlements. A woman screamed as she tried to fight off a rapacious group of invaders. She screamed again and clambered onto the stone wall. Andy held his breath.

'Jesus!' he hissed as the slender figure, clad in a nightgown, fell from the battlements.

There was a loud thump as the stunt woman hit the giant airbag below.

The crew clapped. 'Nice work, Roz,' the director yelled. 'Let's do one more take and we'll call it a day.'

That was Roz? Andy's heartbeat stuttered.

Holy fuck, she was jumping from at least sixty foot up. She could get hurt. Every instinct in his body urged him to rush in and stop her before she broke her fool neck, but he knew he couldn't. No one else was looking the least bit worried, and Roz was grinning as she vanished back into the tower.

It was her job, he reasoned. She was a stunt woman.

Roz was paid to get hit with swords and jump out of towers and fall off horses. Every detail was orchestrated and planned. There was no reason for the cold sweat that covered his back.

The second fall was more spectacular than the first. A gust of wind caught her nightgown and it billowed out exposing pale, slender limbs. The cameraman beside him whistled in approval and Andy beat down the urge to thump him.

Finally, the director called it a day and Andy hurried across the lot. At the airbag, there was no sign of her.

'Looking for Roz?' one of the crew asked him. 'She's gone back inside. She left some gear up there.'

'Thanks,' Andy said.

He stepped back to allow two ladies in period costume to exit and hurried up the broad oak staircase to the landing. Ignoring the sign that warned him not to enter, Andy opened the door to the turret staircase and bolted it behind him. He had promised Roz a reckoning and by god he was going to have it.

The spiral staircase was dark and narrow, but Andy took the steps two at a time. Around the next bend, he almost collided with a woman descending. The linen shift was now covered by a blue gown belted at the waist with a golden girdle. Her strawberry blonde hair was bound in a loose plait that fell over her shoulders.

A vision invaded his head of a painting he had seen as a child – one of a knight and his lady meeting on a staircase. The woman's face was obscured, the knight's full of tender emotion.

The romantic image was utterly at odds with the raging heat bubbling inside him. Lust, frustration and anger battled for supremacy.

Vivid blue eyes widened as she recognized him. Her wide pink mouth didn't have a chance to scream before he dragged her into his arms and fastened his lips on hers.

He forgot tenderness, forgot finesse, forgot every practised move he had ever learnt in the art of seduction. Andy ravaged her mouth, thrusting his tongue against hers. He caught her hair in one gauntleted hand, holding her in place while he continued to kiss her.

Her surprised squeal at the sudden assault changed into a soft moan. Roz tasted sweet, like strawberries. Andy tightened his grip around her waist. He wanted to devour her and never stop.

She wound her arms around his neck and returned his kiss with a hunger of her own. A lustful fire raced through his blood, making his nerve endings scream. He tore his mouth away from hers to kiss her jaw line and down her neck, biting and nibbling on the tender flesh.

Damned costumes. They were wearing far too many clothes.

Andy McTavish, in the flesh. When she saw him, Roz was convinced she was dreaming. Or that he was a ghost. She had been in Charleville long enough to learn that it was the most haunted castle in Ireland and was surprised to hear how many of the crew claimed to have seen something moving in the old tower.

She had ignored them all. She had seen enough real-life horrors to pay any attention to silly ghost stories.

But when she saw the chainmail-clad figure on the stairs, with a face straight out of her darkest dreams, she had wondered if she was losing it. The few times she'd seen him, Andy McTavish had been elegant and polished. This rough-edged soldier was different. He could have stepped out of any of her fantasies.

He climbed up to her, and she could smell sweat and oiled leather. All male. His eyes were narrowed but his nostrils flared, like a hunter closing in on his quarry.

She had a feeling she was his prey and she didn't know if she should run to him – or from him. For endless moments, she stared at him, the tension rising between them.

Andy swooped, pulling her into his arms and kissing her.

The shock of it, of him, kept her motionless for ten heartbeats. Then the heat of his body, the pressure of his mouth, broke through her defences and she took a breath. Before she could move, he pulled her hair, tipping her head back so he could ravage her mouth more deeply.

His mouth was hot, intense, tasting of hungry male. His tongue tangled with hers, giving no quarter.

God, he could kiss. Roz knew she shouldn't succumb, but she couldn't resist the intensity and passion he was focusing on her. She put her arms around his neck so she could kiss him back and lost herself in his embrace.

Reality retreated and the hard muscled arms around her became her world.

She had no idea how long she spent kissing him until

the banging at the door below echoed up the tower. Sounds carried in this old castle and she was jolted back to the present.

She jerked herself out of Andy's arms, trying to steady her breathing and pretend that nothing had happened.

'What are you doing here?' she demanded. She was standing a step above him, so she didn't have to tilt her head back to look into his dark eyes.

'I came here to get you.' His words were stark, uncompromising.

For a moment, she thought he meant he wanted her. Then common sense returned. This wasn't a man hunting for his woman; this was an investigator searching for a witness. Interpol hadn't given up looking for her. They had sent someone else instead. Did they not realize that Hall would kill her before she ever got to testify? She wasn't going back there, ever.

'Tough. I'm working here. I'm not leaving.'

'I'll look after you.' The words seemed to promise more than personal security. And she was shocked to realize how tempted she was.

'Dream on.' She wasn't giving in to temptation. 'I have a job. Go away and stop bothering me.'

She wasn't prepared for Andy's grin. That mouth should be licensed. It teased and promised all at once.

'As it happens, I have a job too. I'm working on the movie. It looks like we'll be seeing a lot of each other.'

Roz escaped down the stairs, desperate to get away from him. How the hell could she cope with Andy here?

It wasn't like she didn't have enough to worry about. She was out of money until she got paid. Frankie was determined to involve her in what looked like a tempting scam. Cheyenne was making moves on Frankie and Hall was out there searching for her. And now Andy McTavish was here, kissing her like a starving man.

She headed back to wardrobe to get rid of the old-fashioned robe. How did women wear those things? Especially in a time when there were no zippers and buttons were a luxury.

Cheyenne was in the trailer, shaking. 'Thank god you're here, Roz. I don't know what to do.'

Roz stripped off her gloves and began the long process of unlacing her robe. 'What's wrong?'

'The director wants me to be naked in the lake scene.'

Roz had been about to pull the unlaced robe over her head, but stopped. 'Is that a problem?'

'Yes.' Cheyenne clenched her fists, looking like a militant chipmunk.

'You've done nude scenes before, in that series you were in.' Roz couldn't remember the name of it, but she did have a vague memory of a bedroom scene.

'That was years ago. It was on a closed set, and it was carefully filmed so you couldn't see my thighs or ass.' Cheyenne paced up and down, three steps in each direction, all she could manage in the limited space of the trailer. 'No one mentioned this when I signed the contract.'

Roz pulled off the robe and handed it back to the wardrobe mistress. She stood in her brief panties and a pair of sandals while she searched for her own clothes. 'So what's the problem? What do they want this time?'

'They want me to walk naked into the lake, and swim, and then have a sex scene with Jack.' Her voice rose. 'Do you have any idea what's involved in a scene like that? Every bit of cellulite will be obvious. I won't be able to hide a thing. Everyone will see my grotesque thighs and ass.'

'There's nothing wrong with your thighs.' Roz, still semi-naked, pointed down at herself. 'Look at me. We're the same size. I'm wearing your clothes and they fit me. Am I grotesque?'

Cheyenne paused in her rant. 'Of course not. You're young and beautiful. It's different at your age. I'm old and fat.'

'For fuck's sake!' Roz tugged on a pair of jeans. 'Get a grip. You're a beautiful Hollywood star. Millions of men dream about you. And if you don't believe me, ask Frankie if you're old and fat.'

But Cheyenne had stopped. She looked like a cartoon character who'd been hit on the head. 'We're the same size. You said it yourself. Why don't you do the scene?'

'Are you mad? I'm not an actress. I can't do that.' The thought of actually acting in a film, as opposed to just being a double, was horrifying. Way to tell Hall where she was. But Cheyenne's distress was getting to her. No matter how often she told herself to let people sort out their own problems, she always managed to get sucked in.

How did her dad do it, she wondered? He could work out what people wanted, and use it against them. Somehow, Roz always ended up trying to give it to them. She wasn't mad about the idea of being naked either, but she didn't hate it as much as Cheyenne did.

Cheyenne was delighted with her idea. 'You can be my body double. You won't have to act, just walk naked into the lake and swim a bit. They can make you up to look like me. It'll be great. And of course, the money is much better.'

That stopped Roz's objection. She could do with extra money. If she were made up to look like Cheyenne, maybe it would work. And – an imp of mischief pointed out – it would really piss off Andy.

'Okay, I'll do it.'

11

Andy paused to catch his breath. Today had been even more backbreaking. Frankie was worse than a drill sergeant and each fight scene was shot over and over again until he was satisfied.

'Let's call it a day, lads. The beers are on me tonight.'

Andy shrugged out of his chain mail – he was beginning to hate the sight of it – and handed it over to the wardrobe assistant to be repaired for the following day. The other guys joked and teased each other as they changed. Tullamore was a lively little town at the weekend but he had no interest in chasing other women.

He had barely seen Roz in the last twenty-four hours, but that was going to change tonight. If Frankie was out for the evening, he might finally get some time alone with her.

'Aren't you coming with us?' Frankie called from the doorway.

'No. I think I'll head over to see what's going on at the castle.'

'I wouldn't bother, my son. It's a closed set tonight. Crew only. Jack Winter is shooting a love scene and they don't want clips appearing on YouTube before the movie is out.'

'I'm sure he doesn't.' Andy laughed. Jack didn't have a shy bone in his body. He worked out as hard as a squad of

Rangers to keep it in top shape. For him, a personal trainer was a necessity.

'And you should have heard Roz this morning when she heard that she had to be fitted for a merkin.'

'A merkin?' Andy's head shot up.

'You know. A wig for –'

'I know what a merkin is, but why the hell would Roz need one?'

'Didn't you hear? Cheyenne and Mike had a blazing row last night. She thinks the scene is too graphic and point blank refused to do it. Roz is doing it instead.'

'She's what?'

But Frankie was already gone. Andy grabbed a dark padded jacket from the back of a chair. The yellow lettering said 'Crew'. It should be enough to get him past security.

The area around the castle was quiet, but Andy could see the lights in the distance. It looked like they were shooting down at the lake. He picked up a toolkit and followed the road through the woods.

The security men straightened when they saw him approach. 'This is a closed set, mate.'

'I know.' Andy lifted his tool box. 'I got a call from Matt – one of the booms is acting up.'

'You better hurry then.'

Relieved, Andy almost ran the rest of the way to the set.

Despite the warmth of the lighting, the evening was chilly. Jack Winter, swaddled in a thick towelling robe over his costume, was sipping a hot coffee while he and Mike discussed the scene. There was no sign of Roz.

Sitting in one corner of the set was Abbie Marshall.

Andy grinned. He knew that Jack was crazy about the New York reporter, but her presence on set kept the rumour mill churning.

Abbie flies in to watch Jack make out. Andy could almost see the headlines in the next day's papers.

He set the toolkit down and took up position near the sound crew.

The door of the small trailer opened and Roz emerged. She was wearing a wig and had been made up to look like Cheyenne. From a distance, it would be impossible to tell them apart. The dark robe was several sizes too big for her, and she hugged it around her, trying to keep out the evening chill. Beside Jack, she looked tiny and vulnerable.

Andy didn't know whether to stay or leave. He was still reeling after that kiss on the stairs but seeing Roz naked wasn't something he wanted to share with a bunch of other guys. The director moved back and Jack and Roz exchanged a high five before Jack walked into the woods beside the lake.

A wardrobe assistant hurried onto the set and with the briefest hesitation, Roz unbelted her robe and handed it over. The boom operator beside him whistled under his breath and Andy resisted the urge to snarl.

Roz was beautiful, long limbed and slender with surprisingly full breasts, a flat, toned abdomen and a round ass. The sight of her nipples peaking in the icy air made his cock stir.

His breath caught. He had imagined this moment for a long time, but he had never done justice to her. The tight nipples looked like raspberries and his mouth watered. He wanted to suck them until she trembled. And then . . . he clamped down on the rest of his fantasies.

The lights were dimmed and the fog machine vented a light mist across the lake. Everyone on set fell silent. A wave of possessiveness washed over Andy. He wanted to punch every guy who was staring at her, but mostly he wanted to beat the crap out of Jack Winter.

'And action.'

Roz stepped into the lake, moving slowly through the water until it was waist high. She turned to the camera and washed her body slowly, allowing her palms to linger on her rounded breasts.

Andy smothered a groan as his cock hardened and he doubted if he was the only guy on set who was turned on.

Roz submerged herself in the water and rose again seconds later, her long hair stark against her pale skin, forming wet tendrils on her breasts.

Dear god, the sight of her like that was going to kill him. She was as seductive as a siren.

'Gormflaith,' Jack Winter's voice carried across the lake.

'Husband,' Roz responded with a slight tremble in her voice.

Andy swallowed. He didn't know how a single word could unnerve him so much. Cheyenne's voice would be dubbed in later, but the hint of invitation in that single breathless word made him want to wade in there and drag Roz out.

Jack dropped his cloak and shrugged off his sword belt.

The rest of his clothes swiftly followed and he stepped into the water, eager to claim his new bride.

The contrast between the tanned, muscular hero and the pale, trembling woman was startling. The director smiled his approval as Jack swept Roz up in his arms, hugging her wet, naked body against him. Their searing kiss went on far too long for Andy's liking. Surely the guy didn't have to enjoy it that much? Abbie Marshall shifted in her chair. He was willing to bet that Jack would pay for that kiss later.

Or maybe Jack was doing it to tease her. Hell, it was teasing the hell out of every red-blooded male on set.

Tightening his arms around her, Jack carried Roz from the water.

'And cut! Nice job guys. That's a take. Let's do the cloak scene and we'll call it a night.'

A shivering Roz was wrapped in a gown by the wardrobe assistant and someone handed her a hot drink. The sight of her pale hands, tinged blue with cold, again made Andy want to punch something.

Jack towelled himself off and pulled on his robe before having a brief conversation with the director. There was a flurry of activity on the set as a blazing fire was set up on the lake shore. The set hands laid a quilt on the damp ground before setting Jack's cloak on top.

At the edge of the water, both actors disrobed and were sprayed with a mixture of oil and water. Roz giggled nervously as Jack lifted her up in his arms. 'Behave,' Jack teased her.

Andy wanted to clamp his eyes shut as the director called for the scene to start but he couldn't resist watching. The naked bodies in the firelight, Jack's hands and mouth on Roz's skin, the passionate expression on his face as he became utterly engrossed in the scene.

If the director didn't yell cut soon, Andy would do it for him. His raging erection was almost painful. He was angry as hell and more turned on than he had ever been in his life. How had she got him into this state? He didn't know whether he wanted to kill Roz or fuck her senseless.

'Great job, guys. That was smoking hot.' The director could barely keep the glee from his voice.

As Andy watched, Jack stood up and helped Roz into her robe before he pulled on his own. He mouthed the words 'Good girl' to her before dropping an almost brotherly kiss on her forehead.

It was the final straw. Andy picked up a pile of towels and hurried towards Roz. They almost collided as she turned suddenly to avoid one of the crew who was intent on putting out the fire.

'Thanks,' Roz murmured as she reached for the towel and then her eyes widened in recognition. Her face was flushed, her mouth pink and tender from her recent encounter with Jack.

Andy barely resisted the urge to throw her into the lake and wash every trace of the other man from her. 'You need a hot shower,' he told her.

'I'm fine. I –'

'Now.'

Her mouth opened and then closed again at the stern tone in his voice.

Andy looked around him. The Jeeps that the set crew

used were parked along the road and he knew that most would have keys in the ignition. Ignoring her protests he bundled her into the nearest one. The engine growled as they shot through the woods at breakneck speed.

Andy pulled to a halt at the castle. Racing around to her side of the vehicle he opened the door and reached for her.

'What the hell do you think you're –'

Andy silenced her protest with a kiss and kept on kissing her until her body sagged against his. He slipped his hand beneath her robe and stroked her breast, pinching the nipple between his fingers until she gasped.

He had to get her alone before he lost control entirely. Andy's thoughts raced. He couldn't risk going back to the caravan she shared with Frankie, but the tower room in the castle had a bed. Andy slid one arm beneath her knees and lifted her from the Jeep.

He put his shoulder to the castle door and it opened with a protesting creak. Andy kicked it closed behind them. He marched up the wide staircase and along the corridor to the east tower.

'Are you crazy?'

'Completely and certifiably,' he agreed as he pushed the door open and tumbled her onto the bed. They were both breathing heavily. Damn, he was losing it if he couldn't carry a woman up a couple of flights of stairs.

Her cheeks were flushed and her eyes sparkled in the faint light that came through the leaded windows. Andy wound a handful of damp hair in his fist and bent his head to take her mouth.

This time he restrained himself, teasing her with all the skill he possessed, drawing little breathless whimpers from her. Roz arched against him mindlessly, brushing her breasts against his chest. With a groan, he rolled off her.

'Shower,' he ordered.

'What! Are you out of your mind? You can't start something like this and stop.' The Roz he knew was back, but he was damned if he was laying a finger on her until Jack Winter's touch was washed from her skin.

He shrugged off his clothes and dropped them on the floor. The tiny bathroom had been squeezed into a corner of the tower room and the oddly shaped space was barely big enough for both of them.

He checked the temperature of the over-bath shower. Tepid, but at least it was warmer than the lake. Andy pushed a protesting Roz beneath the water and brushed her hair away from her face. 'God, you're so beautiful.'

She stared at him, her expression torn between lust and disbelief. How could she doubt that she was beautiful? What imbecile lovers had she taken up to now that hadn't told her?

In between kisses, he washed her hair and soaped her limbs. Something landed in the bath between them and Roz gave a throaty laugh. 'I think I've lost my merkin.'

Andy laughed and towelled her long hair, but it reminded him of the wig she had been wearing when he met her. Roz had been in disguise. Hiding. At some stage they would have to talk about the murder in Paris and why she was still on the run.

But not tonight.

'What about the rest of me?' she protested when he took the towel from her hands.

Andy gave her another lingering kiss and smiled. 'Baby, I'm going to lick you dry.'

Her pale skin was a feast, an uncharted territory he longed to explore. He kissed and licked every inch of her arms, pausing to sample her pebble-hard nipples before kissing her toned stomach.

Curious, he asked her, 'What do you do to work out?'

'Parkour.' She groaned as he found another delightfully sensitive spot. 'Shut up with the questions and kiss me.'

'Yes, ma'am.' Andy pushed her back onto the bed and nuzzled at the tender spot again, drawing another moan.

He paused between her thighs, bracing her legs apart with his shoulders. He couldn't understand guys who said they didn't like giving oral. They must be crazy.

The first long, slow lick almost made her come off the bed. Andy ignored her throaty murmurs and licked again, deeper this time, lingering on her clit.

'Oh, god. Yes.'

Her breathless cries spurred him on. He was willing to bet that it had been a while since anyone had really taken care of her. Andy took the tender bud of her clit between his teeth and nibbled.

Her first orgasm rolled out of nowhere and her high pitched cry was music to his ears. Roz grasped handfuls of his hair, begging him to stop. He ignored her and continued to work with lips and tongue until a second wave overtook her like a flash flood, obliterating everything in its path.

Andy waited until she stopped trembling before he raised his head.

'How did you . . . What did you?' She raised her head sleepily.

The dazed expression on her face filled him with pride. 'Baby, I'm only getting started.'

He crawled up her body, pausing on the way to nuzzle her breasts, before kissing her again, letting her taste her own sweet musk. His cock was as hard as a pikestaff. If he didn't have her soon, he was in danger of disgracing himself. She moaned.

'Hold that thought,' he said as he slipped off the bed.

Damn, it was getting darker in here, with only the glimmer of the rising moon, but he didn't want to switch on a light. He had noticed a candle on one of the fireplaces earlier and he prayed that there were matches to go with it. His luck held. The light from the single candle cast dark shadows around the room. The flame flared as he brought it closer to the bed.

He hadn't been flattering her when he told her she was beautiful. Her pale thighs were an invitation to sin. An invitation he couldn't refuse.

Protection. Some rational part of his brain was still working and he went in search of his jeans. Andy located his wallet and almost cheered. Three condoms. That should be enough, but he would have to find a pharmacy tomorrow.

Roz rolled to watch him and patted the bed in invitation. Andy set the candle down and went to join her. 'God, you're –'

'If you say beautiful again, I may bite you.'

139

Andy laughed. 'God, you're vicious, aren't you?'

Her look was blatantly challenging. 'You have no idea.'

In a move that surprised him, she rolled on top of him and Andy found himself pinned beneath her. He resisted the urge to retaliate and waited to see what she would do next. Her small hands stroked his chest, exploring him, and she smiled in approval. She wriggled her way down his torso until she was poised over his aching shaft.

'Condom.' She held her hand out.

'Only if you ask nicely.'

'Pretty please, give me a condom.' She smirked at his discomfort.

Witch. She was so going to pay for that, Andy decided. But first he had to concentrate on controlling himself when she touched him. She shimmied down the bed to sit on his thighs. Her cool hands stroked him lightly and Andy clenched his jaw. *Do not come. Do not come.*

As if she understood the sudden shift in power between them, Roz took her time rolling the condom onto his rigid cock. The woman was trying to kill him. He patted the bed beside him. 'Lie down.'

'I like being on top,' she protested.

'I'm sure you do, but lie down.'

Roz ignored him, and knelt over him and hovered, her sweet pussy inches from the swollen head of his shaft. She raised her arms above her head and moved in a sensuous dance, undulating and swaying, her eyes never leaving his for a moment.

His palm itched to spank her. No. He would save that pleasure for later. Instead he sat up and grasped her wrists with one hand before tumbling them both over.

Breathless, she stared up at him. Merriment lingered in her blue eyes. 'You didn't say please.'

Andy bent his head and nipped at her breast. 'That's for making me crazy.'

He gave the other breast a matching nip. 'And that's for almost giving me a heart attack when you jumped off the tower.'

Andy nudged her thighs apart with his knee. If he didn't have her soon he would die. He clamped one hand around the base of his cock and rubbed the tip against her wet core. He wasn't going to last. Not the first time anyway.

The sight of her running her tongue along her bottom lip sent him over the edge. In a single thrust into her slick, hot cleft, he drove home.

Roz forgot how to breathe. Every single atom of her body was concentrated on the cock that had invaded her.

She thought she was prepared. She had been convinced she was so ready that he could do what he liked and it would be a nice extension of what had gone before. Instead, she had to fight to breathe.

She was stuffed, impaled, overcome. And god, it was amazing. Andy McTavish was buried deep inside her, and she never wanted it to end. All her nerve endings were tingling and little sparkles of pleasure danced under her skin.

'All right?' he asked.

Dazed, she opened her eyes, taking him in as he rose above her like a conqueror.

She tried to unscramble her brains to answer him. Why did he want to talk? 'Yes,' she gasped. She wiggled, arching her body against his. 'Now move!'

He laughed and the movement sent fresh ripples through her. Oh god, that should be illegal.

Then he flexed his hips, pulling back and thrusting forwards again. Every movement of his hips sent fire racing along her nerves. He was smooth, controlled, and not nearly fast enough. It was the most exquisite torture she had ever experienced.

'More!' She wrapped her legs around his hips, and dug her heels into his ass. She didn't make a dent in the hard muscle, but he laughed.

'Your wish is my command.'

If there was a hint of mockery there, she ignored it. All she cared about was the heat and tightness that was holding her captive. She had already climaxed twice, which was twice more than usual, but she knew that if he didn't speed up and let her come again, she was going to kill him.

'Now.' She pulled him down to her and kissed him. She grabbed handfuls of his hair to keep him in place so she could tangle her tongue with his and show him exactly what she wanted him to do. The taste of her own juices on his hard lips should have turned her off. Instead it was an aphrodisiac that drove her higher.

She was reduced to begging. 'Andy, please.'

As if the words were a trigger, his control broke, and he lunged into her, faster and harder, taking her higher until she was mindless. This was her world: his scent, the feel of his skin, the sound of their bodies against each other, and the heat of him inside her.

Just when she thought she would die if it continued much longer, a final thrust pushed her over the edge. The tension broke so hard she wondered if she could survive it, then she didn't care, as she pulsed with endless spasms of pleasure.

Vaguely, she was aware of Andy's yell as he followed her over.

12

The log in the fire crackled and Roz opened her eyes slowly. She was utterly boneless. She couldn't remember when she had been so relaxed. The various aches and pains and scrapes on her body reinforced the lovely floating sensation.

She turned her head with an effort. Andy was there, grinning at her. So damn pleased with himself that he had turned her into mush. She would be annoyed with him about that. Later. When she had energy.

'How are you feeling?' he asked. Looking for praise.

She wanted to purr like a cat, but she wasn't going to feed his ego. 'I think I've warmed up now.'

The tower room was warm with heat blasting from the enclosed fireplace. A small forest worth of logs sat beside it, ensuring it would keep going as long as necessary. The low, wide bed they were lying on had a jewel-coloured velvet cover, probably hand-sewn. It was decadently luxurious against her sensitized flesh, but not as good as Andy's smooth skin.

She rested her head on his chest, listening to the thump of his heart. So strong and solid. Reassuring. Hypnotic.

How had she ended up in this bed with this man? It was like a fantasy, something not real, something she could luxuriate in without having to think about consequences and aftermath. For this moment, Andy McTavish was hers.

'You okay, babe?' he prompted her.

Oh yes, he wanted to know how she was feeling.

'Not bad,' she said, licking her lips and watching his eyes follow the movement of her tongue. 'This is an excellent way to warm up. I must remember it next time I do a nude scene.'

She wasn't going to let him have things all his way.

Oh yeah. That worked. Andy sat bolt upright, all masculine outrage. 'Next time? What next time?'

'The director was delighted with the scene, and I know Cheyenne Knight doesn't like doing nude scenes, so there will probably be more.' She watched, fascinated, as his eyes narrowed and his nostrils flared. He went from relaxed, well-fed lion to hungry predator in a heartbeat.

'There will be no next time. You're not doing any more nude scenes.' He announced it as if he genuinely expected her to obey. 'And especially not with Jack Winter.'

Now she was outraged. 'Who do you think you are to tell me what I can or can't do? You're not my father.'

'Thank god,' he said, with a meaningful glance at the bed, which was rumpled from their frantic love-making. No, from their sex session. It had been amazing, but she had to make sure she didn't fool herself. Whatever that had been, it wasn't love-making.

This was Andy McTavish. He was temptation on two legs, a deliciously enticing specimen of masculine beauty. Just looking at his angular face made her heart race. His spicy scent caused heat to bloom between her thighs. His voice, with that addictive accent, raised goose bumps on her skin. Every inch of his body begged to be licked. But she had seen the way he flirted with every woman he met in Geneva. And there had been a rumour about him and Princess Samara Shaloub Safar in Paris. This man would never be hers. She had to keep reminding herself of that.

'I'm telling you, Roz, no more nude scenes.'

All lethargy disappeared. He was serious. 'Are you out of your mind? What makes you think I'll take orders from you?'

A determined expression crossed his face. 'Doing another scene like that will create too much media interest. You have to lie low. I'm here to protect you until Interpol –'

How could she have been so stupid? Andy McTavish was a seducer. He was using sex to get her to do what he wanted. Get the girl in the sack and take her into custody. Well, there was no way she was going back there. Hall would kill her.

'Not a chance.'

She climbed off the bed, surprised to find her legs wobbling. Roz locked her knees against the trembles which shook her, and searched for something to wear. She had to get out of here.

'Roz, be reasonable. Come back to bed, we can talk about this in the morning.' The charming smile was back, the hint of anger gone, but she wasn't falling for it.

'Reasonable? You seriously expect to sleep with a woman and get her to do whatever you say afterwards? You're nothing but a man whore.'

Andy got up, prepared to continue the argument, so

she pulled the velvet cover off the bed and wrapped it around herself. It smelled of him and a pang shot through her. It stiffened her determination not to give in. She wasn't going to be one in a long line of women who succumbed to his charm.

'You're great in bed, I'll give you that. Practice clearly makes perfect.' She faced him squarely. 'Why don't you go carve another notch on your bedpost and practise on someone else?'

She didn't let him say anything more, but swept through the old sitting room and down the wooden stairs to the front door of the castle. She might be dressed in nothing but a bedspread, but she held her head high and refused to let him see how her heart was breaking.

She stomped back to the caravan she shared with Frankie, aware that Andy had pulled on a pair of jeans and was running after her. She risked a quick glance back to see that he was bare-chested and he hadn't stopped to fasten his jeans.

Her mouth dried. Even after sampling that delectable body, it had the power to stop all rational thought. His shoulders were broad, with sleekly defined muscles under his tanned skin. How did an Irishman get a tan like that, she wondered, trying to distract herself. A light dusting of hair across his chest narrowed to a trail that ran down over his sculpted stomach muscles. He had a six-pack. Or was it an eight-pack? God, she wanted to trail her fingers over his abs, counting and tasting.

Bastard.

That tantalizing trail of hair disappeared into his jeans, which were loose and inviting. She could slip them down, put her hands on that perfect ass . . . No, stop it. Eyes forwards.

Roz pushed open the door and almost leapt into the caravan, anything to get away from the enraged male following her.

'Are you all right?' Frankie looked up from the worksheets he was completing.

Roz had a moment of semi-hysterical sympathy for the poor accountant who had to decipher his appalling handwriting to work out which extras had worked for how long.

'Cheyenne was here looking for you.'

Before she could answer, the door of the caravan was pulled open again. Instinctively, Roz took a step closer to Frankie, who rose, ready to defend her.

Andy stood there, a predator seeking his mate, ready to drag her out and finish their conversation. He looked from her to Frankie, and his eyes narrowed. 'So this is what is going on.'

He focused his attention on her. 'And to think . . .' He didn't finish that. Instead, that clean-cut mouth twisted into a sneer. 'You do know he's at least twice your age, don't you?'

Roz gasped, shocked at his implication. Frankie was more of a father to her than her own father. How dare Andy even suggest that?

'But I suppose that's your favourite type. Old and obedient. Good luck with this one. Make sure he pays you up front.'

Andy slammed the door and stalked off. She watched

148

through the front window of the caravan as he disappeared into the dark.

Frankie put away his glasses. 'Want to tell me what that was about?'

'No.'

Roz was suddenly conscious that she was naked under the bedspread. It was pretty obvious what had happened. She grabbed a change of clothes and locked herself into the tiny bathroom. She was not going to cry. She didn't cry. She never cried.

Andy zipped up his jeans as he stormed back to the castle. His head was reeling. What the fuck just happened? Even in his fury, his analytical mind pored over the events of the evening, cringing as he remembered his rampant jealousy and uncontrolled lust. He had practically kidnapped Roz from the set. What had the bloody woman done to him?

Andy Campbell McTavish didn't do out of control. He was a player. He ran the game and he decided when it would end. He liked women. Cared for most of those he'd been with but he didn't do messy emotional trauma. And he never touched another man's woman – unless it was a job.

This half naked man standing in the open air on a cold spring night was not him. Roz Spring was a bloody witch. Damn her to hell.

He turned, wincing when he stood on a particularly sharp piece of gravel. He should go back there and sort it out tonight. But he couldn't. He needed to think. Stepping carefully, he made his way back into the castle and up the stairs to the bedroom. The fire burnt in the grate and the air was perfumed with the scent of their lovemaking.

Andy sat on the bed and dropped his face into his hands. *Think man. Think.*

A trickle of blood leaked from his foot and onto the wooden floor. Fuck, he had cut himself. Andy limped to the bathroom and cleaned the wound. The sight of the merkin lying sodden on the bottom of the bath made him smile wryly. The more time he spent with women, the more he realized that he knew fuck-all about them.

Until now, he had treated his dealings with women like a game of chess, move and counter-move, strategy and counter-strategy. When he was on a job, everything was carefully planned. He'd never had such a spectacular failure and if he was honest with himself, it hurt like hell.

Andy huffed out a long breath and turned off the water. Roz wasn't a game. She was a siren and somehow she had managed to get under his skin. The texts, the flirting designed to intrigue and reel her in, had backfired spectacularly. He liked her. He found himself thinking about her all the time. Somehow, he didn't know how, what had started as a job had turned real and for the first time in his life, he didn't know what to do. Andy dried his foot and limped back to the bedroom. His shirt was on the floor, along with the robe she had worn on the set.

Picking it up, he pressed it to his face and closed his eyes. 'You're a fucking muppet, McTavish.'

With an effort, he dragged his mind away from the

memories of their love-making and focused instead on her words.

Man whore.

Another notch on the bedpost.

Insults designed to push him away from her. But why? The sex had been mind blowing, no matter how much Roz had tried to play it down. She had gone off like a rocket within minutes of him touching her. What sort of useless lovers had she taken up to now that they didn't know how to please her or make her feel beautiful? Sometimes he despaired of his own sex. Useless bunch of bastards.

The memory of Roz, breathless and trembling in the aftermath of orgasm, made him ache for her again. Andy replayed the scene in his head. God, she was magnificent. There had been no games, no artifice, she was naturally sexy. And those little breathless noises she made when he . . . His cock stirred again and he looked down ruefully at it. 'You and me both.'

Andy shrugged off his jeans and crawled between the sheets. He wasn't going back to the trailer that he shared with the other guys tonight. Besides, Fletcher would probably be waiting for him, armed with a sword to chop his nuts off.

Fletcher. Now, there was a thought. He could have sworn that the older man had a thing for Cheyenne. And what the hell was he doing sharing a caravan with Roz? He felt an urge to throttle him.

If his woman had arrived home dressed in nothing but a sheet, he would have beaten the crap out of the guy responsible. But Frankie Fletcher had done nothing and that wasn't a normal reaction.

There was something between them, but there was no way that they were shacked up together.

He rolled out of bed and hunted for his phone. Some-one at Moore HQ must be on the graveyard shift. Andy punched in the number and waited for a response.

'Reilly? How did you get landed with working nights?'

Tara yawned. 'One of the guys got food poisoning. What do you need at this hour?'

'I want you to run a check on a guy called Frankie Fletcher. I don't know what branch, but he's definitely ex-military. He works as an adviser on movies now. He specializes in old weapons, that kind of thing.'

'Okay. Leave it with me.'

She disconnected the call and Andy returned to bed. He needed to get some sleep before the big battle scene tomorrow. After that he would talk to Roz and find out what the hell was going on.

13

'Listen up, you miserable bunch of people.' Frankie's clipped tones were audible across the sea of men and women waiting for direction. 'This is one of the most crucial scenes in the movie and I want to see your best work. Let me have your meanest fighting skills. I want to see your swords slash, your spears find their target and you dying in agony. Do I make myself clear?'

'Yes, sir,' a few actors at the front of the crowd mumbled.

'I said, do I make myself clear?' Frankie roared like a drill sergeant.

'Yes, sir.'

'Okay then, take your positions and good luck.'

The crowd dispersed and Andy was left with a handful of fighters who were doing close-up work.

'You five are needed for a scene on the battlements. Andy, you're with me.'

'Fuck,' Andy muttered beneath his breath. Maybe he'd been wrong about their relationship after all.

The older man gave him a considered look. 'You won't be needing the chain mail this morning. I've got something else planned for you.'

Whatever Frankie had planned wasn't going to be pleasant.

'This way.' Frankie turned and headed for the set

where the carpenters had reconstructed a native settlement. The story called for the village to be overrun by invaders after some fierce hand-to-hand fighting. It would be one of the bloodiest scenes in the movie, with lots of scope for 'accidental' injuries.

Frankie was a clever bastard. Andy had underestimated him and hoped that he would be a match for him.

The director was already in place. 'Okay, I want some nice peaceful footage before the invasion starts.'

With a grin that could only be described as diabolical, Frankie thrust a woollen tunic at him. 'You're peasant number four and today you'll be fighting for your life, and your wife.'

Wife? Andy didn't need a map to see where this was going. He pulled the woollen robe over his head and turned to meet his new bride.

They had done something to her hair to make it more red and vibrant. Despite the shapeless clothing, Roz was as beautiful as the day he had first seen her in Paris, and almost as sullen.

'Okay, I want you both in bed for this scene. It's a dawn raid. You hear screams and you reach for your weapon. This is the woman you love and you'll do anything to protect her. Understand?'

Andy nodded at the director. Beside him, Roz was as stiff and taut as a bowstring. He hoped she wasn't armed.

Andy sat down on the fur covered pallet and pulled off his boots. Beside him, Roz shrugged out of her cloak and lay stiffly beside him, wearing nothing but a dingy shift that concealed her curves.

'Okay, we need some affection,' the director roared.

Andy lay down and pulled her into his arms. She tucked her head beneath his chin and her small hand splayed across his chest.

'I will kill Frankie for this,' she muttered into his tunic.

Andy bit back a smile and kissed the top of her head.

'Great, guys. Now eyes closed. You're sleeping, remember?'

The lights on the set were dimmed and the fire light flickered in the silence. 'I'm sorry for whatever I did wrong.' He murmured against her hair.

Roz said nothing, but he swore her body softened a fraction. Andy tightened his arms around her and something hard pressed into his side. Roz had ignored the 'no phones on set' rule.

He shifted a fraction and settled down again. This was how they should have spent the previous night. Not sleeping alone.

'And action.'

Outside, a woman screamed and children began to cry.

As the wooden door was kicked in and a Viking invader entered, Andy went into battle mode. He shoved Roz off the pallet for protection and reached for the nearest available weapon. The wooden staff was no match for a Viking blade, but he jabbed upwards and managed to send his opponent's shield flying.

Andy scrambled on the floor and grabbed it. In his hands, a shield was a weapon. He parried the next sword thrust and sidestepped the following one. Roz screamed as a second invader entered the hut. Two armed warriors against a helpless native. He was definitely going down.

The men fought with relish. They were two of the best

fighters that Frankie had trained. Andy wished that he could have given them a better battle, but he was under orders to fight and die.

Crouched in the corner behind the bed pallet, Roz screamed again as she watched the brutal slaughter. She had a fine pair of lungs, Andy noticed, and couldn't help remembering the noises she had made the previous night in bed with him. 'And cut. That was great.'

The lights went up again and the invaders and crew departed to wreak havoc elsewhere. Andy and Roz were left alone.

Andy helped her to her feet and searched the upturned bed for her tunic.

'Thanks,' she murmured but she wouldn't meet his eyes.

'About last night. . .'

The door burst open again and Andy turned quickly. The new invader surveyed the makeshift room before focusing his attention on Roz. What was the guy playing at? Didn't he know the scene was finished?

'The director wants you.' The stranger's voice was muffled behind the helmet, but Andy caught a hint of an American accent. His blood froze in his veins. He hadn't heard that voice for a year, but he recognized it immediately.

'Coming,' Roz said as she picked up her cloak, oblivious to the danger.

'Which director wants her?' Andy asked as he moved towards the abandoned shield. It wasn't much, but better than nothing and he needed everything he could get his hands on if he was going up against Darren Hall.

When a former Navy SEAL turned bad, virtually nothing would stop him. And Hall was one of the worst excuses for a man that Andy had ever met. If he got his hands on Roz, he would murder her, the same way he had butchered that poor antique dealer in Paris. There was no way that was happening.

The only way Roz was leaving with that scumbag was over his dead body. Andy picked up the shield and smashed it into the invader's face.

Roz screamed as the American staggered on his feet and then righted himself. He kicked Andy.

Christ. That blow would have felled an elephant. Andy pushed the rough wooden table into the man's path and searched the room for something he could use as a weapon. His eyes fell on the torch. One of the crew should have returned to extinguish it.

Andy wondered if he had run into Hall. Poor bastard.

He needed to get Roz to safety as quickly as possible. From her dazed expression, she had finally realized that this wasn't another mock fight. Or maybe she had recognized Hall?

Andy swung the blazing torch in a wide arc and Hall stepped back. 'Roz, get the fuck out of here and find Frankie. Tell him to take you to Niall.'

Reilly had come back with an interim report on Fletcher. He had been involved in a few schemes which could have been considered dubious, but he had never spent time in prison. The guy had been a sapper for ten years and that was good enough for him. Frankie would protect Roz. He would bet his life on it.

'I'm not leaving you.'

He cursed as Hall lunged again, almost knocking the torch from his grasp. Andy recovered and jabbed at the man's face. This was no time for fighting fair. He had to get the stubborn woman out of here.

Hall gave a muffled roar and backed away, crashing into the flimsy partition wall which crashed under his weight. Dropping the torch, Andy grabbed Roz by the arm and pulled her to the door. They had seconds to make their escape.

They had barely made it outside when Hall appeared again. Holy fuck. This guy was worse than the Terminator.

Hall's first punch sent Andy reeling. He staggered and then righted himself.

'Is that the best you've got?' he taunted, anything to get Hall's attention away from Roz.

'Oh, I think you'll enjoy this more,' Hall sneered as he reached into his pocket and drew out a Beretta M9.

The single round was startling in the silence of the forest. Andy heard a shocked cry and Roz dropped to the ground. Disbelief fought with shock and he moved automatically to help her.

Roz had been shot.

Roz was aware of pain all over. She couldn't move, couldn't breathe, couldn't scream. She was one searing mass of unending agony.

Her last memory was seeing the gun aimed at her, hearing the shot and feeling the shock of the bullet hitting her.

I'm dead. This is what it's like being dead. I didn't think it would hurt so much.

She was about to find out who was right. Would there be heaven and hell, or nothing? Would her life, such a mixture of good and bad and who-knows, send her up or down? She had time to regret all the things she'd done wrong, and all the things she hadn't done. To her surprise, Andy McTavish was on the top of her list of things she hadn't done.

Where was the white light? It should be here by now. She forced her eyes open, looking for the light, and saw a cloudy sky above her. There were clouds in the afterlife? How disappointing.

She blinked and her eyes watered. Was she dead? Why wasn't she breathing? She had been shot.

With a jolt of pain, her lungs heaved and she pulled in a desperate gasp of air. God, the agony of the moment was proof she wasn't dead.

She managed to turn her head and saw Andy and Hall on the ground, struggling. Hall was on top, forcing Andy's head back at a dangerous angle.

She tried to yell, and no sound came out. Her starved lungs refused to work, refused to make a sound.

Roz ignored the screaming of her ribs as she forced herself to her feet. She had to help Andy. The dizziness and weakness that washed over her made her realize she wasn't going to be any use.

Phone. She could call for help. She reached into her pocket and fumbled out her phone. It was cracked and distorted, with the back bulging out, and a bullet lodged in it.

She stared at it for long seconds before her brain made sense of it. Her el cheapo phone had saved her life. Who'd have guessed that a phone could stop a bullet?

Now that her brain knew she wasn't dead, she could make sense of the aches in her body. She had a spot on her chest which screamed in agony, where the bullet had driven the phone into her ribs. Her back and head were a mass of bruises from being slammed into the ground and having the air knocked out of her.

But she wasn't dead. All she had to do was get enough air into her lungs and she could scream for help.

Hall was bashing Andy's head into the ground, even while he grunted with pain from whatever Andy was doing. She was no expert, but it looked as if the former SEAL was going to kill him.

It took six desperate inhalations before she could force her voice to work. Finally, she was able to yell, 'Frankie! Frankie! Help!'

Her voice sounded too small and rusty to carry, and she tried to yell again.

It cost Andy. At the sound of her voice, he turned his head and saw her standing.

'Roz!'

He believed she was dead, Roz realized. He had seen the shot and thought Hall had killed her. She flapped a hand at him, trying without words to reassure him.

Hall took advantage of Andy's distraction to hit him in the gut and the eye. Andy's head snapped back, hitting the ground with a force that made her wince. Where was Frankie?

She heard a roar in the distance. Frankie came running from the castle and saw the fight on the ground. He was holding a bow and arrow in his hands, and even as he ran, he nocked an arrow and aimed.

It flew true, and hit Hall on the shoulder. Had it not been for the chain mail he was wearing, and the leather armour underneath, it would have done the job.

Hall reared back from Andy, saw the new opponent and pulled out his gun. Seemingly without aiming, he fired and Frankie fell.

Holding onto the nearest tree in an effort to stay upright, Roz gasped. No, not Frankie. Please no.

Hall turned back to Andy, now with his gun aimed at him. He stood over him, taking aim. His finger tightened.

The second arrow hit him on the thigh as he fired, and the bullet went into the ground beside Andy's head.

Frankie, bleeding from his shoulder, had struggled to his knees and was holding his bow in a defiant grip. He yelled, 'Extras, soldiers, over here!' Even with the shake of pain, his voice contained authority.

Andy rolled, knocking Hall to the ground, but it was obvious that Hall had the upper hand. On the ground, Frankie couldn't fire again, and Hall had the gun in his hand.

A storm of yelling heralded the arrival of the extras. Still dressed in Viking and Celtic costumes, they stormed around the corner of the castle, as beautiful as angels to Roz's eyes.

Relief weakened her knees and she slumped to the ground.

Andy yanked her to her feet again. 'Come on, we have to get out of here.' He hauled her away from the sounds of battle raging behind her.

'What's happening?' She managed to get the words out in a strained whisper. Her lungs were reluctant to waste any oxygen on talking. Andy kept pulling her, not giving her time to rest, and it took her dazed brain a few minutes to realize he was heading for the car park.

'The guys will keep Hall busy while we get away. We have to move now.' He shoved her into his Jeep, not giving her time to do up her seatbelt before he jumped into the driver's seat and turned the key. 'I reckon we've got about five minutes before he comes after us again.'

14

The country roads passed in a blur but it was almost an hour before Andy thought it was safe enough to stop. His body ached all over and he probably needed stitches for the cut over his eye but at least they were both alive.

He had almost lost her. Damn it, he was a complete fuckwit. He had known that Hall was after her, but had been so obsessed with the attraction between them that he hadn't taken enough precautions. Now he knew exactly why 'Don't fuck the client' was the unofficial motto of Moore Enterprises. It made him careless, and Roz had almost paid the price.

No more, he resolved. From now on, he would do a better job. He would keep his distance and not let himself get distracted again.

Beside him, Roz was in shock. She had gripped her hands together to conceal the shaking but the fine tremble in her body was obvious. He turned up the heating as high as it would go and pulled a coat over her to keep her warm.

They needed a plan. If he let her go back to London she would disappear again. He needed to take her somewhere he could keep a close eye on her. Hall had caught up with her once and there were no guarantees what he might do.

Up ahead, a sign announced a service station and he pulled over. He had forgotten how ridiculous they looked until he saw the expression of the girl behind the coffee machine. He was still wearing his native Celt outfit, splattered with a mixture of fake and real blood, while Roz looked like an extra from a King Arthur movie.

'Fancy dress party,' he explained with a wink. Damn. They would have to get proper clothes in the next town. He shoved his wallet into his pocket and, balancing two cardboard cups and a couple of sugary pastries, he walked to the corner booth where Roz was waiting.

Even though her clothing was grubby and dishevelled from the encounter with Hall, she was stunningly beautiful. The sight of her shocked face in that field outside Tullamore would haunt his dreams for a long time. When that shot was fired, he'd thought it was the end, that she was dead.

Possessiveness flared inside him as he remembered last night when she had been his. He needed to experience that again. He wanted her back in his bed and he wouldn't mess up this time.

He made up his mind. He would break his most solid rule and take her home to Lough Darra. He had given a Belfast address when he had joined the army and had never alluded to his family's wealth. He was plain Andy McTavish – nothing to do with the wealthy Campbell McTavish family who bred horses. He had always guarded his parents' home with absolute privacy. There was no connection between him and them. No one would look for her there. His parents would adore her and she could hide out there for months.

The prospect of time alone with Roz cheered him. It was a perfect solution but first he had to convince her. 'We need to get some fresh clothes and then I'm taking you home.'

'London?' She set her coffee cup down.

'No. My home, it's called Lough Darra.' He went on, 'Look. You have a former Navy SEAL on your trail. He'll have someone watching the ports and airports waiting for you to leave Ireland. And you can't go back to Frankie.'

Andy wanted to kick himself when her face crumpled. It was pretty underhanded to play the guilt card, but Roz had to see the reality of her situation. She was alone and penniless in a strange country and she had nowhere to go. 'I'll get onto Niall. He'll see that Frankie is taken care of.'

Suspicion flared in her eyes. 'And what do you get out of it?'

It was time for honesty. 'A fiancée.'

Her lips parted, then firmed. 'Are you asking me to marry you?'

He couldn't read her face, but her voice was strained. Fuck, of course she didn't know his situation, and thought he was trying to mess with her head. 'No, of course not. It's for my parents.'

She picked up her cup and took another sip of the coffee before she replied. 'Yeah, I can see why you'd need a fake fiancée. Your technique could do with a lot of polishing or you'll never get one by normal means.'

Ouch. He had asked for that one. 'My parents want me to settle down. I've been home less than a week and already they're parading me about the place like a stallion at Tattersalls.'

A smirk twisted her mouth. 'Poor little rich boy. My heart bleeds for you.'

He reached for her hand. 'Please Roz. If I can't find you a safe house, then Niall or Interpol will. The time for running is over.'

'That's blackmail.' Roz tugged her hand away and folded her arms across her chest. As she stared out the window, Andy watched her reflection. He had always thought that she was identical to her sister Sinead, but there were subtle differences.

Roz had a tiny scar beneath her chin. Her cheekbones were a shade higher and her nails were short and unpolished. He was coming to realize that there was a world of hurt and anger simmering beneath the tough, uncaring façade she presented to the world.

Finally, she turned to face him. 'Okay. I'll do it.'

'Great.' Andy smiled, waiting for the catch. With Roz, there would always be a sting in the tail.

'But I need clothes. Your house is posh, isn't it?'

To him, Lough Darra was home, but he supposed it would look posh to an outsider. He nodded.

'Then I need a new wardrobe. I can't arrive dressed like this. Oh, and I want a ring.'

He swallowed. 'A ring?'

Roz didn't bother to hide her glee. 'Yes, a nice, big, expensive one, the kind that you'd buy for me if I really was your fiancée.'

She sat back, waiting for him to refuse. But he wasn't going to back down.

'Done. Now, let's go.'

They couldn't go shopping for a ring dressed like two

extras from *Braveheart*. Security would stop them before they got into the first store. First stop was an outlet store off the motorway, where he purchased a dress for Roz. When he returned to the car wearing a cheap new shirt and dark jeans, Andy allowed her to clean his cuts with baby wipes, enjoying the small, tender touches. He was turning into a sad bastard.

While he drove, Roz managed, in a complicated manoeuvre, to wriggle out of her costume and into the new dress without revealing an inch of flesh.

'Stop perving,' she snapped at him. 'I can see you looking at me in the mirror.'

Andy kept his eyes on the road, trying not to grin.

In Belfast, with a vague memory of where a former girlfriend shopped when she was in the city, he took her to Cruise. Roz stroked the fine fabrics with pleasure until she saw the price labels. She immediately headed to the sale rail to study what bargains were left over from last season, looked at the price tags and backed away from that.

Andy remembered the wardrobe in her flat in London. Cheap clothes and expensive shoes and gloves. He cursed himself for not thinking about it sooner. Roz would never spend money on herself. He would have to do it for her.

'My girlfriend's luggage got lost on the flight here,' he informed the sales assistant quietly. 'Why don't you help her select a whole new wardrobe?' Andy placed his credit card on the counter.

Roz was bundled into a dressing room and one outfit after another was passed to her to try on. A couple of times, he heard her laugh at the more outrageous selections, but eventually, they emerged from the store carrying half a dozen bags.

Her face was flushed and her eyes had an unfamiliar sparkle. 'What's next?' she asked.

As they passed a lingerie store, she stopped with a wistful expression. Wisps of lace and satin were draped artfully on a velvet chaise longue and the mannequin in the window wore a steel boned corset that reminded him of Lottie le Blanc. The thought of Roz wearing something like that made his cock stir. Andy relieved her of the bags and inclined his head towards the doorway. 'You have one hour. Make the most of it.'

He found a coffee shop nearby where he could observe the entrance to Orchid Lingerie and settled down to wait for her. He had to file a report and he wasn't looking forward to it.

'Andy,' the voice responded almost immediately. 'Report. I have reports of a shooting on a movie set in Tullamore.'

Trust Niall. Nothing escaped his attention. 'How did you hear –'

'Because it's a fucking movie set and Jack Winter is one of our clients.'

Andy closed his eyes. Jack had been nowhere near the shooting but the media would hype it up within a couple of hours. 'Sorry, boss. Hall turned up unexpectedly.'

'Is Roz – ?'

'She's fine.' Andy reassured him. 'I'm taking her to a safe house until things calm down.'

But Niall wasn't put off so easily. 'What safe house?'

'Lough Darra.'

Andy heard an intake of breath, followed by a charged silence. 'Let me get this straight. You're bringing a former dominatrix home with you?'

'Yes,' Andy mumbled.

'And how do you plan on explaining her to your parents?' Niall was the only person in his professional life who had ever met his parents. Or even knew they existed.

'That she's my fiancée.'

Andy held the phone away from his ear while Niall vented his feelings. He couldn't blame him. It was barely lunchtime and already he was in the middle of a cluster-fuck. 'Make sure she doesn't get into any more mischief until I have a chance to sort this out.'

'Don't worry, boss. Roz will be completely under my control at all times.'

Niall snorted and hung up.

Andy glanced at his watch. It had been over an hour but there was no sign of Roz. She couldn't be shopping for all this time. He collected the bags and walked slowly to the entrance and slipped inside.

In the curtained-off changing area, he heard two women laughing. One of them was Roz. 'Absolutely not,' she said. 'There is no way that I'm buying this.'

'But it's perfect. Look at your curves.'

'It costs over two hundred pounds.'

Andy very much wanted to see what was behind the velvet curtain and he wasn't overly concerned what it cost. 'She'll take it,' he announced.

The shop assistant turned around and Roz popped her head out from behind the curtain. 'Thanks, but I've spent enough.'

He didn't want to add up what he'd already spent. A couple of hundred quid wouldn't make that much of a difference. 'Wrap it,' he mouthed to the sales assistant.

He handed over his credit card again. There was no point in wincing. They had yet to hit the jewellers and he had no idea what that would cost.

Roz was positively glowing by the time they left the shop. She had changed into one of the outfits she'd bought in Cruise, a figure hugging dress that celebrated her body, and a pair of soft leather boots.

'So we're done?' he asked.

She glared at him. 'Are you stupid, or joking? I need make-up.'

He looked her over. She was naturally pale, with the sort of creamy skin that cosmetic companies promised to the gullible who used their products and her lips were wide and kissable. 'You look great to me. Why do you need anything?'

Roz blew him a kiss. 'Okay, you've redeemed yourself a little. But I really do need a bit of slap. Trust me, this is not my best.' There were dark circles under her eyes and he supposed that she probably wanted to do something with paint.

'Waste of time, as far as I'm concerned, but see what you can find in the Castle Court Centre.'

Twenty minutes later, she had a bulging cosmetics bag and an evil grin on her face. Andy took her arm and led her to a nearby jewellers. The brightly lit window contained dozens of rings, all gleaming and shiny. He stopped at the entrance. If he was putting a ring on her finger, it wasn't going to be something ordinary.

'Getting cold feet?' Roz smirked at him.

'No. But this isn't my kind of place. Let's go somewhere else.'

Roz looked at the entrance to Malcolm's with apprehension. Its understated display whispered class but at least the rings in the window had more character than those in the high street jewellers.

Andy's hand at her back guided her in. Three men in business suits had stopped him to say hello. Their strong Belfast accents were hard to understand but she picked up that they were asking about his father's health.

Andy was at ease answering them. Roz was good at reading body language. In spite of his cheap jeans and the stubble giving him a dangerous air, he was an equal to these men who wore expensive suits and carried leather briefcases that probably cost five hundred pounds.

Roz didn't want to think about the bill she had racked up so far, but she was feeling guilty about demanding a new wardrobe from him. She hadn't actually expected him to carry through, and certainly not in such style. A couple of pairs of jeans and a dress from M&S was usually her limit. She stroked the sleeve of the simple wool dress that clung to her curves, making them more dramatic while giving the impression that she was stylish and demure. Whatever this dress had cost, it was worth every penny.

A large-bosomed woman walking along the street paused to give Andy the once-over, then smiled and nodded towards a nearby pub. Roz scowled. Could the woman not see that he was with her? Her red hair made her hard to ignore, but the cow seemed to think she was invisible.

'Are we going inside or not?' she snapped at Andy.

'Anxious to get my ring on your finger?' he asked. 'So many have tried . . .'

'I'd rather put a ring somewhere else.' Damn it, she was not going to fall into the trap of being attracted to him. The cow had reminded her that she was dealing with Andy McTavish. He flirted with every woman he met. And every one of them flirted back. He was a walking, talking vision of male perfection. And he knew it.

That was an image which should keep her heart safe. She couldn't afford to fall for him. Her only advantage was that she knew from the outset that he wasn't interested in her. She was a job to him, nothing more. Andy knew the real Roz Spring. He wasn't fooled by a leather cat-suit, dark eyeliner and a stern voice into thinking she was some sort of kinky goddess.

He wasn't going to fall in love with her. She certainly wasn't going to fall in love with him. Simple. Everyone happy.

'Most women don't think I need a cock ring, but if you insist . . .' Andy's words jerked her out of her depressing reverie, and she gasped.

She recovered and said in her most crushing voice, 'I'm not sure they have one small enough, but we can ask.'

'It's not that sort of shop.' Andy grinned wickedly. 'But we can go to Gresham Street later and get one, if you like.'

She didn't want to ask what was in Gresham Street, but she could guess.

Inside the shop was dim, with the jewellery on display in discreet cases. Idly, she worked out three scams for stealing something from it. Her dad would have come up with at least six. But she was finished with that business now.

She missed the conversation between Andy and the owner, and was surprised by the tray of rings being pulled out for her to peruse.

They were gorgeous. Old and valuable. There was a delicate band of diamonds. A ruby solitaire gleamed at her and she shuddered. After stealing the Fire of Autumn from her sister's museum, she never wanted to see another ruby. Taking that stone had been a big mistake and she was still paying for it.

She turned her attention back to the display. There was a trio of black pearls that teased her. An eternity ring which looked older than Charleville Castle. She picked up an antique sapphire flanked by two diamonds and slipped it on. It fitted as if it were made for her.

She admired the way it caught the light, until she saw the small label with the price tag. Seventeen thousand pounds. Roz shuddered and put it back.

The pearls were nice, and she could imagine wearing them. The ring only cost three hundred pounds. That was okay. She turned to the owner to say she had decided on her ring, and found that Andy was putting away his credit card. He opened the velvet box containing the sapphire and took out the ring. 'It had to be this one,' he said.

She was all too conscious of the sales assistant

watching as he slipped it onto her finger and took her into his arms to kiss her.

His kiss was hot and possessive, and all too brief.

He raised his head. 'Later, darling,' he said.

Only Roz could hear the mockery in his voice.

Andy's stomach growled on the drive north. Had they eaten today? He couldn't remember. Roz was quiet, watching the scenery fly past. She was a real city girl. He wondered how she would cope with Lough Darra. 'Before we arrive, we need to work on a cover story.'

'Okay.' She nodded. This was something Roz was familiar with, getting into the part, hiding behind a character.

'Stick to the truth as much as possible. We met in Paris when I was working for the O'Sullivans.'

Roz frowned at the memory.

'We met again in London a few months ago and we've been in touch every day since then. You missed me so much when I returned to Ireland that you hopped on a plane and followed me.'

'Okay, I can do that. So, where do I live in London? Please say Chelsea? Please. Please. I've always wanted to be posh.' Roz batted her eyelashes outrageously at him.

Andy suppressed the desire to laugh and then shook his head. He was certain that his mother had friends in Chelsea and it could lead to all sorts of complications. 'No. You live in Greenwich.'

'Fine. And what do I call you? Do I have a pet name for you?'

'No pet names,' Andy said, horrified at the thought of it. Knowing Roz she would come up with something outlandish to torture him with. Pet name indeed. He would make her pay for that later, but first they had to run the gauntlet of his parents and the staff.

Almost there. He turned off the narrow country road and swung through the iron gates. He would have to think about improving security. Open gates were an invitation. If he got his hands on the teenagers who had tried to rob the place, he would teach them a lesson they wouldn't forget.

'This is it?' Roz perked up and looked around her as they drove up the tree-lined drive.

His inner imp made him park the Jeep at the front of the house instead of the rear as usual. The gardens ran down to the lake, the waters glittering in the spring sunlight. To someone who hadn't looked at it almost every day of his childhood, the view was pretty spectacular.

Wide eyed, she turned to stare at him. 'Please tell me you're joking. You can't actually live here?'

'It's just a house.'

'And Charleville Castle is a charming country cottage. Damn it, Andy, I'm nervous as hell. What if your parents hate me? What if they –'

'Come here.' He pulled her into his arms. The slight tremble in her shoulders brought out his protective streak but he knew better than to mention it. 'They'll adore you. Just remember that I'm completely and utterly in love with you.'

'Oh.' For once, Roz was speechless. A delightful flush stained her cheeks. She was confused and embarrassed, but she rallied quickly. 'I really want to see you pretending to be in love with me.'

'Do you now?' Andy cupped her face and brushed his

lips against hers. He hadn't intended it to be more than a teasing kiss to reassure her. But hunger flared, bright and hot as a flame.

With a soft murmur, she opened her lips to his and then they were both lost. Hot, open mouthed, the kiss was endless. Nothing existed but her and the soft curves of her body against his. He cursed the dress she was wearing. He wanted to touch her bare skin. Andy stroked her hip, sliding his palm down to the hem of her dress and working his fingers beneath. Stockings and suspenders. Sweet Jesus, she was trying to kill him.

A tap on the window jerked him back to reality.

'Andrew. Is that you?'

Roz jerked herself out of his arms. What the hell was she doing? Letting Andy McTavish under her skin was the worst idea she'd ever had, and she'd had some humdingers.

She looked around to see who had interrupted them.

A small, stylish woman with short, grey hair stood there beaming at them. She was dressed in a pair of well-cut trousers, a white shirt, wellies and a sheepskin jacket. There was something familiar about her eyes.

'Mother,' Andy said, with what sounded suspiciously like a groan. Yes, that was it. Her brown eyes were the feminine version of his.

Oh great. She had been caught necking in the car by Andy's mother. A wave of heat crawled up her face.

'You idiot,' Roz snarled. 'This is all your fault.'

He grinned shamelessly at her. 'Come and meet my mother. She'll love you.'

Roz knew better. Mothers of men like Andy did not like women like her. She would take one look at Roz and peg her for what she was. Out of her class. Out of her depth.

This was the sort of fancy rich woman who was begging to be fleeced. More money than sense. She made herself watch as Andy swept his mother up in a rough hug, kissing both her cheeks and telling her she needed to button her jacket.

'Silly boy, put me down,' she told Andy, patting his cheek, even though she had to stand on tip-toe to reach. 'But I'm cross that you didn't tell me you were coming or that you were bringing a visitor. Please introduce me to your friend.'

Her eyes were perfectly welcoming as she smiled at Roz, but she fancied she heard a hint of censure in those precisely modulated words.

Now it was Andy's turn to blush. He grinned his familiar grin, the one that looked like a pirate about to take a lady prisoner and kiss her senseless, but there was a definite darkening on his high cheekbones. He put his arm around Roz, holding her possessively to his side. It looked like a lover's embrace, but Roz could feel the grip preventing her from running away.

'Mum, may I introduce Roz O'Sullivan? Roz, this is my mother, Mrs Dougal Campbell McTavish.'

The older woman frowned at him. 'Why so formal?' She turned to Roz. 'Call me Poppy, dear. Everyone does.'

She advanced on Roz. The woman was tiny, she barely reached Roz's chin, but she pulled her into a decorous embrace. 'So glad to meet you.'

She smelled of lavender and turpentine and her hands were cold.

In spite of the cool, slender fingers, her hug was warm, and Roz felt unexpectedly bereft. She had never had motherly hugs, and she hadn't realized how much she had wanted them.

Get over it, she told herself. This is part of a scam.

Poppy stood back and surveyed Roz carefully. 'Roz O'Sullivan? I don't believe I've heard of you before this week, dear.'

That was a fishing hook if she had ever heard one. Roz stood up straighter, pulling back her shoulders. She wasn't going to grovel in any way. 'That's Roisin Philomena O'Sullivan-Spring. Andy never gives my full name.'

Andy's exclamation derailed his mother's gentle cross-examination. 'Philomena? You never told me you were called Philomena. I'm sorry, that's it. It's all off. I can't date someone called Philomena.'

But Poppy's brow had scrunched thoughtfully. 'Philomena O'Sullivan sounds familiar.'

'I was named after my grandmother,' Roz admitted. Her dad had told her the story of how she had been named after her mother's mother, and Sinead had been named for Jane Spring. He had cursed that decision every time he mentioned her O'Sullivan grandmother while she was growing up. She had been the demon from hell, according to his stories. She had cut her daughter off without a second thought when she had refused to break up with Roz's father.

Peter Spring wasn't the best father in the world. Okay, he was a long way from being the best. But he had tried, and in his own way, he had loved her. Philomena O'Sullivan hadn't loved anyone, certainly not her daughter.

Thoughts of her dysfunctional family helped to steady Roz. She wasn't a part of this world. She was hiding out here until Hall was off her back, and it didn't matter if they liked her or approved of her.

'Oh, that's right. Andy told me you're one of those O'Sullivans. Welcome to Lough Darra,' Poppy said. She tucked Roz's hand into her arm as she turned towards the house. Andy took his mother's other arm and shortened his long strides to accommodate her as they tramped along the driveway. 'So tell me, how did you meet my son?'

Roz stumbled slightly, but recovered her step. 'I'm sure you'd rather hear it from Andy.' Let him take the heat for a change.

Lying to his mother clearly didn't bother Andy at all. 'We met in Paris last year and I've been chasing her ever since. She moved back to London a few months ago, and I haven't let her out of my sight,' he said smoothly.

'So you're good friends?' Poppy asked.

'A bit more than that.' Andy stopped, picked up Roz's hand and kissed it. His mouth was warm against her frozen skin. 'I never want to let her go. Mum, meet my fiancée.'

'Your what?' Poppy squealed and threw her arms around Roz. 'My dear. You should have told me at once. I know I'm going to love you.'

This time her hug wasn't elegant, but it was enthusiastic. 'I'm going to have a daughter-in-law. I can't wait.'

He wasn't supposed to feel guilty. This was a job, wasn't it? It was for Roz's protection. His mother had seen girls come and go before now, it shouldn't have been a big deal.

But the expression of joy on her face was worse than a kick in the nuts. He must have been crazy. How could he have thought that this was a good idea?

And Roz was like a rabbit caught in the headlights. She shot him a look filled with venom. It was time to rescue her. He caught up with them. 'It's kind of new to us too, so maybe we should keep it quiet for a while?'

'Nonsense! Do you know how long I've been waiting for this? Oh wait 'til I tell Hilary Adams.'

Fuck. His mother's best friend was the biggest gossip in the county. The news would be all over the neighbourhood by dinner time. Andy forced a smile onto his face. 'Great.'

He grabbed the shopping bags from the car and followed them into the house. They had barely made it to the hall before two noisy bundles of energy came racing at them. Mini and Maxi, his mother's cocker spaniels.

'Down.' He injected as much sternness into his voice as he could muster but the dogs ignored him, leaping and jumping at Roz who stood frozen to the spot. She stretched out a tentative hand to pat one of them.

'Ladies, please behave.' His mother clapped her hands and the dogs sat obediently, waiting for her next command. 'I'm so sorry. Andy, take Roz into the library and I'll organize some refreshments.'

He dropped the bags near the stairs and ushered Roz to the book-filled room. It was his mother's favourite spot, mostly because it was the warmest place in the house.

Roz whistled. 'Holy freaking hell, this room is bigger than my flat in London. You actually live here?'

Andy ached to take her in his arms again. That kiss had been far too short. He led her to the couch in front of the fire. The leather was worn and cracked in places, a testament to generations of McTavishes who had curled up with a book over the years. He sat down and pulled her onto his lap. 'I'll give you the tour later, but first can I tell you how much I love this dress?'

His fingers found the hem and slid underneath. If there was ever an invention designed to torture a man it was stockings and suspender belts and she was wearing both.

'Stop that.' Roz slapped his hand away. 'Your mother will be back in a minute. And if you think that I'm going to –'

The door opened and Andy heard the clink of glasses. Damn his mother's timing. Maggie followed behind, balancing a tray containing an ice bucket and champagne. He hurried to help her and set the tray down on the table. The champagne was opened with a satisfying pop and his mother poured four glasses. 'Maggie, did you ever think you'd see the day?'

Her joy was so evident that Andy felt a pang of guilt. He had no idea how long they would be here or what his mother would do when his 'engagement' suddenly ended.

Poppy raised her glass. 'A toast – to the next generation at Lough Darra.'

'The next generation.' Maggie's words echoed his mother's as they clinked their glasses together.

For once, Roz was stunned into silence and Andy wanted to kick himself for being an idiot. Why hadn't he noticed how pale she was? She'd been attacked, shot at and engaged within the space of half a day. Her head must be spinning.

Poppy sipped her champagne and then said, 'Let's sit down by the fire, my dear, and you can tell me all about yourself.'

She gave Andy an arch look. 'Men are so reticent when it comes to the important things.'

They returned to the sofa and Andy pulled Roz down beside him, resting his arm along the back of the couch. Roz relaxed into his embrace and rested her hand on his thigh as if it was something they did every night.

'So tell me, dear, how did you meet my no-good son?' Poppy asked. 'Was it romantic?'

Roz smiled and Andy braced himself. The little madam was up to something. 'We met in Paris last year, at the Eiffel Tower. Andy bought me a ticket to go up to the top.'

Poppy sighed happily. 'How romantic.'

Roz's smile turned evil. 'Unfortunately, the ticket was for the stairs, not the lift. I had to climb the entire two thousand-odd steps to the top. He seemed to think I needed the exercise.'

Andy narrowed his eyes at her, silently promising retribution.

'Oh, what a rascal. You have a perfect figure, how could he say that?' Poppy looked genuinely distressed.

'And when we met again in London this year, he complained that I had put on weight.'

Oh yeah, Roz was trying to drop him into it. 'You have to admit that you had a cute little belly,' he said. 'It suited you.'

Roz choked on a sip of champagne. 'It did not.'

'Sure it did. I'd like to see you like that again.'

'You are so full of it.'

He was teasing her, but for some reason, the idea of her round and pregnant had a certain appeal. 'Try me and see.'

She had sense enough not to reply to that one.

'More champagne, darling?' His mother's question broke the tension.

Poppy poured some more champagne and insisted on toasting them again. 'You have no idea how wonderful it is to have you here. Dougal will be thrilled to meet you.'

That would be a first. Andy had never seen his dour father thrilled about anything that didn't involve horses.

'He'll be down for dinner. Andy probably told you that he's been ill.'

'Yes,' Roz murmured and took another sip from her glass.

Andy could tell that she was flagging. 'Roz is dying to meet him. Aren't you, darling? But she's been up since 4am and –'

'How dreadful. You must be dead on your feet. Why don't you unpack and have a nap before dinner?'

Relieved, Andy stood up and took Roz's glass from her hand. She really was shattered. A nap would do them both good. 'Great. We'll go upstairs and get settled in.'

'I'll see you both later. Maggie has made up the blue room for Roz.'

His mother had put them in separate rooms? She couldn't be serious.

Andy was about to protest when his mother smiled

sweetly. 'The blue room is traditionally used by the lady of the house.'

Yes – if she was ninety or widowed or her husband snored like a freight train. Andy didn't want Roz sleeping somewhere that was almost a five minute walk away. 'I'm sure Roz doesn't want to put you to so much trouble.'

'Nonsense. It's no trouble at all.'

Andy picked up the shopping bags and led Roz up the staircase.

'Your mum is a classy lady.'

'Yes. She's something,' Andy muttered under his breath. On the landing he paused. 'Would you like to see my room first?'

'No thanks. I'm good. Lead the way to the blue room.'

They walked the endless corridor and he opened the door at the end. 'The blue room, M'lady. Will you be needing anything else? Undressing perhaps? Or a turn down service?'

Roz paused in the doorway. 'Well, there is one thing.'

Thank you, god. Andy took two steps into the room.

'I need to use your phone to check on Frankie.'

He fished in his pocket and handed her his new BlackBerry.

She punched in the number quickly and walked away from him. 'Frankie, it's me. How are you? Yes. Yes. Okay. I will.'

Roz disconnected the call with a frown. 'He says he's fine but he sounds a bit off.'

'He's probably stressed after his encounter with Hall.'

Roz nodded. 'I know. It's just that . . .'

She swayed and Andy rushed forwards. He was a

thoughtless bastard. She might be tough, but she wasn't trained. Even experienced operatives weren't used to getting shot at every day. 'Get undressed and go to sleep.'

She bent down to take off her boots and gasped. 'My ribs!'

'Here, let me help you.' Damn! He should have realized she'd been coasting on adrenaline up to now. He hadn't intended to undress her, but it was obvious she wouldn't be able to manage on her own. Gritting his teeth, he eased the dress up over her head, taking care to be as gentle as possible.

The sight of the emerging bruise on her chest shocked him, and reminded him how close she had come to dying. 'You need a doctor.'

'No.'

Roz should have looked enticing, standing there in underwear, a lacy confection of a bra and cream suspenders holding up her stockings. But he couldn't tear his gaze away from the massive purple bruise that spread over her ribs. If someone had hit her with a hammer, it would have done less damage.

He was scared to touch her.

'No doctors,' she insisted.

He unfastened her bra, and eased her into the bed.

Her eyelids fluttered closed and then opened again. 'I'm usually tougher than this.'

'Yeah, being shot at close range, escaping a psychopath and having champagne on an empty stomach is child's play. You're falling down on the job, Spring.' In spite of his attempt at humour, his voice was rough.

She opened one eye and glared at him. 'Well, fuck you too, McTavish.' Then she snuggled into the bed and allowed her eyes to close again.

Andy hesitated. She looked so pale and vulnerable lying there and it was his fault. He was supposed to be looking after her. Instead, he had allowed her to come within inches of dying. Losing a client would be bad enough but losing Roz? He didn't want to think about that. He wanted to kill something – preferably Hall.

Roz gave a soft snuffle. She was already asleep. Exhaustion was beginning to catch up on him too and the aches and pains of his recent fight were kicking in. He needed a shower and some sleep. In that order.

He had never really thought about settling down and, somehow, this wasn't how he expected to be celebrating his engagement. Andy eyed the space beside her wistfully. The far end of the corridor was a long way away. He could always climb into bed with her. Make sure that she was okay.

You're a bad bastard, McTavish.

He and Roz in the same bed could have only one conclusion. Her naked and gasping his name, while he made up for the night they had spent apart after their encounter in Charleville Castle.

Despite his exhaustion, his cock stirred and he sighed. The only way either of them would get any sleep would be in separate rooms.

16

The ringing of a bell woke Roz. She jerked awake, alert in spite of her exhaustion, primed for danger, then winced as the movement reawakened the pain from her bruises. She heard the bell peal again somewhere in the bowels of the house.

House nothing. This was a freaking castle. The view of it from the driveway had been terrifying enough. Nothing could have prepared her for the inside, all marble and mahogany and leaded glass. That library had more books in it than most of the public libraries she had been in, and half of them looked like valuable antiques.

She flopped back on her bed and stared at the ceiling above her. Typical. Even the ceiling wasn't ordinary. It was covered with tiny cherubs, picked out in blue and gold.

How rich was Andy? And if he was this rich, why was he slumming it, working as a glorified bodyguard for Niall Moore?

Roz was painfully aware of the gaps in her education. The flat she shared with her dad had been raided the night before her exams. She'd barely had two hours' sleep before school. She had nothing – not even a GCSE – to her name. But while she had no fancy degrees, one thing she could do was hack computers. Roz had checked out Niall Moore in detail.

She knew Moore Enterprises was considered the best

operation of its type in Europe, and that Niall had a good income and a very comfortable lifestyle. But it was nothing compared to this. Andy sure as hell wasn't paying for this house out of his salary from Moore Enterprises.

What else hadn't he told her? she wondered, getting up and finding an old-fashioned bathroom through the side door of the room.

Andy hadn't been wrong about the plumbing. The water pipes gurgled and the over-bath shower was noisy. The stream of water that eventually came never got really hot, but it was a distinct improvement on the make-shift showers on the film set. Roz stood still, allowing the warm water to soothe her aches.

She had no idea what she should wear to dinner but was pretty sure that jeans wouldn't be acceptable. Roz sorted through her new clothes and picked out a demure black dress. She wanted to tease Andy with another pair of stockings, but her injured ribs wouldn't let her bend enough to put them on. Bare legs it would have to be.

She had finished dressing when he knocked on the door. 'I've come to escort you to dinner –' he started, and stopped, stuck. He looked her up and down, and whistled. 'Wow, you clean up well.'

'You're not so bad yourself,' she said.

She wasn't going to admit how the sight of him in a dinner jacket caused her breath to catch and a ball of heat to curl low in her belly. Andy was sexy in jeans, but in formal clothes, he was devastating.

He held out his arm to her. 'Come and eat. I'll show you around, otherwise you'll get lost in this rabbit warren of a house.'

'I'll leave a trail of breadcrumbs so that I can find my way back,' she told him.

'Are you Hansel or Gretel?' he asked, leading her down the wide staircase.

'More like the wicked witch.' She wasn't some helpless child whose father had allowed her to be abandoned in the woods.

'The witch came to a bad end,' Andy pointed out.

'She was stupid and short-sighted. I'm not.'

'We're eating in the breakfast room,' Andy said, guiding her through the door.

Roz was stuck dumb. The round table might be a reasonable size for four people, but it was antique mahogany covered with Irish linen. A chandelier dripped from the ceiling, with dozens of small bulbs lighting the room and glinting off the crystal droplets. The table was set with far too many knives and forks, real linen and crystal glasses.

'Mum is determined to impress you,' Andy murmured into her ear. 'I'd be lucky to get a seat at the kitchen table.'

Roz would have much preferred to eat in the kitchen. She wondered if she would be relegated to the scullery if she screwed up.

'Well, bring her in so I can see her,' an irascible voice said from the corner. She had managed to miss the elderly man sitting in an armchair, reading a newspaper.

'Don't worry, he'll love you,' Andy said.

Dougal Campbell McTavish did not love her.

Andy seated her at the table, with her back to the fireplace where whole logs blazed and crackled.

Once Andy had helped his father to his seat at the end of the table, the inquisition began.

'So you're from London?' His tone made it clear that this was a mark against her.

Poppy helped Roz to a ladle of soup from the tureen in the centre of the table. To her relief, there was no army of servants standing over them. Maggie had brought in the soup and both Andy and Poppy had jumped up to help her.

'Yes,' Roz responded with a smile. 'But I was born in Ireland.'

'And your family?'

Oh yeah, this is what it was all about. Was she a suitable brood mare to carry on the bloodline? She was tempted to tell the truth, to see the look on Dougal's face, but she needed to stay here, and fit in.

You're a rich girl, you're a rich girl. Time to get into character.

'My dad has his own IT business. My mother died when I was four.'

Poppy was all sympathy. 'Oh dear, your poor father. How on earth did he cope?'

While Maggie brought in roast venison, carrots, cabbage and new potatoes, she elaborated her story. 'He didn't. My dad was broken hearted. Of course, the O'Sullivans tried to help as much as they could. They took my sister Sinead to live with them.'

She glanced at Poppy to watch which knife and fork she picked from the three at each place setting. 'I stayed with my dad. I couldn't bear to leave him.'

Beside her, Andy choked. He moved his hand under the tablecloth to grip her leg in warning. She thumped him hard on the back and the grip became a caress, sliding up her thigh, teasing as it went.

The trick, she knew, was not to tell an outright lie. Tell the truth in such a way that your mark believed the lie.

Dougal chewed a piece of meat before he asked, 'O'Sullivans? Do you mean those airline people?'

Roz nodded, taking a bite of her meal. It tasted unlike anything she had ever eaten before; simple but full of flavour. 'Yes, my uncle is Tim O'Sullivan.' And there was something she never thought she'd admit.

Andy's right hand was holding his wine glass. His left hand was making tiny circles on the soft skin of her thigh, distracting her from the questions.

'New money.' His father grunted as he cut into his meat. 'And too flashy. But he does have an eye for horses.'

'So I'm told,' she said, trying to ignore the hand now tracing the dampness of her panties. She clamped her thighs shut and glared at Andy, while a small part of her wanted to open her legs and let him do whatever he wanted. He was much too good at this.

'Have some more venison,' Poppy interrupted. 'Everything on the table is from our own farm. Except the wine, of course. We never managed to make good wine.'

'Everything?' Roz surveyed the table in awe. In her world, food came from Tesco. She could understand people growing vegetables. She had once managed to grow lettuce and radishes in a window box, but the rest? She was pretty sure venison came from deer. And the bread and butter? Her mind reeled.

'Are you involved with horses yourself?' Dougal asked.

All she really knew about horses was that one end bit and the other end shit. And that Nagsy liked carrots. She shrugged modestly. 'A little.'

'Well, you can take out a horse while you are here. Andy will find you something suitable to ride. Perhaps Flamingo or Kestrel.'

'Are they horses or birds?'

He glared at her. 'Very funny. I see you've inherited Tim O'Sullivan's sense of humour.'

Poppy intervened. 'And do you see much of your Uncle Tim?'

Andy's hand had not stopped his tormenting tease, his index finger flicked lightly against her clit, provoking an insistent throb.

'Not much, I've been working in Europe.' Roz put her cutlery down with some relief and nipped Andy in the side. This meal was hard enough without him distracting her. She slipped her foot out of her shoe and slid it up his calf.

To her relief and a little regret, he left off his sensual torture while he took a mouthful of wine. Poppy collected the plates and Roz, horribly conscious that her dress was bunched up at the top of her thighs, had to sit still without helping. Any movement would reveal the state Andy had left her in.

Dessert was poached pears and crème fraîche, also from the farm, which she had to eat using another knife and fork.

Dougal returned to the attack. 'Andrew went to Queens. Which college did you go to?'

Roz's fingers tightened around her knife. For a moment, she considered plunging it into the suspicious old man's gut. Or at least his dinner. Scare him into another heart attack. It was clear he didn't consider her nearly good enough for his precious son.

Andy must have noticed the danger signal and put his arm around her in what looked like a loving gesture to anyone who couldn't see how tight it was.

She pinched him hard and he laughed.

She couldn't admit she hadn't even done her A-levels, never mind gone to college. What colleges were in London? Her mind blanked. She remembered the local Polytechnic and she was pretty sure that wouldn't do. 'Oh,' she said casually, 'I went to the Sorbonne and Oxford.'

She had been inside the Sorbonne once, posing as a research assistant when she was there to meet a submissive client. When he had failed to show she had almost been arrested. That had been a lesson in getting paid upfront. And she had a vague memory of a windy weekend in Oxford while Dad visited a new girlfriend.

At least Dougal looked impressed, and returned his attention to his place. Andy took the opportunity to caress her in that delicate spot between her shoulder blades, the one that always turned her to mush.

She stopped eating, having lost her appetite – for food. 'Do you mind if I skip coffee? It's been a long day and I'm shattered.'

Poppy fussed anxiously, exclaiming at how pale Roz looked. Dougal raised his eyes from his dish, grunted something that sounded like 'No stamina', and waved her off.

'I'll escort her to her room,' Andy said, but the wicked glint in his eyes promised that he didn't intend to leave her there on her own.

'I'll pour your coffee, so don't be long.' Poppy wasn't exactly subtle – she expected him back.

His hand at her back was warm and reassuring as he guided Roz out of the dining room.

'He'll love you,' she mimicked when they were out of earshot. 'Yeah right!'

Andy winced. 'Sorry, I wasn't expecting him to give you the third degree. He's usually pretty nice to the girls I bring home.'

That stung. 'Sure, girls who are from the same background.' It was painfully obvious to her that she was not.

'Don't worry, he'll come around. In a few days, he'll love you.' They had reached her door by now. He turned her around, tipped her face up and kissed her.

The kiss was light, delicate, almost sweet. There was no body contact at all. But it inflamed something inside her.

Here, in this monster of a house, this was something she knew. Something real and honest and familiar. And, oh, so tempting.

She leaned into him, her breasts aching for the feel of his hard body.

Andy groaned, holding her back. 'Don't, please. I have to go downstairs to my mother, and preferably without a hard-on. And you're still bruised.'

With a grin, she pulled his head down to hers again. She didn't attempt to touch him anywhere else, but she opened her mouth, inviting his tongue to tangle with her, and kissing him back with all the seductiveness she could muster.

His arms trembled as he kept a distance between them, but he didn't pull back. His kiss got hotter, and she allowed herself the luxury of enjoying it. She could kiss him forever, without wanting more.

Time lost all meaning, and she was shocked when he pulled himself out of her grip. 'So much for that plan,' he groaned. She looked down and giggled when she noticed the bulge tenting the front of his trousers.

'Witch! I'll get you back for that.'

'Oh yeah? Do your worst.' Roz was almost hoping that he would.

'Oh I plan to.' He gave her a warning look before planting a swift kiss on her mouth, then pushed her into her bedroom and headed down the stairs.

She watched him until he was out of sight, then closed the door and sighed. Her nipples were hard achy points and she pressed her thighs together to contain the throb his kiss had caused. Andy wasn't the only one who would need a cold shower.

Damn it, how was he going to face his parents with a hard-on the size of the Dublin Spire? The inquisition Roz received earlier was nothing compared to what was waiting for him. The next lady of Lough Darra was a thief, a liar and god knows what else. And there was no way that he was able to stare his mother in the eye and lie to her again. Fuck.

He pulled out his phone. There was only one thing for it. 'Reilly?'

'Identify yourself, and bear in mind that I may kill you,' she whispered.

Shit. Andy winced when he heard what sounded like restaurant noise in the background. Was Reilly on a date? 'I need a call in ten minutes.'

Reilly excused herself from the table and a couple of moments later the background noise faded. He had to admire her. The eloquence with which she rapped out two dozen expletives would have made half a dozen squaddies run home to their mammies. 'You owe me your first born child,' Reilly snarled.

'Grand, you can be godmother.'

'If this is not official, it better be good.'

'It's personal.'

'Oh?' There was almost a twenty second silence before she laughed. 'Flynn Grant owes me a ton. I told him you'd need someone to protect your sorry ass. I can't believe I got one over on him.'

'Reilly, I want a phone call, not one of your kidneys. Play nice.'

'As if.' She disconnected the call and Andy smiled.

The Rangers were brothers and sisters in arms. If one needed, the other gave. That never changed. And at least his dick had stopped throbbing. He strolled downstairs to face his parents.

His mother stood poised, silver coffee pot in hand. 'We were chatting about Roz. She's such a lovely girl.'

'Feisty,' his father announced.

'Aye, she is that,' Andy said as he accepted a cup of coffee from his mother and stirred the dark liquid with a silver spoon.

'Do you love her, Andrew?'

Poppy's expression was pensive and it gave Andy pause for thought. He didn't know Roz. Oh yes, on paper, he knew everything about her. But not the real Roz.

No matter how he felt, he couldn't lie to his mother.

The phone in his pocket vibrated. He would kiss Reilly the next time they met.

'It's work.' He shrugged apologetically. 'Sorry, I have to take this. We can talk later.'

He left the room quickly and bounded up the stairs, phone pressed to his ear. 'You are a darling. I may let you shag me next time we meet.'

'Thanks, but I'll pass. You're not my type.' Niall Moore's voice rumbled down the line.

Fuck. Andy grimaced. 'Sorry, boss. I thought you were Reilly.'

'Keep digging that hole and I'll bury you in it. Do you ever stop thinking about sex? On second thoughts, don't answer that.'

Something had to be wrong if Niall was contacting him at this hour. 'What's up?'

'Do you want the bad news or the bad news? Hall smashed through a police checkpoint a couple of hours ago.'

'Fuck.' Hall was a slippery bastard and too damn good.

'The guys at Interpol are freaked too. I've told them we've found the girl. They want her in witness protection until we can bring Hall in.'

His heart dropped like a skydiver in freefall. They wanted Roz? If she went into protective custody, god knows when he would see her again. Months? Years? And he couldn't contact her without breaking her cover.

Roz would be gone for good.

'When can you bring her to Paris?'

Andy played for time. 'We left Tullamore in a hurry.

She'll need some new ID to travel. And she's pretty bruised and shocked after yesterday. Hall shot her at close range. If it wasn't for her phone she . . .'

He left the rest of the words unsaid. They had both faced danger, but they were professionals, Roz was a civilian.

'Understood. Do you need back up?'

'No. It would draw attention to her if another operative turned up.'

'I could send in Reilly.' Niall didn't even try to keep the amusement out of his voice.

Andy could imagine his mother's face if the tough-as-nails former Ranger turned up. If Roz was rough around the edges, Reilly needed to be sandpapered before she could be allowed indoors.

'Thanks, boss, but I have enough trouble already.'

'Is Roz being a handful?'

'You could say that. She survived an interrogation by Dougal and she barely blinked.'

'Interpol will have fun with that. Okay. Can you hold onto her for a week or so? I'll get things organized.'

'No problem.' Andy ended the call and tossed the phone onto the bed. How the hell was he going to tell Roz she was going into protective custody?

He shrugged out of his jacket and hung it on the back of a chair before loosening his tie. He could always return to Roz, but then he would have to tell her and he didn't want to do that. Not yet.

Coward.

It was one thing that he wasn't. Reluctantly, he opened the door and walked to her room. He tapped lightly on the door but there was no reply. He opened the door and peeked inside.

A bedside lamp cast dark shadows in the room. Roz was lying in the middle of the bed wearing a rose silk chemise. God, she was beautiful. Her pale skin was like cream. A cloud of red hair drifted across the pillow. The only thing wrong with the picture was that she was asleep. It was just as he had imagined her a thousand times. Except that she should be in his bed, not sleeping in a guest room.

She moaned softly in her sleep and shivered. The urge to warm her, to climb into bed beside her and spend the night doing nothing but holding her, was overwhelming. He was getting soft. This was just another job. There was no way that he could get involved. Andy pulled the duvet over her and switched off the lamp.

He had almost made it to the door when he heard her moan again.

'Hall, no. No.' Roz moved restlessly in the bed.

She needed him. Separate rooms be damned. He couldn't leave her like this. He undressed quickly and slid into bed beside her.

'Hush now,' he murmured softly as she turned into his arms. Her distinctive perfume rose from her sleep-warm skin. He couldn't help reacting to her slenderness and the fragility of her bones. When she was awake, her forceful personality blinded everyone to the fact that she was a small woman, one with no military training. She needed to be protected.

Andy pulled her closer. He couldn't remember when he had last cuddled a woman unless it was part of a strategy to seduce. A flicker of shame made him wince. The game was fun at the time, but empty afterwards.

Her hand trailed across his abdomen and came to rest on his chest. The restless touch woke his cock. Oh fuck. How was he going to lie beside her like this? He shifted slightly, trying to put a little distance between them, but Roz moved with him, still clinging. Now her thigh was in contact with his balls. *Down, boy.*

Staying perfectly still, he began to count backwards from one hundred. Sheep, goats, horses, he didn't care; anything to distract him from the images filling his head. A naked, wanton Roz on top, riding him like a stallion. Her head thrown back, her glorious hair messy, her mouth wet from his kisses and her eyes heavy-lidded with passion.

Nope. That wasn't going to work either. This was pure torture. His arousal was becoming painful. There was no way that he could stay here, he would have to leave.

With a soft murmur, she raised her head from his chest to stare at him. A chink of moonlight from the half-drawn curtains gave him enough light to see her face. Her eyes were dark, her expression knowing.

Siren.

Roz brushed her mouth against his in silent invitation and lay back against the pillows. He rose to his knees and ran his palm along the length of the chemise. God, she was beautiful but he wanted her naked.

He put his fingers to his lips, signalling her to be quiet before urging her up and lifting the lace-edged hem over her head, tossing it onto the floor.

The bruises on her ribs were a shocking reminder of

what she had gone through. No wonder she was having nightmares. He was determined to make her forget them.

'We're going to play a little game. I'll give you pleasure but you have to stay absolutely silent.'

Roz opened her mouth and snapped it closed again before nodding. Tempted by her breasts, he fastened his mouth around one nipple and suckled hard. She fingered his hair, urging him on. He turned his attention to her other breast, sucking, tasting, licking at the tender peak until it was as hard as the first.

He sat back on his heels, surveying the feast before him, from her toes to her face. He wanted to taste all of her. Cupping her foot in his hand, he raised it and dropped a kiss on the inside of her ankle. He nibbled his way along her calf and licked at the tender spot behind her knee.

She writhed but didn't protest when he kissed a path along her inner thigh. Her panting gasps were music to his ears. Bracing himself between her open thighs, he licked the length of her exposed cleft.

Roz arched off the bed, a tiny whimper escaping her open mouth.

Oh yes, she liked that. He licked again with purpose, holding her thighs firmly so that she couldn't escape. With the tip of his tongue, he flicked all around her clit, teasing her but never giving her quite what she needed. Her restless hands grasped handfuls of his hair, begging him wordlessly, trying to guide him to the sweet spot.

Usually he would have done what she wanted, satisfying her before he took his own pleasure, but not yet. He wanted more from Roz.

Her muffled groan of frustration made him smile. He

wanted her mindless. With mouth and hands, he paid homage to every inch of her, savouring her taste and scent, licking the salty sheen of sweat from her skin in a deliberate and sensuous torture.

Roz tossed her head from side to side, her movements becoming more frantic. She opened her mouth to protest. He put his finger to her lips. The implication was clear: *quiet or all of this will stop.*

Her mutinous expression made him want to laugh.

'Do you want to come?'

She narrowed her eyes at him, silently promising revenge, but he didn't care.

'Roll over.'

Roz lay face down. Her rounded ass made him want to cheer. He hated scrawny women. He kneaded the glorious globes with reverent hands. Roz was a wet dream of delicious curves. Bending his head, he bit her creamy flesh.

She gave a protesting squeak and tried to roll away from him.

Andy swatted her lightly and she lay still. He knew that she couldn't take much more, that the silence was killing her. 'Poor baby,' he murmured.

Roz wasn't the only one suffering. His cock was aching. If he didn't have her soon, he would die. When she rolled again he didn't try to stop her. Her cheeks were flushed and her mouth was a luscious pink temptation. How could he have forgotten about that mouth?

Andy lowered himself along the length of her so that they were skin to skin. Grasping his head urgently, she drew him down, holding him in place so that she could tangle her tongue with his. Her lips tasted of mint and her own unique flavour. Roz arched her hips urgently against his. With a groan he pulled away from her. Holy shit. How had he forgotten protection?

Andy leaned down, grabbing his trousers and groping for the wallet. He muttered a silent prayer when his fingers encountered a single foil packet. They would have to make the most of it. He tore it open and sheathed himself quickly. The time for games was over. He nudged her thighs apart with his knee and braced his weight on one arm. Clamping his hand around the base of his cock, he rubbed the tip against her opening and drove home.

She was slick and tight. The heat enveloping his cock was amazing. Andy reined back the urge to move hard and fast. If Roz had been impatient before, he was going to drive her crazy now. Flexing his hips, he pulled back and thrust again, keeping his movements slow and controlled, feeling the pressure build.

Roz wrapped her legs around his hips, urging him on.

There was nothing but her. Every movement of his hips increased the sensory overload. Buried deep inside her, Andy never wanted it to end. Their gazes locked. His balls tightened. He increased speed, thrusting harder.

'Oh god. Andy.' Her breathless cry as she came broke the silence.

He was beyond caring. Every nerve ending along his spine tingled in warning. Eyes wide open as he gave a final thrust, burying himself inside her, shuddering helplessly as he came.

17

Roz was smiling when she woke the following morning. Her body hummed with satisfaction and pleasure. She stretched, enjoying the after-effects of a wonderful night of love-making, before her mind caught up with her body.

She stiffened. What the hell had she done?

She had made love with Andy McTavish. Or if it wasn't love, it was something damn close to it. Far too close and too dangerous. She knew a player when she saw one, and Andy was one of the best she had ever met. She couldn't allow herself to fall in love. That way led to a broken heart.

Besides, the bastard had made her submit to him again. She squirmed in embarrassment when the details of the night before replayed themselves in her mind. She liked being on top, calling the shots. She gave the orders and her lover obeyed. That was how it was.

Of course, it had been a very long time since she'd had a lover of any sort. Maybe she was just out of practice, and that was why she had allowed Andy to take control like that. She felt vaguely guilty that she had allowed him to lavish pleasure on her, while she had meekly followed his directions.

She wasn't submissive. She didn't do what she was told. No one gave her orders. Not even Andy McTavish.

Resolve strengthened, she groped under her pillow for

her phone, before she remembered she had none. Since it had saved her life, she wasn't going to complain about losing it, but now she had no way of telling the time. She hadn't been wearing a watch during the fight scene.

Was that only yesterday morning?

She'd have to borrow Andy's phone to check on Frankie again. In the meantime, daylight was sneaking in under the curtains, so it was time to get up. She winced getting out of bed, but she knew she'd work it out in an hour or two. And there was that enormous bathtub to help her soak out her aches.

Roz flung open the curtains and caught her breath at the view outside. God, she hadn't realized how beautiful Ireland was. All that stuff about the Emerald Isle didn't do it justice. The sun glinted off a lake while green hills rolled into the horizon with barely a single building to interrupt the vista of patchwork fields and hedges.

A herd of cows grazed in the distance. Or were they horses? She squinted. She was sure they weren't sheep, but that was all. She was a city girl, no doubt about it.

She got lost once on the way to breakfast, and found it laid out in the dining room. Poppy was there, sipping tea and nibbling on a piece of toast. She had obviously been waiting for her, because as soon as Roz came in, she jumped up to embrace her and insist that she eat.

Roz hated missing meals, and had every intention of eating, but it was nice to be fussed over. Poppy seemed to think Roz was planning to starve herself and pushed her towards the sideboard where a small heater kept eggs, bacon, sausages, mushrooms, fried soda bread and potato farls warm. 'Don't let it go to waste. Andy will keep you busy showing you around and you won't have time to snack –' She stopped. 'Is there something you usually have for breakfast that we've forgotten?'

Roz didn't want to tell her that her usual breakfast was a Pop-Tart or a quick bowl of cornflakes with semi-sour milk. She helped herself to the eggs and bacon as well as mushrooms and toast, feeling a quick pang for poor Frankie. By the time she sat down, Poppy had poured her a cup of coffee.

Was this how the rich lived? It seemed like far too much trouble for her taste.

'Eat up, make the most of being young and active, it's all so different when menopause hits and the weight creeps on.'

As Roz ate, Poppy outlined all the things she had planned to entertain her for the next couple of weeks. 'And after that, we'll see. I'm sure you'll be organizing the wedding by then.'

Roz put down her fork. Did Poppy really think she and Andy would do things that quickly? 'Oh, we haven't thought that far ahead.' The last thing she wanted was Poppy making wedding plans.

After breakfast, Poppy showed her around the house, and Roz got dizzy trying to keep track of where everything was. There were a ridiculous number of rooms. Most of them were under covers and barely half a dozen were open and heated, but the faded opulence was beyond her imagination. She had never been anywhere like this, and with each room filled with genuine antiques, she worried that she was going to show herself up.

She had worn a beautiful jersey dress and court shoes to breakfast, before realizing that a pair of jeans would have been more suitable. Poppy was wearing an elderly pair of tweed trousers and a pair of ratty runners. In France, it had been easier to fit in, to blend with the crowd. Any mistakes could be blamed on being part of the nouveau wealthy English set. Old money was different. She resolved to pay closer attention to how people behaved here.

The closest she had ever come to a house like Lough Darra was an invitation to a BDSM party in a chateau near Versailles, but she had never got there.

She had been driving to the chateau when a police car had signalled her. Old instincts had kicked in and she had accelerated away. After a chase through the suburbs of Paris, she had been caught and arrested. Although she had done nothing but drive away, and might have been able to explain that, the police hadn't been impressed by the collection of kinky toys in the boot of her car. The handcuffs and riding crops in particular interested them, and she ended up in custody for three days before she managed to convince them she had done nothing more criminal than drive with a broken tail-light.

Funny, that evening had been the start of a major change in her life. She had realized she didn't want to be one of the usual suspects any more. She didn't want to have to run every time she saw a police officer. She wanted a regular life.

Or this one.

Poppy was telling her the history of a large Chinese pot in the west drawing room, a young maid was cleaning ashes out of the grate, and Roz was overcome with the contrast between this house and her pokey apartment in Peckham.

This is the life she could have had if the O'Sullivans had bothered to come looking for her. If Sinead had told them about her. Instead of living hand to mouth, no education, no stability, not always enough to eat, she could have been living like this.

Roz sank down on a silk-covered sofa, and one of the dogs, Maxi, she thought, climbed into her lap and licked her face. Roz buried her face in the dog's coat. She'd never had a dog. They had never had a house where she could keep one. She'd never had the sort of life where walking the dog was an option. She'd never had anyone to cuddle up to her like this, to lick her face and pant with pleasure to see her.

Anger simmered beneath her surface. She could have had a dog like this. And a life like this. Instead, she was the beggar at the feast. Life wasn't fair. But she was used to that.

Andy arrived, heralded by Mini. 'There you are. I want to take you riding.'

Roz pulled her hard-won control into place. 'Sure. But lend me your phone so I can ring Frankie first.'

He handed it over. 'Go and put on some jeans and I'll find you a spare pair of riding boots and hat.'

In her room, Roz dialled Frankie's number and it rang out. That was odd. She rang again, in case she had got the number wrong. This time, it was picked up after six rings and a woman said, 'Hello?' in a careful whisper. 'Who is it?'

It took a moment for Roz to recognize the voice. 'Cheyenne? It's Roz, I'm looking for Frankie.'

There was a sob in Cheyenne's voice. 'He's going to be okay. Really, he is.' She sounded as if she were trying to convince herself.

The penny dropped. No wonder Frankie had sounded odd last night. 'What did the doctor say?'

'That he had no business discharging himself from hospital. He's got three broken ribs and a broken nose and torn muscles. The doctors said the chain mail and leather shirt saved his life. But he wouldn't stay in the hospital. Something about being too vulnerable there.'

Damn macho men everywhere. 'Where is he now?'

'In my trailer, asleep. I told the doctor I'd keep an eye on him and make him take his meds. He can't work until he's better. He can barely feed himself right now and he won't believe he's not Superman.'

Roz wasn't surprised. 'Tell him I was checking on him and to get well soon.' She forced a smile into her voice. 'And this is your chance to unleash your inner Domme and make him do what he's told.'

Cheyenne laughed, wobbly but real. 'Actually, I was hoping it would be the other way around.'

'When he's better.' She closed her phone. Typical of Frankie to insist there was nothing wrong when he had been injured because of her. How was he going to manage now? No income and bills mounting up. At least she had a few days to find a solution while Cheyenne was taking care of him, but it was up to Roz to find a long-term solution. She couldn't allow Frankie to suffer for saving her life.

Frankie's scheme to sell Nagsy to Tim O'Sullivan popped back into her head. It was a crazy idea, but at the moment it was the only plan she had. But first, she had to learn how to ride and she wasn't looking forward to it.

'Find a pair that fits you and put them on.' Andy pointed at a row of riding boots lined up against the wall in the tack room. 'I'll get you a helmet and a back protector.'

The boots were well-worn, but made from hand-sewn leather. A couple of pairs of wellies stood at the end. Up above them, a row of black helmets and velvet-covered riding hats crowded on a shelf.

While Roz checked the boots for size, Andy pulled down a pair of suede chaps and zipped himself in. Her mouth dried. Those chaps framed his ass in a way that should be illegal. She couldn't prevent an image forming in her mind of him wearing chaps without the jeans underneath, and imagining how the soft suede would feel against her inner thigh.

Down, girl she told her libido. She wasn't going to get any more deeply involved with Andy than she already was. That was the way to get her heart broken.

She watched as Andy put a saddle and bridle on a horse. He was skilled and deft, and the horse stood quietly for him.

'I didn't know you could get ginger horses,' she said

from outside the door. Now that the moment was drawing near, she was getting more nervous about riding. This horse looked like a giant.

'She's not ginger, she's chestnut. Her full name is Lough Darra Diamond, but you can call her Minty.' He led the horse into a big shed which turned out to be a covered arena, with a wood chipping floor, flood lights, mirrors high up along one wall and a little balcony for spectators.

Reluctantly Roz went to his side. Learning to ride didn't seem like such a good idea any more. Minty shuffled her feet, they were half the size of Nagsy's but still big enough to do serious damage. She smelled of leather and horse, and her back was level with Roz's eyes. 'I don't think,' she began, but Andy had grabbed hold of her left leg and boosted her into the saddle.

Roz shut her mouth with a snap. Now that she was up here, she'd make the best of it. If she was going to pull off a scam to convince Tim O'Sullivan that she owned a potential Gold Cup winning horse, she needed to be at home in the saddle. She paid attention to Andy's instructions about how to hold the reins.

'Keep a light tension on them, so that you have a gentle contact with her mouth.'

Bad choice of words. It reminded her vividly of the gentle contact with his lips last night, the one that had turned her into a mushy puddle of lust. From this angle, she could reach down and kiss that perfect mouth. Stop him talking about horses.

Andy went on. 'Now sit up straight, balance yourself so there is a straight line from your ears, through your shoulders, hips and heels. Good, that's nice.' He took the leading rope and led Minty around the little arena.

She was so high up. She had never realized how big a horse was. The ground was miles away and she had a horrible suspicion that if she fell, Minty would stand on her with those dinner plate-sized hooves.

She knew it was stupid. She had fallen from much higher while free running, but this was different. Minty stumbled slightly and Roz dropped the reins to grab her mane.

'Don't do that,' Andy snapped.

'Sorry, she startled me. This is all new. Which pedal is the brake?' she asked.

Andy stared at her with narrowed eyes. 'Okay, we're going to do this differently,' he said. He took the reins out of her hands and tied them in a knot out of her reach. Then he took away her stirrups, leaving her sitting on top of the giant horse with nothing to hold on to.

Andy backed away, playing out the leading rope and picking up a whip from the middle of the arena. He flicked it at Minty who gave him an offended look but walked on.

'Hey, what's the idea?' Roz called.

'I'm going to control the horse. Your job is to stay upright and balanced. Learn to move with the horse. Put your hands out if you need to but don't hold anything. Let your legs balance you.'

Minty walked around while Roz tried to get used to the motion, and she planned ways to torture Andy. Her spell as a Domme had taught her lots of interesting things to do that would reduce the average man to a pleading wimp. She's make him rub Deep Heat on his balls. Nipple clamps with weights on them. Freshly peeled ginger. A chastity lock. Oh yeah, now that would be real torture for Andy.

'Good, much better.' His voice recalled her surroundings. 'Now we're going to trot.'

He flicked the whip and Minty moved faster, into a jarring march that bounced Roz almost out of the saddle. She leaned forwards and grabbed the mane again.

'Sit up,' Andy said sternly. 'Balance yourself. Slide your bum deep into the saddle, feel the movement.'

'That's all I can feel, you bastard,' she muttered.

Andy laughed. 'Now, while she's trotting, I want you to recite the alphabet backwards.'

She risked taking her eyes off Minty's ears long enough to glare at Andy. 'Are you crazy?'

'Just do it.' He didn't sound as if he would change his mind.

With a bad grace she began. 'Z, Y, X, W.' She paused. It wasn't as easy as it sounded. She had to concentrate to remember what came next. 'V, U, T, S, R.' Another pause while she tried to recall the order of the letters. Andy flicked the whip gently and the horse kept trotting around. Eventually she got to 'C, B, A'.

'Well done,' Andy said. 'And do you notice how much more relaxed you are?'

Damn him, it was true. She had been so busy with the letters that she had forgotten to tense up against the movement of the horse.

'This time we're going to canter. And you're going to have your eyes shut.'

He must be out of his mind. 'You've got to be kidding me. Not going to happen.'

'Yes, you are. Trust me, I won't let anything happen to you. And I know you have courage.'

Her insides knotted, but she didn't want to back down. Resolutely, she shut her eyes. 'Go for it,' she managed.

She heard the whip crack, and Minty moved faster, going from the now familiar trot to a rocking canter. Roz fought the urge to grab onto her and concentrated on staying upright.

'Good girl,' Andy said, and something inside her warmed. 'But relax. You're not going to your death.'

'Easy for you to say,' she muttered.

'Now, keeping your eyes closed, tell me in what order her legs are moving.'

'You have got to be kidding me,' she snarled, but kept her eyes closed and paid attention to the movements she could feel beneath her. She had no idea how much time had passed before she called out, 'Right back leg first, left back leg and right front leg together, left front leg.'

'Well done, you clever girl. I've never known anyone who got it right first time.' She preened a little. 'Open your eyes.'

She was startled to see how fast she was moving. If she had known Minty was moving at this speed, she'd have freaked. Now it didn't seem so bad.

'Good girl, that was excellent,' Andy said. 'I think we'll call it a day now. You deserve a reward.'

She was stunned, pleased and a little off balance, exactly how he liked his submissives. Except that Roz wasn't his sub. But, god, the desire to get his hands on her ass was almost overwhelming.

It was her first time in the saddle, but she had the makings of a good rider. Roz had endured his commands, done everything he told her and displayed remarkable balance and a feel for the horse.

'Well done,' he said as he helped her down.

He let Minty into her stable, un-tacked her and got the grooming kit to clean her up. Roz wanted to help, so he showed her how to brush off the saddle marks. He picked up the mare's feet one by one to clean them out, and showed Roz how to do it. She was tentative picking up Minty's hooves, but handled the hoof-pick with assurance.

'Good girl,' he told her.

Her euphoric smile churned something inside him. She loved it, really loved it. A perverse imp in him decided to push her. He picked up a grape fork and handed her the long-handled tool. 'Here you go.'

A puzzled look crossed her face. 'What's that for?'

'Cleaning up after Minty.' He nodded towards the piles of horse droppings in the stable. The four-pronged tool was perfect for mucking out.

She wrinkled her nose in disgust. 'That's taking the horsey stuff too far. Why can't you do it?'

'She's your horse for now. It won't take you long. I'll see you back at the house when you're done.' Whistling, Andy headed for the door.

The clatter of the grape fork against the ground told him that she was less than pleased.

He coughed to disguise his laughter, but from the curses he could hear behind him, he knew Roz was near meltdown. Andy turned. 'You really shouldn't have done that. I'll get her settled. Have this place cleaned up when I get back.'

When he returned, the stubborn woman was standing where he had left her and the fork was lying at her feet. Oh, he loved the ones who resisted. He affected a stern voice. 'Not done yet?'

Her response was unrepeatable.

'We can deal with this in another way.'

Narrowed eyes glared at him and the set of her mouth was stubbornly defiant. 'Bring it on, Irish.'

That was a challenge if he ever heard one.

'Oh, I will.' Before she could resist, he took her firmly by the wrist and led her from the arena. It was lunchtime. The lads were probably headed for the kitchen. The tack room should be empty.

There was something about the smell of leather that went straight to his cock. Had he always been like this? He couldn't remember a time when he hadn't taken pleasure in the earthy smell. Propelling her inside, he closed the door behind them.

In the dim light of the tack room, uncertainty flickered across her face and then her mouth firmed. 'You're not my boss. You don't get to tell me what to do.'

'No,' he agreed, 'but I am your teacher, and while we're here, what I say goes.'

Roz snorted in disbelief. 'So, spank me.'

'I fully intend to.' Andy didn't bother to disguise his amusement as he towered over her. Whether she realized it or not, that was an invitation.

Outraged, she glared up at him, her blue eyes filled with anger and a hint of something else. 'You wouldn't dare.'

'Oh, I would.'

Andy rested his hands on her waist and let them fall to her hips before cupping her ass and drawing her against him. He rubbed lightly against her and his cock swelled. 'That's a virgin ass if I ever saw one. Haven't you ever been curious to know what it feels like?'

'Not a bit. I've always believed it was better to give than to receive.' She smiled sweetly at him.

Her sarky response was typically Roz, but the pink flush that coloured her cheeks made him wonder. He decided to push. Lowering his head Andy kissed a path along her jaw and bit gently on the lobe of her ear.

Her indrawn breath was delightful.

Squeezing the globes of her ass in his hands, he pulled her tightly against him. His cock had gone from half mast to raging flagpole. 'Do you know what you do to me? And in particular what a sub with an ass like this does to me?'

'Either you've got a really bulky belt buckle or it turns you on big time. What a pity that I'm not a sub.'

Andy turned his attention to her mouth, small teasing kisses that danced around the outside of her lips, but never giving her quite what she needed. 'How do you know until you try?'

Roz had been playing one role or other all her life. She might have played at being a Domme in Paris, but he didn't get the impression that her heart was in it. It was simply another disguise. Maybe he could help her find out. Reluctantly he took his hand from her jean-clad ass and brushed his thumb over one nipple. Beneath the cotton of her shirt her nipples peaked into two hard points.

Andy unbuttoned her shirt. She was wearing a pale

pink satin and lace creation that did incredible things to her breasts, pushing them upwards for his attention. Her breasts rose and fell rapidly as he kissed the valley between them.

'Andy!' The word came out in a throaty moan as she arched against him, seeking more of his searching hands and mouth. God, he was going to hell for this, but her ass was too tempting. 'Soon, baby but first . . .'

He would have loved to have taken her over his knee, but the bruise on her ribs was still purple, though now with green around the edge. He was terrified of putting any pressure on it.

Andy led her to the back of the tack room where the saddles were stored.

'Put your hands here.' He patted the seat of one saddle. Standing behind her, he brushed her hair over one shoulder so that he could see her face.

'Feet apart.' He nudged his thigh between hers, widening her stance. Pressing his palm between her shoulder blades, he made her lean forwards.

'How do you feel?' he asked.

'Weird, and strangely aroused,' she admitted.

'Go with it. I promise not to hurt you.'

Much, he added under his breath. In this position, he didn't know whether he wanted to fuck her or spank her. Probably both.

'You can stop me at any time, but I promise you won't want to.'

'Cocky bastard,' she murmured.

His first blow landed on the middle of her right cheek and she jerked in surprise, but didn't cry out. He rubbed the spot gently before raising his hand again. He found his rhythm, alternating light spanks with soothing rubs. Her breath quickened and Andy increased the force of the blows, watching her face and body for signs that it was too much.

His cock ached for release. He had never been so hard in his life. Andy paused to kiss her, brushing away the damp tendrils of hair that clung to her face. 'Six more. Can you take it?'

She turned her head and smiled at him. 'Oh, you've started? I thought that was a massage after the riding.'

The brat. He'd make sure she felt the last six.

The sharp crack of his hand against her ass was loud in the darkened room. Her jagged breaths turned to gasps and she cried out at the final blow. Roz sagged against the saddle and Andy gathered her in his arms. Her eyes were bright, her expression slightly dazed. She had never been so beautiful.

How the hell did he do it? The delicious warmth from her ass interfered with her indignation that he had spanked her. What had come over her to allow it?

But she knew. It was the riding lesson, where she had put herself into his hands and had committed to obeying all his directions without question. He hadn't let her down. She was no expert, but she knew that she had come further in one single lesson than most people did in several, all thanks to Andy.

Those instructions had triggered a submissive side of

her she hadn't known existed, allowing her to put herself into his hands, trusting him to take care of her.

She grinned. And she had a bratty side too. Who knew? But the temptation to tease him had been irresistible. He had looked so outraged when she had asked him if he had started yet.

She couldn't wait to tease him again.

18

He had been home less than a week. Andy didn't know how his mother had mustered together a celebratory lunch for twenty so quickly. Poppy should come with a health warning. What sort of torture was she planning to inflict on him today? The crunch of tyres on gravel told him that the guests were already beginning to arrive.

He hurried along the corridor to the blue room and tapped on the door before entering. Roz was standing in front of the mirror and every stitch she possessed was strewn across the bed. She wore a dark grey silk bra that pushed her breasts up like an indecent offering. The tiny thong concealed far too little. Those things should be declared illegal.

She held up another dress against her before discarding it.

'I have nothing to wear,' she complained before reaching for another outfit.

'That's not what my credit card says.'

Roz shot him a dark look. 'It's okay for you. You know all of these people. When I go downstairs, every one of them is going to judge me.'

So that was what the panic was about. Andy crossed the room quickly and took the offending garment from her hands, tossing it over his shoulder. He turned her towards the mirror.

'Those people are my friends and they are meeting the

new lady of Lough Darra. Of course they will judge you, and I'd be a liar if I told you otherwise.'

Roz closed her eyes. She was as taut as a tightly drawn bowstring and he suspected she was battling tears. Roz never cried.

'Open your eyes and look at me.'

Reluctantly, she blinked and opened them, holding his gaze in the mirror. Andy cupped her breast, marvelling at how it fitted perfectly into his hand. He adored women, especially their ripe, fleshy softness. Give him a happy woman with curves any day, over a miserable one who spent her life on a diet.

He tweaked her tender nipple until it peaked. 'Yes, they will judge you but I want you to remember that this belongs to me and that you are amazing.'

When she didn't respond, he pinched hard, awaiting a response.

'Bastard,' Roz hissed, but passion was already stirring in those sapphire blue eyes.

Andy laughed. Her response wasn't the one he wanted but if she was angry at him, she wouldn't be anxious about meeting the others. 'A lady shouldn't use language like that and expect to get away with it.'

Still holding her breast, he pulled her against him while he stroked the soft skin of her abdomen.

Roz closed her eyes and leaned into him.

He slipped his fingers inside the scrap of silk. Christ, she was already wet. Her head fell back on his shoulder, her breath quickening as he stroked her clit lightly.

His cock roared to life at her soft moan. Andy rubbed against her, letting her know how much he wanted her.

The perfume of her sex filled his nostrils. He wanted to bury his face between her thighs, to devour her. But this wasn't about him. This was supposed to be teaching Roz a lesson about approval.

She was magnificent. There wasn't a man downstairs who wouldn't want her the moment he saw her. Why did she doubt herself? Abandoning the tender nub, he plunged his index finger inside her.

'Oh god.' She arched against his searching hand, seeking more pressure.

Andy pushed a second finger into her, fucking her slowly, stopping and starting with no apparent rhythm so that she came close, but couldn't come. Her inner muscles squeezed his fingers, needing something hard.

The urge to fuck her was almost overwhelming. His cock was rigid against his zipper, almost painful. Andy withdrew his fingers and her eyes flew open.

'You can't stop like . . .'

'Oh, I can.'

To make a point, he plunged his fingers inside her again, using more force this time, giving her the pressure that she needed, bringing her right to the edge, before withdrawing them once more. Concentrating instead on her clit, he rubbed lightly until she was squirming mindlessly against him.

He stopped again.

She was still fighting him. He ignored the muttered expletives. 'Open your eyes and look at me.'

He eased down the straps of her bra, exposing her breasts, before plumping them in his hands. 'While we are together, these belong to me.'

Cruising along the curve of her waist, he stroked his way down her body. The scrap of grey silk was darkened with dampness. He slipped one hand between her thighs. 'And this belongs to me.'

This time, her gaze was defiant but she remained silent. Changing tactics, he brushed her hair over one shoulder and nibbled a path along her shoulder and neck. Her eyelashes fluttered closed and opened again. Her breasts quivered as her breathing quickened.

'Stop worrying about what other people think of you. When you go downstairs there isn't a man that won't want you or a woman that won't be jealous of you.'

'Andy, I —'

'Hush, baby. No matter how you see yourself, you'll be wonderful.'

Her nod was barely perceptible. Not a ringing endorsement or an enthusiastic agreement, but then nothing with Roz would ever come easily.

Blood raced in his veins and his cock throbbed urgently, seeking release. He couldn't go downstairs in this state and neither could she. Andy released her gently and fetched the antique footstool from the window alcove. It was exactly the right height for what he had in mind. The lesson wasn't over yet.

He placed the footstool in front of the mirror, watching with amusement as realization dawned in her eyes. Roz wanted him. Her body craved him. He had brought her to the cusp, time and time again until she was quivering, but would she submit to him like this?

'Take them off. I want you naked for this.'

Lust and defiance fought for the upper hand. If looks

could kill, he would have been a dead man. Her chin shot up and she reached for the clasp on her bra and tossed it onto the bed. She shimmied out of the damp thong and his breath caught in his throat. No matter how many times he saw her naked, it always filled him with wonder. How could she think that she was anything but beautiful?

A soft dusting of red covered her mons and the pale creamy skin of her thighs made him want to lick every inch of them. His balls ached. He couldn't wait until he was undressed. He grabbed a condom and fumbled with his leather belt. He wished they had more time to play, but that would have to wait until later.

'Good girl,' he said as she bent over the footstool.

He wanted to lick every inch of her perfect back, every bone of her spine and the small beauty mark above her rounded ass. He nudged her thighs apart and held his cock poised at her entrance. Dragging his eyes away from her he looked in the mirror at the vision before him.

Him, fully clothed. Roz, gloriously naked, awaiting his pleasure. It was the perfect portrait of submission, except that he was the one who was enslaved. He pressed his finger inside her, pleased when she moaned loudly and squirmed beneath him. Slowly, he inched inside her tight, wet sheath. His balls tightened, threatening to explode like a horny teenager on his first outing. This hard, aching, never-ending wanting of her was more than sex. Andy withdrew almost to the tip and plunged in again, harder this time.

'Oh please, Andy. Yes. Like that.'

There was no time for finesse. This would be a short, hard ride. Grasping a handful of her hair, he pulled her head back, forcing her to look at their reflections. He thrust again and again, setting a hard, relentless rhythm that had them both gasping.

The primal in him was claiming his woman. Fucking her. Owning her. The urge to mark Roz was savage in its intensity. He wanted to bite her and the thought both horrified and excited him. Slowing his thrusts, he leaned over her, pinning her against the striped damask.

He licked at the tender spot where her neck joined her shoulder and bit.

'Harder,' she gasped, writhing against him. Roz was mindless, hovering, about to fall.

He bit down, sucking at her flesh, licking and swirling his tongue. When he pulled away, the mark was livid against her skin. His mark on his woman. He straightened, and slammed into her once more, sending her over.

She shuddered beneath him, screaming into the padding of the footstool. As he continued to thrust, her tight sheath convulsed around him. It was too much, he couldn't hold back any longer. He roared as his own release overtook him.

Andy clung to her until the thundering of his heart slowed and his breathing returned to something that resembled normal. He raised his head. He was too strong, too big and too heavy for her. 'Did I hurt you?' he asked anxiously.

Her small, self-satisfied sigh reassured him and he relaxed, closing his eyes, savouring the musky scent of her sweat and the feel of her passion-damp skin. What he had experienced with her was more than the sum of all his previous sexual encounters. Roz was a siren. She had lured him in, fed his fantasies and now he was as helpless as she was.

Andy ignored the Medusa-like gaze his mother fixed him with when they arrived late for pre-lunch drinks. But her expression softened when they were suddenly surrounded by friends and relatives, all anxious to meet the new lady of the house.

Roz bore the attention well, although Andy knew from the tension in her shoulders that she wasn't comfortable or enjoying it. To a rapt audience she re-told the story of their meeting at the Eiffel Tower – although her version was a sanitized version of what had really happened. Worse still was her story of how he had pursued her for almost a year before she agreed to date him. That was stretching it a bit, but he let her have her little victory. He shot her a look which promised retribution later.

Roz batted her eyelashes at him before alluding to his reputation with the ladies and everybody laughed. She had them in the palm of her hand.

'You're well caught now, laddie,' his elderly uncle proclaimed.

Even his father smiled at that one. Dougal believed that he was finally getting the stay-at-home son that he wanted. Andy didn't know how he was going to break it to him that they would be leaving within a week.

The gong in the hall sounded the call to lunch. As they moved down the hallway, the doorbell rang. Maggie opened it and a tanned brunette greeted her with a beaming smile.

Spotting Andy, she launched herself at him, planting a wet kiss on his mouth.

Behind them, someone coughed and she pulled away and laughed. Ariana McMahon hadn't changed a bit in the two years since he had last seen her.

'Sorry, but I'm so excited to see you. My answering machine garbled some of my messages. When were you going to tell me you were home?'

Fuck. How the hell was he going to get out of this mess?

Gently but firmly, he disentangled himself from Ariana's grasp. 'You're just in time for lunch.'

Ever the gracious hostess, Poppy stepped forwards and took Ariana's arm and led her towards the dining room. 'I'll have Maggie set another place.'

Although his mother had seated them side by side, Roz might as well have been a million miles away. She was poised, even gracious when someone asked her a question, but icily polite to him. Was she upset about Ariana kissing him? Roz knew their engagement was a fake. Not that there was anything serious between Ariana and him, but he couldn't ignore the waves of hostility aimed at him.

Across the table Ariana was staring at him, shocked. His mother had obviously told her the news and she wasn't happy about it. That was another mess he would have to clean up.

They had been lovers a long time ago, but both spent so much time abroad that their relationship was impossible to sustain. They had settled into a pattern of hooking up when they were home for some pleasant, no-strings fun. Or at least that's what it had been to him. But looking at her face now, he realized that he had seriously miscalculated.

After the main course was cleared away, Maggie carried in a towering croquembouche decorated with spun sugar. She hadn't forgotten that profiteroles were his favourite dessert, and this creation was spectacular.

Dougal poured champagne and tapped his glass, demanding attention.

'My dear friends, the past few years have been quite eventful for Poppy and me. We have known great sadness after the loss of our son, Robert, who was a driving force in modernizing the Lough Darra stables.

'Now we are entering a new phase. Although you might not have noticed, Poppy and I are getting on a bit and we feel that it's time for us to hand over the reins.'

He glanced across the table. 'Andrew has never failed to surprise me and this week he has surpassed himself by bringing home a new filly. Roz is a feisty girl and she has proven that she is more than capable of handling my son. I hope that they can look forward to a long, happy run together.'

His speech was followed by applause and the clinking of glasses.

Damn it. Andy's eyes were suspiciously wet. His father was handing over the estate to him if he wanted it and he didn't know how he was going to tell him the truth.

He slipped his hand beneath the table seeking Roz's hand, but had to grit his teeth when she dug her nails into his wrist. She was worse than a feral kitten. What had happened in the hall wasn't his fault. How the hell was he to know that Ariana would turn up? Roz might be mad at him, but there was no way that he was putting up with that.

Andy stood up and raised his glass. 'I'd like you all to join me in a toast – to my darling Roz, who has led me on a merry dance for the past year. May she enjoy everything that Lough Darra has to offer.'

And he would ensure that she did.

He bent his head to kiss her, knowing that she couldn't refuse without causing the mother of all scenes. Not content with a perfunctory embrace, he took full advantage, teasing her mouth open and flicking his tongue against hers. When he broke the kiss and pulled away, her eyes sparked at him.

'You'll pay for this,' she murmured.

Andy smiled. 'I fully intend to.'

After lunch, Poppy took some of her guests to see the gardens while his father headed for the stables to show off his latest acquisition. Andy watched as Roz slipped upstairs. He needed to speak to her, but he couldn't do it now.

'I hope I didn't upset your fiancée,' Ariana said.

'Do you usually snog a guy at his own engagement party?' he asked.

She glared at him. 'It would have been nice to know about that before I made an ass of myself. I got back from Africa last night to a garbled invitation on my machine from Poppy. But nothing at all from you. No hint that you were settling down to play house with someone else.'

Even when they were together, their relationship hadn't been serious. Ariana had no right to act like this. And there was no way that he was telling her the truth about his relationship with Roz. 'Sorry, but your little display was a bit awkward. Roz is new here, she doesn't know anyone.'

'Which is about as much as anyone seems to know about her! I never heard of her before today. What's going on? And before you give me some bullshit answer, this is me, remember? Not some bimbo blonde you picked up in a bar.'

'I do not pick up bimbos.'

'Really? Do you give them an IQ test first?'

Her chest heaved. Andy had never seen her in such a temper. She was hurt and jealous and he couldn't face another woman who was angry with him. 'Maybe I should have told you first. But things with Roz happened pretty suddenly.'

Like a week ago. Andy closed his eyes when he remembered his first sighting of Roz in the moneylender's shop. But even if it hadn't been her, he would never have settled down with Ariana.

'You told me that you wouldn't get involved because of your job.'

'Aye, I did.' Until now, his life had revolved around blowing up the world or trying to save it. Nothing had changed.

Ariana huffed out a breath. 'I waited for you. I thought that if I gave you your freedom, you'd eventually come home.'

Something crystallized inside his head. He didn't want this life. There was nothing for him here. He didn't want the life that had been mapped out for him by someone else. He didn't want to be part of another generation of McTavishes who sacrificed themselves for a few acres of land or a rambling house that had seen better days. Whether she realized it or not, Roz and he were alike. Two halves of the same coin.

'I'm sorry.' There was nothing else he could say.

Ariana blinked and nodded. 'I'm sorry too.'

Andy was tempted to hug her, but that might make things worse. Instead, he patted her on the shoulder. 'What will you do now?'

'I'm involved in organizing the big fundraiser next week. I have to hang around for that but afterwards? I don't know. Go back to Africa, maybe. We won't meet again.'

He didn't want their friendship to end like this. 'You promised Poppy you'd come to dinner tomorrow night.'

Ariana shook her head. 'That will be the last time.'

She let herself out the front door and didn't look back.

19

The following morning Roz was almost grateful when Dougal insisted on taking her out to show her around the estate. Not that she wanted to give the suspicious old man any more opportunities to grill her, but at least it meant she didn't have to think about Andy and Ariana.

Even their names were a perfect match. Andrew and Ariana. Ariana and Andy. They sounded so good together. Both tall and beautiful and assured.

Roz knew that this interlude with Andy was no more than that, an interlude. She wasn't his fiancée, had no real claim on him. The sex was amazing, but she had a suspicion that Andy had amazing sex with everyone. He could rock her world, but she wasn't rocking his.

She had let him spank her, and had enjoyed it. The intensity of the connection between them had been a revelation. When he came to her room, she had surrendered to his command. That had never happened with her before. Andy did something that no one else could. He had gotten under her skin, and she had to get him out.

Dougal stamped along beside her, leaning on a stick but holding his own weight. For all that he complained about being slow, he kept up a fair pace, refusing to allow his weakness to prevent him doing what he wanted. An elderly greyhound trotted along beside him, a silent shadow to her master.

Fortunately for her, Dougal wasn't any more loquacious outside than he was at the table. He led her out through the walled yard. 'Chicken coop,' he said, pointing at a wooden house on stilts. There was a fence around it, but the gate was open, and a couple of dozen hens were dotted around the field, pecking at the ground and occasionally chasing each other. One pulled a worm out of the soil and ate with enthusiasm.

She had never considered where eggs really came from, beyond refusing to buy eggs from battery farms, and had never seen real hens with her own eyes. 'Can I have a look inside?' she asked.

'Sure.' Dougal held the greyhound's collar to stop her following Roz. She climbed up the little gangway plank into the wooden coop. Inside were rows of hay-filled boxes, two of which had eggs sitting in them. She touched one. It was warm. An egg so fresh it was still warm from the hen. A hen sitting in a box in the corner clucked threateningly at Roz, so she didn't approach any closer.

There was something soothing about the smell and dim light. This was real.

She climbed out, blinking in the sun, and allowed Dougal to show her around.

The kitchen garden was huge, full of vegetables that she had never seen growing before. Roz was wide-eyed at the sight of cauliflowers, cabbage, broccoli, beetroot and carrots. 'What is that?' She pointed at the green bushes that dominated one side of the garden.

Dougal gave her an odd look. 'Potatoes.'

Damn, she was giving herself away. 'I grew up in London, we never grew our own food.'

He led her out to the fields surrounding the house. 'These are our dairy cows, Holsteins and Jerseys. They supply all our milk for drinking, butter, cheese and plenty left over to sell to the dairy. I'll show you the milking parlour later.'

There were beef cattle, goats, sheep and deer.

She loved the orchard and couldn't resist a wistful thought that Lough Darra would be a great place to live. There was something about it that appealed to her. The slow pace, the predictability of it, was completely different from her usual life.

Andy was so lucky. And he had no idea how lucky he was. He took this life for granted.

'Did you enjoy riding Minty?' Dougal asked, showing that in spite of his talk about retiring, he knew everything that went on.

What could she say that wouldn't blow her cover? 'It was good. I was out of practice, so Andy put me through the basics again.'

Dougal grunted.

There was no sign of Andy when she got back to the house. It was no business of hers where he was, she reminded herself fiercely. He was a free agent, able to spend time with anyone he liked.

She spent the afternoon posing for Poppy, who insisted on painting her until it was time to change for dinner.

The dining room was full of glitter and colour when she arrived downstairs. Damn it, her beautifully cut navy blue dress was just a shade too conservative. The men were in black dinner jackets and the women wore slinky silk dresses and sparkling jewels.

Poppy, resplendent in black satin and pearls, came forwards to greet her. 'My dear, you look so elegant. Come and meet your future neighbours.'

Of course Ariana was there, wearing a white dress which showed off her tan, and what looked like a fortune in diamonds. She greeted Roz warmly and introduced her to a string of local girls and their brothers.

How many of the girls had Andy slept with? Roz wondered. It was none of her business.

She sat beside Andy at dinner, with Ariana on his other side.

She was starving, but waited to see what spoon everyone else picked up before she started to eat. As usual, the soup was wonderful.

When she tuned back into the conversation, Ariana had the table rolling around in laughter.

'Once, when I was eating in a tribal chief's house in Namibia, I tried to stick a fork into what turned out to be a sheep's eyeball and ended up flipping it at him.'

Andy laughed. 'Why am I not surprised? You were always a klutz. Remember the time you tripped up when you were getting your prize from the Dean and ended up pulling his trousers down?'

A dark haired man with a Northern accent so strong Roz had difficulty understanding it, joined in. 'You can pull mine down any day.'

Ariana narrowed her eyes at him. 'Another comment like that, Rory Baxter, and I'm telling your mother about you and the Hayes twins.'

Rory threw up his hands in defeat. 'Please, not that. My mother is terrifying, the worst example of an Irish mammy I've ever met.'

'I'll back my Irish mammy against yours any day,' Ariana said. 'Andy has no idea how lucky he is to have Poppy.'

'You haven't seen her when she's annoyed,' Andy said. 'Were you there the time she was judging at the gymkhana and someone beat a pony? I thought blood would flow.'

The banter flowed around the table, and Roz could feel herself becoming invisible. She had nothing to contribute to the conversation. These people all knew each other, had a history together. It was Ariana who noticed her silence. 'So tell us what you got up to when you were at college? I'm so jealous of you going to La Sorbonne. You must be fabulous at languages.'

This was worse. Every eye turned to her, waiting for stories of life at a French university. Roz shrugged. 'It was uni, you know. Nothing special except it was in French.'

Ariana gave her a funny look. 'Yes, I suppose most unis are much the same,' she said with a smile. 'What were you studying?'

Crap, crap, crap. Was Ariana suspicious? What could she say? Her mind blanked. 'Philosophy,' she managed.

'Oh, I'd love to know what the French make of Bishop Berkeley,' Ariana sighed.

Who was that? Why the hell hadn't she said computer science? She could talk about computers without making a fool of herself.

She concentrated on her plate and listened to the conversation. Rory was a civil rights lawyer in Belfast, Ariana headed up an agency which worked for famine relief. Roz couldn't even hate them with a clear conscience.

It wasn't their fault. They were perfectly nice people who had grown up together and had known each other all their lives. She was the interloper, the one who didn't belong. And she didn't want to be here, it was all Andy's fault for dragging her along.

He didn't owe her anything. She was probably getting in the way of his affair with Ariana. He was keeping her safe until Hall was arrested. He wasn't really her fiancé. She was just being stupid.

Of course, ignoring him like this was making her conspicuous. She could feel the eyes on her, wondering what Andy McTavish could see in her. She was the stranger, the one who didn't fit in. At least he could pretend to be in love with her.

Instead he was flirting with Ariana who would probably end up winning a Nobel peace prize, and Isobel and the other girl whose name she couldn't remember.

Her anger grew as the meal progressed. When the coffee was being served, she fumbled the cream jug. A trail of pale liquid spattered across the front of the navy dress. It was the last straw. She excused herself, went to her room and changed into a clinging red dress that displayed all her curves in loving detail. She might not have grown up with a silver spoon in her mouth, but she had her own talents. And it was time Andy got a taste of them. She'd show him that she didn't care. She'd have every man in the room at her feet.

By the time she was ready, coffee was finished and the

guests had moved into the large sitting room. Poppy had told her earlier that she was going to clear the space in the centre of the room to allow room for dancing.

This house was so old-fashioned that Roz wouldn't have been surprised to find Poppy had imported a string quartet to provide the music, but she could hear 'So What' on the other side of the door. Unless Pink had been invited, it was courtesy of a modern sound system. Of course, it was entirely possibly that someone like Poppy was best friends with Pink.

Roz smoothed her dress over her hips, making sure that her tightened bra made the best of her boobs. She checked her reflection in the big mirror in the hall. Her eye shadow was smoky, her lashes ridiculously long and her mouth was scarlet.

Breathe, breathe, breathe. She was Roz Spring. She was a goddess.

Time for action.

Roz pushed the door open wide, waited for three heart beats and walked into the room. No, she didn't walk, she stalked in, allowing the height of her heels to make her hips sway seductively. She moved deliberately, allowing the men to see her as she made her way to the sound system.

Andy was there, chatting to Lily and Ariana. No, not chatting, flirting. She could read body language, and she knew when women wanted a man. They were welcome to him.

'Can you put on 'Halo' by Beyoncé?' she asked the awe-struck blond guy who had a stack of CDs.

He stuttered something and dropped two discs before he fumbled one into the slot.

Yes, it was working. It was amazing. This guy had been sitting opposite her at dinner and had barely noticed her. One red dress, a slick of lipstick and a new attitude later, he was practically slobbering.

Roz had never understood what it was that men saw when they looked at her. She had the normal bits of any other woman, breasts a bit smaller than she'd have liked, hips a bit bigger, lips an odd shape. She liked her legs which were lean, but worried that the calves were too muscular. All ordinary. When she was running a scam, she could look like Ms Average. She could blend into the background.

But when she put on her Domme attitude, she could reduce men to a quivering heap.

Andy thought she was some helpless girl who needed his protection? She'd show him how much she needed his attention.

The beat began and she sauntered out into the centre of the improvised dance floor. She spotted Rory chatting to Brenda, who was gazing up at him with rapt attention. She caught his eye and beckoned him over.

As if mesmerized, he abandoned Brenda and went straight to her side. 'You look amazing,' he told Roz.

'Thank you,' she said throatily. 'You're looking pretty hot yourself. Do you like to dance?'

'Love it,' he said, and took her into his arms. With her five-inch heels, she was almost on eye-level with him. She didn't allow him to pull her too close, but swayed slowly to the beat. As she danced, she smiled at him. 'You dance well.'

He was dazzled. She knew from experience that if she

had ordered him to his knees, he would obey. This wasn't the time or place, but she had him. When the music ended, she pulled away from him slowly.

She allowed her eyes to drift around the crowd. Every man in the room was looking at her. She caught glances and subtly indicated that they could approach her. Ten seconds later, she was in the centre of a masculine crowd, all vying for her notice.

Andy kept one eye on Roz as he pretended to pay attention to his elderly aunt. He should have known he'd pay for Ariana's little stunt at lunch the other day. Roz had frozen him out – completely.

He was supposed to be building her up, making her feel more confident, not undermining her. Roz was a rough diamond. He had seen her file. All the stuff she had told his family about the Sorbonne and Oxford was a pack of lies. She was an outsider who wanted to fit in. Hell, it didn't matter to him that she didn't have a fancy degree. He'd hated every minute of school. In a lot of ways, she fitted in here better than he did.

After the disastrous lunch, she had locked the door to her bedroom and refused to open it when he tried to apologize. She pleaded a headache the following morning until he left for Belfast on an errand for his father.

Miraculously, she recovered almost the moment he was gone and had spent the day posing for Poppy and admiring his father's livestock. His father pronounced that she had a good eye for an animal. High praise indeed, coming from Dougal. They were already falling under her spell, so much so that they hadn't noticed what she'd been up to for the past hour. But he had.

Roz had finally shown her true colours. She was a vixen in a red dress and there wasn't a man in the room that wasn't lusting after her. Including him. Rory, the impertinent bastard, had the nerve to put his hand on the bare skin of her back while they were dancing. He had glowered at him until, sensing that he was treading on dangerous ground, Rory had put his hands in his pockets.

Andy wanted to kill every man in the room. Instead he smiled politely and tilted his head to listen to his aunt rambling on about property prices. When Poppy distracted his aunt long enough for him to make his escape, Andy picked up his drink and made a beeline for the laughing group at the other end of the room.

Ariana intercepted him. 'I don't think she needs to be rescued.'

'That wasn't what I had in mind.'

She raised one dark brow and then broke into a grin. 'I don't believe it. Andy McTavish is actually jealous. Someone pinch me.'

'Don't tempt me. You may not like the results.'

Andy ignored her laughter and took a deep breath. She was right. He couldn't wade in there like a bull in a china shop. Roz might be mad at him, but he was willing to bet that she wouldn't make a scene in front of her new friends.

He left the room and went in search of Maggie. 'I need a favour. I want you to wait for precisely ten minutes and then take this to Roz.'

Andy handed her a folded piece of paper. He didn't believe in fighting fair, but then, neither did she. He took up position in the library, closed the curtains, switched off the lamps except for the small one beside the old-fashioned telephone. As an afterthought, he locked the second door. He didn't want anyone disturbing them. He and Roz were due some alone time.

He was standing in a dim alcove when the door opened. A scarlet-clad figure moved swiftly to the telephone and picked up the receiver. 'Frankie? How did you get this number?'

Andy locked the door and pocketed the key.

She turned, receiver still in hand. It didn't take more than a few seconds for her to realize that she had walked into a trap. He had to hand it to her. Roz barely blinked. She carefully replaced the receiver and walked past him, until she reached the other door.

'It's locked,' he said.

She muttered something under her breath and released the handle. Roz turned, straightened her shoulders and sashayed towards him with all the confidence of a runway model.

She held out her palm. 'Key.'

'Kiss, and I'll think about it.' He knew that he was provoking her, but Andy didn't care. Anything was preferable to being ignored.

Roz smiled sweetly at him. 'I'll kiss you again when hell freezes over. Now, why don't you be a good boy and give me the key? I'm sure Miss Sweetness and Light is missing you.'

'Ariana?' He pretended not to understand.

The slight flush on her cheekbones and the tiny pulse

that hammered in her neck were the only signs that she was struggling for control.

'Why would she be looking for me?' he asked.

An impatient noise escaped her and her blue eyes filled with anger. She was going to blow. 'You kissed her at our engagement party. You spent the whole time discussing Bishop freaking Berkeley and you couldn't wait to get back to Belfast so that you could hook up with her again.'

'Did anyone ever tell you that you look beautiful when you're angry?' His words were enough to push her over the edge.

Andy almost welcomed the blow that struck his cheek. She didn't get a chance to repeat it. He grasped her wrist and twisted her arm behind her back. Roz stumbled on her heels and he took the opportunity to immobilize her other arm and pull her into his embrace.

Roz stood stiff and unyielding in his arms, her chest rising and falling quickly, drawing attention to the magnificent breasts he had lusted after all evening.

'My face is up here,' she snapped.

'Why, so it is.'

His first assault was on her jaw, a light, barely there brush of his mouth. Taking his time, he worked his way down her neck, nibbling, and sucking at her tender skin. He blew softly on her pulse point and she shivered, but she wasn't giving in so easily.

'If you think that you can romance me into forgiving you with a few kisses –'

'I have no intention of romancing you. In fact, I believe you're due a punishment.'

'What?'

Andy took advantage of her outrage. He released her hands and quickly hefted her over his shoulder, giving her a sharp smack on the ass for good measure. Ignoring the thumps on his back, he carried her to the corner of the library and with his free hand found the locking mechanism which made a section of shelves swing out.

'You bastard. Where are you taking me?'

Andy switched on the light and made his way down the narrow staircase. Behind him he heard a thunk as the shelves swung back into place. 'I thought you'd like a tour of my dungeon.'

The secret room was one of the oldest parts of the house. His father speculated that it had been intended to be used as a small wine cellar, for the stuff that had been smuggled during the Napoleonic wars. Thankfully, Dougal had never got around to fitting it out.

A few rusted metal fittings on the walls had made Andy speculate that he might have had a kinky ancestor or a serial killer in the family. Either way, he had long ago commandeered the space as his personal gym. Most of the equipment was innocent enough, but with a little imagination, it could be used for a naughtier purpose.

Roz was spitting like a feral kitten when he set her down on a padded bench. 'Are you out of your freaking mind?'

20

She stared around her. The windowless space was illumin-
ated by recessed lighting and looked modern and
luxurious. There was a sinister wooden frame in one corner, a padded bench, a wide divan covered by red plush
covers that looked temptingly soft to the touch, and shiny
new hooks on the walls and the roof.

'What do you think you're going to do to me, you overgrown ox?' Roz wasn't going to let him get away with this.
'You can't just drag me off to your man cave.'

Andy smiled, not a nice smile, and something quivered
and melted inside her. 'I just did. You've had enough time
showing off. Now it's time to pay the piper.'

'I was enjoying myself for the first time all evening. Up
'til then, everyone was ignoring me, including you.' It was
surprising how much that hurt.

His narrowed eyes were intent on her. 'I'm not ignoring
you now.'

No, the intensity that radiated from him was so strong
she was branded by it. The room was warm enough that
she felt overdressed. She had a suspicion that Andy
intended to remedy that soon and a tiny part of her welcomed the idea.

Not that she would ever tell him. It was time to put him
straight about something. She straightened up so that she
could look him in the eye. To her annoyance, he was taller

than her. 'Let's be clear here. You're pretty, and I think with the right training, you could be a good sub. But I don't have time to train you.'

She spoke with the tone of absolute certainty that she used when she was dealing with a new submissive. One of the things Dad had taught her was that people reacted according to your attitude. Of course, he had been thinking of dressing like a cop and getting people to hand over their car, shop takings or credit card details, but it worked in other ways too. Adopt an 'obey or die' attitude and men always did what she told them.

Always.

Andy laughed. 'Oh Roz, you're magnificent. I could watch you command every man in the house. But not me. While we're here, I'm in charge.'

He picked her up and kissed her open mouth before she could splutter at him.

The kiss was hot and proprietary and said more clearly than words that Andy was claiming her.

'You must be out of your –' Before she could finish the sentence, he kissed her again, even more forcefully.

'And now it's time to teach you who is in charge.'

He set her on her feet and pulled her zipper down slowly. The form-fitting dress was tight enough that it would peel apart as soon as it was unzipped. By the time his hand had reached her hips, only the pressure of his chest was keeping it up. If she pushed him away, her dress would fall to the floor.

Roz was torn between wanting to see his eyes when the dress fell, and enjoying the feeling of his arms around her.

They'd had sex. Hot, sweaty, breathless sex, but she

craved the feeling of his skin against hers more than an orgasm.

Hell, orgasms were easy. She could do that herself with her fingers and a few wicked images, not necessarily of Andy. Throw in a battery-powered rabbit and she could come in under a minute. It was a physical reaction. Nothing more. Do this and this at that pressure for this amount of time, and enjoy the ride.

But the heat and smell and feel of another human being holding her in his arms? That was valuable and something she didn't want to lose. If he wanted to delude himself that he could dominate her, it was a small price to pay to feed her skin hunger.

Andy pushed her back enough to allow the dress to fall and unclipped her bra. A small, detached part of her mind noticed that he was far too practised at that. But the heat in his eyes as he looked down at her was real. Her nipples pebbled under his intent gaze and he touched them with a wondering fingertip. 'Such beauties. The things I'm going to do to them.'

She stood before him wearing a tiny pair of red panties and smoke-grey hold-up stockings. She was five foot seven, and when she wore heels, she was taller than most men. Andy topped her by a few inches and next to his sinewy strength, she felt petite and delicate.

The expression in his eyes was avid and determined. Andy was going to have her.

She couldn't decide if she was hopelessly turned on, or annoyed. Damn it, she wasn't one of his mousey little country girls who did whatever he said. He didn't impress her with the Lord of the Manor thing. But the firmness of his mouth, the flare of his nostrils, was impossibly tempting.

'Very nice,' he said, his voice a little hoarse. 'I usually like suspenders but those hold-ups look good on you. Now, lose the knickers.'

'What?'

'You heard me.'

He expected her to take down her own panties, bare herself to his eyes? Make herself vulnerable and available to whatever he planned to do to her? He must be out of his mind. She wasn't going to do that.

'This isn't fair. I'm almost naked and you're fully dressed.'

It was almost funny how fast Andy ripped off his shirt. Buttons flew as he yanked at it. Too late, he realized he had forgotten to take off his cuff links and had to pull the shirt up again while he fought to get them free. He dropped the pieces of gold on the floor, not bothering to see where they landed.

His chest was as magnificent as she remembered. His muscles were sharply defined and the tanned skin gleamed. The light dusting of hair was enough to stop him being too pretty and looking like a model. His chest rose and fell as he stared at her.

'Now you.'

Roz slid a finger inside the elastic and eased it away from her skin. It slipped down an inch. She gave a little wiggle and it fell all the way to her feet. 'The stockings stay on,' she told him.

'If they do, I will rip them off,' he warned her.

He had paid for them, so he would be ripping his own

stockings, but damn it, Roz wasn't used to owning anything this gorgeous. She didn't want to ruin them. She eased them down her thighs, making a point of drawing it out like a burlesque dancer, teasing him. It was fun watching his eyes narrow as she slowed her movements still more. She had him. Men were so predictable.

But when the stockings were off, he dragged her close, his grip showing no weakness. Her breasts were pressed against his chest and she caught her breath at the sheer perfection of the contact. He had the right amount of hair to cushion and tease her nipples to aching hardness, and his heat warmed her from the inside out.

To her surprise, he turned her around so her back was to him as he picked up a coil of rope. It was pink and she caught the distinctive scent of hemp.

'I don't like to be tied,' she said. Allowing someone else that much power over her had always freaked her, even in her imagination. She knew, with a bone deep certainty, that she had to stay in control, no matter what. She couldn't afford to be vulnerable. The risk was too high.

Andy shook his head. 'You need it. I've watched you. You're always planning, always thinking four moves ahead.'

'Five,' she snapped.

'And you need to relax. I'm going to tie you up, so that you don't have to do anything.'

'You're going to tie me up, no matter how I feel, is that it? Don't I get a say?' Her anger was rising at his high-handedness.

And something else, which she refused to acknowledge.

'Sure you do. Say the word "Bunny" and I stop. In fact, everything stops. I tell my parents what we're doing and tell Niall to get someone else to look after you.'

'That's blackmail.'

'No, it's your safe word. It safe words you out of this entire situation, but I don't want you to use it lightly.' He held up the coil of pink rope. 'Shall we begin?'

She turned her head to stare at him in frustration. Damn it, she didn't like being tied up and out of control, but she didn't want to stop him either. The thought of Poppy's face when she realized Roz wasn't her future daughter-in-law haunted her. She didn't want to see her disappointment.

'Oh, very well. But don't take all night, I'd like to get back to the party,' she said.

Andy laughed. 'I'll do my best to keep you entertained.'

He whipped the rope out to its full length, before looping it around her chest, above and below her breasts, knotting it at the back, then wrapping a couple of loops around her breasts.

'Rope gives me better uplift than a Wonderbra,' Roz told him, amazed by the effect.

'You ain't seen nothing yet,' Andy drawled in a fake American accent. His expert fingers fastened the knots rapidly before pulling her hands behind her and tying those too.

'Hey!' she protested.

It didn't stop him; he did something to the loops and her wrists were securely tied behind her. She tugged. The position wasn't uncomfortable and nothing was pressing or tight, but she wasn't going to get free until he untied her.

He stood back to admire her. 'You look so beautiful like that, very sexy.' He bent to give her nipples a quick kiss before picking her up and putting her on the divan. 'But you're not finished yet.'

The covers were soft against her skin and she was tempted to burrow into them. The way her arms were tied behind her felt odd, but wasn't too uncomfortable on the padded divan. This room was warm and softly lit, and it occurred to her that she couldn't hear the party that must still be going on.

'It's soundproof,' Andy told her when she asked. 'You can scream as loudly as you like. Don't worry about disturbing anyone.'

'I don't scream.' She was offended by the idea. She wasn't some silly child who thought that screaming would make any difference to what happened. Over the years she had learnt that it was what you did that mattered.

'We'll see.' Andy took one of her legs in his hands and admired it. He kissed her knee before bending it so that her ankle was close to her bottom, then he proceeded to tie it into place. Andy tied her other leg quickly. She was immobilized.

'And the last detail.' Andy took out a length of white muslin, put it around her eyes and tied it. She wasn't in pitch dark, but Roz couldn't see anything. 'Now for the fun.'

Her legs weren't tied together and she could move around but her hands and feet were out of her control, and the blindfold had reduced her world to her sense of hearing, smell and touch. She twisted and found she could move from front to back or even sit up, but with great difficulty, and she couldn't go anywhere.

Roz flopped around, struggling against her bonds, trying to see how tightly they held her. Andy, damn him, knew what he was doing. The knots were out of reach of her fingers and were slither-proof. She was trapped. Roz had no choice but to endure whatever Andy had in mind, and a tiny shiver shook her at the thought.

He pulled her up so that she was leaning back against his chest. She could feel his trousers against her bum and she wondered why he was still wearing them.

Then he trailed his hands over her sides and she forgot everything else. She had to accept whatever he did to her. Every caress was magnified. The gentle drag of his fingertips was like a brand. She gasped.

No, she wasn't going along with this. Andy had tied her up, but that didn't give him power over her. She wasn't some little sub who got turned on by a man who bossed her about. She was the one who gave orders and men rushed to obey her.

'Tell me when you're done,' she said in as bored a tone as she could manage.

He laughed, and nipped her neck. She was surrounded by him, by his heat and masculine scent, a mixture of sandalwood, musk and pure Andy. The nip wasn't hard, but there was something primitive about allowing it. She was female, imprisoned and controlled by a powerful male.

Andy turned his attention to her ear, which he explored with tongue and teeth, driving her mad. Her ears were so sensitive that she could never decide if she loved or hated having them touched. He flicked his tongue into a whorl and whispered, 'You're mine.'

Even while she fought to remain impassive, to be as inert as possible, she reacted.

She melted at the possessive note, her insides clenching with need as his big hands found her breasts. Her skin was on fire, eager for his touch. He pinched one nipple and she gasped.

Andy took advantage of her open mouth to kiss her, a hard kiss that was claim and brand and promise all at once. 'You can fight all you like,' he told her. 'It can only end one way.'

Another kiss. 'My way.'

His tormenting fingers continued to play with her breasts, teasing the nipples, advancing and retreating. It was going to drive her crazy. She struggled against her bonds again, but they held firm.

'Forget it, Roz. We're going to be here all night. And all day tomorrow, or as long as it takes.'

How long had they been here? She had no idea. With no outside sounds, there was a womblike quality to this room. She could be anywhere in the universe, outside of time and space.

No matter how much she wiggled, Andy kept up those sense-shattering caresses. She fought to keep her mind detached, to think about the scam she was going to run. She needed to talk to Frankie soon about buying the horse and –

Andy bit her other earlobe; fire streaked through her and she forgot her own name.

'Are you still there?' she managed. She had to get him to stop.

He laughed. 'All in good time.' He sucked gently on the tender lobe, as if to apologize. 'We have all the time in the world.'

'Please hurry it up, I have things to do.'

And if he didn't, she'd go insane. Already she was a panting, aroused, quivering wreck from his touch on her breasts and neck. What would happen when he moved further down?

She found out. Holding her upright against his chest, he stroked down her stomach, feeling the muscles under her skin, tracing the indentations of her ribs, dipping into her belly button. Were his hands magic? Every touch was more intense than before. The rasp of fingernails along her sides was a pleasure so sharp she could barely breathe. He repeated it on the other side and she gasped, unable to stay silent.

'Enjoying yourself?' asked that tormenting voice.

'Doing algebra in my head,' she replied.

He laughed, a low, knowing sound that made her shiver. 'I'll have to work harder.'

He pushed her thighs apart and trailed one finger down over her sensitive clit.

Roz screamed. There was nothing else to do. The flash of sensation consumed her whole body.

'And I thought you never screamed.'

Roz turned her head and snapped her teeth, almost hoping that she could take a chunk out of his arrogant mouth. But he was gone, and with a laugh, he flipped her onto her back and positioned himself between her legs.

She wanted to kick him. But although she could open and close her thighs, her efforts were futile. Andy was still wearing his trousers. He laughed again, damn him.

'I think you're warmed up now,' he said. 'Let's get on with business.'

Andy leaned down and kissed her stomach, dipping his tongue into her belly button and fluttering it. Every muscle she had clenched and she tried to curl up to make him stop. Nothing worked, he was like a man at a banquet, determined to taste everything. And she was the feast.

For an endless time, she fought against him. Against the pleasure he was lavishing on her, the way he was using her own body against her.

She must resist, must resist.

He took a gentle bite from her inner thigh, awakening nerve endings she had never been aware of, and short-circuiting her brain.

Why was she fighting? Andy was going to win. He was always going to win.

She shuddered, accepting the truth of that, and gave herself up to the dark eroticism. 'Kiss me,' she begged.

He obeyed so promptly he must have been waiting for it, and the kiss was deep and dark and dominating. His tongue took possession of her mouth while his body pressed hers into the divan. Even now, even when she was urging him on, he went slowly, taking his time as he branded her as his.

The fight was over and Roz surrendered to his capable hands and mouth and body. She no longer tried to work out what he was doing, but allowed him to do what he wanted. He was the master puppeteer and all she had to do was relax and allow him to pull her strings.

The darkness behind her eyelids became streaked with red and silver and black as Andy pushed her body to heights she had never experienced. She didn't bother trying to keep track; remembering how to breathe was enough of an effort.

A lick of his tongue, a nip of teeth, a scrape of nails, and sparkles fizzled through her, so intense she had to gasp and pant and scream. She had no idea what he was doing, except that he wasn't doing the one thing she wanted.

She needed him, pounding hard, obliterating the hunger he had drawn from deep inside her, but Andy refused. A long finger slid into her pussy, while his other hand pressed on her stomach and she wailed. She needed to come, needed it so badly she was begging.

'Not yet,' he whispered. 'Not for a long time.'

She heard the sound of a bottle opening, and suddenly his hands were covered with oil. The smell of coconut perfumed the air, mingling with the scent of her arousal. He massaged deep into her muscles and flicked her nipples.

'I expect you're a bit sore after that riding lesson the other day,' he said. His strong hands dug into her thighs, finding aching spots and working out the stiffness. Then those oily fingers teased her clit before sliding into her pussy.

Roz opened her mouth to scream an orgasm, but he withdrew them.

'Naughty, naughty. We're not ready for that yet,' he said and turned to massage her toes.

Time lost all meaning. She gave herself up, allowing Andy to take charge of her body, and letting her mind go wherever it wanted. She was helpless, unable to form a rational thought. Her mind was dominated by the hunger driving her body, which Andy wasn't going to satisfy until he was ready.

She floated on a rainbow, able to see the entire universe, while experiencing all the pleasure in the world. Too much. Too much and never enough.

'Such a good girl, you deserve a reward,' Andy whispered, nudging between her thighs. He took her clit into his mouth, sucking and licking while three fingers pushed inside her, the pressure a counterpart to the delicate nibbling. His other hand reached up and pinched her nipple.

She shattered, all the tension inside her breaking, so that she couldn't draw breath, could not scream, could do nothing but ride out the waves of pleasure that Andy was forcing on her.

For once his bed didn't feel like the inside of an icebox. It had been worth carrying her up the stairs to his room after that amazing scene. Andy stretched, luxuriating in the unfamiliar warmth and slowly opened his eyes. Her naked back was inches away. Soft strands of Titian hair stretched across the pillow. His cock, already at half mast, stirred when he remembered the events of the previous night.

He had never known a woman who had challenged him so much, or submitted to him so beautifully. Oh, she had fought against it, but her surrender was a gift, rather than a victory. A warm glow of pleasure swept over him. It had been one of the best nights of his life.

He curled up to her back, brushing her hair aside so that he could nuzzle her neck. Andy cupped her breast, pleased when her nipple peaked against his palm. His cock stirred again. This was his ultimate fantasy – Roz Spring, naked and willing in his bed. He had to have her.

'If you put that thing near me again, I will chop it up and feed it to you for breakfast.'

'You don't mean that, baby.'

'Oh, I do mean it. And I am not your baby.' Roz sat up and tugged the sheet around her as she scanned the room for her clothes.

'It's a bit late for modesty, don't you think?'

Her answering flush delighted him.

Who would have thought that she could blush? Andy patted the place beside him. 'Stay. It's too early to get up yet.'

Roz eyed his erection. 'Tell that to your cock. Now, where are my clothes? What did you do with them?'

Andy frowned. He had a vague recollection of dropping the red silk outfit on the floor of the dungeon before he . . .

'Did you tear my dress?' Roz lost her grip on the sheet as she lunged for him.

'You vixen,' he muttered as she made a full-on attack on him with her fists and teeth. He should have remembered from the night before. Roz liked to dish out pain as well as receive it. He rolled them both over, using his weight and strength to pin her beneath him.

'I did not tear your dress. I swear. You'll be able to wear it again.'

'To what?' The anger in her eyes subsided and she relaxed in his arms. 'If you're organizing another meeting of the wimpy intellectual society, count me out.'

Andy snorted with laughter. 'Maybe we can have a romantic dinner somewhere when Dougal and Poppy are at the ball.'

'What ball?'

'It's the social highlight of the equestrian year. All posh frocks, champagne and the horsey set getting their social rocks off.'

'How posh?'

'Oh, stud farm owners, the odd sheik or two. The Aga Khan turned up last year. Tim O'Sullivan is guest of honour this year.'

Roz perked up considerably. 'We should go,' she said, with more enthusiasm that he would have expected.

He would have liked nothing better than to walk into the ballroom with her on his arm, but she was supposed to be lying low. With the number of photographers in attendance, she could end up in one of the newspapers or society magazines and there was no way he could let that happen.

'Sorry, but with Hall on the loose, Niall wants me to keep you under wraps.'

'We could go and stay out of the way.'

Why was she so keen to go to a horsey ball? 'Not a chance. Sorry, but there is no way you can go. It's out of the question.'

Roz pouted. 'Fine, but you better make it up to me.'

Her ready capitulation made him uneasy.

Following a tepid shower which she refused to share with him, Andy made his way to the kitchen. Roz was already drinking coffee and chatting with Maggie. He had to admire her. Roz was a natural empath. She seemed to be able to connect with everyone from the stable hands to his elderly aunts.

Everyone except Ariana.

Andy patted his pocket, checking for his phone. In the past, he would have met Ariana for lunch but after that discussion with her, not to mention Roz's insecurity, that wasn't going to happen.

Submission had been a big thing for Roz. He doubted that she had ever trusted anyone else enough. The thought made him feel privileged.

He would have liked to spend longer exploring her

boundaries, finding out what made her tick and what made her scream. Their time together was trickling away like grains of sand in an hour glass and he didn't know how he was going to tell her that she was going into protective custody or how he was going to let her go.

Damn, he was falling for her. He didn't know when or how, but there was no denying that she had got under his skin.

He was in danger of falling in love. Real, happy-ever-after love. The kind that involved resigning his membership in Club Noir and the other fetish clubs.

Except, of course, that none of that was possible. Roz was going into protective custody and probably into witness protection. They only had a few more days together before they said goodbye for good. He had to make sure he didn't let this go any further.

Poppy entered the kitchen, her coat draped over her arm. 'Ah, there you are. I thought, as Andy was going to Belfast, that we could go along and do some shopping. I have to buy some shoes for the ball and I'm sure Roz could do with a new dress for it.'

Andy shook his head. 'Sorry, Mum, we won't be able to make it.' He didn't want to tell his parents why it was so essential that Roz stayed in Lough Darra. They had enough problems without worrying about Hall. 'I'll be working and Roz won't go without me, will you?'

He pinned Roz with his eyes, willing her to tell Poppy she didn't want to go. Instead, she smiled sweetly. 'I'd love to visit Belfast with you. I need to buy a new phone. My old one isn't working for some reason.'

Like a bullet from Hall's gun. Damn. He did owe her

a phone, but they could have spent the day in bed not traipsing around town. But when he saw the delight on his mother's face, Andy forced a smile. 'Great. I'll drop you into town and I can buy you a new phone while you're shopping.'

At least it would save him from hanging around outside dressing rooms.

Roz waved to Andy and watched him disappear into the crowd. She would have preferred to torture him by dragging him around the clothes shops, but at least she would get a new phone out of it. She patted her pocket, checking for her purse. There wasn't a lot of money in it and she had no credit cards now. She hoped that Poppy didn't have expensive tastes.

The city was bustling with shoppers. 'This is lovely.' Poppy beamed at her. 'I barely get half an hour in the stores when I'm out with Dougal.'

'Where would you like to go?' Please don't mention the designer place that Andy had taken her to.

The laughter lines around Poppy's brown eyes crinkled. 'I'm awfully fond of a good rummage around the second-hand places but Dougal won't set a foot in them. Would that be okay?'

Relief swept through Roz. Vintage was her favourite kind of shopping. Mostly it was her only kind. 'That sounds great.'

Poppy patted her arm. 'I can see we're going to get along fine.'

The first store she dismissed with barely a flicker of

interest. 'Too bridesmaid,' Poppy pronounced before heading out onto the street again.

The next store was better. While Poppy and the owner discussed the merits of an original fifties evening dress, Roz turned her attention to the open door leading to the stock room at the back of the shop, where unsorted clothing was piled high.

She knew from experience that most of the good stuff never made it onto the hangers. It was bought for a pittance by staff. This shop had obviously just got a new consignment. Keeping one eye on Poppy and the assistant, she made her way to the back of the shop.

At the sorting table, she fingered the fabrics. Most of the clothing was high street, but there was the odd gem. A dark green satin dress caught her eye, it would be fabulous with her hair, but it was too big. `

Through the open door, she could see that they had moved to the display case. Poppy asked to see a small gold bangle.

'That's genuine art deco, love,' the middle-aged assistant pronounced. 'I'll fetch the key.'

Roz didn't have much time. Beneath a black velvet evening dress, she saw a flash of cobalt blue. The label said Valentino. Even second hand, she couldn't afford it, and where would she wear it anyway? Andy said they couldn't go to the ball.

The imp in her made her pick it up anyway. She waved to the assistant. 'I'm going to try this on.'

She slipped out of her clothes and pulled the dress on over her head. To die for. She had heard the expression but never truly appreciated it until now. It fitted her like a glove. If Andy saw her in this, he'd be hard for the night. Maybe she could wear it for their dinner date?

'Are you decent?' Poppy called.

Roz laughed. 'No, but I'm dressed.'

She pulled the curtain back and watched as Poppy's mouth formed a perfect O before she announced, 'It's beautiful. You simply must let me buy it for you.'

When she dropped the curtain, Roz frowned at her reflection. The dress would probably cost a few hundred pounds. Poppy had already been so kind to her. She couldn't let her spend that kind of money.

Roz dug into the pocket of her jeans for the hoof pick she had used on Minty. The tool had a large pointed spike, and a small folded knife that was sharp enough to remove the label. It wasn't stealing exactly, more like renting. She broke a nail pulling the blade out, and got to work. She would pay for the dress and send it back to the shop with the label on after she had worn it. Then they could sell it again.

She made her way to the cash desk. 'How much is this?'

'No tag, love?' The assistant shook out the dress and cocked her head, considering. 'Fifty quid then.'

Poppy was about to open her purse when Roz stopped her. She would need shoes too.

'Forty,' Roz countered. 'And I'll take the silver sandals in the window. Size six, aren't they?'

Andy put down his newspaper when they came through the door of the pub. They were both smiling. His mother carried a bag which obviously contained a box of shoes, but there was little else to show for a whole morning of shopping.

Poppy spotted a friend at the bar and went to greet him while Roz pulled up a chair opposite. 'You can buy us lunch with all the money I've saved you.'

Andy knew better than to dispute her peculiarly female logic. Damn. Why hadn't he thought to give her money before he left them? For a penniless woman on a shopping trip, she was in a remarkably good mood. Beneath her impish grin, excitement bubbled. There was something she wasn't telling him. But what sort of devilment could Roz have been up to with his mother in tow?

'Please don't tell me you stole something,' he whispered.

'Of course not,' she said, affronted.

'I could always search you,' he offered, eyeing the plain black plastic bag she carried.

'Don't even think about it. Besides, it's only a dress I picked up in a charity shop.'

There was something she wasn't telling him. Roz might be able to fool other people, but he was beginning to learn her habit of not lying, but not exactly telling the truth either. 'What are you not telling me? What did you do?'

Roz huffed a breath and reached into her pocket. 'You are such a –'

'Dom?' he offered as he held out his hand.

She dropped a scrap of fabric into his open palm and waited, defiance written all over her face. Was this what all the fuss was about? A dress label?

He smoothed the fabric out. *Valentino*. 'How much would it have cost with the label on?'

'I don't know. A few hundred, maybe.'

He examined the scrap of cloth. 'How did you cut the label off so neatly?'

Reluctantly she held out the hoof pick. He pulled it out of her hand. 'Jesus, I can't believe you used my hoof pick to steal.'

'I didn't steal it,' she insisted.

'What would you call it then?'

He caught a glimpse of hurt in her eyes before she hid it. 'I borrowed it so that I'd look good for your posh friends. In case you haven't noticed, I'm not exactly a dress-up girl. I won't be wearing any of this stuff afterwards.'

She pushed back her chair and hurried for the door.

She had said 'afterwards'. Roz was already thinking of when this was over. When they stopped playing at being lovers and she was out of his life for good. Her words hit him like a slap. He remembered her meagre wardrobe in London. Until he'd taken her shopping, she barely had more than the clothes she stood up in. Roz always travelled light.

Andy raced after her and caught her in his arms, ignoring the glances from the middle-aged shoppers. 'I'm sorry,' he said.

'Go to hell.' She pushed against his chest, but he refused to release her.

Andy held her tightly until she calmed down. He kissed the top of her head: 'That's better. I can see that I'm going to have to do some more work on your trust issues. Tell you what, let's play again tonight. A fantasy each, no holds barred.'

The speculative look she gave him almost made him nervous. Roz was a kinky bitch but no match for him. Let her bring it on.

'Okay, toss you later for who goes first.'

Poppy was chatting away at the bar when they returned. She hadn't noticed that they had left. They settled down again, but Roz was quiet. Andy reached into his pocket and touched the velvet-covered box. While waiting for the phone to charge, he had wandered around an antique store and a small gold compact had caught his eye.

'Gemini,' the middle-aged assistant informed him, pointing out the pair of embossed faces that decorated the top.

Roz was a twin. He had almost forgotten that lately. The more he got to know her, the more he realized that she was nothing like her sister Sinead. How could he have ever thought that they were the same?

Sipping her coffee after their shopping, Roz busied herself checking out her new phone and admiring the Victorian décor of the Crown pub while trying not to remember the night before. Trust issues, her ass. What had Andy done to her? She scowled, trying to recreate what had happened. Her mind, usually so sharp and dependable, had shut down and she had been operating on pure hunger and instinct and emotion.

Yes, it had been the most amazing night of her life. She had given herself over to Andy, and he had given her an experience unlike anything she had ever had before. She hankered for it again, but knew it couldn't happen. Tonight, she would have to take control and turn the tables on him.

This was Andy McTavish. She sneaked a glimpse at him. He was flirting with the waitress who was taking their food, and those dark eyes were smiling warmly at her. It didn't matter that the waitress was easily sixty years old. She was under his spell, assuring him that she'd get him exactly what he wanted, even though it wasn't on the menu.

Andy didn't do faithful. He was the guy who flirted with every woman at the party, the one who could make any woman he met feel special. Just as he had done to her last night.

She had to remember that the intensity of the connection between them wasn't due to Andy having special feelings for her, it was because he was always this way with women.

To give him his due, Roz thought, trying to be objective, he was good at his job because he really did like women. He loved Poppy in a way that made Roz feel jealous. What must it be like to have a mother there for you, one who loved you no matter what?

She told herself that if Maggie O'Sullivan had lived, she would have been that sort of mother. Of course she would.

Her memories of her childhood were vague; odd snapshots of sharing a bed with Sinead because there was only one. She remembered eating cornflakes out of the box because there was no other food and petting the puppies that lived beneath the hedge. She shivered when she thought of the icy cold caravan site in winter.

Her childhood had been like that because the O'Sullivans hated her dad. He had tried his best, but they had disapproved of him from the start. It had nothing to do with Maggie being a bad mother.

It was all the O'Sullivans' fault that she had never had a mother like Poppy.

Andy adored Poppy, and his regard for her spread to all of the other women he met. He genuinely enjoyed women's company and liked them. He was laughing as warmly at the waitress as he had at Isobel at the party last night. But that didn't mean anything.

Andy McTavish was the ultimate one night stand. He was amazing in bed, and while he was with a woman, he could make her feel as if she was the only woman in the entire world. She had gotten lost in those amazing eyes, thought the dimple was for her alone, forgotten that she wasn't the only one who loved feeling those abs. But while Roz could lie convincingly to everyone else, she didn't believe in lying to herself.

Andy wasn't for her. He would marry Ariana, or someone like her. Someone from the right family, someone educated and cultured. Roz liked to think that if he married, Andy would be a faithful husband, but she had seen too many men who played away.

There was no point getting involved with him. It would never lead to anything except heartbreak and disillusion. Andy would do his job. She trusted him one hundred per cent to keep her safe. But keep her heart safe? No way in hell. It was time to remember that they moved in different worlds.

The phone that Andy had bought for her was already set up. Clever boy. Her old number was now ported over, so she opened up her address book and checked that her numbers were still there.

She usually rang her dad once a week to see how he was doing. She didn't enjoy the conversations where he was full of schemes that were never going to work, particularly not with the Ramos brothers after him.

This was a call she wanted to make in private. She told Andy she needed the ladies, and locked herself into the wheelchair toilet before she called.

'I'd like to speak to Peter Spring, please,' she told the office. Ironic, after so many years using so many different names, he had been arrested under his own name.

'Who is it?'

'Roisin Spring, his daughter.'

There was a pause while the man searched through his list of allowed contacts, then he said, 'You won't be able to speak to him, but I'll transfer you to the hospital wing.'

'What?' But before she could demand more details, she was listening to 'Greensleeves'. It seemed to be ages before the phone was picked up at the other end and she could ask what was wrong with her father.

She lied to herself frantically – it was no more than something minor, an infection or flu – before the nurse told her the truth.

'He was attacked in the yard,' she said. 'He's got three broken ribs, twenty-three stitches and numerous contusions from kicks and blows. But he will recover.'

Roz clutched her phone. 'What happened to him?'

The nurse sounded exasperated. 'Your guess is as good as mine. Everyone swears they didn't see it and the security camera was down. He says he doesn't know who did it.'

'Can I speak to him?'

'He's sleeping now. You can ring tomorrow or the next day. Don't worry. He'll be put into the protection unit until he's released. They won't get another chance at him.'

Roz hung up, promising to ring back soon. Damn, damn, damn. She knew exactly what had happened. The Ramos brothers had delivered a warning that they wanted their money or he wasn't going to live long.

The thought of life without her dad was terrifying. He might be a giant pain in the ass, but he was the only relative she had who wanted anything to do with her. She was well aware that life would have been a lot easier for him if he had dumped her with the O'Sullivans, but her dad had always wanted her with him. He loved her. He had taken care of her.

Now it was her turn to look after him.

Roz stared at her reflection in the mirror blankly. She had to come up with half a million to get her dad out of hock and enough money to take care of Frankie. What the hell was she going to do now?

22

Andy lifted his eyes from his book to watch Roz emerge from the playroom. He should have known better than to play bar games with her. When Roz wagered, she never lost. He had promised her a fantasy and bet that she couldn't Domme him. He was a fucking idiot.

Roz was being secretive all evening and he guessed that he was in for it. What would she have in mind? His cock stirred. Whatever it was, he was game. He knew that she had raided Maggie's kitchen (luckily it was her night off), his mother's workroom and his father's wine cellar. It was looking very promising.

'Need any help with that?' he asked as Roz returned carrying a cloth-covered tray.

'No thanks.' She flashed him a smile that bordered on evil.

Yes, he was definitely in trouble. But it was the kind of trouble that he was looking forward to.

The sound of her steps on the stairs made him return his attention to his book. If she wasn't going to tell him, there was nothing he could do about it. His cock begged to differ.

'Go downstairs and wait for me.'

The stern voice made him respond, 'Yes, ma'am.'

Andy stood up eagerly and moved towards the door to the dungeon.

'Oh, and I want you naked.' With that, she shut the library door behind her.

Punching the air, Andy hurried downstairs.

Fifteen minutes later he glanced at his watch. Did naked mean watch or no watch? He decided to put it away and added it to the pile of clothing in the corner. Anticipation tingled in his veins. What would he do tonight? Bondage? A light spanking? He wouldn't hit her hard, not hard enough to leave a mark. Her skin was like warm cream. It would be a shame to bruise it.

A flogger, he decided. His red and black deerskin could be sensual or sadistic, depending on how hard he wielded it. For Roz, he would hold back. No marks, only a pretty pink glow.

The sound of heels on the stairs made his mouth water with anticipation. Roz had made him wait. He would add that to her list of sins. He folded his arms across his chest and waited for his submissive.

The door opened.

Holy mother of fuck!

'Like it?' her voice was almost a purr.

She was wearing a black velvet corset that showcased her breasts, turning them to quivering white globes. Underneath, a black suspender belt was attached to silk stockings and a tiny thong did nothing to conceal her gorgeous ass. He almost licked his lips. A phrase from his Catholic education came back to haunt him. An occasion of sin. Roz was all that and more. Vying for control he said, 'Nice outfit. Shame you won't be wearing it for long.'

Her blue eyes were glacier cold. 'I think you're forgetting something. Tonight is my fantasy.'

'Baby,' he began.

Her carmine lips tightened. 'Don't *baby* me.'

She was serious? Andy raised an eyebrow, waiting for the punch line. There was none and he swallowed. 'I have a question.'

Her smile held a touch of pity. 'You mean, may I ask a question, Mistress?'

Fuck and double fuck. She was serious about this. 'What did you have in mind? Mistress.'

He kept the last word light, but almost choked on it. He had played a lot when he was the Dom, in charge, the boss. This was a new, uncharted world.

Roz lifted a cloth from the padded bench revealing an interesting collection of objects. An ice bucket, jars from the pantry, two squat candles, a bottle of massage oil and, if he wasn't mistaken, vintage champagne. 'Any problems?'

Relief washed over him. The bench contained nothing more than a good night in. He dropped his head to hide his smile. 'No, Mistress.'

'Good. Do you need a safe word?'

Andy lifted his head and raised one dark brow in warning. Was she joking? The firm line of her mouth told him that she wasn't.

'Bring it on.' He held her gaze in a direct challenge. 'Mistress,' he added mockingly.

Roz sashayed towards him, her heels clicking on the flagstone floor. 'I can see that you have an attitude problem. Let me take care of that for you. Turn and face the wall.'

Andy turned.

'"Red" is your safe word,' she whispered before the first blow of the crop landed square across his bare buttocks and he flinched. The little –

Five more followed in quick succession, followed by another six. Harder this time, and Andy bit his lip as heat bloomed. She was really doing this. His cock stirred, rising to attention. No. He was not turned on by this. He wasn't, but Christ, it was . . . Oh, god, it felt . . .

The blows stopped and he closed his eyes. He would play along with her. For now.

'Like that?' she whispered in his ear.

'Not much.'

'Good, I wouldn't want you getting too comfortable. Lie down.'

Smiling, Andy took his place on the bed. She really thought she could Domme him? Roz was in for a surprise. He lay on the padded bench and waited to see what she would do next. The soft muslin had been 'borrowed' from Maggie's pantry. Expecting that she would blindfold him, he was surprised when she raised his hands above his head and tied his wrists. The suggestion of restraint was more erotic than he had anticipated.

'I thought you were going to blindfold me,' he chuckled.

Roz shook her head. 'No. I want you to know exactly what's going to happen. I usually find that anticipation is half the pleasure.'

'If you say so.'

Roz ignored him and turned her attention to the bench. She lit both candles and dimmed the lights before opening the oil and pouring a little into the palm of her hands.

She was right. His cock was already anticipating the touch of her hands and it rose to half mast.

'So smooth,' she said as she massaged the oil gently into his chest.

Andy heaved a sigh of pleasure. She was good at this. Why hadn't they done it before? He would have to promote her to personal masseuse.

'Like that?'

'Mmm, yes.'

'Good, because you may not like what's coming next.'

His eyes flew open. Roz held the burning candle over his abdomen. Shit. He'd heard of guys who got off on wax play. He didn't anticipate being one of them. 'Baby, are you sure about this?'

'I'm sure.'

The first drop landed square on his abdomen. The flare of heat quickly dissipated as the liquid wax turned into a solid blob.

'You know,' she said conversationally, 'it's not the pouring temperature but the impact temperature that matters. The closer I get to the skin the hotter it is.' To prove her point, she brought the candle closer and poured a single drop.

'Sweet suffering –'

Andy bit down on the last word. It didn't burn exactly. The melted soy wax was no worse than stepping into a hot bath, but the anticipation of where and when the droplets might fall next made him shiver. Andy noticed how careful she was not to tease areas where his skin was thinner. He grunted when she allowed some wax to fall on skin which hadn't been oiled. That hurt like a bitch.

He lost track of time. Trails of pale wax snaked over his skin, vibrant against his tan, layering over each other like strands of rope. Was this what it was like to be at someone else's mercy? He wasn't helpless. He could rip the muslin from his wrists in seconds. No, he decided. It was a mental thing, the giving up of control to someone else. Surrender.

Andy jerked when another drop landed on his chest and the movement pulled on his skin, sending a mild sensation of pain along his nerve endings.

She was definitely a witch.

'Poor baby,' she said with a throaty purr. 'Maybe we should try something else.'

He sighed with relief when she replaced the candle on the bench. The flickering flames cast eerie shadows on the walls and ceilings of the cellar room. Andy closed his eyes.

An icy cold sensation against his nipples made him jerk to attention. His sudden movement made the wax break, pulling and tugging against his skin. She had done it on purpose. 'You evil . . .'

Roz laughed and pulled away. 'What's the matter, can't a big strong Ranger cope with a little ice-cube? I thought you were meant to be tough.'

'I'll show you how tough I am. My hands are especially hard. In fact, one palm is very itchy.'

'Promises, promises. I have a few more treats and then you can rest. Now, close your eyes.'

Andy cheated, watching her through lowered lashes as she tugged the cellophane from two paintbrushes before opening the jars she had brought from the pantry. He doubted if Maggie or his mother would be pleased with what Roz intended to do with them. Excitement thrummed in his abdomen and the blood rushed south.

The sable brush was featherlike against his skin, teasing his nipple to attention. He loved women's breasts, adored their fleshy softness, but who would have known that his own nipples could be so sensitive?

He caught the faint scent of chocolate before the brush made contact with his nipples again, circling and teasing him so that he wanted to shake off his bindings and ravish her until she screamed.

A warm, hot mouth fastened on his nipple and he arched off the bed as she licked and nibbled the tender flesh until he was mindless.

'Did I mention that I love chocolate?'

'I'll keep it in mind,' he gasped.

'But not as much as I love something else.'

Slow, slick strokes circled his nipples. Not chocolate this time. Andy sniffed, trying to figure out what she had used, but the blooming warmth on his skin confirmed his worst suspicions. Chilli.

'Fuck.' He almost arched off the bench. 'That stings.'

'Use your safe word then.'

There was no way on god's earth that he was doing that. He gritted his teeth as the heat increased. It was worse than the candle wax, much worse.

'Need help with that?'

Her impish grin made him want to bite something, preferably her ass. 'I wouldn't mind.'

'Good.' She lowered her head and fastened it on his burning flesh, licking and flicking her tongue, circling the tender skin.

Finally, she released him. 'We lived over an Indian take away for a couple of years when I was a kid. Since then, nothing is too hot for me.'

'Really?' That was a challenge if he ever heard one. If Roz thought she could out-kink him, she was mistaken. Ms Spring was about to get a lesson she wouldn't forget. Not for a long while.

He ripped the muslin binding from his wrists and sat up. 'If you're finished playing, I think it's my turn.'

Roz had been so high on what she was doing to him, seeing how he was reacting and getting into his experience, that she had forgotten their bet. Now she had to let him do anything he wanted to her. His fantasy.

What had he in mind? Suddenly she was nervous, and wondered if she should have played with the wax. Who knew how he would take his revenge?

'What are you going to do?' She was proud she managed to keep the tremble out of her voice. She was used to being in control. This would always have been difficult for her, never mind after what they had just done.

'Get you naked first,' he said, and proceeded to strip off her scant clothing with ruthless speed. It had taken her twenty minutes to lace herself into the corset. He had her out of it in twenty seconds.

'What now?' she asked, standing before him.

'Don't worry, you'll like it.' He held up a heavy silver chain. She studied it with an expert eye. It was almost certainly antique, probably Victorian, smooth with age and frequent wear. She tried to price the chain if she were to sell it and reckoned it would fetch at least a couple of thousand. It was much longer than the Alberts she was used to, but too short for anything kinky.

But then, Andy McTavish took kinky to a new level.

'What have you in mind?'

He guided her to the divan and handed the chain to her. It was cool and slightly damp. 'It's wet.'

'I sterilized it.' He slid her back on the divan, making sure she was comfortable. Somehow, it didn't reassure her. 'You can warm it up in your hands. I don't want you to be cold.'

She shut her mouth with a snap. She wasn't going to ask. He was enjoying this too much. Bloody smart-alec Irishman. She didn't even comment when he opened a cabinet and took out a bottle of Liquid Silk, but tried to look bored.

'Now lie back and enjoy. Do I need to tie you?'

'No!'

The last time he had tied her had been amazing, but she wasn't sure how often she wanted to do that. It required a huge amount of trust to allow any man to have so much power over her body, never mind her emotions. 'You enjoy that far too much.'

He laughed. 'True, you're a dream rope bunny. I can't wait to suspend you some time. But for now, hold onto the bars at the top of the divan.'

She hadn't noticed them before, but she obediently gripped them. This she could handle: she could let go at any time she needed to. She'd always had a slight phobia about being tied up and not being able to scratch an itchy nose. Silly, but there it was.

'Good girl.' His approving rumble warmed her. This was Andy, she reminded herself. He wasn't a dick. He wouldn't torture her because she had said he could do whatever he liked. She ached to know what he liked.

Lying this way, Roz was vulnerable, open to him, even though she could lift her hands from the bars at any moment. Maybe it was the way he settled himself between her thighs and looked at her with that hot, possessive expression.

'So pretty. So soft.'

He traced a finger down between her breasts to her belly button. She flinched at the touch, startled by the intimacy of that single finger. His finger continued down, over her trembling stomach to the small puff of hair that proclaimed her a natural redhead. She wished she'd had the forethought to shave until he said, 'So sexy and exciting.'

That questing finger dipped lower, investigating, and he smiled. 'Oh, you are wet. You were as turned on as I was, weren't you?'

She shrugged, still gripping the bars. 'Hey, it was fun seeing you writhe.'

'Now it's my turn to see you wiggle. And wet as you are, more lube is always a good idea.'

The uncapping of the bottle was shockingly loud in the quiet room, before the cool wetness startled her again. 'That's cold,' she protested.

'You're hot enough for ten women.' He picked up the chain from where she had dropped it on the divan, and slid one link inside her hot pussy.

She gasped. 'That's perverted.'

He laughed. 'I know. Fun, isn't it?'

Andy picked up the length of muslin. 'I've noticed that you're quieter if I blindfold you, so here goes.' He was careful but thorough as he tied the light cloth around her eyes.

Andy had noticed something that she'd only just realized. If he had tried to gag her, she would have fought and chewed her way out, but for some reason, when she couldn't see, she became quiet and receptive.

His voice sounded far away. 'If anything hurts, tell me at once.'

She nodded, not bothering to reply in words.

The next link slid in, smooth and cool. The sensation was odd, but not uncomfortable. She would relax and let him play. She needed a rest anyway; Domming him had been hard work and taken all her concentration. 'Proceed,' she said, and even that took more energy than she wanted to waste.

'Oh, I will.' She heard his smile, as the next link slid in. And the next.

He continued, link by slow link. One after the other.

'Time for more lube,' he said, and she braced herself for the cool wetness. More links.

Her insides felt full, stretched in ways she had never experienced before. One finger pressed inside and she gasped. It hit a nerve and pleasure zinged through her body, tightening all her muscles in a spasm.

'Enjoying that?'

'Mmmm,' was the best she could manage. He couldn't seriously expect her to talk, could he?

He laughed. 'I am. You're such a good little sub.'

Annoyed, she opened her eyes behind the blindfold and glared in his direction. 'In your dreams, Irish.'

'You have no idea how much I've dreamed about this. Now be quiet and let me play.'

Oh well, if he was having fun, who was she to stop him? She relaxed back into the pleasurable darkness.

Another link. They were graduated in size, with the larger, heavier links in the middle. That one was definitely bigger. 'How much is in?' she asked.

'About twenty percent.'

Wow. He had to be joking. She felt stuffed already.

More links slid in, slowly, so slowly. She realized her internal clock had switched off and she had no idea how long they had been there. 'Aren't you bored?'

He chuckled. 'Are you kidding? I'm having a great time watching you.'

What did he see, she wondered, then forgot about it. If he was enjoying himself, she could relax and zone out. She allowed him to continue, feeling the weight of the chain increase gradually. He stopped to blow on her clit, then licked and sucked, making her shiver in pleasure. The movement caused the chain inside her to shift, echoing and intensifying the feelings.

'So sexy,' he murmured as he eased one long finger inside her. He hooked it, pressing against her G spot, and she nearly came off the bed. An electric current of pleasure shot through her erogenous zones, going straight to her brain. Her toes curled and her legs flexed involuntarily.

'So responsive,' he murmured.

She was out of control, and it didn't matter. Andy had

her, he was in charge and she could allow him to look after her. The thought provoked another orgasm.

Now that he had her fully aroused, he kept her there, playing her body like a guitar. His hands were everywhere, pushing her to come over and over, sometimes holding back, bringing her to the edge and back before she toppled over.

She lost her ability to think. Andy's lips were hot and sweet, easing hers apart slowly and allowing his tongue to sink into her depths. His knowing hands pinched her nipples, teased her bellybutton, flicked her clit, tickled the back of her knees. She reached for him, but he gently put her hands back. 'This is my time. I get to do what I want to you. Just enjoy.'

She did.

Her entire world consisted of the sound of skin on skin, the smell of Andy's unique musk and her own arousal, and the pleasure that washed through her in wave after wave, too many to count.

Andy. Andy. Andy. He was her world.

When her body was worn out, and she thought she would never be able to move again, he whispered into her ear. 'And now for the big finale.'

That was all the warning she had. He pulled the chain out in a smooth movement that jerked all her nerve endings back to shocked life. As he pulled he pressed on her clit and she screamed as she tipped into one last, magnificent orgasm.

Then Andy's arms were around her and his mouth was on hers and she let go of the bars to hold onto him as if she would never let him go.

23

'Andy.'

He lifted his head from the book he was pretending to read while he savoured the memories of the night before. He had never met a woman who matched him so well in the bedroom. Roz was unique, sexy, beautiful and kinky as hell. How could he even think of letting her go?

Right now, she was quiet. Maybe she had a touch of sub drop? Tonight, there would be no play, only cuddles. He would take such good care of her.

'Andrew,' his mother called again. 'Have you seen my diamond necklace?'

Poppy was always losing things. His mother had her own unique sense of fashion and was liable to wear the necklace with a pair of wellies if the mood took her.

'Have you been wearing it in the garden again?' Dougal asked.

Poppy glared at him over her reading glasses. 'No, dear. And I do wish you wouldn't keep harping on about that. We did find it in the end.'

'With a metal detector,' Dougal said, with a chuckle.

She looked to Roz for support.

'I'll help you search for it.'

Roz put her book down and Andy caught a glimpse of the title on the spine. Why would Roz be interested in horse breeding? He couldn't put his finger on it, but she had been a little distant since the day they went shopping together. She was spending a lot more time with his parents, especially his father, who adored taking her around the farm, but there was a tension about her that hadn't been there before.

Roz stood up. 'Where did you last have it?'

'The conservatory, I think. Or maybe it was the dining room.'

As they passed his chair, Andy reached for Roz's hand. 'You didn't "borrow" it, did you?' He winked at her.

He meant it jokingly, but the look she gave him cut him dead. She pulled her hand from his grasp and followed Poppy from the library. He had put his size elevens right into it. He stood up quickly and hurried after them.

'Andrew,' his father roared after him. 'That blasted phone of yours is ringing.'

He patted his pocket. The bloody thing had slipped out again and the Tardis ring tone was blaring from the wing-backed library chair where he'd been sitting.

'McTavish,' he said.

'I need you. Pack a bag,' Niall Moore said without preamble.

'What's up?'

'Jack Winter. He's in Dublin and he wants someone to look after Abbie.'

Winter was a high-profile client and whatever Jack wanted, Jack got.

'What's wrong with Abbie?'

'Not a thing, but since the shooting incident in Tullamore, Jack won't let her out of his sight. She got a note and he thinks it had something to do with some South American crazies she was involved with three years ago.'

'But the shooting had –'

'I told him that. But he wants protection ASAP and you're the nearest operative. Be there for dinner. It's only for a couple of days. They're staying at the Shelbourne.'

'But I'm looking after Roz and Hall is still loose,' Andy protested.

'Does anyone know where she is? Will she run? Is she in danger?'

Damn it, Andy wanted to say yes, but . . . 'No, she's safe here.'

'Then get to Dublin and protect Abbie until I can relieve you.'

Niall disconnected the call.

Damn and blast. He knew that Roz was safe at Lough Darra. There hadn't been a sighting of Hall since Tullamore and there was nothing to draw him here. But he didn't want to leave her right now.

'Work?' his father asked, frowning.

Andy sighed. 'Looks like it. I have an assignment in Dublin but I'll try to get back soon.'

'Well, if you must,' Dougal said, but Andy could see that he was annoyed that he was leaving again so soon.

'Look, Dad. I can't really talk about it, but there was an incident on a movie set in Tullamore a few days ago. Roz was involved.'

'What happened?' The old man sat up, alert and looking five years younger.

'A stalker. I want you to look after her while I'm gone.'

'Of course.' Dougal straightened his shoulders. 'I can still battle with the best of them. You only had to ask.'

Maybe he should have kept quiet. God help him if his dad became involved in another fight. 'Promise me, no guns.'

Dougal looked almost disappointed.

Back in his room, Andy packed quickly, choosing clothes that would help him blend in. Fitting in with the client's lifestyle was part of the job. The perfect body-guard was invisible, and every job was different. He stowed his bag in the back of the car and went in search of his mother and Roz.

The search for the necklace had moved to the conservatory where Poppy had been working the previous day, but his mother had been distracted by her latest painting. She was doing a series of botanical studies of orchids. Roz listened as his mother explained about the fluctuation in temperature necessary for an orchid to bloom.

From her rapt expression he could tell Roz wasn't being polite or dutiful, she was genuinely interested. Despite her background, she was a perfect fit for Lough Darra and Poppy obviously adored her. Pride welled in his chest. If things had been different, if their engagement was real, Roz could have been happy here.

He cleared his throat, interrupting the lecture. 'Sorry, but I have to go to Dublin. Something's come up.'

Roz was immediately on the alert. 'Do I need to –'

'No. Stay here. I'll be back in a few days.'

A flicker of hurt crossed her face and Andy wanted to kick himself. He hadn't meant to be abrupt with her, but this was what his life was like when he was working. He could get a call at any moment and he couldn't discuss his assignments with anyone.

He glanced at his watch. With rush hour traffic, he would barely make it to Dublin in time for dinner and he didn't want to piss off a client who was already anxious. Andy bent his head to kiss her, but Roz evaded his mouth and offered him her cheek instead. She was annoyed with him and wouldn't play nice.

He didn't have time for this now. He would put the little madam over his knee and spank her for that later. His cock stirred at the prospect. Damn, just what he needed on a long drive. Roz Spring would be the death of him.

Roz glared after his departing figure. He actually thought she had stolen Poppy's necklace? He believed she was a thief?

Well, she was, of course, but she stole from people who deserved it and who could afford it. And it was nothing to do with the rich people being the ones who had the most money – it was scarily easy to steal from poor people. Rich people dealt in credit, poor people carried cash.

No, there was something magical about getting one over on someone who deserved it. Who had got rich by their own scams, or by profiting from other people's hard work.

She wouldn't steal from someone like Poppy, who had been so good to her. Poppy might be rich and live in a ridiculously large home, even if it had a plumbing system that was at least fifty years old and didn't even have proper heating. It was clear that she worked hard, didn't indulge herself with senseless luxury and valued her family more than her bank balance. That necklace had belonged to Poppy's great-grandmother, and that meant more to her than the insurance value.

And Andy fucking McTavish thought she would steal it?

The pain that welled up as she absorbed that thought was more than she could bear. The house, cold as it was, was stifling to her. She had to get away. She sprinted for the stables where she could hide from everyone.

The yard was full of stable hands when she arrived, but Minty stuck her head out over her stable door and whickered a greeting to Roz. Her big brown eyes were friendly and didn't accuse her of anything.

Roz slipped into the stable, bolting the half door behind her. Now she was out of sight.

Minty butted her head against Roz, looking for a treat. Roz patted her pockets but the only thing she had on her was a packet of Tic Tacs. She shook one out on her hand and looked at it dubiously. It seemed far too small, but she offered it on her palm.

Minty lipped it up with enthusiasm and Roz swore the horse was smiling at her. At least someone liked her. The horse shoved her nose against Roz for a caress.

Roz patted her gingerly, then with more assurance when the horse stayed still. Finally she leaned against her neck, absorbing the warmth and strength of the animal.

'He thinks I'm a thief,' she murmured to Minty. 'In spite of everything we've done together, he thinks I stole Poppy's necklace. He didn't even ask me, he assumed.'

Her hand stilled as she was struck by a horrible possibility. 'I wonder if Poppy and Dougal think the same?'

She had no way of knowing what Andy had told his parents about her background. Surely he wouldn't have told them she was the daughter of a convict? They wouldn't have her in the house if they knew. Or would they? She could almost see them taking her in as some sort of charity case.

She hugged Minty tightly. She couldn't bear to be someone's charity case. Life had been hard over the years, but she had always got by on her own. She had never gone begging to anyone and she wasn't about to start now.

Well, that solved one dilemma. When she had realized how rich Andy was, she had toyed with the idea of asking him for the money to get her father out of hock. She had been reluctant because she could see that even with an estate of this size, there wasn't half a million in cash floating around to throw away on a small-time conman.

Now there was no way she would consider it. She had to find the money on her own, and she knew how to do it.

She pulled away from Minty with reluctance. Who'd have guessed that horses were cuddly? In the back of the stable, she pulled out her phone and called Frankie.

Cheyenne answered immediately, panting slightly as if she had been running before she picked up. 'Hi, Roz, want to talk to Frankie?'

She had barely finished before Frankie spoke, sounding equally breathless. 'Yo, what's up?'

'You sound better.'

'Yep, getting back into the saddle, so to speak.' There was a smile in Frankie's voice. 'How are things with you?'

She wasn't going to dump all her problems on him. 'Good. I'm at Andy's home, and I want to get moving on the Shergar sting. What do we need?'

His voice muffled as he said, 'Sweetie, could you get me a coffee?' A door slammed, and his voice returned to its usual crisp tone. 'Okay, first up, you need to buy Nagsy and make sure the paperwork is tight. Then we need to convince O'Sullivan that he is worth half a mill. That will take DNA testing, but I'll leave that to you. And some sort of race, where he looks good. That will be harder to rig.'

'Leave that to me.' Roz had no idea yet how to do it, but she trusted her fertile imagination would come up with something. 'I'll have to find somewhere to put him, until I'm ready to spring the trap.'

Her thoughts raced. This was going to be a long con. But she had to do it.

'I'll get working on it. Anything else you think of, text me about it. When are you back at work?'

There was a pause, small but she caught it. 'Soon enough. It won't be long before the docs will sign me fit again.'

Yeah right, and pigs would fly. Roz knew Frankie well enough to know when he was lying. He was injured, even if he was fit enough to keep Cheyenne happy for now. She added Frankie to the list of things she had to do. But first, she needed a crash course in horses and she knew the man to teach her.

Dougal had become keen on their hikes around the estate, and she didn't think it was her imagination that he was moving more easily and leaning on his cane less frequently.

'Here, time you earned your keep,' he told her. Pointing his cane at a small white bucket of warm milk, he instructed her to carry it out to the paddock. Mystified, Roz obeyed.

The paddock, a small field close to the house, contained a gangly, knock-kneed foal. 'Oh, he's adorable.'

Dougal grunted. 'That's Harmony. His mother, Serenade, died last week, so he has to be hand-fed. That's your job from now on.'

This poor little thing was an orphan. Roz carefully carried the bucket of milk into the field and braced herself in case Harmony tried to knock her over. But he extended a curious nose and stood back. She moved towards him and he backed away.

'Hey, hey, easy,' she murmured. 'I'm going to give you some nice milk. Here, try a bit.' She made her voice as soothing as possible and he took two cautious steps towards her. 'Lovely warm milk, you'll like it. Try a little.' One more step and the foal buried his face in the bucket.

It was better than being awarded a medal. She continued to mutter nonsense to him as he drank greedily, and he rewarded her by occasionally raising his head to sniff at her. His mouth was milky and dripped on her, but she didn't mind.

When the bucket was empty, Harmony let her pet him and pull his ears gently.

'You've a nice touch with horses,' Dougal grunted approvingly. 'When he's old enough, you can put Harmony into training.'

'How long will that be?' she asked.

'He's got the breeding for a steeplechaser, but I think we may keep him as a hunter,' he said, 'so when he's three.'

He thought she was going to be around in three years' time. Something inside Roz warmed at that. She ignored the feeling, it was too dangerous.

'So what's the difference in training a racehorse?' she asked. It was time to get down to work.

Although it was a while since Andy had worked in Dublin, the concierge at the Shelbourne greeted him like an old friend. 'I'll have your bag taken up to your room, sir. Mr and Mrs Winter are expecting you. They're in the Horse-shoe Bar.'

There was something about Dublin that was cool and laid back. Jack and Abbie were able to sit at the bar without being plagued by fans. Everyone knew who he was but Dubliners would never be vulgar enough to interrupt his conversation with requests for autographs or photographs. It was the one city in the world where Jack could relax.

Although he didn't look particularly relaxed at the moment.

Jack was glaring at his Oris diver's watch, while Abbie laid her hand reassuringly on his thigh. His expression brightened considerably when he spotted Andy heading towards them.

Jack clapped him on the shoulder. 'Great to see you again.'

'You, too. Niall said that you needed me. What's up?'

Although he had spoken to Reilly about Jack's concerns on the journey, it was always better to get the client's story direct.

'Show him.' Jack nodded to Abbie.

She shook her head at his peremptory tone and gave him a look that was openly challenging.

Andy was tempted to laugh. Abbie was a brat if he ever saw one and he was willing to bet that the film star had his hands full keeping her in line.

'Jack is being an idiot. I've told him that it's probably a teenage fan, but he won't –'

Jack snatched the crumpled note from her hand and promptly received another glare. 'Look at this.'

Andy skimmed through the note. The paper was cheap and the writing was large and curved. Female, definitely, and from the text-speak phrasing, probably young. Still, it couldn't be ignored.

'What do you need me to do?'

Jack raked his fingers through his hair. 'There's been a technical glitch on my last movie. I need to do some voiceover work in the studio for a few days.'

'I'm not staying in my room while he's working,' Abbie snapped. The stubborn set of her jaw reminded Andy of someone else. He had been away from Roz for a few hours, but already he was missing her.

'So you can see my problem.' Jack gave Abbie a pleading look which would have earned him another Oscar.

Her mouth twitched before breaking into a smile. 'Stop that. Okay. Andy can babysit me for a few days, but I hope he likes shopping.'

'I love it,' Andy replied with as much sincerity as he could muster.

The following day, Andy was bitterly regretting the enthusiasm he had shown the evening before. Abbie Marshall was nothing like Roz. Whereas the sarky redhead could scan a store in under a minute, Abbie insisted on examining every piece, piling stuff over her arm and spending an age in the dressing room.

'I used to hate shopping,' she called to him through the curtain as she tried on yet another outfit. 'My sister could have made a career out of it, but vintage stuff is my one weakness. It's great that you're here. Jack hates doing this kind of stuff.'

Andy sighed. His instinct told him that the most dangerous thing in the shop was a 1920s fur stole, complete with tiny claws. If Abbie asked him if her butt looked big in that he would say yes – anything to get out of here.

He stood up when she emerged from the dressing room and headed for the till. Thank god the torture was over. 'Where to next?' he asked.

'A gift for Jack, and then we're done.'

Abbie's gift for Jack proved to be lingerie. A friend in New York had tipped her off about a new Irish range called 'Embrace' and Abbie looked as if she was going to purchase their entire stock.

He was almost relieved when his phone buzzed.

'Where are you?' Niall asked.

'I'm trapped in BT's lingerie department. Please send someone to shoot me.'

'Maybe next week – I have a job coming up in Afghanistan. But that's not why I called. Can you talk?'

Andy moved to a quiet corner, where he could observe the dressing rooms. 'Okay, go ahead.'

'Interpol have a lead on Hall, but they want to bring Roz in first.'

His heart plummeted. He had known this was coming, known that this thing with Roz couldn't last, but he had to force himself to ask the question, 'When?'

'ASAP. I'll send someone to Lough Darra to fetch her.'

'No. She's safe where she is for now. I'll do it when I finish here.'

'If you're sure.'

There was a question in Niall's tone but Andy ignored it. How could he explain to Niall when he didn't understand it himself? This thing with Roz was getting out of control. Over the past week he had caught a glimpse of another life. One he could have had with her if things were different.

'Fine. I'll delay things for a few days.'

'Thanks, boss.' Andy disconnected the call. He had to face reality. He wasn't the kind who settled down and she was going into protective custody. It was never meant to be. Their short time together had been nothing more than a hiatus, a time out of real life. He had known from the start that a future with Roz wasn't on the cards. So why did he feel like someone had torn his heart out?

24

'You look like someone broke your favourite toy.' Abbie stood before him, smiling and carrying more shopping bags. 'Come on, we can drop these back to the hotel and I'll buy you dinner.'

Abbie insisted on taking the long way back to the hotel. They passed Trinity College and strolled along the damp streets, passing rows of elegant Georgian buildings on the way back to the Shelbourne. After they freshened up, Abbie insisted she wanted sushi and they braved the rain again.

It should have been a pleasurable evening. How many guys could boast that they had dinner with the wife of a Hollywood A-lister? But although he was on full alert and kept his attention focussed on Abbie, his thoughts strayed back to Roz. How was he going to tell her that she was going back to Paris?

Abbie sat back in her chair. 'So tell me about the woman?'

'What woman?' Andy sat back, startled.

Abbie waved at a waiter and laced her fingers together, the picture of innocence.

'The one who's putting the frown on that handsome face.' She laughed. 'The last time I met you, you checked out every woman we met, but you haven't looked at a woman here all evening.'

Andy stalled for time. 'I don't know what you mean.'

She shook her head. 'And I thought Jack was secretive. What is it with you Irish guys?'

The waiter's interruption was welcome. 'I'll have a Black Bush, no ice.' Abbie said. 'What will you have, Andy?'

'Nothing. I'm on the job.'

She widened her eyes in mock horror. 'You can't let me drink alone. Who's the client here?'

'Bitch.' He laughed, knowing that his insult wouldn't faze her in the least. 'But I'm still not having any. Coffee please.'

'I am so telling Jack you called me that,' she warned him.

'Yeah, yeah.'

The waiter returned almost immediately with the coffee and Abbie's whiskey. Andy raised his cup and clinked it against her glass.

Abbie sipped her drink but, being a typical reporter, she didn't let him off the hook. 'Well, are you going to talk to me, or do I have to use the thumbscrews?'

'You brought thumbscrews?' He smiled. 'How did you get them through customs?'

Abbie waggled her glass and the amber liquid swirled. 'You know, I like this stuff, but not so much that it would distract me, so spill.'

What could he tell her about his relationship with Roz? Hell, he didn't understand it himself. They were polar opposites who should never have clicked, but they had and now he didn't know what to do about it. Andy took a sip of coffee. 'I met a girl, but it's hopeless. She's a client and she's going into protective custody as soon as I get back home.'

'She's staying with you?' Abbie perked up at the thought of Andy McTavish bringing a girl home to meet his family.

'She's pretending to be my fiancée. It was supposed to be a cover story, but my parents adore her. She's helping my father with the estate and my mother is teaching her to paint.'

He remembered his mother's face flushed with pleasure when she and Roz returned from their shopping excursion, giggling like a pair of teenagers. 'I have to hand her over to Interpol on Saturday and I have no idea what I'm doing anymore.'

Damn, he sounded worse than a lovelorn lad. He was grateful Abbie didn't laugh at him.

'Do you love her?' she asked.

Love? Andy McTavish didn't do love. He did flirting, seduction and sex, and he was pretty good at it. But love? 'Roz and I have the worst timing in the world. Next week she'll have a new home and a new identity and there's not a damn thing I can do about it.'

Abbie reached across to squeeze his hand in sympathy. To his left, a camera flashed and Andy came to attention. Damn, someone had papped them. God knows where the shot would appear. He rose to his feet but Abbie placed a hand on his arm.

'It's okay. Let him go. I'm used to it by now.'

They strolled back to the hotel where Andy escorted her to the penthouse and insisted on checking each room before he left.

In the elevator, his phone vibrated, announcing a message from Niall. Flights booked for Saturday from Belfast

302

and there was a check-in code. Someone would meet them with temporary ID for Roz.

He returned to his own room and switched on his laptop, wondering if Roz was online.

<Hi> he typed.

The words flashed on screen but there was no response. Andy checked Yahoo Detector to see if Roz was online, but invisible. He found her almost immediately. She was still mad at him and his stupid remark about the necklace.

<I know you're there.> He pressed send.

<I'm surprised you want to talk to a thief.>

Now, that little comment deserved a spanking when he got home. If they had time. <I was teasing you. My mother loses things all the time. One Christmas, she cooked her wedding ring inside the turkey.>

<Giggles. She did not.>

<She did. Dougal found it and broke a filling.>

<Yeah? One year, my dad left all my Christmas presents on the bus.>

Andy was glad she believed that story, but he wanted to punch something. He was willing to bet that her deadbeat dad had forgotten to buy her Christmas presents in the first place.

Roz was typing.

<But that wasn't the worst Christmas. Another year he came home drunk and forgot to defrost the chicken. We had to make do with veg and all the trimmings while we watched the Queen's speech.>

Jesus. He had spent years in the field, sometimes eating MREs on Christmas day. But the lads always made an effort and there would be a bit of cheer during the evenings.

<How old were you?>

<Nine. But Dad insisted on buying a big turkey when the shops were open again on Boxing Day. We were eating it for a week.>

He was definitely going to punch Peter Spring when he met him. Trying to turn the conversation to a more cheerful topic, Andy typed <How are things at Lough Darra?>

<☺☺ You won't believe this, but I'm a mummy! Dougal has given me a baby foal to take care of and he's going to show me how to train it.>

Training a horse would take two or three years. Roz had days at most before she had to leave Lough Darra. Should he tell her now? Why ruin the rest of her time there? *Coward*. A little voice inside his head taunted him. He couldn't lie to her. She had the right to know and there was no easy way to tell her.

<Niall had a call from Interpol today. They have a lead on Hall.>

There was a pause before she responded. <That's good, isn't it?>

<Yes and no. They want to make sure that you're safe. They need you to be a witness at his trial.>

Andy closed his eyes, feeling like a first class bastard. He took a deep breath and opened them again. His fingers hesitated over the keyboard. He had to tell her.

<They want to take you into protective custody.>

<When? When do they want me?>

<Saturday.>

The word flashed on the screen like a danger sign. Andy typed on. He couldn't stop now.

<Niall is organizing the travel arrangements. We're flying to Paris on Saturday afternoon.>

Her status changed to offline. Andy checked Yahoo Detector again but she was definitely gone this time. Fuck. He tried his phone. He should call her. He punched in her number. It rang several times before the call was rejected. Maybe he should try the landline? No, he couldn't do that, because then his mother would know that something was up, and he still had to tell them the bad news.

He raked a hand through his hair. The situation was spiralling into a clusterfuck.

'You complete dickhead, McTavish.'

Andy paced the hotel room, feeling like a caged lion. He was stuck here. Niall would have his nuts if he left Dublin before this job was done. He had a duty to his client, but the thought of Roz alone in her room at Lough Darra made his heart ache.

And he knew what his heart was telling him. He had to take her to Paris but there was no reason that she had to stay there alone. He had leave due – tons of it, and more money than he knew what to do with. They could live in Paris or wherever Interpol wanted them to live, but he wasn't losing her.

He couldn't let her face this alone. He had to be with her.

Paris? Witness protection? No, no way. Even if she was willing to spend the rest of her life doing some dreary job in a French factory, deliberately never doing anything to attract attention, it wouldn't fix anything else. Her dad needed that half a million, and Frankie needed a retirement fund.

She knew what witness protection involved. The police had explained it to her when they had caught up with her in Geneva after her sister's trial. Damn Andy and Niall for tracking her down.

Someone had seen Hall in the area where the antique dealer was killed and they knew he had been murdered with a knife commonly used by Navy SEALs. Hall was their number one suspect, but they needed a witness. A baker making his first batch of dough had seen her leaving the shop. Now they needed her to stand up in a courtroom and tell the judge what she had seen that night and she couldn't do it. It was more than her life was worth.

It would mean moving to a strange town, getting a low-profile job and never contacting anyone she knew for the rest of her life. She was used to moving from place to place and not calling anywhere home, though a pang went through her at the thought of leaving Lough Darra.

For someone who thought she was rootless and fancy-free, she discovered she had too many people who were holding her in place. Her dad, Frankie, Poppy, Dougal. And Andy. Okay, she knew she was never going to have a happy ever after with him, but the thought of never seeing him again drove a jagged shaft into her heart. The hollow ache would never go away.

Life without Andy would be just that, hollow.

So witness protection was out. She would have to make sure there was enough money from the Shergar scam to provide for her future.

Roz turned out the light and lay in silence, listening to the noises of the house. She usually didn't sleep well in strange places, but the odd creaking sounds of the house settling for the night were comforting.

For the next couple of days she busied herself with preparation for the Shergar job. Despite Andy telling her to lie low, the ball was her best chance to scam Tim O'Sullivan. He would be relaxed in the company of his rich horsey friends and he wouldn't expect anyone to try to trick him. She had to look the part and sound as if she was part of the horsey set. This was the biggest hustle of her life. Her dad was depending on her, Frankie was depending on her. She couldn't let them down.

She knew she had very little time to learn the horse business so she was determined to soak up everything she could. Dougal was a fountain of knowledge about racing, and she listened attentively. Among his ramblings about racing was the story of a Fairyhouse winner that had been trained on a dude ranch. She knew Nagsy would have to get some training if he was going to be convincing, and the fees for training a racehorse made her wince.

She added up the cost of buying Nagsy, transporting him to a suitable trainer, training fees, bribery, suitable documentation and all the other costs, and realized she was going to need seed money.

A lot of seed money.

She closed her fist over her engagement ring. Andy had bought it for her and kissed her as he put it on her finger. She hated to part with it, but it was the only way she could raise the money she needed. She vowed that the first thing she would do when she had money in hand was to redeem it and return it to him.

Dougal didn't believe in taking time off. Not only was she giving Harmony four small buckets of warm milk a day, he was taking her around more of the estate every morning. She got a shock one morning when she got out to the yard and found him sitting on a tall horse with Minty saddled beside him. By now, she knew the horses well enough to know he was riding Tully, a former race-horse. Beside him, Minty looked small.

'Thought you'd miss riding when that rascal was away, so I tacked up Minty for you. She could do with a good run.'

Roz gulped. She had ridden once and that was with Andy controlling the horse. 'I wasn't expecting to ride today, I'm not dressed,' she said weakly.

'Don't worry. I'll wait while you put on a pair of chaps over your jeans. There are some in the tack room.'

Damn, why hadn't she told him that she had her period? Dougal was the generation that would let her get away with anything if she pleaded 'women's trouble'. But it was too late now. She put on the chaps and came out slowly. Dougal was holding Minty, but a stable hand was there to give her a leg up into the saddle. He even tightened the girth for her. One less thing for her to worry about.

She got into the saddle and settled herself, trying to remember exactly what Andy had told her. She took the reins and the pedals – stirrups, she reminded herself – and hoped Minty was in a good mood. A quiet, docile mood.

Dougal led the way into a big field, somehow closing the gate behind them without getting down.

'I don't want you to overdo it. After all, you've had a heart attack recently,' she said.

He winked at her. 'Don't tell Andrew, but it's hard to kill a tough old countryman like me.' Then he turned his horse and trotted off.

Damn, damn, damn. There was nothing to do but follow. Without waiting for any instructions from her, Minty took off after Dougal. Roz set her teeth and tried to remember everything Andy had told her. Sit tall, head up, heels down, bum deep in the saddle. Absorb the movement.

Just when she thought she was getting the hang of it, Dougal broke into a canter. Oh crap. It looked far too fast. Without waiting for any signal from her, Minty picked up speed and did the same.

Roz resisted the urge to yank back on the reins. She had a vague memory that this could make a horse rear up on its back legs. Instead she grabbed a handful of mane and hoped this didn't hurt Minty either. Then she concentrated on staying on.

The ground rushed past far too fast. She knew she wasn't that high up, but it looked so far down. She looked out in front, between Minty's pricked ears, and watched Dougal as Tully began galloping in front of her.

She caught the rhythm and the balance she needed to stay on, but she had no idea how she would stop. In the meantime, she would enjoy the ride.

She had always loved speed, and had acquired more than her share of speeding tickets on her Ninja, but this was different. The wind was in her face, and underneath her was half a ton of muscle and strength whose joy in the gallop was infectious. She let out a yell, which encouraged Minty to stretch her legs even more.

By the time the end of the field came rushing towards them, she was so high on adrenaline that she had stopped worrying about how to stop. It didn't matter, Minty had that under control. When Dougal stopped, so did Minty. Roz had to catch her balance not to be tipped forwards with the sudden decrease in speed, but she made it.

'You've got an unusual style, but it works,' Dougal said. 'Tomorrow I'll get a faster horse for you.'

'Oh, I like Minty. She's a sweetheart.' Roz petted her damp neck. The smell of sweat and horse rose to her nose, pungent and exciting. She could get addicted to this.

'The two of you get on well together. So a quick gallop back, and maybe a hack around the roads to cool them off?'

Roz had no idea what he was suggesting, but she agreed. She had a few more days here before it would all end. She wanted to store up memories while she could.

25

The day of the ball was bright and clear. Roz did her usual routine, feeding Harmony, riding Minty, talking to Dougal about what makes a Gold Cup winner at Cheltenham, posing for Poppy and taking the dogs for a walk. All normal. No reason for her heart to be breaking while she did any of them.

She knew Andy believed she wasn't going to the ball. That he had told her parents to give their tickets to someone else. But this was the best opportunity she would ever have to meet Tim O'Sullivan, not as a poor relation, but as the owner of a prize racehorse. So she had told Poppy that she would love to go and Andy would try to come as well. When he found out, Andy would know she had been stringing him along.

She thought she had herself in full control, but Poppy put down the brush after half an hour. 'You're not yourself, my dear. Why don't you go and get ready for the party? The painting will wait.'

No, it wouldn't. Tomorrow she would be gone. She would never see Poppy again. Why did that thought make her insides ache with a hollow pain? Poppy was a nice lady, but she wasn't related to Roz. She was Andy's mother. Not hers. Never hers.

She had to blink back tears. 'Thanks, I'll do that.' She was proud that the quiver in her chin didn't affect her voice. A long, hot shower would calm her. And if a few tears fell while she was there, no one would see.

Poppy washed the paint off her brushes and put them away carefully. Roz had never realized that a smell like white spirits and linseed oil could be so evocative. She would never be able to see a painting again without being transported back to Poppy's studio.

This painting would never be finished. She hoped Poppy wouldn't hate her for it.

'I have something for you, dear,' Poppy said. 'Come with me.'

'You shouldn't have.' They had done too much for her already. But Roz followed Poppy to her room and looked around with curiosity.

Andy's parents still shared a bed, a massive, hand-carved mahogany monstrosity. The room was warm, heated by a fireplace where logs burnt, and would have been gloomy if it wasn't decorated by Poppy's paintings and family photographs.

Roz couldn't prevent herself examining them. There was Andy as a baby, held in Dougal's arms, a Dougal who looked remarkably like Andy now. There was another boy, too, a boy with plump cheeks and a beaming smile. 'That was Robert, my eldest,' Poppy said quietly. 'It broke my heart when he died.'

There were pictures of the two boys growing up, and it was obvious that even though he was younger, Andy was the leader. The mischief in his eyes was a clear indicator that no matter how angelic their smiles, the boys would be in trouble as soon as they were released from sitting for the photo.

Another photograph showed Andy and Robert wearing uniforms, sitting on an old-fashioned trunk, on their way to boarding school. Next they were dressed in formal evening clothes. More followed – Andy in his Ranger's uniform. Robert in climbing gear – determination in his eyes and the set of his chin.

Then a single painted portrait of Robert, blurred and misty, with a grave in the background.

Looking at the paintings broke Roz's heart. How could Poppy cope with losing a child? How could she get up in the morning and force herself to pick up a paintbrush?

'Don't cry,' Poppy said.

Roz hadn't been aware that her cheeks were wet.

'No mother should bury her son. But life goes on, and now that Andy has you, there will be another generation of McTavishes running around the house and breaking the china.'

Oh god, this was worse. Roz gulped, trying to swallow the tears. How could she tell Poppy that it was pretend, that there would be no wedding, no grandchildren, no happy ever after? She nodded, not trusting herself to speak.

'I didn't bring you here to upset you,' Poppy said. She rummaged through her drawers and pulled out a long, shallow box. 'I wanted to give you these.'

'You shouldn't give me anything,' Roz protested.

'Oh, they're not valuable. But I wore them the night Dougal proposed to me, and you're the first girl I've ever met who loves to wear gloves. I hope you like them.'

Roz opened the box and drew out a pair of long silk gloves in a deep blue colour. They were fastened by a row of at least twenty tiny buttons and would be a perfect match for her engagement ring.

They were so beautiful.

She picked them up. The feel of them was gorgeous. Roz couldn't remember when anyone had ever given her something like this, a gift from the heart. She worked for things, or she scammed them or occasionally she stole them. No one gave her something as precious as these gloves without a reason. But she had no doubt Poppy had the purest of motives.

Despite herself, she burst into tears.

She was stunned to feel arms around her. Poppy hugged her tightly, allowing her to cry herself out. Eventually she said, 'I can take them back if they are upsetting you.'

'No!' Roz clutched the gloves. 'I love them.' And she did.

'Then go and get ready. I'll need a bath to get the paint from under my fingernails.' She held up her hands, thin and hard-working and so gentle, to show the dirt under her nails. 'Dougal will be expecting us to be ready on the dot of half past seven.'

Roz took a long time bathing and getting ready, and by the time she was dressed, she was able to apply her make-up with a steady hand. Lots of smoky eye shadow and a bright red lipstick drew attention away from the traces of pink under her eyes.

Putting on the gloves, however, was a different matter. Poppy's hands were smaller than hers, and though she was able to get the left one on and do up the twenty-five buttons, she couldn't manage the right one. She slipped her ring over the glove and admired it as the sapphire glittered. She would need help doing up the right glove. She hurried downstairs to the front door where Dougal was standing, smart in a formal tuxedo and bow tie.

The car waiting outside was a Rolls Royce. A real Rolls Royce.

'Just how rich are you guys?' she asked before she could contain herself. Who the hell owned a Roller?

Dougal laughed, not offended. 'Don't get excited. My father bought this little beauty over thirty years ago, but it runs nicely. And as long as we don't take her out too often, the insurance isn't bad either.'

The inside was all white leather and luxury and Roz couldn't resist running her hands over it, marvelling at the way it had been kept. 'The back seat is more comfortable than my bed at home,' she said as she sat down.

'You should try driving it,' said Poppy from behind the wheel. 'I miss power steering.'

Poppy was wearing what looked like an original Chanel dress, and a string of pearls which had the roughness and glow of the real thing.

'You two clean up well,' Roz said.

Poppy looked down the empty drive. 'Where is that boy? We'll have to go without him and he can catch up afterwards.'

Roz hoped not. Andy had already made his opinion quite clear and would be furious if he discovered she had gone to the ball. But this was something she had to do, no matter what Andy thought.

She and Dougal sat in the back while Poppy drove, and

he fastened her glove for her on the way. For some reason, his simple act of kindness made her want to cry again.

'Are you sure Jack will be okay about the picture in the paper?' Andy asked, as he walked Abbie Marshall back to the hotel. He had hoped that the photographer in the restaurant was a fan and was annoyed that the photo had appeared so quickly.

She considered. 'He doesn't like me being in the media, but he won't think I'm having an affair with you, if that's what you're thinking.'

Andy watched the crowd, alert for anyone paying them more attention than usual, or suspicious bulges under coats, or the body language that spelled military. 'Oh good,' he said absently. 'I wouldn't like to cause trouble.'

Abbie laughed. 'I know you think you're god's gift to womankind, but I'm married to Jack Winter. *THE* Jack Winter. He doesn't worry about other men. And because he's Jack, I don't worry about other women.'

Andy marvelled at her confidence, even as he envied it. What would it be like to have a woman who felt that way about him? Correction. To have Roz feeling that way about him?

With Roz he would be so busy keeping up with her that there would be no time to think about other women. The hunt had always appealed to him, but life with her would be a constant chase. He would never get bored.

And he couldn't wait to see her again. His parents were going to the big charity do this evening, so he'd have Roz all to himself at home. What would he do first? There was so much he had planned for her that he was as giddy as a kid in a sweet shop.

He couldn't wait.

'Reilly will be arriving soon to take over from me,' he told Abbie, while he continued to watch the crowd. Something was up. His Spidey sense was tingling. 'She's as good as they get.'

Abbie perked up. 'She was the first female Ranger, wasn't she? I can't wait to talk to her and find out all about it.'

Typical reporter. She couldn't meet someone without wanting to know all about them. He flicked her a glance and she was alight with curiosity. 'Good luck with that. She won't tell you anything.'

'Oh, come on, it sounds like a great story. The Rangers are like the Irish SEALs, right?'

He nodded. 'Something like that. But we're better. And we don't talk about it.'

'I'll get it out of her.'

They reached the Shelbourne and Abbie pressed the button for the lift. 'I'll drop the bags in my room and join you in the bar.'

Andy shook his head. 'When will you learn? You go nowhere without me.' He stepped into the lift with her and pressed the button for the sixth floor. When the lift arrived, he told her, 'Stay in the lift with the door closed until I come to tell you the room is clear.'

She pulled a face at him, but closed the door of the lift as he headed for her suite. Once inside, he examined it carefully, checking for any sort of booby-trap as well as anyone hidden there. He had no reason to think there was any danger to Abbie, but he was always thorough and there was something in the air today. He gave an extra sweep to be sure, but there was no sign of any intruder.

He made one more pass, but before he had finished the door of the penthouse was pushed open. He looked up and there she was. Damn it, she should have waited for him. 'I told you –' he began.

'Not my idea,' she said. Her voice trembled, and now Andy could see the man behind her.

Hall pushed Abbie in through the door and closed it behind him, locking it. His arm was around her, holding a diving knife at her throat. The point of it was under her ear, and was rock steady. SEALs, even disgraced, dishonourably discharged ones, didn't make mistakes.

'I'd ask for your autograph,' Hall said to Abbie. 'But something tells me you won't give it. So how about he tells me where he's stashed Roz?'

Fuck, fuck, fuck. A dozen different scenarios raced through Andy's mind as he thought of ways to take down Hall. But every single one of them would put Abbie at risk. 'Who?' he said, playing for time.

'Nice try.' Hall shifted the knife slightly. 'But I saw her face when she looked at you in Tullamore. She has the hots for you. I'm betting you two are an item.'

Funny how quickly Hall had spotted something that it had taken him so long to realize. Andy shrugged. 'Lots of women have the hots for me. I'm pretty.'

He gave the other man a dismissive once-over. 'Way prettier than you.'

Hall was tall, broad and blond, with a sort of wholesome handsomeness which was wholly false. He sneered at Andy. 'I eat pretty boys for breakfast.'

'So I heard. They talk in the locker room.'

Hall's face tightened. 'Tell me where Red is or your client gets it.'

Andy moved half a step closer, and stopped when the point of the knife broke Abbie's skin, causing a single drop of blood to run down her neck. 'For fuck's sake, think about what you're doing. You're already wanted for one murder. Do you think killing someone else will help?'

'Who said anything about killing?' His knife stayed perfectly still, but his other hand moved, grabbing Abbie's breast and twisting it. She screamed.

The sound tormented Andy but there was nothing he could do. Hall didn't take his eyes off him even as he tortured Abbie. Hall repeated it, and Abbie's scream was louder. 'This is the warm-up. I can do permanent damage that doesn't leave a single bruise. Want me to show you?'

Andy shook his head. 'I don't know where she is. Niall has her safe somewhere.'

Hall buzzed. 'Wrong answer.' He moved his hand again, and Abbie's resulting scream was even louder. Damn the soundproofed penthouse walls. This was one time Andy would have been glad of neighbours complaining about the noise.

'Try again. And this time get it right.' He did something that caused Abbie to sag in his arms, gasping and gagging.

The sight tore at Andy, making him sweat, but Hall

never took his eyes off him. 'Stop. Let her go and I'll tell you.'

Hall didn't let Abbie go, but he did loosen his grip on her breast. 'I'm listening.'

'Don't tell him,' Abbie's voice was faint but clear.

The door opened, and Jack Winter stumbled into the room.

He swayed as he stood there, staring around him with stupefied wonder. 'What you doin' here?' he asked Hall. His words were slurred and his Irish accent was stronger.

'Fucking drunk,' Hall sneered.

'Wha's that mean?' Winter held onto the back of a chair. 'Why you hugging m' wife?' His head tipped and he straightened up with a jerk.

'Go get help,' Andy told Winter, his attention on the knife at Abbie's throat. Jack couldn't see it from where he stood. Was he sober enough to understand? The one thing he didn't need was another hostage in Hall's power.

'Help?' Winter blinked owlishly. 'Don' need help. I can walk.'

How drunk was Jack? Andy sniffed. There was something wrong. No smell of alcohol. The eyes behind the slitted eyelids were bright and intelligent.

Damn it, Andy couldn't even signal to Winter. Hall didn't make the mistake of forgetting about Andy.

'You were saying,' Hall reminded Andy.

Andy opened his mouth to recite the address of the flat in Rathmines he had shared one summer in Dublin. Winter let go of the chair and stumbled towards Abbie. He tripped over his feet and lurched into Hall.

It took a split second for Hall to push him away, but it

was all Andy needed. He launched himself at the bigger man, breaking his hold on Abbie as he did.

The next few minutes were a blur. Andy was determined to do whatever it took to take Hall down, but he had to stay away from his lethal knife hand. He grabbed Hall's wrist and tried to pin him down with his body. Hall punched him hard, the blow snapping his head back and making stars dance in front of his eyes.

Andy prayed that Abbie had got away.

He and Hall rolled over and Hall, now on top, aimed the knife at him. Andy twisted, catching the weapon under his body and making the most of the chance to knee Hall in the ribs and punch him. He was aware of a table falling in the melee, the crash of the crystal glasses almost as loud as the punches falling.

Finally, when he wondered if he could hold out any longer, a siren outside heralded the police. Hall fought his way to his feet, knocking over Abbie and dashing for the corridor.

By the time four Gardaí arrived into the room, he was gone, and the only evidence of his presence were the bruises on Andy's body.

26

If she hadn't been so nervous about finally meeting Tim O'Sullivan and putting the Shergar scam in motion, Roz would have been tempted to whistle. The gigantic ballroom was lit by dozens of chandeliers shedding glittering light over the white-clothed tables, laid out in splendour around a dance floor.

'We're sitting at table ten,' Poppy said, leading the way. 'I expect Andy will be here by now.'

Andy was not at table ten. His place was empty. 'Really, that boy is always missing for meals,' Poppy said crossly. 'We never know when he's going to turn up.'

Roz didn't have time to worry about that. The other places at the table were already occupied.

'Little Red, is it you?' The heavy French accent didn't disguise the astonishment in the words.

No, it couldn't be. In the FemDom circles of Paris, she was known as Little Red. This was Ireland. Northern Ireland at that. But it was. Claudine Blé, the French Minister of Cultural Affairs, who Roz had last seen at a FemDom party in Paris. And beside her, grinning like a shark, was Anton Fox, a former client.

'Hello, Red, here to play?'

She was supposed to have met him in Paris to Domme him but got arrested instead. Clearly he hadn't forgotten her. 'I haven't seen you since Paris,' he said, his voice oily with innuendo.

She wasn't going to make life easy for him. 'I don't remember seeing you at all.'

'How quickly you forget,' he laughed. 'But then you always did play hard to get.' He moved to seat her but Dougal got there first.

She smiled at Dougal but kept her attention on Fox. 'In your case, consider me impossible to get.'

Poppy looked from one to the other. 'Do you two know each other?'

Roz shook her head. 'Barely acquainted.' She picked up her napkin and shook it out.

Fox grinned, showing a lot of teeth. 'If you say so, Red.' The threat was clear.

'Still in stocks and bonds?' she asked him sweetly.

He glared at her. The last time she had seen him, he had been locked in the stocks ready for her to flog him. She couldn't remember why she hadn't and she wasn't going to let him discomfort her. But she was glad when a couple arrived to join them at the table – until she saw who it was.

Tim O'Sullivan and an older woman. Her heart pounded. This wasn't her usual mark, a stranger she was going to cheat. Oh dear god, how was she going to go through with this?

You can do it, she chided herself. This is your uncle, remember? He's the man who raised your sister in luxury and left you to rot in a council flat in London. The O'Sullivans ruined your life. It's their fault you're in this mess.

'I'm glad you came with me, Tim. I would never have managed those stairs.' The older woman with him had a strong Cork accent which stood out among all the Belfast and Dublin voices. Roz's breath froze in her chest while she tried to process the thoughts racing around her head.

She had thought she was prepared for meeting Tim O'Sullivan. It wasn't as if she didn't know what he looked like – he was rarely off the news, complaining about governments interfering in how airlines ran and thinking up interesting new ways to charge passengers for extras. In the flesh, he looked taller than on screen.

But she hadn't been expecting the woman sitting beside him. Roz's stomach tightened into a knot as she looked at her grandmother. This wasn't part of the plan. She leaned into Dougal's shadow, watching as Tim helped the older woman into her chair. Her grandmother was at least seventy, petite and buttoned up in a black silk suit, and wearing a string of pearls much smaller than Poppy's. But her mouth pursed as she surveyed the opulence around her, and her expression tightened even more when she saw the McTavishes.

Over the years, she had heard lots of stories about Granny O'Sullivan. How she had told her own daughter that she couldn't come home unless she abandoned her lover, Peter Spring.

Her father had no doubt that if Maggie had gone home, their twin daughters would have been sent away to prevent a scandal. Granny O'Sullivan wouldn't have her good name dragged through the mud. A daughter who lived in a hippy commune was bad enough. Living with a man with criminal convictions, even if they were for minor offences, and having babies out of wedlock? It would have scandalized the entire town of Castletownbere-haven.

The good name of the O'Sullivan family was more important than her love for her daughter.

In her imagination, Roz had always pictured her grand-mother as being tall and broad-shouldered, with hands like shovels and a voice calling down the wrath of god on sinners. The woman beside Tim was a surprise.

Roz braced herself. This was why she was here, what all of this had been leading up to. She was going to lay the bait so Tim O'Sullivan would buy Nagsy for at least half a million.

Get into character, Roz. It's show time.

Tim was dressed in an expensive suit, which almost concealed his rounded belly, and a clashing tie. She would have recognized him anywhere. Roz hated that she couldn't ignore the family who had managed to ignore her for so long, but she devoured anything on the news or in the papers about O'Sullivan Airlines and Tim in particular.

Poppy, ever the gracious hostess, asked, 'Does every-one know each other?' She performed the introductions, starting with the trim chic Frenchwoman, while the staff served soup. 'Madame Blé, please allow me to introduce the man who donated our top prize of the evening, two round-the-world airline tickets – Mr Tim O'Sullivan, and his mother, Mrs Philomena O'Sullivan.'

They nodded to each other, smiling politely.

Poppy turned to Roz. 'And may I present my soon to be daughter-in-law, Miss Roz O'Sullivan.'

Fox smiled at her, showing a lot of teeth. 'Charmed to meet you, Miss O'Sullivan.'

She wasn't going to let this go. 'Actually, it's Roz O'Sullivan-Spring.'

Tim's bushy eyebrows bristled as he glared at her. 'Is that so?'

His accent was stronger in person, but she would have known his voice from his frequent television appearances.

His mother put her hand on his arm. 'Ah, Tim don't –'

To Roz's surprise, O'Sullivan actually shut his mouth. Philomena's hands shook as she fumbled in her evening bag for a hanky. A real one, Roz noticed, not a tissue. The elderly woman dabbed at her face and when she turned to Roz her eyes were bright with tears. 'I'm sorry, this is a bit of a shock. Lord, Roisin, but you're the spit of your sister.'

The reference to her sister startled her as much as the tears, but Roz reined in her feelings. Of course they knew Sinead. They had raised her, hadn't they? But they hadn't given a damn about her twin sister. Years of bitterness welled up, but Roz reminded herself of what was at stake. This was no time for a confrontation.

'Thank you. It's nice to finally meet you,' she said, using the poshest voice she could manage.

Poppy looked from one side of the table to the other. 'A family reunion. How lovely.'

'And long overdue,' she said under her breath, hoping no one else could hear it. Why did Philomena have to be here tonight? Meeting her grandmother could ruin everything.

Fortunately, Madame Blé intervened. 'You 'ave not met?'

Roz watched the O'Sullivans carefully while she replied to the French minister. 'No, I was brought up by my father in England. Sometimes I forget I have a family in Ireland. I'm sure they feel the same.'

Tim glared. 'Well, it wasn't as if you didn't know where we were.'

So now it was her fault? 'You'd have welcomed me with open arms, I'm sure.'

For an old woman, Philomena's voice was surprisingly strong. 'You're family, Roisin. You're always welcome.'

The sympathy in her grandmother's voice unnerved her. She almost sounded sincere. Yeah right. Roz snorted. If she really meant that, the O'Sullivans would have searched for her. *Don't do this now. You'll ruin everything.* Roz took a deep breath and managed to sound polite. 'How nice to know that.'

Fox seemed unaware of the tension gripping the table. He had finished his soup and was determined to talk. 'So what are you doing in Ireland, Red? Change of pace for you, isn't it?'

'Don't call me that.' The horrible man made her palms itch and she had a sudden desire to flog him hard. 'I'm staying with the Campbell McTavishes at Lough Darra.'

Poppy beamed around the table. 'Isn't it wonderful? She's engaged to my son, Andy. We thought he'd never settle down. And she's such a lovely girl.'

Trying to sound modest, Roz said, 'We're a good match.'

She was glad when the waiter put a plate with a fillet

steak and potatoes au gratin in front of her. She busied herself moving food around so she could avoid the asparagus, which she hated. Another waiter arrived at her side with a bottle of red wine. She was horrified to realize she had already finished a glass.

Roz shook her head and held up her water glass. When she was working, she needed a clear head. A discussion about where to get the best steak dominated the conversation for a while, allowing Roz to observe the O'Sullivans. She had to make her move soon.

Her chance came when the plates were being cleared and Poppy waved. 'Dougal, look, there's Ariana and Rory. We must go and say hello.'

The Campbell McTavishes got up, leaving Roz at the table.

This was her chance to bait the hook. She turned to Tim. 'So, no luck in the Gold Cup this year?'

He took a swig of his wine. 'Not a bit of it. It's easier to run an airline.'

She smiled. 'I'm sure you're right. But I'm hoping to do better myself.'

His eyes lit up. Gotcha. 'Oh. Has Dougal found himself a winner?'

'No. I have.' She shrugged. 'It was one of those one in a million flukes. At least the next Gold Cup winner will be in O'Sullivan colours. But not yours.' She smiled at him.

'Is that so?' he asked, too casually. She wanted to laugh at his expression.

'Yes. And I'll make a fortune in stud fees, when his bloodlines are revealed . . .' She left it hanging. Let the mark do the work.

'What are his bloodlines? I know Dougal's bought in a few lately, but they're too young for the Cup.' Relaxed and friendly, one horse person to another, but the curiosity in his eyes gave him away.

Roz sipped her water. 'This is nothing to do with Dougal, although I am considering allowing him to buy a half share if he can afford it.'

Make sure the mark knew what sort of money they were talking about.

Tim snorted dismissively. 'And what would you know about horses?'

Was her uncle such a patronizing bastard to everyone, or had he saved it for her? Her determination to take him for a fortune mounted. 'Well, I haven't bought as many also-rans as you have. But even a city girl like me knows about the bloodlines of this horse.'

'And what would those be, eh?'

Gotcha! She smiled. 'I'd rather not say until after he's won the Cup. The odds will be ridiculous, and the media circus would be crazy.'

Claudine Blé intervened. 'But how is this? No horse is certain to win a race.'

Roz could have kissed her. A perfect opening. 'True, but this horse is amazing. His father won every race by the greatest margin in history. I'd say the odds are in my favour.'

Fox laughed. 'And you're such a connoisseur of flesh . . .'

Gruesome man. She fixed him with a steady look. 'I do consider myself skilled with a riding whip, true.'

'*Touché.*' He mangled the French word.

329

Tim harrumped. 'I'd be interested in seeing his time trials. If he's as good as you say, I might be interested in chipping in a few bob. Keep it in the family, eh?'

Claudine Blé looked interested. 'You should enter him in the Prix de L'Arc de Triomphe.'

'I probably will. I hope you're not fond of that trophy, because I'll be taking it home.'

'So, what did you say his breeding was again?' Tim asked, trying to sound casual.

She laughed. 'I'm not telling. Let's say his father won the Epsom Derby by ten lengths.'

She watched as O'Sullivan processed that and saw the instant the penny dropped.

'You don't mean . . .' Tim laughed derisively. 'Someone's sold you a pup. That horse only had one season at stud.'

Hook, line and sinker. Roz smiled. 'Officially. But semen freezes.'

With perfect timing, Poppy and Dougal returned to the table. Poppy stuck a fork into her apple crumble before she turned to Philomena. 'I know it's traditional for the bride's family to organize the wedding, but do you think I might? I never had a daughter.'

Her grandmother turned to examine Roz and seemed to make up her mind. 'No. If there's to be a wedding, we'll do it. She's an O'Sullivan after all.'

Roz almost had whiplash from the sudden turn in the conversation. Had she fallen down a rabbit hole? Poppy and Granny O'Sullivan were planning *her* wedding as if she wasn't there.

She couldn't stay silent. 'Andy and I are planning a quiet ceremony. And we'll organize it ourselves, thank you.'

She had to get away. Roz pushed her chair back and headed for the toilets. If she stayed here any longer, she would commit violence and it would ruin the work she had done setting Tim up for the scam.

Roz splashed water over her face, not caring that it was ruining her make-up. The door to the ladies room opened and footsteps sounded on the tiled floor. Please don't be Poppy. Roz lifted her head and saw the last person she wanted to see. Philomena O'Sullivan.

'I didn't mean to upset you. Mrs Campbell McTavish caught me off guard with all the talk about weddings.'

'I bet you're relieved you won't be doing it.' Roz couldn't resist biting back. How dare her grandmother pretend that she actually cared about her at the table? It was all for show. Don't sully the precious O'Sullivan name in public.

Philomena stiffened. 'Nonsense. Didn't I do the weddings for the other girls?'

This was too much. She couldn't control herself any longer. Roz glared. 'I wouldn't know. I didn't get an invite.'

For a moment she thought there was a flash of hurt in the faded blue eyes. Eyes, she realized, that must have been the exact colour of her own fifty years ago.

Then the older woman squared her shoulders. 'I'm your grandmother, young lady. The only one you have. And you will not take that tone with me.'

Roz gasped. 'How dare you? This is the first time we've met. You have no right to tell me what to do.'

'As Tim said, you knew where I was. You could have contacted me at any time.'

Roz could hardly believe her attitude. How dare she do this? How dare she pretend that she would have welcomed her? The O'Sullivans never gave a damn about her. 'Oh yes, I'll go crawling to the woman who threw her own daughter out of the house. You killed my mother.'

The older woman's face blanched with shock. 'I did not.'

'You told my mother that if she stayed with my father, you would have nothing to do with her. You told her she wasn't welcome in your home. Her home.'

For long seconds, Philomena held Roz's gaze. A single tear rolled down her powdered face and she didn't bother to wipe it away. 'Whatever you've been told about me, I loved my daughter. Maggie was a hothead, always getting into trouble and I didn't handle her well.' Her eyes clouded and she shook her head. 'We were too alike.'

There was a betraying quiver in her voice, and despite herself, Roz was shaken. She patted the old woman's shoulder, unable to think of anything to say. When her father talked about her, Philomena O'Sullivan was a virago, a fire-breathing dragon, not a tearful old woman.

Philomena gathered herself. 'Maggie was a beautiful girl. She could have had anyone she wanted. I couldn't bear to watch her throw herself away on a useless bla'gard like him.'

Roz snatched her hand back. 'That useless bla'gard is my father.'

How dare she blame her father for what happened? Roz turned and marched back into the large dining room, furious at the entire O'Sullivan family. She had almost fallen for it. Almost believed that they weren't a crowd of new-money, snobbish bastards.

Roz paused at the entrance to take a deep breath and calm down. The price for Nagsy had just gone up. Forget half a million. Roz was going to take Tim O'Sullivan for at least a million. She was going to take every spare penny he had, and when it was over, she would tell everyone and make him a laughing stock. It would serve him right. It would serve all of them right.

She pushed open the door to the ballroom. In her absence, the orchestra had tuned up and started to play.

She saw Anton Fox heading straight for her, and decided she couldn't deal with him without a whip in her hand. Instead, she made a beeline for Rory Baxter. 'I have a sudden urge to dance,' she told him.

Mesmerized, and ignoring Ariana, he rose to his feet and held out his arms to her. She smiled as they took to the dance floor.

27

The traffic on the road back north drove Andy crazy. It was the weekend, and every lunatic in the city seemed determined to get in his way. He took one hand off the wheel to rub his jaw. It ached from the punch Hall had landed. His parents would go crazy when they saw the state of his face.

He was looking forward to relaxing when he got home. His parents would be at the ball, and Roz would be there all on her own. Wicked ideas of what he could do to her made him smile. As soon as Maggie left, he was going to chase a naked Roz around the house, armed with a bottle of oil and a feather duster. He wondered how fast she would run.

And after that, they would have to talk.

He had no clue what he was going to say to her. A declaration of love would make her laugh her head off and he couldn't blame her. Mr Love 'em and leave 'em didn't have a plan for this – fate, karma, or whatever it was that had turned around and bitten him on the ass.

Andy thought of the women before her. He remembered most of their names – he wasn't a complete bastard – and wondered if any of them, well, any of them other than Ariana, had ever cared for him, or whether he was no more than a passing fancy. The thought set off another ache in his jaw. Damn Roz for making him feel like this.

The traffic ground to a halt and a chorus of beeping horns sounded, followed by the sound of a siren. Accident. He was going to be late.

It was dark by the time he arrived at Lough Darra. The lights in the library were off. Good. His parents had already left. Grabbing his bag from the trunk, he headed into the kitchen. 'Hi, Maggie.'

'Oh, you've missed them. Poppy had to drive and she wasn't too pleased. You know how she hates driving that antique thing.'

'The Rolls?' The Phantom was a souvenir from his grandfather's time. It was a beautiful car if you didn't like heating or air conditioning, and apart from the occasional car rally, it rarely came out of the garage.

'Well, your dad said that it was a special occasion. He had the lads polishing it all day.'

Andy grinned. Dougal was worse than an army sergeant and there was quite a lot of chrome on the Phantom. His stomach growled. He had missed lunch and something bubbling away on the top of the range smelled appetizing. 'Has Roz eaten yet?'

A puzzled look crossed Maggie's face. 'Eaten? No. Sure, they'll be having a five course dinner at the ball.'

'She went with them?' He had warned her that the place would be full of photographers. The last thing they needed was Hall making an appearance at Lough Darra.

'Oh, she looked beautiful. Poppy made Dougal take a photo of the pair of them together. Your mother was so proud of her.'

Fuck. He was going to tan Roz's hide when he got his hands on her.

335

'Will you be wanting dinner?'

'No thanks. It looks like I'm going to a ball.'

Andy dashed upstairs and had a tepid shower. He riffled through his wardrobe until he found a tux. Slinging a bow tie around his neck, he raced downstairs again, almost colliding with a startled Maggie in the hall.

'Don't wait up.'

Ignoring the speed limit, he kept his foot to the floor until he reached the FitzWilliam hotel. The former mansion was now a five-star hotel favoured by visiting heads of state and golfers with more money than sense. He tossed his car keys to the valet stationed at the entrance and made his way inside.

At the entrance to the ballroom, he paused, scanning the tables until he found the one he wanted. Andy whistled under his breath. Holy hell. His parents, Tim O'Sullivan and his mother, the French minister for something or other – he couldn't remember her name – and Anton Fox. He hadn't seen him since the party at Versailles. What was that bastard doing here? Roz must think she'd fallen into the seventh circle of hell.

And speaking of hell, where was she?

The small orchestra was playing a waltz. Older couples circled the floor sedately while the show-offs displayed their best *Strictly* moves. At the centre of the floor one couple moved gracefully. The figure-hugging dress flared out around her calves as she moved. The demure jewelled collar was the only thing that stopped the dress being indecent. He made a mental note that she wasn't allowed to wear such an outrageous garment in public again, not unless he was with her. Some of her hair was artfully pinned with silver stars that sparkled under the lights. The rest of her curls cascaded down her bare back like a Titian waterfall.

Rory fucking Baxter was touching Roz. No one was permitted to do that except him.

As Andy watched, Rory bent his head to whisper something in her ear and she threw back her head and laughed.

Andy was going to kill him.

'Welcome, sir.' The maître d' obscured his vision of the dancing pair and Andy was temporarily dragged away from his homicidal fantasies. 'I'm afraid you're a little late for dinner. Can I get the chef to prepare something for you?'

As if on cue, his gut rumbled again. He couldn't beat Baxter to death on an empty stomach and there was one guaranteed cure for the munchies. 'I'll have a basket of bread and a cheese plate, please. And some brown sauce.'

'Brown sauce?' The man's horrified expression was quickly hidden behind a polite mask. This was a five-star hotel, after all. Nothing was too much trouble for a guest, even one with a battered face, not as long as he was wearing a tuxedo.

'Yep,' Andy replied, taking perverse enjoyment from the maître d's discomfort. 'The kind that comes in a bottle will do fine. Drop it over to table ten.'

Andy made his way carefully around the outskirts of the ballroom. There was no point in alerting Fred and Ginger that he was here. Nodding to the other guests, he kissed his mother on the cheek and ignored her hissed questions about his appearance. He didn't take his eyes off the dance floor for a moment.

He would eat, then he would deal with Roz.

The music changed to a sultry rumba and Andy smiled. He was willing to bet that Rory didn't do Latin American. The guy waltzed as if he had a poker up his ass. It was time to lock on to his target.

As he left his chair, his mother placed a warning hand on his arm. She glanced at the dance floor where Rory and Roz were swaying. 'Andrew, I know you've had some sort of argument, but –'

'Don't worry, Mum. I'm only going to dance.'

He approached the couple with the stealth of a predator. Roz had her back to him. Either she hadn't noticed his arrival or she was doing a damn fine job of ignoring him. Rory spotted him first. From his shocked expression, his face must be worse than he'd thought.

Andy tapped Roz on the shoulder and she whirled around. Up close, he could see that the dress was a perfect match for her eyes. The expression 'hotter than hell' popped into his head, but the facial expression that greeted him was colder than ice.

'Care to dance?' He didn't wait for her to reply, but pulled her into his arms. Automatically, she placed her hand on his shoulder and before she could protest, he whirled her onto the dance floor.

He was a good dancer, but she was better. Roz lived the music. She had a natural rhythm that drew the eye of every man in the place. If it weren't for the storm brewing in her eyes, it would have been one of the most erotic experiences of his life. Andy pulled her closer. He'd almost forgotten how good it was to hold her in his arms.

Drawing a deep breath, he inhaled the fragrance of her hair. Her scent was soft, like flowers. 'Miss me, baby?'

She held herself stiff and unyielding in his hold. 'Not a bit, but I'm sure Abbie Marshall does. Why don't you go back to her?'

'Because I don't want her and, besides, Jack would probably kill me.'

'Are they selling tickets? I'd pay money to see that.'

Roz almost managed to twirl out of his arms, but he yanked her back and clamped his hand around her wrist, holding her tightly against him. 'That sounds like jealousy,' he murmured against her ear.

She pulled away from his embrace. 'I've known from the start exactly what you were. Any woman that falls for you would have to be crazy. Why should I be jealous?' Her glare would have melted a glacier. 'Don't flatter yourself. This *thing* between us is nothing more than fucking. We had fun and now it's over.'

Ouch. She didn't believe in pulling her punches, but Andy could sense the hurt welling behind her words. Something had happened. It would take more than a Photoshopped picture in a tabloid newspaper to make her this mad at him.

Her cheeks flared with colour as she continued, 'I've had enough of you and your imbecile friends. I'll be glad to get back to Paris.'

'That's what we need to talk about.' He glanced around him. They were drawing attention and it wasn't entirely to do with the way they were dancing. 'But not here. Let's go to the lobby.'

'If it will stop you clomping all over my feet, I'd be happy to.' She twisted out of his arms and headed for the door.

Ignoring the bemused stares of the other dancers, Andy followed her.

The lobby was thronged with a party of golfers checking in with enough equipment for a tournament. Andy glanced around, searching for a quiet spot to talk but he was out of luck. They needed somewhere private. A wicked grin curled his mouth. He knew the very place. Placing his hand in the small of her back, he propelled her towards the exit.

Outside, the air was crisp and cold. The warmth of the spring day had faded to a wintery evening. A gust of wind caught the hem of her dress and set it fluttering. Roz shivered.

'Will this take long? I'll freeze to death out here dressed like this.'

Andy shrugged out of his tux and draped it around her shoulders. Maybe cooling down would do them both good. He guided her along the gravelled path towards the artificial lake. It had been one of his favourite playgrounds when he was growing up. Interminable Sunday lunches had been made bearable when he and Robert were released to play in the 'jungle'.

Back then, there had been ornate metal seats at intervals around the water. He hoped they were still there. As they walked, the music from the ballroom faded into the distance. A mournful saxophone solo echoed across inky black water. It would have been the perfect romantic setting for a proposal.

Except that she was mad at him.

The power of speech deserted him. Was that what he was about to do? Ask Roz to marry him? That might be a bit hasty, but they could live together in France until the trial was over. The prospect both thrilled and terrified him.

She stumbled and he offered her his arm to steady her. 'Bloody stones,' she muttered. 'What is so important that you had to drag me away from the ball?'

'You're supposed to be at home. What happened to avoiding the media and staying safe?'

'Sod the media. Have you any idea what it's like to always be Cinderella?'

The bitterness in her voice made him wince. Compared to her sister Sinead and her wealthy cousin Summer, Tim's daughter, Roz was the poor relation. But that didn't give her an excuse to put herself in danger. 'You might be the belle of the ball but I should put you across my knee for disobeying me.'

She whirled to face him. The rise and fall of her breasts beneath the fine silk of the dress made his cock ache. She might be the most infuriating, maddening, reckless woman in the world, but, god, she was beautiful. And she would be his.

'Don't even think about it. If you touch me I'll —'

He didn't wait for her to finish. Andy hauled her against him and took her mouth in a savage kiss. Roz gave a surprised squeak and wriggled in his arms, but he had no intention of letting her go. He had missed her, ached for her, worried that she was in danger and she had ignored his warnings to stay out of trouble.

He fisted one hand in her hair and tugged. Roz might

play at being in charge, but he knew how to get her attention. She stilled and her mouth softened ever so slightly. Taking advantage, he changed tactics, flicking his tongue against her lips, begging for entry.

She complied, opening to him with a soft murmur that set his heart racing. Her tongue duelled with his and she wound her arms around his neck. The jacket slipped from her shoulders onto the ground. Andy didn't care. He was lost in her kiss, lost in her scent. Forever wasn't long enough to kiss her.

A gust of wind blew across the lake. She would freeze if he didn't get her back inside. Maybe they could get a room? He would order champagne and show her how much he had missed her. Reluctantly, he pulled away and stared into her deep blue eyes. 'You make me crazy.'

'Not half as crazy as you make me.' She pressed her palms against his shoulders and shoved hard.

Andy caught a glimpse of grim satisfaction on her face as he pitched over backwards and his last thought before he hit the water was that it would be freezing. The icy shock knocked the breath from his lungs. He sank beneath the surface and got tangled in the plants growing from the bottom of the lake.

Andy gasped as he broke through a mass of leaves floating on the surface. Water lilies – the lake was full of them. He headed for shore, dragging the foliage with him. He was going to kill her. No, he was going to give her a bath in the lake and then spank the ass off her.

He clambered onto the bank and dragged himself out. He was conscious of laughter and the crunch of shoes on gravel. Did she really think that she could run away from him? Andy stood up, brushing off the pond weed and bits of greenery he had picked up during his unplanned swim.

A single, pale water lily clung to the mess. The yellow petals appeared waxy in the moonlight. But its fragile appearance was deceptive. Like Roz, the flowers were tough and resilient. They came back every spring despite the weather. They were hardy survivors, just like her.

In the distance, he caught a glimpse of blue. He picked up his discarded jacket, tucked the flower into the pocket of his shirt and set off in pursuit.

28

She was surprisingly fast for someone wearing heels. Andy remembered the day they first met in Paris and her ability to keep up with two ex-Rangers as they made their way across Paris on foot. He would be hard pressed to catch her before she reached the hotel, and he couldn't go back to the ballroom looking like this.

A minibus covered with signs announcing that it specialized in golf tours pulled out in front of her and Roz dodged into the car park around it. He had her now. Without thinking, Andy stepped up on top of a low-slung sports car and jumped from vehicle to vehicle, heading in a direct line for the hotel. Her progress was slower as she wove her way through the rows of parked vehicles. The hotel must be full to the rafters. There would be no possibility of a room.

Adrenaline pumped through him as he pursued her. Andy changed direction, heading straight for Roz. Realizing that he was hot on her tail, she let loose a string of curses, one of which questioned his paternity. He picked up speed and slid off the roof of a Mercedes, straight into her path.

Roz looked around her wildly, desperately seeking another avenue of escape.

'Oh no, you don't.'

Andy lunged for her and picked her up, ignoring the

blows that she rained on him. For someone who had no training, she was effective and they hurt, but if they were going into protective custody together, he would have to teach her how to do real damage.

'Put me down, you bastard. You'll ruin my dress.'

Andy ignored her and carried her, kicking and protesting, to the valet parking area. She was worse than a feral kitten. He set her down, reached under the Rolls for the magnetic box that held a spare key in case Poppy lost hers, opened the rear door of the big car and pushed her inside.

Roz crawled immediately for the other door. Andy lunged after her, pinning her down. 'You're wet,' she protested.

'And whose fault is that?' The silky menace in his voice silenced her momentarily. Roz knew that she was in trouble but it didn't stop her for long.

'Yours. You deserved it for messing around with other women when you're supposed to be engaged to me. How do you think your parents reacted when they saw that picture?'

So that's what this was about. 'I haven't looked at another woman since I met you. Abbie Marshall is a client and a friend of mine. She –'

'Oh yeah? Well, you looked *very* friendly.'

Her blue eyes glared, cutting through him like lasers. Andy's temper rose. He knew that he should have dealt with that perving pap at the time. 'It wasn't like that.'

Roz wriggled beneath him, trying to get free. 'I don't care what it was like. Go find someone who believes you.' She landed another punch on his ribs, right on top of where Hall had hit him.

Andy yanked both her arms above her head to stop the blows. There was no point trying to talk to Roz when she was like this. He would have to wait until tomorrow, when they had both calmed down.

From the glow of the car park lights, he could see that her hair had come loose from its pins, spreading like a Titian cloud over the white leather upholstery. Beneath the thin silk of the dress she shook. Her fragrance caught him, all hot, aroused woman. Whether from the cold or from the excitement of the fight, her nipples had formed two hard points that called to his mouth. Roz was a witch. They were in the middle of a bitter argument, but he wanted her with a hunger that appalled him. He could never have enough of her. Not if he lived to be a hundred.

Roz moved again, suddenly realizing his emotions had shifted from anger to burning lust. 'Don't you dare.'

Andy laughed. Roz might fight him like a wildcat but behind her angry words, her mouth had softened. A hectic blush stained her cheeks. Her pupils were large and dark. Kinky bitch. She was as turned on by this as he was.

He stared into her eyes, not letting her look away and smiled. 'I dare.'

'Asshole,' she spat, but she didn't move when he released her wrists and sat up.

'We don't want to ruin your pretty dress.' Andy shrugged out of his wet shirt, pausing to remove the water lily from his pocket. He toed off his shoes. They were wet and difficult. He reached for the fastening on his pants.

'I hate you.' She made a token protest as anger and lust fought within her.

346

'Good. I prefer it when a woman speaks her mind.'

Tugging his wet bow tie free from the collar of his shirt, he used it to secure her hands above her head.

She made such a pretty picture lying there that he couldn't resist sliding his palm along the length of her torso, pausing to cup her breast and pinch her nipple hard. Her outraged gasp was music to his ears. No bra? Even better.

He opened the jewelled clasp at the neck of her dress and pushed the fabric aside to expose her breasts. The dress opened almost to the waist. Little wonder half the men in the ballroom had been lusting after her.

Bending his neck, he fastened his mouth over one nipple and sucked hard. His fingers found the other and he toyed with it mercilessly, enjoying the feel of her wriggling beneath him as she tried to evade his searching hands and mouth. He wished he had something to blindfold her with to heighten the sensation for her. If he'd had his way, he would have taken her back to the dungeon and shown her exactly how much he had missed her.

How could she think for a moment that he would look at another woman when he had her? Andy raised his head. Her nipples were berry red against her alabaster skin – perfect for nipple clamps. He wondered how she would feel about that. Or maybe a tiny chain that led down to her clit.

He slid his hand beneath the skirt of her dress, mesmerized when stocking gave way to smooth flesh. Andy pushed the fabric up until the dress was around her waist. 'A suspender belt? Naughty girl.'

She gave him a scorching look that promised payback,

347

but right now he was beyond caring. As if they had all the time in the world, he dragged his fingers over her body, alternating between using the soft tips or his short nails.

Roz broke their silent battle when he traced a line up the inside of her thigh, over and over, but never quite reaching her aching core. Her stifled moan made his cock throb, but they weren't going there yet. She wasn't half as frustrated as he intended to make her.

As she writhed, seeking his touch, he returned his attention to her breasts, clasping one tender nub between his teeth while flicking the other nipple hard. When she groaned in protest, he switched sides. She thoroughly deserved this for doubting him.

Andy raised his head. 'You know you can safe word at any time?'

'Fuck you.'

Andy clicked his tongue. 'Fuck you is not a safe word. Let's see if we can do better, hmmm?'

He made his leisurely way along her torso, using every trick he knew to build her excitement. She was panting now, soft moans occasionally escaping. God, she was stubborn. She wouldn't give an inch. It was time to up the ante and drive her wild.

Andy settled between her thighs and dropped a light kiss on the scrap of fabric that covered her mound. Grasping the fragile string of her thong, he ripped it off her. She didn't need panties. Hell, he might make that a rule when they lived together.

Burying his face between her legs, he licked and then stopped. Roz was so close to coming. He held her on the cusp of orgasm until the tide of sensation ebbed away.

She hissed a curse and he hid his smile. Roz deserved this and more. Andy stroked her labia with his thumb, coating it with her slick wetness before turning his attention to her clit. He stroked lightly around it, never quite hitting the sweet spot that would send her over. With his other hand, he dragged his nails along her inner thigh.

'Please.' The single plea was music to his ears.

When Andy plunged one finger inside her, she raised her hips, arching off the seat and seeking more.

He held perfectly still. 'Is that good, baby?'

Stubborn to the core, she refused to respond. Slowly he withdrew his finger and returned his attention to her clit, stroking carefully, with never quite enough pressure to take her over the edge. He could see the tension in her muscles, her body desperate for release, her mind fighting him every inch of the way.

The windows of the Rolls had steamed up. A light sheen of sweat glistened on her pale skin. The scent of her arousal perfumed the air. Ramrod straight, his cock throbbed, begging for release. It took every inch of self-control he had not to bury himself inside her. Not yet. He moistened his fingers again before pumping two inside her.

Her relief was palpable. With a throaty noise of approval she writhed against his fingers. She was slick and wet and so very hot. He could have watched her for hours. Her hair clung damply to her forehead, her hips lifted, seeking the extra pressure which would send her over, but he hadn't tortured her quite enough yet.

Andy stopped.

'Noooo.' Frustration dragged a scream out of her. If looks could kill, he would have died a thousand times.

Andy stroked her thigh, pleased when she opened to him. Her body wanted him, but she was fighting it. The stubborn wee bitch. He bent his head to nuzzle her neck. She was so sensitive there. He loved the little trembling movements that she made when he touched her.

Ignoring the fire that blazed in her eyes, Andy stroked her body from neck to core and back again, letting his hand rest lightly against the base of her throat. 'Who does this belong to?'

She remained obstinately silent. He had to admire her. Most women would have surrendered long before this, but then Roz wasn't most women. She was his woman. His alone. And he had to convince her of that.

'You.'

The single word was barely more than a whisper but it was enough. God, she was magnificent. He would never master her. She would continue to challenge him. Every day together would be a battle. But tonight she was his.

'Oh, baby.' He couldn't say the easy words, the glib phrases that usually tripped off his tongue. None of them were good enough for her.

Andy pressed a possessive kiss on her mouth before he kissed her earlobe and neck tenderly. Positioning himself between her thighs, he stared in awe at the vision that was his. Roz belonged to him. His chest filled with a tender emotion he had never known before this moment.

Aiming his aching cock, he slid a slow inch inside her. She was hot, slick and so very wet. He couldn't wait another moment. One slow delicious thrust and then another, making her ready for him.

'Andy, please. I can't wait.'

He withdrew almost all the way, before plunging back in hard. He wasn't going to last, but then, neither was she. With a harsh cry, he pushed inside her again, relishing the sensation of her hot core gripping him. Mindless, he quickened his pace, setting a rhythm to please her.

She wrapped her thighs around his hips, holding him prisoner. Her breathless broken cries filled his ears. She was so close. Digging her heels into his ass, she urged him on. 'Harder. Fuck me hard.'

He was lost. Plunging as wildly as a stallion, he lost all control. He gritted his teeth against the fire that burnt each nerve ending. His balls tightened. He was going to come. Not yet. Not yet. Please not yet. Her inner walls clamped around him. She shuddered, lost in the maelstrom of orgasm, and, with a guttural cry, he followed her, pumping inside her until he had nothing left to give.

Andy raised his head. The fog around his brain cleared and he eased his weight from her, untied her wrists and pulled her into his arms. 'That was . . . amazing,' he managed to gasp.

With her pale skin and long red hair, Roz looked like she'd stepped out of a fairy tale. Except that he hadn't exactly behaved like Prince Charming. He touched the crumpled fabric of her dress. 'Somehow, I don't think we'll be going back to the ball.'

Roz gave a little sigh as she looked at the rumpled outfit. 'Figures. It's the story of my life. Remind me to shove you in a pond again next time we see one.'

Andy laughed. Roz would never give in. It was one of the things he loved about her. 'I'll buy you another dress, but you look perfect the way you are.'

'Does that kind of stuff usually work on women?'

'Some,' Andy admitted. He didn't want to say that it was true. That she was beautiful and amazing. If he was going to ask her to spend the rest of her life with him, he wanted to do it properly. For the first time in his life, he cursed his reputation. If he said anything to her now, she wouldn't believe him.

He would tell her tomorrow on the flight. She deserved a romantic evening in Paris with champagne. The works. Roz had to believe that he was serious about this. On the floor of the Roller, Andy caught sight of the lily. He reached for it and pushed it behind her ear. The waxy petals contrasted dramatically with her red hair. He brushed her lips with his.

'You look beautiful.'

Emotion fluttered across her face. Surprise, mingled with regret. What sort of idiots had she known before this, that not one man had told her she was beautiful? Tomorrow he would tell her, and the day after that and the day after that. And he would never stop telling her.

Across the still night air, he heard the first strains of 'New York, New York'. The ball would soon be over. They couldn't be caught like this in the back of his parents' car. Sitting up, he smoothed her dress over her hips and legs, before reaching for the top.

She brushed his hands away. 'It's fine. I'll do it. You better find some clothes.'

She was right. His trousers and shirt were sodden. His

dad probably had some waterproofs in the back of the car. They would have to do.

Roz fastened her dress and raked her fingers through her hair. She was careful not to look at him. There was a hint of sadness about her. Something was up and it was more than his photograph appearing in the newspaper.

'Are you okay?'

'I'm fine. Couldn't be better.' She gave him a brittle smile that didn't quite reach her eyes.

They definitely needed to talk.

Outside he heard the sound of the first cars driving away. It wouldn't be long before his parents arrived. They had to hurry. Andy stepped out of the car and opened the trunk, offering a silent prayer of thanks when he spotted some of his dad's old hunting clothes. They would have to do. He yanked them on quickly.

The crunch of gravel announced the arrival of his parents. He had to go, but tomorrow he and Roz were going to have a talk and he would get to the bottom of what was troubling her.

29

It was still dark when Roz got up the next morning. She had barely slept and her eyes were red and gritty, even though she had managed not to cry all night. Now she had to get out of Lough Darra, even though every instinct in her body urged her to remain.

She dressed silently in a pair of jeans, runners and a warm jacket before she packed a small bag with a couple of changes of clothes. Everything she couldn't carry would have to be left behind. She heaved a bitter sigh. The story of her life.

Roz eased her outdoor gloves on and ran her hands over the dresser which she had gripped when Andy had made . . . no, when Andy had fucked her. Just because she was stupid enough to let her messy emotions get twisted into knots by him didn't mean he cared.

She might be a criminal but she deserved better. She wanted a man to herself, not one she had to share with every woman out there.

Roz pulled her hand away from the polished surface. So what if the memories would be bittersweet? It was time to go.

She slipped out of her room, closing the door silently behind her, and made her way downstairs, remembering to skip the third and the fifth stair, both of which creaked. Mini and Maxi appeared from the back of the house but for once, refrained from barking. They circled her legs, and she reached down to rub their silky ears. She had never had a pet, not even a goldfish, but these guys had gotten under her skin.

Maybe when she got settled, she could get a dog of her own. And a horse. And – she cut off that line of thought. First, she had to get away.

This was the last time she would be here. She was never coming back. Closing the door behind her had a terrible finality and her breath caught in her throat.

No, she would not cry. She was tougher than this. Squaring her shoulders, she tiptoed across the path onto the grass, in case her footsteps on the gravel would alert anyone in the house, and headed down the drive.

Dawn was a blazing line across the horizon when she reached the road. She hitched her bag more securely over her shoulder and started walking. It was at least a mile further on when she heard a lorry behind her.

On impulse, she stuck out her thumb.

She had hitched before when she lived in England, but the web of motorways that crisscrossed the country had made it difficult and she had got out of the habit. To her astonishment, the lorry pulled up beside her and the passenger door opened.

This driver was a stout man wearing mud splattered wellies and a tweed cap pulled over greying hair. 'I'm going to Larne, is that any use to you?'

His accent was so thick she could barely understand him, but she nodded and pulled herself up.

The lorry was old and rickety and smelled of the hundreds of live chickens in the back, but the driver was grandfatherly and friendly. He chatted about the state of the economy, idiots who thought they could drive after they'd been drinking, the gobshites running the government, grandchildren who did all their letter writing via Facebook, and how rough the passage to Cairnryan was likely to be.

He asked her about herself, but not in a nosy way. She always lied when people questioned her, but this time, she told the partial truth. 'I had a fight with my boyfriend. I couldn't bear staying there with his mother thinking we were getting married, when I knew we weren't.'

'Could you not give him another chance?' he asked. 'Couples fight all the time. You have to care about someone to fight with them.'

She shook her head. 'Too many things are against us. We have nothing in common. He's rich and, as you can see,' she gestured to her position in the cab of his lorry, 'I'm not.'

'That doesn't sound like a deal-breaker to me. Most women want to marry a man with a bit of money.'

She laughed and even she could hear the bitterness in her voice. 'Didn't you ever hear the saying, "Anyone who marries for money earns every penny of it"? I don't want to be Cinderella, always being reminded how poor I am.'

'But Cinderella got the prince in the end, even when he knew she was penniless. Money isn't the only thing that counts. Seems to me you've got looks and brains and courage. Does he?'

Roz thought of Andy, his sculpted cheekbones and long, lean body, his razor-sharp intellect and the dark eyes that noticed everything. His readiness to throw himself into the line of fire to protect not just the people he loved, but also perfect strangers.

'Yes, he does.'

Andy was everything she had ever wanted. He was her knight in shining armour. Okay, the armour was slightly tarnished, but he was the man she wanted to have for her own. The man she loved.

The man she was leaving forever.

Despite her resolve, she sniffed and her eyes leaked. She grabbed a crumpled tissue from her pocket and scrubbed her cheeks fiercely. She was not going to cry. She was not.

Wisely, the driver didn't comment on her blotched, tear-stained face. Instead, he told her to look under the passenger seat.

Gingerly she did, the state of the cab making her grateful for her gloves. In a brown paper bag was a small bottle of Bushmills whiskey. 'It's a single malt that I was keeping for after a visit to the mother-in-law, but I think you might need it more. Have a swig.'

Roz wasn't a drinker, and it wasn't even noon, but to hell with it. She broke the seal and took a sip. The heat caught the back of her throat, and she coughed, before the honeyed tone soothed and warmed her.

'Thanks, that helped a lot.'

She re-corked the bottle and put it back under the seat. Today was going to be long and hard. She couldn't afford to be drunk.

They chatted as they drove. She didn't offer her name, and he never told her his, but when he heard she was

357

heading for Belfast, he changed direction so he could drop her at the ring road. 'Young girls like you shouldn't be hitching, you know. It's dangerous,' he told her sternly.

Roz swallowed a laugh at the irony of that, and agreed meekly.

When she jumped down and waved him on his way, she was sorry to part from him.

Murray's pawn shop in High Street was small but well positioned, and the guy manning the counter was polite. His eyes assessed her, noting the quality of her jacket and the cut of her jeans. 'Good morning, what can I do for you today?'

It was an effort to take the ring out of her pocket. She had known she would have to use it to get the sort of money she needed, but handing it over was a wrench that shook her.

The pawn-broker whistled when he saw it. 'You can barely see where the Titanic hit it.'

Behind him on the wall was a poster advertising the Titanic Experience. Oh yes, she had forgotten the doomed liner had been built in Belfast. Clearly the city had not.

'Do you have proof of ownership?' he asked briskly. 'I don't handle anything stolen.'

Roz pulled out the receipt she had taken from the desk in Andy's room. It clearly described the ring, as well as showing how much it had cost.

'You could sell this back to them, you know,' he said.

She shook her head. She had considered it, but was certain that the jewellers would have been on to Andy before she was out of the shop. 'I don't want to sell it. I'll be redeeming it soon.'

No, she wouldn't, but she wasn't going to admit it, or she would cry again. And she'd already cried more in the last week than in the previous ten years.

'I can give you eight grand for it.'

'Fifteen.'

He shook his head. 'Ten is my best offer.'

She took it and headed for the train station. There was an Enterprise to Dublin leaving in twenty minutes and she intended to be on it.

She exchanged her sterling notes for euros in a bank across the street from Connolly station and asked for directions to the bus depot. *Busáras*, an elderly woman corrected her as she pointed to a glass building near the station.

By the time she got off the coach in Tullamore, Roz was stiff and lethargic. The journey had taken forever. She couldn't wait to get back to her Ninja. She had never appreciated how easily she had got around on a motorbike until she had to depend on chicken lorries and trains.

The film location machine was still there at the castle, and extras and crew milled around, but without Jack Winter on site the energy seemed to have gone out of it. The noise was less and the voices more subdued.

Roz ducked back into the shelter of the dark forest near the castle as the wardrobe mistress and one of the catering staff walked past. She didn't want to be recognized by anyone who might remember her.

Frankie's caravan was in the same position, far enough away from the others to make it easy to slip inside without being seen.

'Hi, Frankie.' The interior was dim and for a few moments, she couldn't see him.

'What are you doing here?' His familiar voice warmed her, and she smiled until her eyes adjusted to the dim light and she was able to see him clearly.

Frankie was stretched out on his narrow bed, on top of the covers. He was wearing nothing but a pair of jeans, usually a sight to gladden a female heart. But not now. His chest was covered with white bandages, and a sling supported his arm. One leg of his jeans had been ripped up to allow for the cast that covered his left foot.

Almost worse was his face, which was cut and bruised beyond recognition. His normally neat beard was growing out, as it was impossible to keep it trimmed. But he managed a smile for her.

'Wasn't expecting to see you so soon. How are you, pet?'

She wanted to throw herself into his arms, but was terrified to touch him in case she injured him more. 'Better than you, obviously.'

She leaned over, balancing herself on the tiny table, and kissed him gently on the forehead. 'You belong in hospital, you idiot.'

He shook his head. 'Hate the places. Full of sick people.'

'And doctors who could fix you up.' She kept her voice brisk, even though she was shocked at the sight of him.

'There's a doctor on location here, he looks in once a day,' Frankie said.

'Hospitals have pretty nurses too.'

He grinned. 'Nah, the ones in the local hospital weren't worth staying in for. Besides, there are pretty girls here.'

As he spoke, the door opened and Cheyenne put her head in. 'Hi Frankie, I've got –' She waved a bottle of beer at him, and broke off at the sight of Roz.

'Don't wave that, you'll unsettle it.' His words were laconic, but the light in his eyes at the sight of the actress gave Roz a clue about what was going on.

Damn, it looked like nobody was going to have a happy ending. She was never going to see Andy again, and she couldn't imagine any way that Frankie could have a long-term relationship with a Hollywood star.

'What are you doing here, Roz?' Cheyenne asked. 'When you disappeared, they gave the job to someone else. But Frankie did collect your wages for you.'

'I'm not back for my job, but the wages will be good,' Roz said.

She turned to Frankie. 'You remember that idea you had? I'm in and good to go.'

He nodded. 'Cheyenne, could you get a bottle for Roz?'

The actress looked from one to the other. 'Why do I feel like the child being sent on an errand while the adults discuss something important?' The hurt in her voice was obvious and made Roz feel wretched. But it was essential that as few people as possible knew what she planned.

'Oh, never mind, I can see you're not going to tell me.' There was a distinct flounce in her step as she opened the door and got out. 'I'll leave you to talk about me.'

'I swear, this has nothing to do with you, and I'll tell you as soon as I can,' Roz said, but she knew Cheyenne didn't believe her.

'Making friends all around then,' Frankie said, sardonically. He scribbled something in a notebook and ripped out the sheet with the one beneath it. 'That's the farmer who owns Nagsy. I'll give him a ring and tell him to expect you. The horse has gone back to him and you can pick him up as soon as you pay for him.'

She nodded. 'Thanks. I need to go off-grid for a while, but I'll contact you as soon as I can. Don't tell anyone, not even Cheyenne, anything about this.'

'I won't. Where were you staying since you went off with Andy?'

Roz put the pages into her pocket. Front pocket, because it was harder to pick. She knew exactly how easy it was to take something out of a back pocket. 'It's safer if I don't tell you. Remember, if you see Andy, you know nothing about where I am. I've ditched my phone but I have your number and I'll text you when I have a new one.'

She had tossed the phone into the back of the lorry full of chickens. Anyone tracking her that way would think she was in Scotland by now. 'Until then, you can honestly say you know nothing.'

'So who cares about honest?'

She shrugged nonchalantly. 'I'm getting tired of lying. It's too much of an effort. I'll be glad when this is over.' She spotted the keys to her bike hanging on a hook and took them down. She kissed Frankie again. 'Look after yourself. I need you in my life.'

She was long gone before Cheyenne returned.

30

The dull ache in Andy's leg woke him. Fuck it. He was too young to be getting old. But being shot did that to a guy, even if it was almost five years ago. Thank god the pain hadn't affected his cock. He cupped the stiffening organ in his hand and opened his eyes. In the dim half-light of the bedroom he came fully awake. Something was wrong.

There was no one else in the room.

He rolled over. The empty pillow beside him confirmed his suspicions. He was missing a redhead. Idly, he stretched out his hand, but the cold sheet beside him made him sit up in the bed. Roz had been gone for a while.

He sat up and reached for his watch. Almost 9am. Shit. Bounding out of bed, he pulled on a pair of sweat pants. Without bothering to hunt for a T-shirt or shoes, he hurried down the corridor, checking the bathroom on the way. No water in the tub, no residual scent of the lotions and potions that women were so fond of.

The first hint of alarm pumped through his veins. He quickened his pace and, without bothering to knock, he entered her room. The bed was neatly made as if it hadn't been slept in. That didn't mean anything. Roz was almost compulsively tidy. She would have made her bed. Pulling open the wardrobe doors he scanned the contents. It contained the clothes he had bought for her in Belfast. She hadn't packed for Paris yet. Maybe she wanted to go for a last ride before they left? If he hurried, he might be able to catch her.

He returned to his room and dressed quickly. Grabbing his phone from the chipped antique dish on the dresser, Andy hurried downstairs.

Maggie was already busy in the kitchen.

'Have you seen Roz this morning?' Andy hated that even as he strived for casual, he sounded anxious. Maggie wasn't fooled for an instant.

'No. The lads were here earlier but they didn't mention seeing her. Had a row, did ye?' Her knowing smile taunted him.

Fuck, he didn't have time for this. If Roz hadn't gone riding, where was she?

Something softened in Maggie's face at his expression. 'Better snap that one up while you can. She's well able for you.'

She was right. Roz was well able for him. She suited him more than any woman he had ever known. Despite the differences in their upbringing, she matched him in ways he had never expected.

Andy made a quick trip to the stables. She wasn't there, none of the lads had seen her and the horses were all accounted for, so she hadn't gone out riding. Maybe she was with his mother.

Unlike Dougal, Poppy survived on four or five hours' sleep. Loath to disturb his father after a late night, he made his way to Poppy's favourite haunts. The conservatory was empty. So was her studio. Her brushes and tools were cleaned and laid out for another day of work.

On the way to his parents' room, he breathed a sigh of relief when he met his mother in the hall, still wearing her dressing gown.

'Wasn't it a wonderful evening?' she said. 'And there's a lovely photograph of Roz in the *Belfast Telegraph*.'

Andy snatched the paper from her hands. On the front page, a smiling Roz was framed by the O'Sullivans. Fuck. He had warned her not to go to the ball. Niall would have a fit when he saw it.

'Yes, Mum. But have you seen her this morning?' He didn't realize how desperate he sounded until he heard the words out loud.

'No. I presumed she was sleeping. Are you two still arguing?'

'It's nothing,' he said, but his words sounded hollow.

He had tied her up in the back of a car. Used sensual torture as a weapon and had never gotten around to talking to her and telling her the important things. That he loved her. That he wanted to spend the rest of his life with her.

'You bloody asshole,' he muttered under his breath as he turned and hurried down the stairs. He pulled his phone from his pocket and rang her.

The number you have dialled is out of service. The user may be out of range or have the unit powered off.

He shouldn't have let her out of his sight. Could she have taken one of the cars?

'Andrew,' his mother called after him. 'If you've upset that girl . . .'

'It's okay, Mum.'

The garage contained its full complement of cars. No one had seen her. She hadn't eaten, gone riding or left the estate unless it was on foot. Or someone took her.

Could Hall have tracked her to Lough Darra? The prospect was too awful to contemplate. The only thing he was sure of was that Roz was gone. He was willing to bet his favourite Glock on it.

He was behind the wheel of the Jeep before he realized that he had no plan and that he had to file a report that he had lost his client. 'Fuck fuck fuckety fuck.'

He thumped his fist on the steering wheel. He had to talk to Niall and he wasn't looking forward to it.

Andy punched the number into his phone and a sleepy-voiced Reilly answered. 'Bloody boggers,' she snapped when she realized who was calling. 'I didn't get to bed 'til after four. Don't you ever sleep?'

'Roz is gone,' he said starkly.

'What do you need?' Fully alert now, Reilly was already on the job.

'A phone trace.' He rattled off her number.

For a few minutes, the sound of Reilly's keyboard clicked over the phone. Andy tapped the steering wheel impatiently.

Reilly yawned. 'If this is right, she's in the middle of the Irish Sea, somewhere between Ireland and Scotland.'

Roz had taken the ferry? The devious wee bitch. Of course she would. She had no passport and she could have hopped a ferry easily. 'Which one?'

'Do I sound like a magician?'

'Sorry, Reilly. Please. Pretty please.'

Another yawn. 'Hold on 'til I check.'

More clicking on the keyboard. 'Looks like the Larne to Cairnryan ferry. It's not due in port for another two hours.'

'Get someone up there. I want her picked up when she gets off that ship.'

'Andy, there could be a hundred people on board, to say nothing of freight. Do you know what the big guy will do to me if I send a dozen guys up there?'

Andy was beyond caring. 'Send them. I'll take the blame.'

'On your head be it. I'll call you back when I have their report.'

Andy disconnected the call. If Roz was on the way to Scotland, there was nothing he could do until she got there. The team would pick her up for her own protection. Damn it. Why had she run? Why had she disappeared in the middle of the night without talking to him?

He replayed the events of the previous evening in his mind, analysing every word, every gesture. She had been angry about the photograph, jealous even, but they had made up. Hadn't they? The physical connection between them was off the scale. He had never known anyone like her. Okay, she was the worst submissive in the world. She fought him every inch of the way, but, god, she was worth the battle.

Andy glanced at his watch. He couldn't hang around here waiting for news. It would drive him crazy. He made his way back to the house. Maybe he could go for a run about the estate.

Ninety minutes later, he was out of breath and sweating. The run had turned into a search of the back roads and ditches. His imagination produced ever worsening scenarios. Was she alone or with Hall? Was she even on the damned ship at all?

He took a quick shower and while he was changing a tap came on the bedroom door.

'Andy?' Poppy's voice came from the corridor outside. 'We have visitors. Can you come down?'

He was stuck here. He could do nothing until the team from Scotland reported in. He took a deep breath and exhaled slowly. They were meant to be together. He would find her. This was no more than a bump in the road. They would look back on it and laugh at how foolish they had both been. Over the fireplace the ancient family crest mocked him. *Non Oblitus*. Not forgetful.

He couldn't forget her. Roz was emblazoned on his soul like a brand and he wouldn't give up trying until he found her.

'Andy.' His mother called again.

'Coming, Mum.'

Downstairs in the library, the fire was already blazing and Maggie was serving coffee to his parents and their visitors, Claudine Blé and Anton Fox. In a pair of slim-fitting pants and a fine wool sweater, Claudine was sexy in an understated way that Frenchwomen did so well. Her companion was wearing pale pants and a loud tweed jacket which made him look like a well-dressed pimp.

'Fox.' Andy nodded a greeting before kissing Claudine on both cheeks.

'Monsieur Campbell McTavish promised us a tour of the stables and some riding.' Claudine smiled with delight at the prospect.

'I'm not sure that I'll accompany you on the ride,' Fox

drawled. 'I was looking forward to becoming reacquainted with your lovely companion.'

'Isn't it a small world,' Poppy said before taking another sip of her coffee. 'Mr Fox knew Roz when she worked in Paris.'

Worked in Paris? The knowing smirk on his face made Andy itch to punch him.

'And New York,' Fox added. 'Our gal certainly gets around, doesn't she?'

His parents were oblivious to the undertone in Fox's voice, but Andy wasn't. Was this miserable excuse for a man the reason why Roz was upset last night? Had he been baiting her all evening? Andy fought back the urge to throttle the oily bastard.

Dougal set down his cup. 'If we're all finished, why don't we go to the stables?'

'Tell Roz I'll see her when she comes in from riding,' Poppy said before she returned to her painting. Andy followed Claudine and his father to the yard without telling his mother anything different.

The Frenchwoman had a keen eye for horses and was determined to take his father up on his offer. While she mounted a lively hunter, Fox hung back, clearly nervous.

'Will you join us, Mr Fox?' his father asked politely.

'No, thanks, you go ahead.'

They watched as the others left the yard and headed for the fields. 'Claudine's got a great ass,' Fox remarked. 'Speaking of which, where is Red?'

Oblivious to the impending danger, he continued to stare at Claudine's departing figure. 'What kind of money does Red charge for a long term gig like this? Now that I'm based in Europe I might be interested in –'

'Don't call her Red.'

Fox stilled at the curt tone. 'There's no need to be like that. Red is a hot little number. I'd be happy to take her on when you've finished with her.'

The McTavishes weren't generally known for killing their guests but Andy was willing to make an exception. If this was what Roz had to put up with all night, no wonder she had disappeared. Fox might not have driven her away from him, but his boorish behaviour had certainly encouraged her to run.

Andy glanced around him. There were too many lads around the yard. He needed a bit more privacy if he was going to tear him apart, limb from limb. An open stable door beckoned. 'Why don't we finish the tour?'

He propelled an unwilling Fox through the doorway and into the dim space beyond. 'Take off your jacket.'

'Why?' Fox asked, slowly realizing that he might be in trouble.

'Because I'm going to beat the crap out of you and Claudine might notice that you've been playing in the dirt.'

'You're going to fight me? Because of some little –'

Andy grabbed him by the jacket and slammed him up against the wall. 'Do not finish that sentence,' he warned Fox, then let him go.

The other man sneered at him. 'Don't take on more than you can chew. I was on the college boxing team.' Andy stood back while Fox removed his jacket and hung it on a hook. He assumed a boxing stance, knees bent, fists raised in front of him.

Jesus wept. He wouldn't last two seconds against a Ranger. Trying to rein in his rising temper, Andy kept his arms loosely at his sides. 'What did you say to Roz last night? Did you insult her?'

His opponent's face creased in a frown and then he shook his head. 'You can't insult a whore.'

Andy lunged, sending them both to the ground. Fox gasped as the air was driven from his lungs. Boxing champion, my ass. The idiot couldn't defend himself against a five year old. Fox swung his fist wildly towards Andy's head and Andy rolled off him, landing in a pile of straw.

'Are you out of your mind?' His opponent struggled to a sitting position and brushed the straw from his pants. 'I wanted a bit of fun but Red ignored me. She was busy playing lady of the manor, chatting about buying horses with that airline guy.'

O'Sullivan. Was he the reason that Roz had left? Andy climbed to his feet.

'Then his mom joined in with some talk about weddings and Red got up and left.'

'And that was it? You didn't say anything to her.'

Fox's eyes narrowed. 'I might have teased her a little, but she wasn't up for it. Why don't you go ask Red? She'll tell you.'

Andy reached down and pulled the other man to his feet by his shirt collar before slamming him against the wall. His face turned purple as the collar bit into his neck, and a choking sound emerged.

Andy's heart pounded. He wanted to kill him. Between the O'Sullivans and Fox, they had pushed her too far, convinced her that she couldn't stay. He leaned forwards until they were face to face and he could see the nervous tic that fluttered beneath Fox's right eye. Outside, the sound of horses whinnying brought him back to reality

'Listen to me, and listen well. Don't ever call her Red.'

Fox raised his hands in surrender. Andy released him and brushed the dust from his hands. The man was a sleazebag and an idiot, but that was no reason to kill him.

Fox coughed, leaning against the wall for support as he dragged several gasping breaths back into his lungs. 'Okay, you've got something going on with her. I get it. I get it.'

Andy took the jacket from the hook and tossed it at him. 'And now that I have your complete attention, there's one last thing. You can tell your friends and anyone else she's played with that Red has retired. She's mine and I won't ever be finished with her.'

Andy left Fox to catch his breath and hurried back to the house. He had left his phone on the bed and Reilly had promised to call him.

Two missed calls. One less than ten minutes ago. He punched in Reilly's number.

'Reilly, do you have news?'

'Oh yeah, I have news. Niall is on the warpath because you lost a client and I sent a dozen operatives to search for a phone in a chicken truck.'

'Roz?' he asked hopefully.

'Your bird flew the coop long before the driver boarded the ferry.'

Andy closed his eyes. He'd been hoping that they would find her in Scotland. He should have known better.

'Two of the guys spoke to the driver. They said he was a nice old man. He told them that he dropped her at the ring road near Belfast. The girl he gave a lift to was pretty upset. She was crying over some guy who had broken her heart. He offered to beat some sense into him.'

She paused. 'Want me to give him your address?'

He was almost tempted to say yes. 'Thanks, Reilly. I owe you one. Can you run the usual checks? Hotels, car hire, credit cards?'

'I'm already on it.'

Andy disconnected the call. He needed to think. Relief that she hadn't been taken by Hall mingled with regret that she had chosen to walk away from him. He had spent the whole day blaming everyone else for her disappearance when it was his fault. Oh yeah, the others had helped, there was no doubt about that, but the blame was entirely his. He wanted to howl like a beast.

What had made her run? Was it the thought of Paris and the trial? Had she been afraid of what Hall might do to her? Why hadn't she confided in him?

She didn't get much of a chance, did she? A nagging voice inside his head taunted him.

This was more than Roz being jealous about a stupid photograph. He had abandoned her to work on another job. His face had been plastered all over the media with Abbie Marshall and then he had used her own body against her, instead of talking to her and dealing with her uncertainties. How could he have been so blind? He had handled her all wrong. Roz had never been able to lean on any man. Why had he imagined that she could learn to trust someone like him?

He should have talked to her, instead he had fucked her. Like every other deadbeat guy in her life. How could he make her believe that he was different? He didn't care about her past. Roz wasn't the only one who had done things that they were ashamed of. What mattered was the future. He was certain they belonged together, but he had to convince Roz.

And first he had to find her.

Andy grabbed the keys to the Jeep. The truck driver had dropped her off near Belfast. It was a logical place to start. Before he left, he carefully tore the page from the newspaper that contained her photograph. The first twenty-four hours after someone disappeared were critical. It was time to hit the streets.

Michael Brophy's farm was a million miles away from Lough Darra. Roz bounced her motorbike along the rutted laneway that led to the old farmhouse. It had taken her three wrong turns to find the farm up the narrow, unmarked roads. After the motorways she had travelled getting to Tullamore, this was like a trip back in time.

The farmhouse was grey and square, with a latch door and chickens scattering when she rode her bike into the yard in front of it. Three stables lined one side of the yard, and Nagsy stuck his head out of one, greeting her with a soft whinny. Two sheepdogs barked from a few feet away but made no effort to touch her. She stayed on her bike, not sure how well her leather pants would stand up to dog teeth.

On the other side of the yard, a hayshed sheltered more chickens and in the field behind it, half a dozen horses grazed with cattle.

The door of the house opened and the owner came out. He was grey-haired but wiry and waved as he walked towards her.

She smiled at him, dismounting from her Kawasaki Ninja. 'Hi, I believe Frankie told you I was coming?'

He smiled back, revealing several missing teeth. 'You're the girl who wants to buy my horse?'

She pulled off her gauntlets and patted Nagsy. 'Yes, we became friends when he was working on the film.'

Michael pushed a bucket under the tap and let the water run. He tossed a handful of grain to the chickens who rushed up to peck at it. The bucket wasn't full yet, so Michael led the way into the shed and stuffed hay into a net. By the time he was done, the water was an inch below the rim of the bucket. He used an elbow to open Nagsy's door and lifted the bucket in.

Roz admired the smooth efficiency of his movements and understood how one man could run the farm.

'Well, you see, there's the thing,' he said. 'My father always told me not to sell him.'

Roz looked at Michael, who had to be at least fifty, and wondered if he was joking. 'This horse?'

'Well, anything out of old Molly.' He scooped some crushed oats into a basin and put it into the stable. In the next box, Roz saw two young calves licking a block of salt. 'But you can have any of the others that you like. I'll make you a good deal.'

'No, I want Nagsy. What's the problem?'

'To be honest, I'm not exactly sure. When old Molly went in foal, he told me that I was never to sell anything out of her. Pity, because they've all been good and Da used to work with racers so he knew that. But a promise is a promise.'

Damn. All this work and now this? Roz couldn't believe it. He wasn't going to sell. She had to try again. 'How long ago was this? He might have changed his mind.'

Michael pulled Nagsy's ear thoughtfully. 'True. He was a great believer in, "Better be sorry you sold than sorry you didn't" but he refused all offers himself and made me promise to do the same.' He screwed up his face in thought. 'Must be a good thirty or more years ago.'

Nagsy was five, Frankie had told her. She wasn't an expert on horses, in spite of hours spent listening to Dougal talking about them, but she knew horses didn't live that long. 'It can't have been Nagsy he meant then.'

'That's true. Molly was his grand dam.'

A flutter of hope was dashed when he shook his head. 'Sorry, I can't sell him.'

'I'll pay cash. Five thousand.' From the state of the farm, she bet that was more than he usually got for his horses.

Michael looked tempted but shook his head.

'Six.' She took out the money from her pocket. 'Cash in hand.'

His eyes rounded at the wad of five hundred euro notes, but his mouth firmed. 'A promise is a promise, and he's dead now, so I can't ask him to change his mind.'

He backed away, as if from the temptation of her money, and bumped into her motorbike. He examined it carefully and stroked it more gently than he had Nagsy. 'That's a beauty you have there. Is it fast?'

'It's a Kawasaki Ninja, top speed of 180kph, with acceleration that would knock you backwards.'

'Come in for a cup of tea and you can tell me all about it.'

The front door opened directly into the kitchen, a big room heated with an old-fashioned Aga. Michael pushed the kettle onto a hot spot and it hissed within seconds. He made tea in a heavy brown teapot and let it stew. She gazed around while he poured it out and added four spoonfuls of sugar. The kitchen looked like it was from the previous century, with a rickety wooden staircase, a television that was older than she was and a calendar featuring glossy photos of motorbikes.

Roz sipped the over-sweetened tar while she chatted about the Kawasaki Ninja and an idea germinated in her head. Michael found an open packet of biscuits and gave her one. It was stale and soft and she dunked it into her tea. It was that sort of house.

Roz put down her cup. 'You know, I think we could make a deal, one that doesn't involve selling Nagsy.'

Michael tapped his spoon against his mug. 'I'm listening.'

'How about we swop? I give you my bike, and you give me the horse.' She loved her Ninja, and this nearly killed her, but it was the only way she could see to get Nagsy.

There was silence while he considered her offer. The clock in the corner ticked away. Finally, he said, 'Deal.'

They spent a further ten minutes haggling over the details before they emerged into the sunlight. Roz handed over her keys, helmet, gauntlets and leathers but kept the boots, and Michael got out a saddle and bridle for Nagsy.

At her request, he gave her a note saying she was now the owner of the horse and she promised to send on the logbook for the Ninja as soon as possible.

She now owned Nagsy, and the logistics were suddenly impossible. 'How am I going to get him home?'

Michael looked at her as if she was an idiot. 'Ride him.'

'But I'm going to –' She shut her mouth quickly. No point telling him any unnecessary details. 'It's a good twenty-five miles away.'

'If you get on now, you'll be there before dark.' He tacked up Nagsy for her and gave her a leg up into the saddle. As she set off down the rutted driveway, she heard him gunning the motor of his new motorbike.

Sunday morning and it was life minus Roz, plus twenty-four hours. He had toyed with the idea of telling his parents that she had been called back to work, but he couldn't lie to them. Instead, he admitted that they'd had an argument. Poppy was full of sympathy. Even his dad was marginally less brusque than usual.

Andy had slept in her bed, hoping that his subconscious would give him a clue to her whereabouts. Frantic about her missing sister, Sinead Moore had persuaded her husband to use every resource he had to find her. They had hit the bus station, the hire companies and every cheap hotel and B&B within a twenty-mile radius of Belfast, but their enquiries had turned up nothing.

The photograph in the newspaper had been circulated to each of the men, but so far nothing. Her flatmate in London had been traced and although she hadn't seen her, she was a mine of information about Roz's life there.

How come he didn't know that she volunteered at the biggest food bank in London or that she aced parkour and taught it to disadvantaged kids on Saturday afternoons?

The report from Pentonville prison revealed little – except that Peter Spring was due to be released shortly. He had been beaten up on several occasions and had spent time on the hospital wing. He refused to speak to them about his daughter.

Andy rolled out of bed and without stopping for breakfast drove to the city again. Belfast on a Sunday morning was a ghost town. None of the shops opened before noon. Small groups of tourists dragged suitcases around the silent streets or drank coffee and stared through café windows at the rain that drizzled onto the grey streets.

Knowing she didn't have much money, Andy checked out the cafés that offered a cheap Ulster fry that would keep you going for the day. But there was nothing, zilch, nada. Roz was good at disappearing and the trail was rapidly going cold.

The team was meeting at the Europa Hotel at noon for a video-conference call with Niall and the guy from Interpol. He wasn't looking forward to it. Arriving half an hour before the others, he drank strong tea and doodled on a memo pad.

Think, man, think.

She's on the run with no money and no transport. She had few, if any, friends in Ireland and not a lot of people that she could turn to. Andy scrawled a circle with a sword driven through it.

The meeting room door opened and the rest of the team filed into the room. Every man and woman had given up their weekend to help search for her. Andy nodded to each of them in turn. At noon precisely, Niall Moore's face filled the screen. Occasionally, he looked to his right as if someone else was in the room with him. It must be Sinead. He looked tired. Reilly had told him that Sinead was suffering from morning sickness, morning, noon and night, and the big guy was worried about her.

She and Roz had been separated when they were barely four years old. They had met briefly when Roz had carried out a jewel robbery at the museum where Sinead worked. The twins' relationship was fragile at best, but blood was thicker than water.

Niall glared at the video screen and said, 'Report.'

One by one the teams spoke. The places they had searched, the leads which had come to nothing and all the scraps of information they had gathered, which didn't amount to much – a lot of stuff about where she wasn't but nothing about where she was.

Andy went last and he didn't spare himself. He had failed to secure the client when he was pulled away on another job. He had allowed her to appear in public and there had been a media story about her. Hell, he might as well have erected a billboard at the entrance to Lough Darra saying *Roz Spring This Way*.

'Stop beating yourself up,' Niall said. 'Guilt isn't going to find her. So, what other leads have we got?'

Andy glanced down at his notepad. The circle had somehow become a shield and something clicked in his head. 'Tullamore,' Andy offered. 'Someone got her a job on the movie set. I'll drive down there and check that out.'

'And she's the registered owner of a Kawasaki Ninja motorbike,' Reilly's face popped onto the screen. 'The lock-up where she stored it is empty. We think she took it to Ireland.'

'Two reasons to go to Tullamore then,' Niall said. 'But

I want you to speak to our contact in the PSNI tomorrow morning, Andy. I'll send you the details. He's offered to keep a discreet eye in case anything turns up.'

By 'anything' Andy knew that Niall meant Hall.

'Okay, that's about it, everybody. You're all free to go. Andy, if you could hang on for a while.'

Andy shifted in his chair as the rest of the team filed out. He was due a bollocking and Niall could deliver one better than most.

'Inspector Prévost of Interpol is joining the call.'

Andy recognized the name. They had been supposed to meet in Paris the evening before to hand Roz over. He sat through the next few minutes stoically. He had fucked up monumentally and he knew it. Eventually, the inspector ran out of steam and left the call.

'I don't think there's much I can add to that,' Niall said. 'Find her or Sinead will have my nuts.'

Inspector Robert Smyth of the PSNI was a dour man in his early fifties. He had seen too much trouble over the past thirty years and it showed in his waistline and the high colour on his face. He shook Andy's hand, before settling back into a creaking office chair and waving Andy to the one opposite.

'You haven't found her?'

'No,' Andy admitted. 'Mr Moore said you might be able to help.'

Smyth patted the piles of paper on his desk until his hand lighted on the right one and he handed a grainy CCTV shot to him – Roz walking near the motorway, a dejected slump to her thin shoulders. The weary expression on her face was worse than a kick in the balls.

'Anything else?' Andy asked hopefully.

'Nothing on CCTV, but then nobody has reported her missing.'

He was right, they couldn't make it official, or Hall would find out and they didn't want to tip him off. 'There are reasons . . .'

'There always are, but the truth will out. Take a certain tout of mine. He doesn't drink much, but occasionally he likes to go out and get snattered.'

Andy sat back in his chair, unsure where the conversation was leading.

'I got a call last night saying that he'd had a bit too much to drink in the Crown and would I pick him up at the station.'

'And?' he prompted. Tullamore was a three-hour drive away and he had to pack.

'He was celebrating a deal he had made with a red-haired girl who pawned a ring for half of what it was worth.'

Andy swallowed. She wouldn't have. Roz couldn't have.

'An antique sapphire ring which you might recognize, seeing as your name and credit card number is on the receipt.'

'How much did she . . . ?' He couldn't say pawn. The word refused to come out of his mouth. Roz had sold the ring. His ring. Their engagement ring.

'Ten thousand pounds.' Smyth continued with a pleased smile on his face. 'It would appear from her actions that the lady has chosen to vanish.'

The rest of the inspector's words washed over him. She had left him for good and she wasn't coming back. His usual calm in the face of fire deserted him. Roz had pawned the ring and she had plenty of contacts in the underworld. With that kind of money she could buy a new ID and disappear for good. How the fuck had he ever believed that he knew anything about women? *You complete and utter muppet, McTavish.*

'– and do you wish to report the ring as being stolen?' The inspector's words caught his attention and he zoned back into the conversation.

Andy cleared his throat. 'No. That's okay, but can you ask him to hold onto it? I'll redeem it myself.'

'Of course, sir. Anything to help.'

The journey to Tullamore was wet and miserable, what his father would have described as a 'soft' day. Andy took the turn-off for the castle and headed up the rutted driveway. He parked near costume and make-up and grabbed a woollen robe from the rail.

'I didn't know you were back.' The bubbly blonde smiled at him.

Andy glanced in the mirror. He'd hardly need make-up, and as he hadn't shaved for more than a day, he would fit right in with the rest of the peasants.

'Yeah, I got a call for a crowd scene,' he said. 'You know what a perfectionist Benny is.'

The girl nodded sympathetically before turning to her next client, a heavily bearded Viking invader.

Andy took a path through the ancient woods surrounding Charleville Castle. The forest was knee deep in bluebells at this time of year, their delicate floral scent contrasting with their vibrant appearance. The colour reminded him of her eyes. Damn, he was getting maudlin.

He reached the clearing near the castle and found Frankie's caravan. It was empty, but his weapons were there. Andy decided to wait. He used the time to search every inch of the place, but there was nothing to suggest that Roz was staying with him. His heart pounded when he found a few items of lingerie in the tiny bathroom, but the labels were American. What was Frankie up to and with whom? The sound of voices outside drew his attention and he took a seat on the couch.

Andy almost didn't recognize him. The man had aged in the few weeks since he'd last seen him. He was thinner and favoured his right leg when he walked. Andy felt a grudging respect for the older man. He had faced off Hall to allow them to escape.

Frankie didn't seem surprised to see him. 'She's not here.'

'I can see that. I don't suppose you'd like to tell me where she is?'

'You suppose right,' Frankie replied with a half grin.

'But you have seen her?' Andy pushed. He needed to know that Roz wasn't in any immediate danger.

A flicker of sympathy crossed Frankie's face. 'She's safe for now, if that's any comfort.'

'Thank you for that much. Will you be seeing her anytime soon?'

The half-smile turned into a genuine grin. 'If you mean is it worth your while hanging about here, getting under my feet, waiting for her to turn up? Then, no, she's not coming back here.'

Andy nodded. 'Fine.'

Frankie was telling the truth. He was back to square one and his leads were rapidly vanishing. He was outside in the rain again before Frankie called after him.

'Don't worry about the girl. Roz is used to taking care of herself.'

He was right, but her idea of taking care of herself was relying on her wits and trusting no one. No wonder Roz was messed up. He gave Frankie a curt nod.

'I know, but she shouldn't have to.'

32

Time lost all meaning for Roz. The combination of lone-liness, sorrow, back-breaking work and sore muscles had effectively deleted her calendar. She dragged herself from day to day, and gave thanks if the day had been hard enough to help her sleep at night.

She had arrived at the dude ranch before dark a few weeks ago. Patrick O'Hara and his wife Suzanne had been welcoming but, conscious of the number of people who were hunting her, Roz was reluctant to be drawn into their warm circle.

She had watched them bed Nagsy down in a spacious stable and had helped them brush him and make him comfortable. He had coped with the long ride better than she had. Her thighs were chafed and stiff, and she thought her ass would never be the same again.

Andy could spank her as hard as he liked right now, and she wouldn't feel a thing.

Stop it. No more thoughts about Andy. That's over.

'What's his name?' Suzanne asked. She was a petite bru-nette who managed to make jeans tied with a belt made of bailer twine look chic. For a moment, Roz thought she had read her thoughts, until she realized Suzanne was talking about the horse.

'Hagar's Son, but I call him Nagsy.' She would have to register him soon.

'Nagsy it is, then.' Suzanne petted him before looking him over with knowledgeable eyes. 'He's got extraordinary lines. Who does he remind me of ?'

'No idea. I want him fit and trained to race as soon as possible.'

'It will be a nice change of pace from teaching tourists how to ride,' Patrick said. He named a price that made her wince, but she agreed. Who knew racehorses were so expensive?

Once Nagsy was settled, Roz realized that she had made no plans for herself. Her entire worldly possessions were in the duffle bag she had taken from Lough Darra and she had nowhere to go. 'Where's the nearest B&B?' she asked.

'Here.' Patrick pointed to the row of small chalet-style buildings. 'After that, you're looking at McGuigans four miles down the road, but I'm told their cooking isn't the best and they'll want to know every detail about you.'

Right now, Roz thought she would never be hungry again, so that wasn't an issue, but a nosy landlady would be a disaster. They always gossiped.

'Here is fine.'

And it was. The chalet was warm and comfortable, and even had a flat-screen TV to fill the silence with noise.

She went into the office the next morning to pay for Nagsy's livery, and found Patrick cursing at his desktop. 'What's the problem?' Computers were one thing she could do well. She could make them sing and dance and jump through hoops.

'I'm trying to design a website that looks good and keeps track of bookings and everything I need. This is impossible. Doctor Who himself couldn't manage this stupid thing.'

'Bet I could.'

She told him she was hiding from an abusive ex, who had beaten her and was trying to lock her up with no contact with any of her friends or relatives, and no horses. She had no difficulty making herself sound honest; it was the truth, or near enough to it.

Patrick believed every word.

They struck a bargain. She would live at the ranch and eat with the other guests and Patrick wouldn't reveal her whereabouts to anyone. In return, she would help out at the stables and work on his website.

Roz buried herself in work. After a certain point, exhaustion obliterated all thoughts of Andy and how much she missed him, but she could do nothing about the dark eyes that haunted her dreams. About how often she woke up feeling strong arms around her and the slow thud of his heartbeat beneath her ear.

She didn't need any of those things. Not now. Not ever.

At least she had cash, which meant she didn't have to use credit cards. She had no doubt that the first time she put a card into a machine, Niall Moore and Andy McTavish would be on her tail. She didn't even bother buying a new phone.

Roz took a chance one evening and borrowed a phone from one of the American guests to ring Pentonville. Her father was in great form, and had received some good news. He was getting out sooner than they had expected. The authorities believed that after his beating and stint in hospital, he deserved early release. He would be out in less than two months.

Damn, damn, damn. That raised the stakes and complicated things. She had to have the money by the time he got out. She rang Frankie and told him they had to move up the timetable.

That night she dreamed of all the things that could go wrong, ending up with her standing at her father's grave. All alone. In the distance, she heard the O'Sullivans laughing and saying, 'We knew he would come to a bad end.'

Andy's laughter joined them. 'Did you really think you had a future?'

She'd never had such a vivid dream before, and woke up shaking. Even a hot shower didn't make her feel better. When she joined the O'Haras for breakfast, she was still unsettled. She walked into the kitchen and the heat from the stove hit her like a blow. Her legs weakened and she sat down quickly at the waxed pine table.

'Rough night?' Suzanne asked, handing her a steaming mug of coffee. The smell turned her stomach and she had to put it down and escape into the fresh air.

What the hell was going on? Suzanne was an excellent cook. She would never have used bad coffee beans, but that's what the coffee smelled like.

Roz sucked in a few deep breaths and collected herself. Her stomach wasn't the best, but she knew she should eat to fortify herself for the morning in the stables. She had to muck out ten horses before she rode out.

She went back into the kitchen and a cold sweat broke out on her back. Roz ignored it and sat at the table. She forced herself to pick up a fork and take a mouthful of the fluffy eggs Suzanne had scrambled.

Her stomach rebelled and she put her hand over her mouth so that she wouldn't puke at the table. Roz shoved the chair back so violently that it fell over. She dashed outside, not caring that at least half a dozen guests were staring after her, bemused.

Roz barely made it to the yard before she heaved helplessly. She dropped onto all fours and let nature take its course. Her stomach was empty so she brought up only a bitter yellow liquid, which seeped between the bricks.

She sat on her hunkers, hugging her knees in misery.

'Try one of these.' Suzanne was beside her, holding out a bag of barley sugar sweets.

Roz wanted to refuse, but the expression on Suzanne's face made it clear she wasn't going away, so she took one and sucked gingerly. To her surprise, it helped. She sucked until it was gone, then accepted another one.

She was suddenly hungry. 'I think I could eat those eggs now.'

The smell of food drifting out from the kitchen was still as strong, but no longer as nauseating. 'Sorry for making such a fuss, I have no idea what happened.'

'No?' Suzanne raised her eyebrows. 'I think a pregnancy test might give you some answers.'

Roz was so shocked her feet slipped and even her parkour-honed reflexes couldn't stop her from falling onto her ass. 'That's impossible.'

'Is it? You know best.' Suzanne went back to the stove, leaving Roz staring out into space.

Of course it was impossible. Andy had always used a condom, and it had been almost two years since her previous lover.

Wait. That last time at the ball, had Andy used protection then? She had been trying not to examine that heart-breaking memory, it hurt too much. But now she allowed herself to remember, and couldn't recall the sound of foil tearing. And then there was the time before the dinner party . . . she couldn't remember if he'd used a condom then or not.

So maybe . . . She counted back, trying to remember when she had last had a period. Surely it wasn't long ago. What date was it now? She didn't know.

Now that she thought about it, she did feel different. Not only the barfing at the breakfast table, but the lack of PMS, and something extra that was new.

She borrowed the keys to Patrick's Jeep and drove to the nearest pharmacy. Half an hour later, she stared at a double blue line.

She was pregnant.

To be certain, she did the test again with the second stick, and got the same result.

Yes, pregnant.

She didn't know whether to laugh or cry. She clutched the two plastic sticks, uncaring that they were wet with her urine, and danced around the tiny bathroom.

'Oh my god. Oh my god. Oh my god.'

She couldn't take her eyes off the double lines in case they disappeared.

The emotions which flooded her were so tangled that

she couldn't have put together a coherent sentence if her life depended on it.

She didn't want to be pregnant. It was a disaster. It would ruin the rest of her life.

But a baby!

She hated babies, noisy at one end, smelly at the other and expensive all over. She didn't want a baby, ever. She was too young and immature to look after a baby.

Andy's baby. With big dark eyes staring up at her.

Pregnancy. Nine months of retching and throwing up. Weight gain. Swollen ankles. Varicose veins. Maternity clothes. It would be sheer hell.

Her hand pressed on her belly protectively. It was as flat as always, but somewhere in there a tiny human being rested, depending on her to look after it.

She couldn't look after a baby. She could barely look after herself and the other people who depended on her. She had to make sure her father and Frankie were looked after, and she had a ruthless former Navy SEAL hunting her. Her life expectancy could be counted in weeks, not years. Now she had an extra responsibility.

She knew nothing about taking care of babies, but had a vague notion that it involved a lot of breastfeeding and nappy changing. Could she take a baby on the back of a motorbike, or would she have to buy a car? What about clothes? Did babies care if she put the wrong colour on them?

This was a disaster. She'd be a terrible mother. She couldn't cope with a newborn. They'd take her baby away and give it to someone who could look after it properly.

Her hand tightened on her belly. No, they wouldn't. She was keeping this baby. They could do what they liked, but she would protect it with her dying breath. She might be a useless mother, but it looked as if she *was* going to be a mother.

Time to get on with it.

She forced herself to put the pregnancy tests down on the bathroom sink.

One thing was sure. Nagsy's price had just gone up. Way up.

Pregnancy sucked. Roz had never spent so much of her life trying not to puke.

From being someone who wolfed down whatever she could get, whenever she had time, she was now desperately trying to find things she could eat.

Her life had turned into a fight to eat without gagging and to keep the food down afterwards. She now lived on beans on toast, poached eggs, porridge, boil-in-the-bag fish (which drove Suzanne nuts), frozen grapes and cocoa.

Tea, coffee, bacon, green vegetables, potatoes, fried food or anything spicy turned her stomach, and choking down her folic acid tablet was a daily battle.

Oddly, although Patrick's cologne forced her to open every window in the office in an effort not to retch, she still enjoyed the smell of the horses and the stables.

Maybe you're a country girl at heart. Who knew?

She hadn't told Patrick or Suzanne anything about being pregnant. In any case, Suzanne knew. She quietly cooked something bland at every meal and no longer set a wine glass for Roz in the evening.

Roz had taken to spending her afternoons, when she was supposed to be working on the ranch website, obsessing over the tiny life inside her. She logged on to pregnancy websites to see how much it had grown overnight. She worried about the lack of leafy vegetables in her diet and she dumped the packet of hair dye she had bought in Belfast. No matter how sick this baby was making her, she was taking no chances with its health.

The debate about continuing to ride engrossed her, but since there was no conclusion, she continued to ride out every day on the quietest horse in the stable.

Nagsy was coming along at an astonishing rate. Every morning, Roz dragged herself out of bed to watch him being trained and was impressed by his progress. At normal speed, he didn't look like anything much but when his jockey gave the signal to open up, his choppy motion became smooth and elegant and ate up the ground. Sometimes it seemed he barely touched it.

Oh yes, she would have no trouble convincing Tim O'Sullivan that this horse was worth a million.

That was the figure she had set in her head as the price she would demand.

When she wasn't surfing pregnancy and baby websites, she worked out the details of how she could make Nagsy look like a Gold Cup winner. She needed the paperwork to convince Tim he was the son of Shergar, a convincing time trial, and a convincing win. And also an opponent to drive up the price.

The obvious person was Andy McTavish. He was from the sort of family which bought expensive racehorses. Or even Dougal. But she knew that one hint of where she

395

was and what she wanted, and Andy would have her on the first plane to some witness protection hell in France.

She toyed with the idea of insisting that her dad went into hiding with her, but she abandoned it. She loved him, but she knew that Peter Spring would never settle down to a life of law-abiding boredom.

And she had resolved not to think about Andy. He was her past. Now, she was alone.

All day long, she repeated this to herself, and managed to believe it when she was working. It was the evenings which were hardest. Until she had cut herself off from everything personal, she hadn't realized how many friends she regularly contacted by e-mail or Yahoo. She couldn't log into any account under her own name, and she was wary about creating a fake profile to use other sites where she was known. Someone had once told her that writing style was as distinctive as handwriting, so she stayed off the internet. The empty hours jeered at her.

She didn't want to become entwined in the O'Haras' warm circle. She knew she wouldn't be able to resist their friendship for long, and would end up telling them more than was wise. She couldn't put them in danger.

When had her life become so empty?

33

Although she was exhausted all through the day, and had to fight the urge to nap, it was hard to sleep at night. When she did, her dreams were bright and vivid.

She was back in the playroom of Lough Darra, and Andy was naked. The subtle lighting made him a study of dramatic contrasts. His eyelashes were long and dark against his cheekbones, and the muscles of his abdomen were hard ridges. His distinctive scent, a combination of healthy male and spicy cologne, filled her nostrils and she had no urge whatsoever to be sick. Instead, it filled her with hunger.

She licked her lips and was rewarded by the sight of his penis lengthening and thickening. She moved towards it.

'No, you don't. Not yet.' Andy's voice was rough, but the command in it was clear. 'I want to look at you first.'

She blinked. Until he had spoken, she had no idea she was naked.

She stood there obediently while he circled her, examining her from head to toe. What would he think of the changes since he had last seen her? In spite of the cheap shampoo she used, her hair was brighter and thicker. She knew she had lost weight, though she had no idea how much. The ranch chalets didn't run to unnecessary extras like scales. The tiny life inside her didn't show yet.

'I didn't give you permission to lose weight.' Andy

spoke from behind her. One finger traced down her back, sending chills through her body, and ended up on her bottom. 'This ass is mine. I want it in prime condition.'

He came round in front of her again, and frowned down at her. 'Have you been taking care of yourself? You belong to me. You don't have my permission to neglect your health.'

She wanted to laugh. All her energy was going into staying as healthy as possible. She had never been as conscious of what she ate or drank. But she was distracted by having Andy so close. The roughness of his jaw was irresistible. She raised her hands, lured by the texture of the evening stubble. Being so near to him made her breathing quicken and her heart pound.

She stood on tiptoe and pressed a brief kiss on his lips. They were hot and firm, and moved under hers, but he didn't do as she had hoped and grab her into a full embrace.

Instead, he kissed her back, before taking a seat on the divan, facing her.

His pose might be casual to the point of arrogance, but his cock rose proud and demanding, with a pearly drop on the tip revealing his readiness.

Roz moved towards it eagerly, licking her lips in anticipation. She would give him an experience that would drive him out of his mind.

'No, don't touch me.' He pointed at the spot on the carpet where she had been standing. 'Stay there.'

'Are you kidding me? You're turning down a blow job? Have you turned into a woman while I was gone?' It wasn't exactly her area of expertise, but in her experience, no man ever turned down a blow job. Once a woman had that cock in her mouth, he was hers.

He smiled grimly. 'Oh, we'll definitely get to that later. Much later. Now I want you to kneel.'

He couldn't be serious. She was Little Red. Men competed to kneel at her feet. She had never knelt for anyone. 'Or what?'

It might be interesting to see what Andy would do. The prospect of a naked wrestling match had a certain appeal.

'There is no "Or what?" Kneel.' He stayed sitting where he was, waiting.

At that moment, she hated him. She would have enjoyed having him force her to her knees. The big strong man who wanted her to submit so much that he compelled her to obey. But this was torture. Andy expected her to kneel simply because he told her to.

And there was a tiny part of her, deep inside, that wanted to. Her pride fought but, despite it, her knees buckled and she knelt.

'Good girl.'

His voice was a caress and his smile so full of approval that her belly clenched and wetness flooded her thighs. What was wrong with her that it took so little to turn her on? 'Now spread your knees so that I can see you.'

After the struggle to kneel, this was nothing. She had made the mental leap and was his to command. She parted her thighs, allowing him to see how aroused she was.

He whistled. 'Oh, very good.'

Getting up, he moved around her, stroking her shoulders, running his hands down her arms. When he passed in front of her, his cock was so tempting that she stuck out her tongue for a lick. It was hot and jerked in reaction. 'Naughty, naughty.'

He stood and moved to the back of the room. She looked around to see what he was doing, and he grinned at her. 'You're a very bad submissive, aren't you?'

That hurt. 'I knelt for you. What more do you want, peanut butter covered nipples?'

'What strange tastes you have. We'll try that someday, but now I'm going to help you.' He held a long length of muslin in his hand, and he wrapped it around her eyes, tying it carefully so that it wouldn't slip.

Her world was now reduced to the sound of his voice, the feel of his hands and the warmth of his body. 'Clasp your hands behind your head.'

She did, able to feel the muslin and knowing she could pull it off in seconds. She didn't. When she had dropped to her knees, she had given up control to Andy. Now she waited to see what he would do with it.

What he wanted was to drive her out of her mind. He leaned down and kissed her, his tongue plundering her mouth like a conqueror, but without allowing her to respond. He pulled back when, desperate for the taste of him, she tried to suck on his tongue.

Andy kissed his way along her jawbone to her ear, where he nibbled the lobe and explored the whorls. Her breathing deepened, from what he was doing and from the scent of male arousal so close to her. The warmth of his body was like a furnace, but the fire inside her was almost as hot.

His fingers navigated her upraised arms, testing the sensitive skin along the inner arm which was so rarely touched. She gasped, shocked by the intensity of the pleasure.

'Hmmm, you like that, don't you?'

She could hear the smile in his voice, and while one part of her wanted to zing him a smart answer to shut him up, most of her wanted him to continue, to do more.

He trailed his fingernails down her back, rendering her mindless.

She heard silly noises and it took her a moment to realize she was making them. As long as he continued, she didn't care. One finger swiped across her nipple and she forgot how to breathe. They were so sensitive that she could barely touch them, but somehow, he knew that it would take the lightest pressure to taunt them to straining hardness.

Between the hand on her back and the one playing with her nipples, she couldn't support herself, but it didn't matter. Andy was there, holding her, taking her weight.

'Good girl, trust me, I'll take care of you.'

She gave herself up to him, allowing him to hold her up and do what he wanted with her body. The pressure inside her was growing tighter and tighter, getting ready to blow in an orgasm which she feared would take her head off. She didn't care.

'Oh, did I mention that you need my permission to come?'

'What?' she wailed. He couldn't be serious.

'Don't come until I tell you. Let it wash over you.'

No, no, no, he had to be joking. But she knew he wasn't. His hands continued to torment her, lavishing pleasure on her, finding all her most sensitive points and kissing and caressing them until she was writhing in his grasp. The urge to climax was so strong she felt dizzy, but she did her best to obey him, and tried to relax into the pleasure, allowing it to flow over her like water.

She was mindless and dumb, unable to form a single coherent thought or word, but it didn't matter. All that mattered was Andy. Andy. Andy. The ball of fizzing pressure inside grew bigger and bigger. She wasn't going to be able to contain it . . .

The banging on the door woke her. 'Roz, Roz, come on, you're late for training.'

She sat up with a jerk, panting and sweating, the sheets a twisted mass of cotton around her.

Dream. It was a dream. The most vivid, realistic dream she'd ever had, but only a dream. Her insides pulsed with demanding arousal and it would have taken one flick of a finger to bring her to a shattering, satisfying orgasm.

Something held her hand. The memory of dream Andy saying, 'You can't come until I tell you.' She knew it was a dream. Her dream. All from her subconscious, nothing to do with him or what he wanted. This dream was all she wanted. But she couldn't order her finger to make that one movement.

She struggled out of bed and into the shower, scrubbing herself with lukewarm water and being careful not to touch the parts of her body where she was sensitive. Not today. For today, she would obey Andy. She pulled on her jeans and headed to the flats where Nagsy was waiting.

It was going to be a long day.

Andy parked the Jeep in the garage and switched off the engine. Another false lead and another sighting of a woman who looked vaguely like Roz. This one was in Westport. The 'woman' had turned out to be a cross-dressing transsexual. If it wasn't so heart-breaking, it would have been funny. He stretched, shrugged his shoulders and twisted his neck, trying to ease his aches and pains. He was bone tired from driving. He needed a bath and a Bushmills. He couldn't remember the last time he'd taken a night off.

The rest of the team had gradually drifted back to other jobs, but he wouldn't give up. He would find Roz. He was sure of it. The main thing was to stay focused and not give up.

He longed for sleep. Every night he dreamt of her – deliciously filthy X-rated dreams, where she was naked and sorry for running away and breaking his heart. Andy gave a self-deprecating laugh. He had reached the age of thirty-four without someone breaking his heart. A few weeks with Roz had smashed it to smithereens. He welcomed the pain. It made him feel alive. Anything was better than feeling dead inside.

Andy made his way to the house and stuck his head into the kitchen.

'Any sign of her?' Maggie asked.

He shook his head. 'No. It was someone else.'

Her expression was tinged with sympathy. 'They're in the library. Dinner's in half an hour. I've made your favourite – steak and Guinness pie.'

'Thanks, Maggie.' A big plate of comfort food was exactly what he needed. No, he needed Roz, but this was second best.

In the library, his father was doing the crossword while his mother offered suggestions for the clues he was stuck on. 'Eight down – the world's murder capital.'

'Chicago,' Poppy said.

Dougal looked at her over the rim of his reading glasses. 'It begins with "T".'

'Tegucigalpa,' Andy told him.

His mother looked up and smiled. 'You're home, dear.'

She scanned his face and wisely didn't ask about Roz, although Andy knew that she also missed her terribly. Changing the subject, she said, 'We had a visitor today after you left. An American gentleman.'

'Oh, who?' Andy asked as he poured himself a drink.

'He said he was sorry to have missed you. David, no, Darren Hall.'

Andy spun around, almost dropping the glass. 'Hall was here?'

'Big chap,' his father said. 'I gather he's involved in your kind of work.'

Hall was here? Jesus fucking wept. That bastard had walked into his parents' home. He wanted to punch something, preferably Hall. Instead, he took a sip of his drink and forced himself to calm down. He didn't want to frighten his parents, but he would get Niall Moore to put a team on the place straightaway. 'What did he say?'

'Such a pleasant man. Lovely manners,' Poppy rattled on. 'When I told him that you weren't here, he asked about Roz.'

'He did?' His hand tightened involuntarily around the glass until the sharp pattern of the crystal hurt his palm.

'Well, I wasn't sure what to say, but as he's a friend of yours, I told him you and Roz were having a little time apart. That was alright, dear, wasn't it?'

Andy sighed with relief. If Roz had been here, Hall would have killed everyone to get to her. 'That's fine, Mum. Did he say what he wanted?'

'Only that he had something for Roz.'

The words were innocent, but Andy's blood chilled in his veins. He knew what Hall had for Roz – an encounter with his diving knife, or a neatly broken neck. But it wasn't enough to go to the local police with.

'We're not friends. He's not welcome here,' he told her.

He couldn't leave his parents alone. He didn't think Hall would be back. He had delivered his message, but Andy couldn't risk it. They needed protection. His mind raced, seeking a solution.

'I need a favour. A friend of mine from work has broken up with her boyfriend. She needs a place to stay for a few days. I was wondering if I could invite her here.'

'Oh the poor thing,' Poppy was full of sympathy. 'Of course she can stay here. I could do with some company. I miss having Roz about the place.'

His father grunted his agreement. He was already lost in his crossword puzzle.

'Great.' Andy drained the last of his whiskey. 'I'll have a quick shower before dinner.'

He raced up the stairs two at a time and punched in Reilly's number. 'How would you like a week in the country?'

'How would you like a slap in the head? You know I hate all that cow shit and fresh air stuff.'

'Hall was here.'

'Here? Where here?'

'Lough Darra.'

'Are your parents okay?'

'They're fine, but I'm concerned that he might come back.'

Andy held the phone away from his ear as Reilly raced through a litany of curses, some of which he wasn't familiar with. The petite Ranger was the only girl in a family of six boys and Reilly knew how to hold her own.

'Well at least we know that she's in hiding and that Hall hasn't found her,' she offered when she had run out of swear words.

She was right. Hall's resources were almost as good as Niall's and he didn't believe in going through official channels for anything. The fact that he believed Roz was in Ireland cheered him. But if Hall was desperate enough to come knocking on his front door it meant that he would stop at nothing to find her.

Andy couldn't let that happen. He had to find Roz before Hall did. Apart from missing her like crazy, his hand itched. He had an overwhelming desire to spank the ass off her. Where could the bloody woman have got to? He had been to every county in Ireland looking for her.

He heard Reilly tapping the keys of her laptop. 'There's

a flight to Belfast at 10pm tonight. I'll let Niall know that I'm on my way.'

'Thanks, Reilly. I'll pick you up at the airport.'

'Great. Is there anything I need to pack for a visit to a stately house? A tiara? A pair of corgis?'

'No. We have enough dogs. Make sure you bring warm woollies and wellies.'

He heard her snort of disbelief. 'To go with my tiara?'

'I'm not joking.'

He disconnected the call. Despite the bone-tiring day, Andy felt a glimmer of hope. Roz was alive and in Ireland.

34

The night before the time trial was a nightmare of tossing and turning and worrying. Roz played every scenario over and over in her head, looking for things that could go wrong and trying to find ways to deal with them.

There were too many variables. Too many disasters lying in wait. This was the biggest scam she had ever pulled. The biggest scam she had ever heard of anyone pulling. What had made her think she could pull this off? It was bound to fail.

Stop it. You have to make this work. You have one chance. Don't fuck this up.

She heard an echo of Andy's sexy Northern Irish growl in her own words and wanted to laugh. He was invading her dreams, and now her conscience sounded too much like his voice.

That was all she needed. She got up and used the bathroom for the fourth time that night. Andy Junior might only be the size of a lime, but he was making his presence felt. On the plus side, she had only puked twice today, so maybe she was getting over the worst.

Apart from the birth.

She'd heard horror stories about that. What size had Andy been when he was born? She wished she could ring Poppy and ask her. Poppy's warm common sense was what she needed right now, and what she couldn't have.

Roz knew, deep in her bones, that if Andy discovered he had a baby, he would never let her go and neither would Dougal or Poppy. And there was a big part of her that wanted to be caught. But she had a job to do – one which she knew would put the law-abiding McTavish family out of reach.

Stop being maudlin. Concentrate on the hustle.
She forced her thoughts back to the job.

Patrick swore that Nagsy was in peak condition, and would put up a great performance at the time trial. He had been a bit taken aback when he heard the names of the other horses who were running against him, two of the previous year's best newcomers and both tipped to win big. But he agreed with her that Nagsy needed well-known horses to show off his quality.

The horsebox was ready for the trip to Kilbeggan race track for the trial. She had loaded the tack the night before, along with rugs, water, hay, oats and nuts, brushes and hoof pick, and even his favourite snack – carrot – for afterwards.

The O'Haras' jockey, Willie O'Brien, a small, wiry lad who lived locally and rode out before driving to college every day, was keen to show his talents against the well-known jockeys riding Queen of Tarts and Five of Diamonds. He promised he would be ready and would not take a drop of drink the night beforehand. He was determined to win.

Frankie would be there, too. He told her he had a suitable outfit and could play his part, but Roz worried about his health. If he wasn't strong enough, would he give the game away? Could he maintain the façade? Hell, could he walk? He swore he would be ready and could pull it off.

She had the paperwork. It had taken hours with the O'Haras' computer, but the documents should stand up to almost every examination. Except . . . She had no idea what else Tim would want. Suppose he demanded a document she didn't have? Or what if he changed his mind and didn't come? Everything depended on him turning up, and being anxious to buy. Would her carefully worded invitation attract him to the time trial or turn him off?

Panic quickened her breathing and she forced herself to calm down before she barfed again. She didn't need that.

By the time she managed to get to sleep it was almost dawn, and she slept through the knock on her door, the dawn chorus of the birds who arrived to raid the chicken seed, the clatter of hooves outside and the rattle of buckets of horses being fed.

Roz woke with a panicked start at 10am.

Fuck, fuck, fuck, how had she slept so long? Why had no one woken her? This was one day she couldn't afford to miss anything. She leapt into her clothes and raced to the kitchen. She bitterly resented the time it would take to eat, but knew from experience that skipping a meal would result in crippling nausea before long.

'Where is everyone? What's happening?' she panted.

'Everything's fine,' Suzanne said as she heated some milk for her cocoa and dropped two slices of white bread into the toaster.

Roz would have preferred her home-made sourdough, but it seemed the baby didn't. One of her worst bouts of vomiting had been after eating that. She allowed herself to relax a little and reached for a pear.

Suzanne continued, 'There was a bit of a problem with the race track, but Patrick has handled it.'

Roz froze. 'What sort of problem?'

'Oh, a water pipe burst and the whole bottom end of the track is water logged.'

Slowly, Roz put down the pear. 'That's not a bit of a problem. That's a huge one.' And one she hadn't planned for.

'Don't worry, it's all sorted. We're having the time trial here instead.'

'WHAT?' Roz was aware she was shouting, but couldn't control herself.

Unaware of what a disaster this was, Suzanne poured out a big mug of cocoa and put it in front of Roz. 'Yes, he phoned everyone, told them to come here instead. He's got the lads out clearing the old race track now.'

Stunned, Roz held the mug in trembling hands. What could she do now? Even if she managed to find another race track for the time trial, people now knew the address of the ranch, and Hall could track her down.

How long did she have before he traced her? Her thoughts scurried like mice being chased by a cat. She couldn't bring Hall here. His focused ruthlessness terrified her. Patrick and Suzanne wouldn't have a chance against someone like him. She longed for Andy, but knew he would never let her go ahead with the scam.

Could she call it off and start again? She shook her head. That would never work, it had taken too long to set up, and her chances of finding stables like this one, where she and Nagsy could live below the radar, were non-existent.

Besides, she would start showing soon, and had to be far away before that happened.

She had to go ahead with it and pray that she would be gone by the time Hall arrived. She hated to leave without saying goodbye to Suzanne and Patrick, but it was for their own safety.

Roz forced down half the mug of cocoa, ignored the toast and went out to help groom the turf of the old race track for the time trial.

'This is going to be amazing publicity for us,' Patrick said. 'We'll be in the news.'

For all the wrong reasons, Roz knew, but kept her head down and kept clearing. How many people had she hurt? She didn't have the heart to remind Patrick she was supposed to be hiding.

By 1pm, she was hot and sweaty, but the ranch looked great.

She grabbed a handful of dried apricots and ate them as she showered and changed. With the aid of Suzanne and one of the ranch guests, she had put together an outfit that looked understated and expensive. She had lost weight, and though she worried how this would affect her baby, it did have the advantage of making her look elegant, like someone who might own a world class horse.

The other horses had already arrived and been assigned stables. They were on the track being warmed up by their jockeys. She nodded to the men and they nodded back, but no one spoke. There was no need to remind them how much she would give them when Nagsy won the race. If they could arrange it so Nagsy won by at least ten lengths, there was a bonus.

Their owners were being shown around by the O'Haras.

Nagsy was being warmed up too, and looked every inch a champion with the way Willie had groomed and turned him out.

Tim O'Sullivan arrived next, in an Aston Martin that looked like something James Bond would drive. He inspected the well-kept yard with a certain amount of respect. The O'Haras looked after their ranch with love and it showed.

She nodded to him. 'Uncle Tim,' she said politely.

He rubbed his hands, suddenly looking much more like a Cork horse trader than an airline magnate. 'So where's this horse you think I'm going to buy?'

'Buy?' She managed to sound astonished. 'Oh, I'm sorry. I must have misled you. I'm not selling *you* the horse.'

He scowled. 'Then what did you drag me down here for?'

'I thought you'd be interested to see the trial. But I doubt you could afford Hagar's Son.'

His eyes narrowed. 'Now listen here, missy. If, and it's a big if, this horse is all you say, you should keep him in the family.'

She shook her head. 'I'm sorry, but another buyer has first refusal.'

He snorted. 'Load of nonsense. You've probably been sold a pup.' Tim wandered off, but she saw his eyes taking in Nagsy's quality. And, no doubt, his resemblance to his famous 'father'.

So far, so good.

Frankie arrived in a black stretch limo. It swept into the

413

yard and stopped close to the house. The driver, elegant in a black uniform, opened the rear door. When Frankie stepped out Roz had to choke back a laugh. Who would have guessed that he could clean up so well? He must have raided the wardrobe department of the film set, as well as the props department.

He wore a white suit and a neat headdress which showed off his tanned face and newly trimmed beard, while he leaned on an ornate walking stick.

Roz approached him deferentially. 'Your highness. So good to see you.'

If she hadn't known it was her old friend Frankie Fletcher, she would have been impressed. She had been a bit afraid he would overplay the part, but he looked modern and businesslike as well as suitably Middle Eastern.

He bowed slightly. 'Miss O'Sullivan.' Even his accent was perfect, pure English public school with the merest hint of Middle Eastern wealth. 'I'm anxious to see your horse.'

If his dark eyes twinkled at her, she hoped no one else would catch it.

'Of course.' She turned and found that his flamboyant arrival had attracted attention. 'Shall I perform the introductions?'

Permission granted, she turned to do her duty. 'Your highness, may I introduce Patrick and Suzanne O'Hara, our hosts for this event? This is Prince Farhad Al Husseini. He is interested in building up his racing stables.'

They looked over-awed but bowed politely.

Roz continued through the group, introducing owners

and jockeys to the prince, and purposely leaving her uncle last. 'And this is Mr Tim O'Sullivan.'

He glared at her before sticking his hand out to the prince. 'Her uncle, and the owner of O'Sullivan Airlines.'

Frankie, looking bored, allowed him to shake the tips of his fingers. 'I believe I heard of it.' The disdain in his voice was priceless. 'I usually fly in my cousin's personal plane.'

'And who is your cousin?' Tim snapped.

'Why, the Aga Khan, of course.'

He turned away from Tim and back to Roz. 'Now, Miss O'Sullivan, you have the DNA certification?'

Roz guided Frankie away from the crowd, and lowered her voice enough that Tim had to strain to hear her. She pulled out a certificate from Wetherbys which had taken her weeks to fake and handed it to Frankie, allowing Tim to catch a glimpse of the letterhead. 'Here is it, your highness. As you can see, Shergar is clearly the sire of my horse.'

Frankie took it and made a show of examining it. 'Excellent. Now, perhaps you can tell me how my cousin's horse has managed to sire a foal from beyond the grave.'

Roz lowered her voice even more, and from the corner of her eye, she saw Tim take a step closer so that he could hear what was being said. He had taken the bait.

'There are some details that are a little unclear, but it appears that when your cousin's horse was kidnapped from Ballymany stud, one of the kidnappers must have been a racing man. He took semen from Shergar before the poor horse, er, met his fate.'

'My cousin would have loved to have the horse restored to him, you know. He was distraught, and would have paid, if your police had not advised against paying the ransom.'

Roz banished a pang of guilt at the thought of Nagsy in uncaring hands. Was it her pregnancy that made her want to cry all the time? Now she had a deal to seal. 'At least we can rejoice that his son is well and healthy.'

She led them towards the race track where Nagsy was frisky and eager. He pranced along, nostrils flared, tail high and ears pricked.

The other horses, with greater experience and an innate awareness that this wasn't a proper race, were more sedate as they lined up at the start. Roz handed out stopwatches to the spectators. 'This is a six furlong track. I suggest they race three circuits?'

Everyone nodded, the horses lined up and Patrick fired the starting pistol.

It was the first time Roz had been at a horse race. She had never realized how fast they ran, how thrilling the chase, how loud the thunder of their hooves. She, along with everyone else on the ranch, cheered for Nagsy.

The three horses galloped around the first lap. They were close together, first one edging ahead, then another. Nagsy's bay head inched out in front, but he was over-taken by the black Queen of Tarts. On the outside, Five of Diamonds raced along beside them, his long legs keeping pace.

Roz barely glanced at her stopwatch as they finished the first lap. She was too busy shouting for Nagsy. The smell of the horses, grass and expensive cologne combined to fire her energy. She danced from foot to foot as she watched the horses begin the second lap. They had spread out a little, Five of Diamonds in front, Nagsy half a length behind and Queen of Tarts a neck behind him.

'Go on, go. Move your ass,' she screamed as Nagsy passed her at the start of the final lap. The stopwatch in her hand was forgotten and she didn't care who was watching. Nagsy was her horse and he was amazing. She yelled him on.

The hooves thundered, and clods of earth flew as the horses raced on. If Nagsy didn't make his move soon, this could all be for nothing.

Then Willie, perched over the horse's withers, signalled to him, and Nagsy stretched out his legs and raced forward. His choppy stride smoothed out and ate up the ground. He surged ahead, taking the lead and widening it with every stride.

Roz was barely aware of her own screams as he passed the finish line fifteen lengths ahead of the other horses. She swore he was slowing up before he crossed the line.

Suzanne hugged her tightly and Roz realized she had tears in her eyes. It was going to work.

The horses pulled up, snorting and sweating, and Nagsy turned a wide horsey grin on her, looking like a champion who knew how good he was.

She petted him and congratulated Willie on the winning ride. Then she shook hands with the other jockeys and slipped them the money they had agreed. 'Great work, lads. It was amazing the way you managed to look as if you were trying to catch Nagsy while letting him win.'

The wizened English jockey who had ridden two Grand

National winners opened his mouth to say something, but the other one nudged him and he fell silent.

Beaming, Roz returned to the prince's side. 'Your highness, did you see the time?'

Everyone glanced at their stopwatches and blinked at the time displayed. Well, they should, it had taken Roz a week to organize stopwatches that shaved about ten seconds off the time. 'I hope you're happy that this horse is for you?'

Frankie bowed. 'I am truly impressed. It could be his father running again. It is time he was returned to his rightful owners.'

Tim looked from the stopwatch to Nagsy and back as if he couldn't believe his eyes. Was he suspicious? Roz prayed he hadn't used any other timer during the race or she was busted. She turned back to Frankie. 'What price are you prepared to offer?'

The prince spread his hands, an elegant gesture that managed to look both foreign and exotic. 'One million euro.'

There was a startled silence. Everyone turned to stare at him and Roz fought the urge to box his ears. What was he thinking? This was too high. They had to start lower, and allow the bidding to build.

'A million euro, your highness,' she said carefully. 'Are you sure?'

Damn him, Frankie was going to ruin everything.

35

'One million,' Frankie said firmly.

Time ground to a halt. What could she do? She had to accept his offer. No one would believe it if she turned it down. But it was too much, too soon. Frankie was off his head.

She opened her mouth, not sure if she was going to accept or reject. Then a new voice cut across her.

'Don't be so hasty, I'm interested too,' Frederick Von München spoke up. 'That was an impressive time. I'll offer 1.2 million.' As the owner of Queen of Tarts, he had an interest in acquiring a good stallion.

'One point five million,' Frankie responded without a blink.

'One point seven,' Von München upped his offer.

What the fuck was Frankie playing at? There was no point raising the bidding. He didn't have enough money to buy a lame donkey, and she couldn't sell someone like Von München a ringer.

But Frankie wasn't finished. 'Two million. This horse belongs to the Aga Khan.'

Then Tim O'Sullivan broke in. 'Hold on there. This is an O'Sullivan stallion. It should stay in the family. Two point five million.'

Frankie sneered at him. 'Three. The rightful owner of the horse deserves him.'

Tim glared. 'Three point five.'

Everyone fell silent, even the horses seemed to be listening.

'Four.' Frankie planted the end of his walking stick into the ground.

Roz turned to Tim. He took a breath. 'Five. And that's my final offer.'

A long pause stretched every nerve before Frankie shook his head. 'I love my cousin, but that is too rich for me. You win, Mr O'Sullivan.' He bowed deeply.

Tim's face was a picture of uncertainty when he realized he had committed himself to paying five million euro for a horse. Suzanne O'Hara decided for him by throwing her arms around him. 'Oh, Mr O'Sullivan, you won't regret it. This is a fabulous horse. You'll win next year's Gold Cup for sure.'

'So I will.' Tim relaxed a little.

He pulled out his phone and dialled. 'Hey, Summer, buy yourself a hat for the winner's enclosure, I've just bought the next Gold Cup winner.'

Roz couldn't hear what was said on the other end, but Tim's grin widened. 'Sure, tweet away if you want to. I don't care who knows.'

There was another pause. 'From your cousin, would you believe? No, not her, the other one, Roz Spring.'

He hung up and Roz took the opportunity to say, 'This is a cash sale. I'll give you the details of my Swiss bank account.' She handed him a card with the numbers on it.

Tim narrowed his eyes at her, but said, 'Fine. It'll take an hour or so to go through.'

'As soon as it does, you can take the horse.'

Suzanne clapped for attention. 'Please, everyone, come inside for some champagne. This has been an amazing day.'

His mother's speed as she crossed the stable yard alerted Andy. Poppy never ran. She was the most unflappable woman he knew, but here she was, sprinting across the mucky yard as if her life depended on it.

'Andy, Andy,' she called.

He tucked the hoof pick he'd been using into his pocket. He had been carrying it with him ever since he'd taken it from Roz. Every day he told himself to leave it back in the tack room, and every day he held onto it for a little longer. Somehow, he was convinced it held a faint trace of her perfume. He raced towards Poppy. Was his father ill? Was Dougal having another heart attack? He caught her arm.

'What's wrong? Is it Dad?'

'No, your father is fine. You won't believe this, but we've found Roz.'

'What? Where?' Andy didn't realize his grip had tightened until Poppy winced. He released her immediately. 'Sorry, Mum.'

He took a deep breath to calm down. They had found her. His elderly parents had achieved more than a team of skilled operatives.

'Where is she?'

'Your father has just gotten off the phone to that

dreadful Tim O'Sullivan. The man's either demented or drunk. He told Dougal that he'd bought the next Gold Cup winner – from Roz.'

'Where is she?'

'Staying with the O'Haras near Moate. They run some kind of equestrian centre. Roz has been working there.'

None of this made sense. Andy was certain that Roz had never been near a horse until she came to Lough Darra and now she was working at an equestrian centre and selling thoroughbreds to the likes of O'Sullivan.

'And you won't believe the rest,' Poppy continued. 'Five million euros. Tim O'Sullivan has paid five million euros for the animal.'

'Jesus wept,' Andy said. The word 'scam' flashed inside his head in bright neon letters. He didn't know what she was up to, or how she had persuaded a canny business-man like O'Sullivan to part with that kind of money, but he was certain of one thing. Roz might have the money to disappear for good, but there was no way in hell that he was would let that happen.

Ignoring Poppy's shouts behind him, Andy raced for the garage.

He completed the three hour journey to Moate in less than two hours. It was a wonder he wasn't arrested. His knuckles were white from gripping the steering wheel, but at least he had gotten here alive.

Andy slowed down at the crossroads and rolled down the window to ask an elderly man for directions to the stables. How long would it take Tim O'Sullivan to lay his hands on that kind of money? Please god, Roz was still there or he wouldn't have a hope in hell of finding her.

He was well past the turn off for the stables before he realized he had missed it. 'Never take directions from fucking culchies,' he fumed.

Five miles out of town, my ass. He reversed and took the turn. The Jeep bounced on the rutted road and briars scraped along the side windows. This couldn't be the main entrance. It must be the back way in. They couldn't possibly run a business from here.

The lane widened and an overgrown sign announced O'Hara Stables. The rusty gate beneath the sign was tied shut. It was definitely the wrong road. He was about to drive away when he heard the distant whinny of horses. He climbed out of the Jeep and stepped into a muddy puddle. Great.

Andy climbed onto the third rung of the gate and scanned the horizon. In the distance was a cluster of stable buildings and a large barn with a corrugated iron roof. Across the field came the sound of laughter and music. They must be celebrating the deal. He might be in time but he would have to go cross country.

Andy untied the gate and shouldered it open. It swung back with a protesting squeal of rusting metal. He drove into the field and after he closed the gate behind him, he prayed that he wouldn't meet a ditch on the way and headed straight for the stables.

The main room of the ranch was designed to be spacious, but it was stifling and too hot. All these people around her made her skin itch. The smells of perfume and cologne were so strong that she had to swallow down the urge to puke.

Patrick handed her a glass of champagne. She had paid for it, so she knew it was excellent quality. This was not a time to be cheap. He tapped his glass and when the room quietened, he called for a toast.

'To the best horse ever to pass through O'Hara's Ranch, and to his new owner. May they make a successful team.'

Roz raised the glass, but even though she barely touched her lips to the fizz, her stomach rebelled and a cold sweat bathed her back. She couldn't take much more of this. She smiled at the couple beside her. 'Please excuse me, I need a little fresh air.'

The woman – Roz couldn't remember her name – frowned at her. 'You look a bit pale, are you feeling all right?'

'I'll be fine once I get outside.'

She put down her glass and while Tim O'Sullivan was making a speech, she eased out through the French windows. The fresh air smelled sweet and she gulped deep lungfuls of it.

In a few minutes, someone would propose a toast to her, and she should be there, smiling, looking gracious and exulting in the knowledge that she had pulled off the scam of a lifetime. She had more money than she had ever dreamed, enough to keep her father safe and let her do whatever she wanted for the rest of her life.

And all she wanted to do was throw up.

Roz moved away from the house. How long would it take before the money was in her Swiss bank account? One hour? Two? She had heard Tim on the phone, making arrangements to pick up Nagsy and take him back to his own stables.

How much longer?

A restless crawling sensation beneath her skin prevented her from standing still. Roz walked towards the yard and saw Willie O'Brien holding Nagsy while he grazed on the back lawn.

'Go and celebrate, Willie,' she said. 'I'll look after him.'

The jockey looked torn. 'Are you sure?'

'Of course. There's some expensive champagne going a-begging and a couple of owners would like a word with you.'

He handed her Nagsy's lead and rushed away without another protest.

Someone else for her to feel guilty about. What would happen if Willie was offered a job as a result of today's race, and they found out it had been rigged? Willie knew nothing about it, but when Tim O'Sullivan discovered that Nagsy wasn't a wonder horse, but a plain old nag with a passing resemblance to a famous racehorse, who would he blame?

She'd be gone. Tim would blame Willie, who had ridden the race of his life and had no idea it was all a con. And the O'Haras, who had been nothing but good to her.

Bile rose in her throat and she leaned against the horse. 'Oh, god, Nagsy, what am I going to do?'

He looked around with mildly curious eyes, nudged at her with his nose, before putting his head down again to the sweet grass.

'No words of wisdom, eh?' She didn't even know why

she was talking to a horse, but at least he didn't answer back or make sounds of outrage or disgust.

'Perhaps it's as well you can't talk. I'd hate to hear your opinion of what I've been doing.' She put her arm across his back, feeling the solid muscle under her hand. 'I should be thrilled. I've got five million euro. I can pay off the Ramos brothers and keep Dad safe. I can fix Frankie up so he can retire. Hell, maybe he can move to Hollywood and keep seeing Cheyenne if he wants to. I have enough money to disappear, get away from Hall forever and give a good life to my baby. Happy ever after, right?'

Nagsy raised his long tail and pooped on the grass.

'Yep, that about sums it up. Horse shit.'

She'd clean that up later. She burrowed her hand under his mane, now trimmed and short. 'It's all crap. Dad will walk away from this and get into trouble again. Frankie and Cheyenne won't have a happy ever after. He's a crook and she's a Hollywood film star. The O'Haras and Willie will be disgraced for being associated with this. Your life of luxury as a champion racehorse will disappear when Tim discovers you're an ordinary horse.'

She froze. 'He wouldn't put you down or anything, would he? It's not your fault you look like Shergar. None of this was your idea.'

But what good was a racehorse who couldn't win races? Her mind spun, trying to think of some way to make sure Nagsy didn't pay for her crimes. She couldn't stop the sale now, she needed the money, but the temptation was so strong she shook with it.

One more life she had messed up.

She hated to think of the McTavishes, who had opened their home and their hearts to her. Dougal might be dour and taciturn, but he had all the patience in the world for anyone who tried and worked hard. And Poppy, the grief-stricken mother who desperately wanted grand-children to fill the hole in her heart.

Roz prayed Poppy never found out that she was carrying her grandchild, and she would never see him.

And Andy. The thought of him brought pain stronger than losing a limb. The time she had broken her leg in three places had been nothing compared to this. Andy, her lover. The man who made her tremble with passion with a glance of his dark eyes. Whose kisses turned her to putty. Whose touch raised goose bumps on her skin, even when he was shaking her hand. Who had saved her life, over and over. Who had sheltered her, protected her. Made love to her.

'Andy.' Saying his name made her insides twist with need. A need that would last forever and could never be satisfied.

She would be hungry for Andy for the rest of her life.

Roz had no idea how long she stood there with Nagsy, grappling with the realization that she had screwed her life up past redemption. No matter which way she turned, someone would pay the price for her actions. There was no way to fix it.

A familiar sound pulled her out of her miserable rumi-nations. It was her Kawasaki Ninja coming up the drive to the house. She'd know her bike in a thousand. For years, that engine was all that had kept her out of trouble.

She froze. What the hell was Michael Brophy doing here? He could scupper the entire deal. With a few words, he could reveal Nagsy's true parentage and it would be all over. She had to stop him.

Roz pulled Nagsy's head up and started towards the house, then halted. There was something wrong. The figure on the bike was too big to be the elderly farmer.

Michael Brophy was around the same size as her, which was why she had given him her helmet and leathers. This rider was much bigger. Bigger, wider and more muscular. He brought the bike to a skidding halt and she got a clear look at him.

Hall.

Acting on instinct, she ducked in behind Nagsy before he saw her.

Hall was here. And – she caught her breath – the fact that he was riding her bike meant he had taken it from Michael Brophy. Roz wouldn't bet a cent on the old man being alive. Had Hall seen him wearing her helmet and leathers and assumed it was her?

Oh god, oh god, oh god.

She had to get away.

Hidden behind Nagsy, she risked a peep under his neck. Hall was looking around, searching for someone. For her.

Why hadn't she stayed in the house? She might have puked on the floor, but Hall couldn't attack her in front of so many witnesses. Now she was on her own and there was no one within shouting distance.

Roz had seen Hall in action already and had read up on the training of Navy SEALs. This was a man who didn't need fancy weapons; he had been trained to kill with his bare hands and to make a weapon of whatever was available.

How could she get to safety? She was out in the middle of an empty paddock. There was nothing around her to provide shelter. She hadn't a prayer of being able to run to the house before he noticed. Or to the stables which were empty anyway. She was out of screaming range.

Another peep under Nagsy's neck.

FUCK. Hall had stopped and was turning the bike in her direction. He was between her and the house and was going to hunt her down on her own motorbike. She knew how fast the Ninja was; she had no hope of getting away.

Unless . . .

Nagsy.

She didn't allow herself time to change her mind. Roz vaulted onto his back, feeling the fine linen skirt rip as she did. Then she was on top, Nagsy's solid muscles shifting beneath her.

She yelled, 'Giddy up!' as she kicked him.

Nagsy startled, then gathered himself and took off at a full gallop.

She had no saddle or bridle. The horse wore a nylon head collar with a short leading rope attached. She had no way of guiding him but it didn't matter. If she could get away from Hall, she'd worry about stopping later. She grabbed a handful of mane and concentrated on staying on.

The horse was headed for the stables, but that was no good. They were all at the party and there was no one who could help her.

Roz pulled the rope, turning Nagsy's head towards the

race track. He responded, lengthening his stride as he went.

This was nothing like riding Minty. Nagsy was bigger, stronger, faster. The muscles which flexed and bunched between her thighs were fluid and powerful. His warm horsey scent rose to her nostrils, filling her with an odd exhilaration. She was terrified, knowing that she might be moments from death, but at the same time, she savoured every breath as she raced to get away.

She blessed Andy for his riding lesson, where he had made her go without reins or stirrups. This was completely different, but at least she knew how to find her balance.

Nagsy seemed to know what he was doing. Ears pricked forwards, he opened up his ground-eating legs and galloped flat out.

The sound of the engine told her that Hall was in pursuit on the Ninja. Even with the rough going, the bike was catching up.

Why the fuck did I have to buy a bike with so much acceleration?

She urged Nagsy on and he obliged, somehow finding an extra reserve of speed. It wasn't going to be enough. As long as they were on the flat, the Ninja would catch up.

There was one thing Nagsy could do that the Ninja couldn't. He could jump. She had seen him jumping and he had taken a series of five foot fences in his stride. Nagsy could jump. The trouble was, she couldn't. The closest she had ever come to jumping was balance exercises over trotting poles.

Roz looked behind her. Hall was closer now. She could see the grin on his face and the feral gleam in his eyes. There was no alternative. She pulled the rope and turned Nagsy, pointing him at the thick blackthorn hedge that fenced the field.

She kicked him on. 'Go on, boy. Time to fly.'

36

Andy had almost reached the far side of the field when a horse sailed over the hedge less than twenty feet in front of the Jeep. The woman was riding bareback, clinging to the stallion's mane for dear life. Her long red hair flew out behind her.

Andy braked hard, narrowly missing a rider on a motorbike who shot through a gap in the hedge. The rider swerved, before righting himself. He gunned the engine and set off in pursuit of the horse. The military buzz cut was gone, but Andy would recognize that profile anywhere. It was Hall, and he was chasing Roz.

Fuck. Why hadn't he packed a gun? Andy downshifted and pushed the accelerator to the floor as he set off in pursuit. He didn't know how Roz was holding on. He had to cut them off before Hall caught her.

The Jeep bounced like a fairground ride as he pushed the engine to its limit, passing the bike and sweeping in a wide circle around the horse, trying to make the stallion change direction. He saw the ruthless grimace on Hall's face.

Finally, he was racing side by side with Roz. Keeping one hand on the wheel, he rolled down the window and roared across the field, 'Stop him.'

She turned, her face alive with real fear and exhilaration. 'Are you kidding? I can't.'

'You're heading towards the motorway.'

She raised her head and could see the cars and trucks speeding along on the other side of the fence. 'Oh fuck.' Panic crossed her face. 'I can't stop.'

'Then turn him.'

The horse was racing towards disaster at a frightening speed and there was nothing Andy could do to stop it.

For endless seconds, Roz continued to gallop towards the motorway. She was barely four strides away from the fence. Nagsy was already gathering himself for the leap when she leaned forwards, grabbed his collar and hauled his head to the side. For two more strides, Nagsy fought her grip before giving in and turning away from the road.

Then she was galloping alongside the fence, with Hall catching up.

'Get out of here,' Andy yelled. She didn't reply, but pulled on the head collar again until they were headed back towards the stables.

It was time to deal with Hall.

When Andy swerved, trying to get between them, bike and rider almost ploughed into him. Hall whipped the bike around but the wheels skidded and the bike slid sideways. Hall managed to leap free but the Ninja went under the Jeep's wheels with a sickening crunch. Andy fought to control it but didn't manage to turn in time to avoid hitting the ditch.

This was going to hurt.

A maze of birch and hawthorn rushed to greet him and he shut his eyes and braced for impact. The last thought before blackness struck him was relief that Hall was down.

The whoosh of the inflating airbag pinned him to his

seat. He was dimly aware of the sounds of wheels spinning in the mud, mixed with the cawing of disturbed crows. Christ, he had fucked up royally. He automatically carried out a quick inventory of his body. Every bit of him hurt like hell, but nothing was broken. He would have a fine collection of bruises, but that was nothing new.

Andy fought his way out from beneath the rapidly deflating airbag and staggered from the Jeep. In the distance, he caught a glimpse of Roz galloping for the stables. Punch-drunk, Andy shook his head, trying to get some sense back. There was something wrong with this picture. Something was missing.

Where was Hall?

The first blow came out of nowhere, slamming him against the Jeep. Andy raised his arm instinctively and managed to block the next one, following it up with a blow of his own. Hall evaded, dancing away from him. His opponent's face was grazed from his fall from the bike, but the lethal intent in his eyes told Andy that Hall wasn't giving up yet.

'I'm gonna take you apart and after that, I'm going to take care of Red.'

Adrenaline surged, pumping through his veins, mixing with anger and masking his pain. He was the only thing that stood between Roz and Hall and there was no way that he would let that bastard touch his woman. 'Don't call her that.'

Hall cocked his head. 'Well, isn't that sweet? Someone's got the hots for Little Red.'

Andy was glad that Roz wasn't here. He couldn't fight Hall and protect her at the same time. The bastard was out for blood. No matter what happened, this had to end here.

Hall lunged. The blade of his diver's knife came at Andy in a vicious arc.

He twisted out of its path but not quickly enough. A bright sting of pain cut his ribcage, burning like fire. Gritting his teeth, Andy blocked the next blow and landed a series of short jabs while Hall was off balance.

His small victory was short lived. Hall didn't appear to feel a thing. He grinned with the lethal charm of a wolf. 'You'll have to do better than that.'

The next swipe shredded the sleeve of his shirt. A thin line of blood stretched almost from shoulder to wrist. Andy had heard of the death of a thousand cuts; he wasn't sure how many of these he could take. Feinting left, he unbalanced his opponent and managed to kick him twice in the ribs.

The big man winced in pain. 'Not bad. But I'm just getting warmed up.'

Retaliation was swift. While Andy was distracted by the blade, a fist the size of a ham made contact with his jaw. His neck snapped back. Christ, it was like being hit with a mallet.

Shaking the dizziness away, Andy aimed another kick, this time at his opponent's knee. That one drew a grunt from Hall, but didn't bring him down. What was the guy made of? Titanium?

Slash. Feint. Slash. Another burning contact. Andy had lost count of his injuries. He was losing blood from the gash in his side and the lighter cuts made him feel that his body was on fire.

Hall limped slightly but he was still strong. Was he strong enough to kill him? Andy couldn't take that chance. The longer he kept him here, the more time Roz had to get away. If he followed her, they were both dead and he was never letting that happen.

Staying on the balls of his feet, Andy danced away from Hall's next blow. He needed to keep distance between him and that knife. He feinted to the right before aiming a roundhouse kick at Hall's head. He missed his target, but his foot hit Hall's chest, driving him to the ground. It was now or never. Andy followed him down.

In a parody of a lovers' embrace, the pair rolled, each fighting to stay on top. Andy grasped Hall's wrist, digging his fingers deep into the groove between his tendons, trying to get him to drop the knife. Hall yelped in pain, but stubbornly refused to release it.

Andy jerked his head back and slammed his forehead into Hall's face in a Belfast kiss. The sickening crunch of gristle and breaking bone was music to his ears. Hall roared in pain as blood erupted from his broken nose. Taking advantage of his distraction, Andy drove Hall's knife hand to the ground and the blade jerked free and disappeared beneath the Jeep.

Despite the pumping blood, Hall refused to give up. Grasping a handful of Andy's hair, he tugged sharply and managed to roll them both over. The air was pushed from Andy's lungs as he was slammed into the damp ground.

This guy was worse than the Terminator.

Something hard pressed into Andy's hip. He was still carrying Roz's hoof pick. It wasn't much, a tiny blade and the spike for pulling stones from hooves. Beggars couldn't be choosers. Despite the crushing weight of the heavier man, Andy managed to reach his pocket.

Loosening his grip on Andy's hair, Hall turned his attention to Andy's unprotected throat.

Jesus, Hall was strangling him. Andy gasped for air. His vision clouded at the edges. Somewhere in the distance he heard Roz scream and it jerked him back to reality. Andy managed to raise his arm and drove the spike of the hoof pick into Hall's neck.

A look of horror crossed Hall's face as blood spurted like a fountain from his carotid artery. His grip loosened and Andy drew in a deep lungful of air before pushing his opponent away.

Andy staggered to his feet. A terrible wheezing sound filled the silent field as Hall struggled for a breath that would never come. His fingers flailed weakly for the yellow and black handle wedged deep in his neck and then he slumped to the ground.

Andy squeezed his eyes shut and opened them again. A red-haired missile raced towards him across the grass and flung herself into his arms. He buried his face in her hair and held her as if he would never let her go.

He wasn't sure how long they stood there. The sound of sirens carried across the open ground. He was vaguely conscious of people running towards him, but he couldn't have moved if his life depended on it. As the adrenaline ebbed, the pain returned. There wasn't a bit of him that wasn't screaming for attention. None of it mattered a whit.

Nothing, except her.

Roz wriggled out of his grasp, her worried eyes taking

inventory of each blooming bruise and bloody injury. She touched his ribcage and her already pale face turned ashen when she realized he was bleeding. 'You're hurt.'

'No kidding!'

Andy refused to release her hand while the paramedic tended his injuries in the O'Haras' kitchen. A hospital was out of the question. He had refused point blank to go. He wasn't letting Roz out of his sight. He was dead on his feet and almost certain that he was suffering from delusions, because a man dressed in a white suit who looked suspiciously like Frankie Fletcher was being treated like royalty.

Hall's body had been taken to the hospital morgue. There were enough witnesses to the fight to confirm that the killing was self-defence. At least he wasn't under arrest. Andy had managed to fend off most of the Gardaí's questions about Hall, redirecting them to Niall and Interpol. The big guy was already on his way to Ireland.

The paramedic finished dressing the wound on his ribcage. 'If you won't go to A&E, at least promise me that you'll lie down.'

Andy nodded. He doubted that he was capable of doing anything else.

'He's staying with me. I'll make sure that he does,' Roz said.

'Is that an offer? I'm not sure that I'll be up to much tonight.'

The glare she gave him made the paramedic laugh.

'I'll leave you to the care of your good lady.'

Patrick had managed to rescue the Jeep from the ditch

and insisted on driving them back to her cabin, even though it was less than five minutes away. Roz pushed open the unlocked door and helped him inside. He would have to give her another lecture about personal security.

Before leaving, Patrick carried his hold-all and jacket from the Jeep. Roz fetched him a blanket and switched on the heater.

'I'll get you a drink,' she said.

Why wouldn't she sit down? This was more than a reaction to being chased by Hall. Andy patted the couch in invitation. 'I don't want anything to drink. I want you.'

Reluctantly, she sat down beside him, twisting her hands.

Yep. Something was definitely up.

Ignoring her resistance, he pulled her into his arms and wrapped the blanket around both of them. 'It's over. You're free.'

Her answering laugh was harsh. 'I'll never be free.'

'Yes, you will. Now that Hall is dead, everything is different. Interpol won't want you any longer. Tomorrow we'll go back to Lough Darra.'

'I can't. You don't know what I've done.'

'I've a pretty good idea.' Andy reached for her and winced. Everything hurt like a bitch. 'Grab my bag for me?'

Bewildered, she got up and fetched the hold-all for him.

Andy unzipped it and pulled out a small velvet bag. He had carried it everywhere since he had redeemed it from the pawn shop, hoping that he could put it on her finger again.

'You forgot something when you left.'

When she saw the name on the bag she gasped. 'My ring? You got it back?'

'Aye, and I want you to wear it for real this time.'

Roz choked, tears springing to her eyes and she shook her head. 'Oh Andy, I can't. I'm so sorry.'

He'd had a fucking crap day. He'd been punched, stabbed, half strangled and almost killed by a psycho nutcase. He was damned if he was taking 'No' for an answer.

Roz loved him. He was certain of that. He had to find a way to make her see reason. Pulling her into his arms, he settled the blanket around them. 'Fine. If you can give me ten reasons why we shouldn't get married, I'll let you go.'

She raised her head in protest. 'You can't do that.'

'I just did. Come on, if you're so set against us being together, you should have lots of reasons.'

'I scammed Tim O'Sullivan out of five million.'

'He can afford it.' Andy was dying to hear the details of that one, but it wouldn't do to get side-tracked. He had more important things to think about.

'Didn't you hear me? He's going to go nuts when he realizes what I did.' Her voice was rising.

'So give it back.'

'I can't. My dad messed with the wrong people. I need half a million to keep his kneecaps attached.'

Rage surged through Andy. Peter Spring was a bastard. What kind of a parent would expect his child to bail him out every time he screwed up?

He put his finger beneath her chin and tipped her face up so that she was forced to meet his eyes. 'You are not responsible for your father. Let him sort out his own problems. Hell, let him get a job.'

Roz sniffed at his unsympathetic response.

There was no way that he would allow her deadbeat dad to come between them. 'If you want him to disappear, I'll get him a job in Ireland. I'm sure the O'Haras would find work for another stable hand.'

'Are you nuts? My father would never do stable work.' By her tone of voice, he could have been suggesting he go into outer space without a suit.

'Fine. Let him get a sex change and join a convent, I don't care. The point is he has choices. He can disappear if he wants to badly enough.'

Reluctantly, she nodded. 'I suppose so.'

'And I'm waiting for eight more reasons.'

She was quiet for a moment, considering her next words. 'Frankie got hurt when he helped us get away from Tullamore. I owe him.'

'If you owe him, then so do I, but you don't owe him the rest of your life. Actually, he looked pretty good in that fake sheik outfit. I think he'll be okay.'

'Your parents will hate me when they find out the truth. I'm not rich. I didn't go to a fancy university and my dad is a –'

'Have you ever killed anyone?'

'No,' she replied, looking offended.

'Do you have a criminal record?' Andy already knew the answer to that one. Roz had managed to stay one step ahead of the law all her life.

'Not exactly, but what's that got to do with anything?'

'My parents won't care that you're poor or went to the local polytechnic instead of the Sorbonne. They love the real you – the one who helps on the estate and poses for hours for a portrait without complaining.'

Andy caught the faint trace of a smile, but then her mouth firmed. 'I have a past and it's not a pretty one.'

'That makes us even. I wouldn't like to tell you half the things I've done. I'm not a nice guy.'

'You are impossible. Do you know that?'

She gave him a half-hearted thump that made him wince, then mouthed an apology. But her body had softened slightly. Maybe there was hope for them after all. Andy picked up the velvet bag and waved it at her enticingly. 'Are you running out of reasons?'

'No.' She heaved a sigh. 'I can't live off you. I need to work. I've never been dependent on any man.'

Of course she hadn't. Andy was willing to bet that Roz had been forced into independence from a very early age. He wished for ten minutes alone in a dark alley with Peter Spring. 'Live off me? You've got more money than I do.'

Despite herself, she laughed.

'Next silly reason?'

She sobered. 'Your world is a million miles from the one I grew up in. I don't fit in. I can put on a good act, but that's all it is. It's not real.'

Andy tightened his arms around her and kissed the top of her head, inhaling the scent of her hair. The ache in his chest had nothing to do with the beating he'd received at Hall's hands. He couldn't lose her again. Whatever difficulties they had, they would work through them.

'I know that you have trust issues, but I'm not your father and you have to learn to lean on people.'

Roz picked at the blanket, pondering his words silently. 'But what if I can't? What if I mess this up?'

'You might, but I'm willing to try if you are.'

She raised her head and stared unflinchingly at him. 'What about your job? All those other women? I won't let you run around seducing everyone you meet.'

She was jealous. Andy wanted to punch the air and do a happy dance, but every cell in his body protested at the prospect. The prospect of someone getting a call to say that he was injured or missing had kept him single up to now, but it was time to change.

'To tell you the truth, being shot and beaten up has lost its attraction. Niall can move me to something different.'

Roz hadn't given up. 'I used to be a professional Domme.'

She waited for his reaction, looking as if she had dropped a bomb.

'Try telling me something I didn't know.' Releasing her, he forced himself to his feet, cursing his aching body. He took her hands in his. They were small and delicate, and he could feel the subtle tremble in them.

'Tell me, did you have sex with any of them?'

'No!' She tried to pull her hands back, but he wouldn't let her. 'Of course not. I was a Domme, not a whore. Mostly I gave them orders or flogged them. Or let them lick my shoes.'

Andy grinned. He couldn't help it. She looked so adorable confessing like a naughty child. 'I'm as big a fan of a pair of sexy heels as the next man, but don't expect me to lick them.'

'Weren't you listening? I said I was a pro-Domme.'

'I heard. We're going to have fun working out who's on top.' Andy relished the prospect of it. He couldn't imagine anyone who was a better match for him.

'What if we meet someone who knew me? It would cause such a scandal.' The shadows in her eyes told their own story.

Andy took her hands, and forced her to look at him. 'Trust me. No one will ever cause a scandal for Mrs Andrew Campbell McTavish. We are not a family to mess with.'

But it was clear she wasn't finished. 'You don't know what I'm really like inside and when you do, you'll . . .'

The pain in her voice made his heart ache. Tough, sassy independent Roz was all a front. Beneath the wisecracking façade, she was vulnerable. She had learnt how to hide, how to push people away, but he was damned if he would let her do that to him.

'I'll what? Cheat on you? Mess with your head? Leave you?'

'Yes, all of that, but that's not the real reason.' She brushed away a stray tear and Andy sensed that something bad was coming.

'I can't marry you, because I'm pregnant.'

The silence in the little cabin was so deep Roz could hear her own heartbeat. She had promised herself she wouldn't tell him but she'd had no choice. She waited for his reaction. Would he ask whose it was? That would kill her. But if he jumped in and insisted she marry him because she was pregnant, that would be almost as bad. She couldn't bear to spend the rest of her life with him, wondering if Andy had been noble and married her because she was pregnant.

She realized she was holding her breath, and exhaled with a gasp.

Andy stared at her, turned to stone by her announcement. His eyes narrowed. 'How long have you known that you were pregnant?' he demanded.

He didn't sound like a man who was about to get down on one knee.

'Um, about two months now,' she admitted reluctantly. Where was he going with this?

'Two months! For two months you've know you were carrying my baby, and you didn't tell me. Not a single hint. Instead, you were out riding horses and no doubt doing all sorts of heavy and unsuitable work.'

'Well . . .' This wasn't going the way she had expected.

He pounced. 'You were! Ignoring your own safety is bad enough. But now I learn you were taking chances with our baby.'

Was he serious? She straightened her shoulders. 'You have no idea what you're talking about. I researched it, and I didn't take any stupid risks.'

'And do your so-called experts know how reckless you are?' he demanded. 'It's not as if we're talking about an ordinary sensible woman who thinks before she does stupid things.'

She gasped, outraged. 'Reckless?'

'Oh, maybe that wasn't you galloping bareback on a

racehorse towards a motorway? It must have been your idiotic twin.' Andy sounded thoroughly pissed off.

'So I should have allowed that psycho to kill me, rather than risk riding a horse?' She wasn't going to let Andy get away with this shit.

'No! You should have told me two months ago, so that I could have been here to protect you.'

Roz had been working herself up into a fine rage, but that stopped her.

He went on. 'If anything had happened to you, I wouldn't have been able to bear it. Thinking of you in danger like that . . .' He took her in his arms and held her so tightly she couldn't breathe.

Who cared about breathing? 'That's how I feel about you going off doing soldier stuff,' she murmured.

His arms tightened further. 'Then maybe it's time I stepped back, let other men do the dangerous work.'

She wiggled an arm out around his neck. 'Good idea,' she whispered, and kissed him.

He tipped up her chin so that he was looking directly into her eyes. 'There is only one reason that matters. Do you love me?'

She took a breath. Time to tell the truth. 'So much it hurts. I've never loved anyone like this before and I never will again.'

His arms tightened round her. 'Thank god I'm not the only one. To love you this much and not have you feel the same would really suck.'

Who needed words? She pulled him down and kissed him.

37

Roz was silent on the return journey to Lough Darra. She drove, leaving Andy to sleep in the back, wrapped up in a tartan blanket. Despite the arnica that Suzanne had applied to his face, the bruises were more livid today. He looked like he had gone ten rounds with a world heavy-weight boxer.

Andy had fought the bad guy for her. And won. And he wanted her and the baby. She placed one hand on her belly. 'It looks like we'll be taking care of Daddy for a while.'

'What?' Andy murmured, barely waking up.

'Nothing,' Roz replied, blushing. 'Just thinking.' She hadn't realized that she'd spoken the words aloud.

She had offered to buy Nagsy back from Tim, telling him that he had a tendency to throw a splint.

'Tell him it was a scam,' Andy had said.

'And implicate everyone here in a criminal fraud? No, I'll tell him he goes lame easily and refund the money.'

But Tim had refused. He had seen her offer of a refund as seller's remorse and it made him even more determined to hold onto the horse.

Niall had offered to arrange a new life for her father when he got out of prison, but refused to tell her where. Frankie was going to the States with his share of the loot. The Peckham Food Bank had received a large anonymous donation, and for the first time in her life she felt . . . Well, she didn't know how she felt.

Happiness had been so foreign to her for so long that she found it hard to relax and enjoy it. Back at Tullamore, in Cheyenne's trailer, she had drunk from a coffee cup which proclaimed *Life isn't about finding yourself, but creating yourself.* Maybe it was right. She was creating a whole new Roz, and today was the start of her life with Andy.

In the back seat, Andy's wakening stretch was followed by a groan. Yep. He definitely needed some TLC.

She had barely stepped out of the Jeep when Poppy arrived. The older woman seemed a little more frail since she had last been here, but her eyes were bright and her smile was filled with delight. 'Oh, my dear girl. I'm so glad that he found you. Andy's been such a misery.'

'I have not.'

Poppy eyed his bruised face with a considered look. 'I haven't seen you in such bad shape since Afghanistan. Are you sure you shouldn't be in hospital?'

'Positive.' Andy dropped a kiss on her cheek. 'A few days in bed and I'll be fine. I've brought a nurse with me.'

Roz let that one go. He would pay for it when he was well again. 'Let's get you into bed.'

Andy tried to wink but his poor battered face couldn't quite manage it. They made a slow procession up the staircase and into the master bedroom.

'I'll leave you to it, my dear,' Poppy said. 'You need a rest after the drive. Maggie has promised to make his favourite dinner.'

She closed the door, leaving them alone.

Roz busied herself unpacking Andy's bag. His shirt was

torn and blood-stained. She didn't dare let Poppy see that. The dark jeans had been slashed. She rolled them up quickly. She would dispose of them later.

'Nurse,' Andy called and she turned around. 'I think I need some help.'

'You do?' Trying not to laugh, she folded her arms and cocked her head. 'What kind of help?'

He sat on the bed, giving her his best puppy dog impersonation, but the laughter in his dark eyes was tinged with something else.

'Don't even think about it, Andy McTavish. You almost died. Do you realize that?'

'I thought you were going to take care of me? I'm in pain. I need lots of TLC.'

Roz crossed the room and stood before him, brushing a stray hair away from his battered face. 'Where does it hurt?'

'Here.' He pointed to his bruised cheekbone and Roz kissed it gently.

'And here.' Andy indicated his neck where finger-sized bruises were clearly visible.

Roz opened the top button of his shirt to give her better access and nuzzled the tender spot. Battered and bruised as he was, he was still sexy as hell and she had missed him. A tingle of anticipation fluttered inside her and it had nothing to do with the baby. What sort of a wanton wretch was she? She couldn't expect an injured man to . . .

'And I have a really hurty spot on my belly,' he continued.

She raised her head. 'Hurty? Is that even a word?'

'Uh huh. I don't know. I never went to La Sorbonne.'

'Don't push your luck,' she warned him. She would never live that one down.

'But I missed you every night. Haven't you missed me? Even a little bit.'

'I have several little bits that missed you.' She laughed. 'But somehow, I think they're going to have to wait until you're better.'

'I'd hate to leave a lady in distress,' he murmured. 'If we were really careful, we could take care of each other.'

'Andy, it's the middle of the afternoon, you can't possibly –'

His kiss silenced her. He might be injured but there was nothing wrong with his mouth. His tongue duelled with hers in a sensuous invitation and she moaned softly. Oh, that was so good and it had been so long. She pulled away reluctantly. 'Are you sure?'

'The only thing that aches more than the rest of me is my cock. Help me get my clothes off.'

Roz needed no further encouragement. She opened the buttons of his shirt one by one and eased it off. Kneeling on the floor, she pulled off his shoes and tugged off his pants.

In the bright spring daylight, the damage that Hall had inflicted on him was brutally evident. But he was hers, and she loved every battered inch of him. 'I don't know where to touch you that won't hurt.'

'We'll figure something out. Now, strip.'

Giggling, she obeyed his gruff command. Her man might be down, but he wasn't out. There was something liberating about being naked in daylight. Roz struck a pose, waiting for his next order.

'Turn around.'

She turned and pouted at him over her shoulder. The muffled growl of approval from the bed made her nipples peak.

'God, I love your ass.' He patted the bed beside him. 'Come over here.'

Roz decided to tease him. Andy would have to learn that he couldn't have things all his own way. 'There's something I need to do first.'

Climbing onto the high bed, she sat at his feet. For once, Andy wasn't in charge, and she was going to enjoy it. His cock was fully erect, a tempting prize. She bent her head, letting her hair trail over his legs, and pressed a tender kiss to the inside of his calf. Taking her own sweet time, she alternated licks and tender kisses along his inner thigh.

Next time, when he was feeling better, she might bite him there. She liked the idea of marking him as hers. Roz paused when she reached his cock. Giving him her best porn-star gaze, she ran her tongue slowly along her bottom lip before she licked the length of his shaft slowly. His strangled groan was all the encouragement she needed. Opening her mouth wide, she closed it over the head of his cock and swirled her tongue around the sensitive tip.

'Oh yes, like that. Just like that,' he said hoarsely.

Pleased, she raised her head and plunged again, taking him deeper. She loved the sense of power that it gave her. It was more potent than any aphrodisiac. Andy was helpless, and hers.

'I want to see your face. I want to watch you take me,' he said.

'Kinky devil.' But she obeyed, brushing her hair over

her shoulder so that he could watch as she licked him from balls to tip before taking him in her mouth again.

'I need to be inside you.'

Straddling his hips, she grasped his cock, rubbing it back and forth, along her sensitive clit, teasing. Roz lowered her hips, taking only an inch of him inside her before rising again. She repeated the action, knowing that it would drive him crazy.

His eyes flew open. 'Brat. When I'm fit again . . .'

'You'll what?'

Andy grasped her hips and pulled her down hard onto his shaft. 'Ride me.'

The brutal invasion almost sent her over the edge. Every nerve ending screamed. Her inner muscles clenched. She was going to come from one stroke.

'Easy. Not yet. Or you'll take me over with you.'

She held his gaze as she raised and lowered herself again. The temptation to go fast and hard was overwhelming but this slow, sensuous stroking was an exquisite torture. She clenched her inner muscles with each rising stroke, prolonging the agony.

Andy's pupils were large and dark and looked almost black. So good. This was so good. She rocked, grinding her clit against him on each downwards stroke. The desire to come was a hot ache between her thighs. She groaned again.

'I can't. Please let me come.'

He grasped her hips again and slammed her down hard. She might be the one who was on top, but he was vying for control. Andy arched his hips to meet hers, thrusting hard, until it was almost painful. Her nerve endings caught fire. It was too much. Too much. His final thrust drove every rational thought from her head.

She was flying. Riding a wave. No, not a wave, a star. She had no more control than a piece of stardust being pulled along by a comet. When she opened her eyes again, her head was resting on his chest. They were still joined together and Andy's heart was racing alongside hers.

'Give me your mouth.'

After his slow possession, Andy's kiss was hard and merciless. Hands fisting in her hair, he invaded her mouth, branding her with his possession until she was breathless. She belonged to him. Looking into his eyes, she had never felt so naked. Andy knew her soul. He knew the best and the worst of her, but his expression was full of tenderness and acceptance. Overwhelmed, she felt a sudden urge to cry but she didn't know what she was sorry for. For leaving him, for not trusting him, for lying to him? She had dragged them both into danger, but they had come through it. Together.

'I love you,' she whispered,

Andy stroked her face, then lowered his warm palm to her breast before letting it come to rest on her belly. 'Not as much as I love you. I'll always love you.'

It was sunset before he woke. Andy watched his sleeping lover. He couldn't believe that Roz was back in his bed. He didn't want to think of all the terrible things that could have happened to her or his baby. Andy doubted if he would ever be able to erase the memory of Roz flying over that hedge, clinging to a runaway horse.

But she had come through it; they both had.

When he stroked her face, she murmured softly in her sleep. In repose, her face was softer. She couldn't hide her vulnerability. His prickly, defensive girl had been through so much, but there was one hurdle she couldn't avoid for much longer.

Telling his parents that she was pregnant would be a piece of cake compared to a reunion with her sister. Andy sighed. It couldn't be avoided. He had promised Niall and Sinead that he would tell them the moment he found her and he would keep his promise. Roz had stolen from her sister's museum and Sinead had ended up in prison because of it.

Oh, he understood why she had done it. Peter Spring had poisoned her mind against the O'Sullivan family. The bastard had funnelled his own rage and bitterness through an innocent child and made her a pawn in his quest for revenge. But Roz had to make amends. She needed to face her past before they could move on.

He winced as he eased out of bed and went to find his phone. Pulling on a dressing gown, he slipped into the hall. Niall answered on the second ring.

'We're home,' Andy announced.

'Good. I'm almost finished tying up the Hall situation and Sinead is anxious to see her.'

'There's something you should know before you arrive here with all guns blazing. Roz is pregnant too.'

Silence hung in the air. Eventually Niall laughed. 'Well at least they'll have one thing in common.'

'True. When are we going to do this?'

'Given the circumstances, as soon as possible. Do you think your parents can cope with two more visitors?'

Andy laughed. Only a fraction of the rooms at Lough Darra were ever used. His mother would be delighted with the company. 'No problem, I'll see you tomorrow.'

He glanced at the closed bedroom door with regret. Despite his injuries he would have loved to climb back into bed with Roz, but he had to fix things with his parents first. He located his mother coming from the conservatory, her paint-stained clothes evidence of her recent activity.

'What are you doing out of bed?' Poppy was all concern. 'I really wish you would see a doctor.'

'I already did, Mum, but that's not important. We need to talk.'

He had to hand it to Poppy, she listened to his story without comment but her eyes glistened with tears when he told her about the baby.

'Oh my dear, I'm so happy for both of you. Of course I'll help. And we'll have the wedding here at Lough Darra as soon as I can arrange it.'

Wedding? He threw back his head and laughed. He hadn't actually got her to say yes, but he would. He was going to marry Roz Spring.

'Is something wrong, Andy? I know I'm old-fashioned but you can hardly expect the next heir to Lough Darra –'

Andy sobered. 'Of course not. I'll speak to Roz.'

He climbed the stairs back to their room to wake Roz for dinner. He hoped that she was willing to marry him after tomorrow.

Roz blinked at the time displayed on her phone. 11am. How had she slept for so long? She lay still for a few minutes, waiting for the inevitable urge to barf. Nope. Nothing was happening. Maybe this was going to be a good day. Her stomach growled, protesting the lack of breakfast. She'd ask Maggie to rustle her up something baby-proof.

She showered and went to the blue room in search of the clothes she had left behind, then got dressed. Three months pregnant and everything was a little loose. Only the waistband of her jeans was uncomfortable. She caught a glimpse of a car driving up and parking out front but it wasn't familiar. Dougal and Poppy must have visitors.

On the staircase, she heard voices from below before the closing of a door silenced them. One of them sounded like Niall Moore. She hoped he wasn't here to drag Andy away. She hurried to the kitchen, relieved to find Maggie there. Her mouth watered when she spotted a tray laden with warm scones.

'I'll get this,' Maggie picked up the tray and Roz followed her to the library, as eagerly as a stray dog looking for scraps.

Distracted by hunger, Roz didn't notice the woman standing at the window until she turned. Sinead. What was her sister doing here? It was a trap. This couldn't be a coincidence. She had been set up. None of this could have happened without Andy's knowledge. He had betrayed her.

Maggie departed quickly. Roz ignored the tea tray.

Sinead raised her hand but Roz was silent, unable to respond to her sister's greeting.

'Hi, Roro.'

The use of her childhood nickname made her heart

ache and Roz fought against the welling tide of emotion that rose inside her. Sinead stepped closer, her loose silk top swaying with the movement, and only then did Roz realize that her sister was pregnant too.

'Sinead,' she finally choked, wishing she had a more eloquent response prepared. In her darkest moments, this was what she had dreamed of – the chance to confront the sister who had abandoned her, the one who had left her to live in poverty while she had everything.

Her anger ebbed a little when she saw her sister's pale face. The dark circles beneath her eyes were testament to more than one sleepless night. A mirror image of that face had stared back at her each morning when she was living at the O'Haras' ranch.

Things were different now. She wasn't poor any longer. She didn't have to buy her clothes in charity shops or scour the supermarkets for marked-down food. She was going to be the next lady of Lough Darra, if she didn't kill Andy first. And she had serious money in the bank.

She gestured to the tray that Maggie had left. 'Will you have tea or coffee?'

'Tea, please. Very weak, with lots of sugar.'

'I can't stomach coffee anymore either.' Roz didn't know why she was sharing that with her. She reached into her pocket for the supply of barley sugar sweets she always carried. She couldn't find the magnanimity within her to hand them over, but pushed them to the middle of the coffee table.

'These might help.'

Sinead gave a tentative smile as she took one. 'Thanks.'

Roz poured tea the way she had observed Poppy doing

it. She sat up straight in her chair and nibbled on a dry scone while she sipped from the china cup. The picture of a perfect lady. Sinead had loaded a scone with butter, home-made jam and clotted cream.

The tables were turned now. Weren't they? So why didn't she feel good?

Sinead picked up her scone and put it down untouched. The tick-tock of the library clock filled the silence.

'When are you due?' Their questions emerged simultaneously and they both laughed nervously.

'Just before Christmas. You?' Roz asked.

Sinead picked up her cup and sipped her tea before replacing it on the china saucer. 'End of October.'

Roz nodded politely. She didn't know what to say. The last time she had spoken to her sister was in the back of a police van in Paris. She had caught a glimpse of her at the trial in Geneva, but since then there had been no contact.

Neither encounter had been enough to satisfy her hunger for revenge. All the years she had spent dreaming about meeting her sister. She would laugh at Sinead. Taunt her. Find the perfect words to make her cry and plead for forgiveness for abandoning her. Roz had planned out every situation possible. Except sitting across from her in a library, sipping tea and making polite small talk.

She had no plans for this. Her usual response when dealing with a situation she couldn't handle was to run. But Lough Darra was her home. She was damned if she was leaving it.

Roz gestured around the vast library. 'What do you think of my home? It's bigger than O'Sullivan Manor. Not what you expected, is it?'

Sinead stood up quickly, bumping into the table so that her cup rattled in its saucer, splashing tea across the table. The hurt in her eyes was unmistakeable. 'I can't do this. I'm sorry. I have to go.'

She was halfway to the door before Roz realized she was leaving and she got up, spilling more tea. 'You can't do what? Did you think that I'd be delighted to see you? That we'd play happy families? Get real.'

Sinead paused with her hand on the door and shook her head. Her eyes gleamed with unshed tears. 'I don't know what I expected. But you're my sister and I searched for you for so long. I just didn't believe you'd be such a . . . such a bitch, Roro.'

The words were a slap. Roz was the one with the terrible childhood. She was the one who'd lived with a series of 'aunts' while Dad was in prison. No one had cared about her then.

Roz didn't realize that she'd spoken the words out loud until a sob caught in Sinead's throat.

'You weren't the one who was abandoned. Dad took you with him. He didn't want me.' As if her knees couldn't hold her, Sinead slumped to the floor. Her shoulders heaved. 'They took Mammy away. After everyone left I was in that rat-infested place for days with no food. But you had Dad. And you never came back for me. I cried for you all the time, Roro, but you never came . . .'

Roz stood helplessly watching her sister cry. When had she become the bad guy? A vision popped into her head of another O'Sullivan woman crying in the bathroom of the FitzWilliam Hotel.

'You knew where we were. You could have come

459

to us at any time.' Her grandmother's tearful words taunted her.

Her stomach churned with a sickening realization.

Granny O'Sullivan was right. Roz could have contacted the O'Sullivans years ago. Turned up on their doorstep and announced who she was. As a teenager, she'd fantasized about doing that, but her father told her that they didn't want her.

Her father had told her a lot of things.

What if he'd been wrong? Her dad lied for a living. He twisted the truth to suit himself. But he was her father. He wouldn't do it to her. Would he?

A tangle of emotion that she couldn't name burst to the surface, carrying with it waves of anger, regret and bitterness. She had to find a way to fix this, to stop hurting herself and her sister.

With tears welling up in her eyes, Roz staggered across the room and knelt beside Sinead. Awkwardly, she put her arms around her sister and hugged her shaking frame. 'I'm sorry, Sis. I'm sorry. So sorry.'

Epilogue

'Come to Daddy.' Andy held out his arms and Emma Sinead Poppy Campbell McTavish almost wriggled out of her mother's arms in her attempt to reach him.

'You are such a tart.' Roz nuzzled the tender skin of the baby's neck as she handed her over.

Glancing in the mirror, she jammed another hat-pin into the black velvet creation and hoped that it wouldn't blow away. Cheltenham in late March was cold and she was willing to bet that the racecourse would be even colder. 'Are we mad? Dragging a baby to watch a horse race?'

'I'm sure that Tim has a box and, besides, she'd never forgive us if we left her at home.'

Roz suppressed a smile. That was always Andy's excuse. The truth was that he was utterly besotted with the new girl in his life, and Emma could wrap him around her little finger with a flash of her gummy smile.

She watched as Andy deftly dressed the child in a tiny velvet coat and matching hat. He was a more hands-on father than she had expected. Nothing fazed him, not even the nuclear explosion nappies, which he changed without complaint.

Roz shook her head, remembering the previous day when she had gone shopping with Sinead, leaving the fathers in charge of their respective daughters. The former Rangers and their offspring had managed to destroy her sister's house in three hours. Sinead had not been impressed, and their explanations about 'Training the next generation of Rangers early' hadn't gone down well. She knew who was really to blame for the damage.

She glanced at her watch. 'Come on, or we'll be late.'

The racecourse was thronged with fans, fashionistas and punters eager to have a flutter. They made their way to the O'Sullivan box where an excited crowd was gathered around Tim O'Sullivan.

Roz wasn't looking forward to the race. She had made several attempts to buy Nagsy back and Tim had sneered at all of them.

'How is he?' Tim asked his trainer.

'Grand, Mr O'Sullivan. He's dying to get out for a bit of a run.'

'Did you hear that, Summer? I can't wait to show this toffee-nosed shower what a real horse is like.'

His daughter peeked up at him from beneath her Philip Treacy hat. Roz grinned. She was willing to bet that Tim had spoken of nothing else for weeks.

'Yes, Dad, but if he's that good, why is he only running in one race?'

'The element of surprise,' Tim announced. 'My boy is a complete unknown and the bookies are quoting a hundred to one.' He rubbed his hands gleefully.

There had been a few rumours, but the O'Sullivan stables weren't known for producing winners and they had rapidly died down. 'Are you sure you won't sell him back to me?' Roz said.

'I might. For ten million.' He laughed at his own joke before turning his attention to the trainer again.

Tucking Emma into her sling, Roz scanned the crowd for Andy. Where could he have gone? She spotted him fighting his way through the crowd, balancing a glass of champagne and a bottle of alcohol-free beer.

'Are we celebrating?'

He raised his drink to her. 'We will be – in two and a half furlongs and twenty-two fences.' He looked suspiciously pleased with himself, like a child who knew what Santa was going to bring.

Roz prayed that he was right. The Gold Cup was the most valuable non-handicap chase in England, with a prize fund of almost half a million pounds. An unknown hundred-to-one winner would take the racing world by storm.

The race announcement came over the PA, and they surged to the front of the box. 'I'm not sure I can watch,' she whispered to Andy. 'It's going to be a disaster.'

He held her hand. 'Trust me. It will be fine.'

She gripped it. She was learning that when Andy said 'Trust me', she could.

The horses lined up at the start and Roz scanned them until she saw the O'Sullivan colours of green and yellow. Nagsy. Her heart fluttered. She missed her four-legged friend. 'I hope he's not hurt.'

'Will you stop fussing?' Andy laughed. 'He'll be fine. Finish your drink and see if you can get up to the front. I'll hold Emma.'

Roz drained the remains of the champagne. Her first drink in months and she felt sick. She had never had to face the consequences of a scam before and certainly not one on this scale. Every bad thing she had ever done in

463

her life was coming back to haunt her. Nervously, she pushed her way to the front of the box and managed to squeeze into a spot beside her uncle.

The start of the race took her by surprise. One moment, the racers were at the starting gate and next they were thundering up the track in a frenetic jumble of horses and riders.

'And it's Lone Star making the first break,' the commentary came over the speaker. 'Followed by Giant's Causeway, Silverado, House of Worth and Champion's Dance.'

Where was Nagsy? Roz craned her neck. She couldn't see him in the throng. The horses reached the first fence and there was a loud 'ahh' in the crowd as House of Worth lost his rider and galloped on without him.

The next four jumps were uneventful.

'There he is.' Tim almost deafened her with his shout.

Sure enough, Nagsy was hugging the inner rail in the group behind the leaders.

'He's only in an exercise canter!' Tim pronounced.

Roz lost count of the jumps that followed. To her unseasoned eyes, there was little change in the running order until Champion's Dance made what looked a dangerous move. He edged closer to Lone Ranger, and the two horses soon began a neck-and-neck race, duelling for the front spot. The horse in third place inched towards them, but then disaster struck on the next jump. Roz wasn't sure what happened, but two horses fell heavily.

With three fences to go, Nagsy's group raced to the fore.

'And it's Bobby's Dazzler. Bobby's Dazzler is launching a challenge to Lone Star.' The commentator could barely

464

contain his excitement. Bobby's Dazzler was the favourite and carrying most of the punters' money.

As they approached the last fence, Bobby's Dazzler hit the front and Roz could see when Lone Star began to weaken.

Nagsy must have sensed it too. As if he had suddenly woken up, Nagsy hit his stride. Roz couldn't contain herself as he passed the other horses with ease. 'Run, Nagsy. Run, you beauty.'

Tim O'Sullivan was beside himself with excitement. 'Shift your ass,' he roared.

Beside him, the expensively dressed crowd in the adjoining box tittered, but the smiles vanished from their faces as they watched the drama unfolding on the track below.

Nagsy's lead widened and widened, until he was a full ten lengths ahead of his nearest rival. He raced across the finishing line, barely out of breath. The crowd erupted. The commentator ran out of superlatives in his effort to praise the unknown winner and place the remaining horses.

'And it's Hagar's Son. Hagar's Son followed by Bobby's Dazzler, Lone Star, Giant's Causeway, with Totem Pole taking fifth.'

'Ten lengths. Did you hear that?' Tim O'Sullivan elbowed his daughter. 'Ten fecking lengths. What did I tell you?'

'Yes, Dad.' Summer rolled her eyes. She would never hear the end of this.

Tim turned to the crowd in the box and beamed. 'Who wants to be first to announce to the media that I own Shergar's great-grandson?'

Roz gasped. 'Great-grandson?'

Tim's grin turned evil. 'Didn't I tell you? I had my own DNA test done. Didn't get quite the same results as yours, but he's got the bloodlines all right.'

She was stunned when Tim swept her into a crushing embrace. 'You're a grand girl. A true O'Sullivan. Just like your mother.'

He released her and turned to greet the media who were doing their best to invade the box. Tim stopped and looked over his shoulder. 'Tell that old coot at Lough Darra that when Hagar's Son goes to stud, he can send down his best mare and I won't charge him.'

With that, he walked into the excited crowd.

Roz clutched the railing, not sure whether to laugh or cry. *A true O'Sullivan – like her mother.* And maybe she was. Her mother had been young, and wild, but Maggie never had the chance to settle down.

Not like her.

Roz scanned the crowd and spied two dark heads close together. Emma was tired with all of the excitement and Andy was singing in an effort to distract her. Her heart welled up with love and pride and tenderness until she thought it would burst. Fighting her way through the crowds milling around the O'Sullivans, she wrapped her arms around both of them.

'Let's go home.'

Acknowledgements

Caroline and Eileen wish to thank:

The management of Charleville Castle who allowed us to take all sorts of liberties with it, with special thanks to Dudley and Damien.

Our beta readers, Mary, Silje, Frances. Aoibhinn and Jack, for their encouragement and for pointing out the obvious.

Patricia O'Reilly, who continues to inspire and mentor us.

Our editors Patricia Deevy and Davina Russell, and Michael, Cliona and all the staff at Penguin Ireland, with special thanks to Catherine Ryan Howard, our publicist.

Our wonderful agent, Madeleine Milburn.

Website designer Seoirse Mac Gabhann, for the IT support and endless pots of coffee.

Stella for allowing us to use her flat and Dave for his weapons expertise.

Our unshockable friends on FetLife for their kinky suggestions.

And all those too numerous to mention, who answered our questions – no matter how strange – during the writing of *The Pleasures of Spring*.